The Cults of the Worm

Scott Hale

THE CULTS OF THE WORM

Copyright © 2017 Scott Hale
Cover art by Natasha Mackenzie
Map by Jacquelyn Graff
Edited by Dawn Lewis

First Edition: November 2017
Copyright © 2017 Scott Hale

ISBN-13: 978-0-9964489-6-3

BOOKS BY SCOTT HALE

The Bones of the Earth series

The Bones of the Earth (Book 1)

The Three Heretics (Book 2)

The Blood of Before (Book .1)

The Cults of the Worm (Book 3)

The Agony of After (Book .2)

The Eight Apostates (Book 4)

Novels

In Sheep's Skin

The Body Is a Cruel Mistress (Coming Soon)

KEY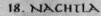

1. CALDERA
2. ALLUVIA
3. TRAESK
4. RIME
5. ELD
6. LACUNA
7. GEHARRA
8. NORA
9. ELDRUS
10. NYXIS
11. ISLAOS
12. HROTHAS
13. BEDLAM
14. GALLOWS
15. CATHEDRA
16. PENANCE
17. CADENCE
18. NACHTLA
19. LYNN
20. TRIST
21. MARWAIDD
22. RHYFEL
23. ANGHEUAWL
24. COMMUNION
25. SKYGGE
26. FORMUE
27. BRANN
28. HVLAV
29. KRES
30. THE DISMAL STICKS
31. GARDEN OF SLEEP
32. DEN OF UNKINDNESS
33. SKELETON'S KEEP
34. SCAVENGER'S TOWER

 CORRUPTED   NIGHT TERROR

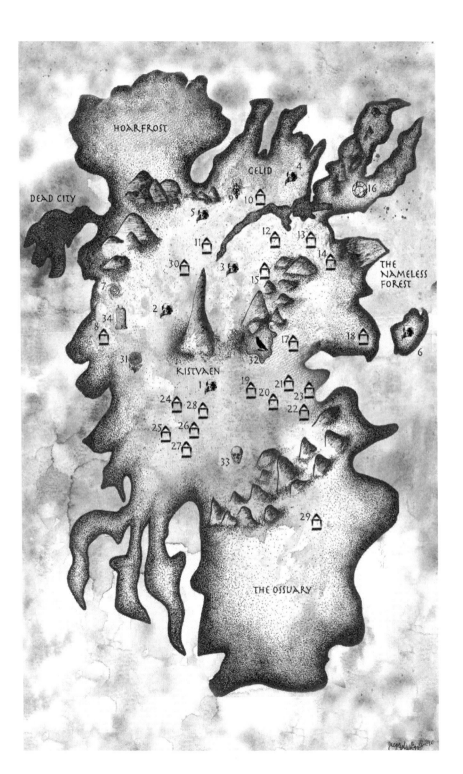

CHAPTER I

R'lyeh wasn't the church-going type, but even she knew priests weren't supposed to have tentacles flailing out from the back of their heads. Whereas others would have been disturbed by the vermillion growths, R'lyeh was just jealous. Freaky as they were, they did kind of put her octopus mask to shame.

Shrouded in shadows, Vrana's ax in hand, she moved across the church's rafters to follow the priest as he went about the room, lighting candles. He prayed while he did so in a language she couldn't make sense of. The words were thick, the syllables muddy; and yet the sentences themselves had a sharpness to them that pierced R'lyeh's ears. Every time the priest spoke, she imagined a shovel plunging into the ground, unearthing unholy utterances. Considering the man belonged to King Edgar's new religion, the Disciples of the Deep, she wasn't too surprised. In the end, unearthing God was their ultimate goal.

Noises outside the front of the church. First, scuffling feet, and then a knocking on the door. With a sick, sucking sound, the vermillion tentacles slithered into the priest's skull. The only trace of the appendages having been there were the sweaty patches on the holy man's scalp. But this was Bedlam. Sweat and secrets went hand-in-hand. All things considered here, he was invisible, which was exactly how he and his faith had been so successful so far.

R'lyeh repositioned herself on the rafters to better see the entryway. For being a place meant to hold the light of God, the church was host to a whole lot of darkness. It was a small and stuffy building with no windows, let alone cracks. It had been built with driftwood and rocks from

1

the river it now sat beside. According to James, up until about two months ago, it used to be a worshiping site for the Holy Order of Penance. When and how the Disciples of the Deep had taken over ownership of the church, no one could say for sure. It was as though they had been here the whole time, waiting for the right moment to make themselves known. Not just here, though, in Bedlam. Everywhere.

Again, another knock on the door.

"The way is open," the priest said.

R'lyeh smirked. She wanted a job like that, where she got to sound fancy and no one batted an eye about it. Most of the time, when she killed someone, she just cussed out their corpse until the adrenaline died down. But that wasn't very cool. She needed some one-liners. Something snappy.

The front door creaked open, and an older woman shuffled in. She was short and stubby with stiff shoulders and big knuckles. She wore a tattered veil from behind which she sniffled and wept. Like some other humans R'lyeh had seen lately, this woman's Corruption looked different. The Corruption was still crimson, still on the right arm, but now in the right light, at the right time, the stretch of flesh almost seemed to... move.

"Ms. Louisa," the priest said, his voice smooth, emotionless. "Are you ready?"

Ms. Louisa shut the door behind her. Going to the priest at the pace of a slug, she said, "That's just it, Father. I'm not sure that I am."

"Have you been spreading the Word to our fellow Bedlamites?"

"Yes, yes. I have, yes." She took out a few crude rolls of parchment from her pocket. "I think we will have a few additions to our congregation tomorrow. But Father—"

"Excellent." Close enough to take Ms. Louisa's hand, he did. His wild eyes inches away from her own, he said, "You have shown yourself a most dutiful servant of our Lord during these trying times."

"Yes, Father, I am trying." Ms. Louisa scrunched up her face behind the veil. "The Holy Order were deceivers. You have shown me the true God. I am grateful, Father, but my... my son."

"Your son was a good man, was he not?"

Ms. Louisa nodded so hard R'lyeh thought for a moment her spine was going to snap.

"The good suffer enough in life as it is. They should not suffer in death. Ms. Louisa—" he pulled her into an embrace that looked about as

2

comfortable as hugging a rock, "—let me send your son to heaven."

Now we're talking. R'lyeh shifted the octopus mask to get some fresh air flowing through it. The Skeleton had insisted she wear it whenever she went on a mission. As a thirteen-year-old girl, she was an easy target that no one would take seriously. As a thirteen-year-old Night Terror, she would appear twice her age and even more frightening. Or something like that. The Skeleton always played up her background. It made her blush.

Ms. Louisa bowed her head. "Father, it just doesn't seem… natural."

"After everything the Lord has shared, still you doubt?" The priest clicked his tongue against his teeth. "Do not forget. This is all very new. Surely those who had never heard of the Holy Order before thought they were mad, too."

Ms. Louisa nodded, the veil swishing across her face.

"It is human to doubt. I can tell you and the others worry that you've made a mistake. For years, you've been comfortable with the Holy Order of Penance and their teachings. How could you know that they were leading you astray? You couldn't have, Ms. Louisa. You couldn't have. Not until now. Have I not shown you miracles?"

"You have." She cleared her throat and laughed. "Oh, yes, Father, you have."

The priest slipped a hand into his robe. "Would you like to see another miracle?"

Did she? It didn't seem like it. Ms. Louisa had gone silent, and she started to shake.

"Is Jeremiah out there on the porch?"

She nodded weakly. A few candles went out.

"Bring him in." The priest took his hand out of the robe. He was holding something, but it was too dark to tell what exactly. "We'll see him off to heaven together."

Ms. Louisa scrunched up her face and started to cry. She turned on her heels and headed toward the front door.

"It is a kindness we offer him," the priest said.

She wrapped her hand around the doorknob. Over her shoulder, she said, "I won't be punished for this?"

The priest shook his head. "You will be exalted."

Ms. Louisa drew three sharp breaths and then opened the door. Stark sunlight and the general commotion of Bedlam poured over the threshold. In this stuffy closet of a church, R'lyeh had been so focused on the mission at hand she had forgotten she was smack-dab in the middle of a Corrupted town. For a split second, the sounds brought her back. Back to Alluvia, to Geharra, to the pit, and her—

Ms. Louisa pushed her wheelchair-bound son into the church. She had to hold the back of his shirt to keep him from falling forward, because he was dead. R'lyeh's nose twitched as the smell of rot drifted into the rafters. There was dirt all over the wooden wheelchair, as if his mother had started to bury him, and then changed her mind midway through.

"Close the door behind you," the priest said.

Ms. Louisa did as she was told.

"Lock it."

And she did that, too.

"Bring him to me."

Ms. Louisa shuddered. She took the wheelchair, pushed it forward. In his Sunday's best, Jeremiah slumped over the armrest. His dead weight seemed to be giving his mother a hard time, as if he were dragging his heels from beyond the grave.

The priest went to Jeremiah and took his head in his hand. "The Holy Order buried our people with blessings and prayers. Empty words and empty gestures. Promises they never had to keep."

Ms. Louisa let go of the wheelchair. She put her hands together and started praying to the ground.

"God has given his most trusted Disciples a piece of Itself." The priest opened his hand, finally revealing what he had taken out of his robes. "A seed of heaven."

R'lyeh took off her mask and leaned forward. *Son of a bitch.* In the priest's greasy palm, a red, bristly, walnut-sized mass sat. Small tendrils, not unlike the tentacles stowed away in the priest's skull, whipped around it. Seed seemed a stretch of the word, and heaven even more so. The thing looked like something a cat with cancer might cough up.

The priest opened Jeremiah's jaw as if it were a jewelry box. Holding the seed over the corpse's lips, he said, "Where is God, Ms. Louisa?"

She stopped praying and sputtered out, "In heaven."

"And where is heaven?"

"In the..." Old Holy Order habits had her looking up, but instead she cast her eyes downward and said, "In the Deep."

The priest nodded, pleased. "To bring out God, we must bring out heaven. When we die, we should not die with heaven on our breath but in our breasts. In each one of us, Ms. Louisa—" he smiled, "—we hold the seed to heaven. And when our bodies bloom, God will come to save us all."

Ms. Louisa shivered. "Praise be to the Deep."

"Praise be to its boney shores," the priest responded.

"Praise be to the Red Heaven."

"And our slumbering Lord."

The priest slipped the seed past Jeremiah's teeth. It sat on the dead boy's tongue. With a will of its own, it used the tendrils to force itself down his acrid throat.

Ms. Louisa went around the wheelchair. She touched his face, felt his bones. She smelled him. It was as if she was an animal, and she wasn't so sure that the child that sat before her was her child anymore.

"What h-happens next, Father?"

"Take him home and bury him beside his sister." The priest touched the small of her back. "Does it not comfort you to know you will have a piece of heaven in your backyard?"

Ms. Louisa turned around. Tears whipped out of her eyes, across the priest's robes. "It's just… I've heard terrible things about those who… who—"

Jeremiah shot out of the wheelchair. Eyes wide, mouth agape, he sank his clawed fingers into Ms. Louisa's shirt and dragged her to the ground.

"Father, Father!"

Jeremiah, now no more than a mere puppet to the thing inside him, dug his nails into her skin until she bled. His mouth stretched open; the sides of it split into a permanent smile. His throat ballooned. Small, black spikes tore through his neck, as if something were working its way up his choked esophagus.

Ms. Louisa tried to push her son off her the same way one would an overzealous lover; that is, carefully, considerately, with weak shoves and even weaker kicks. Holding back his face, she begged the priest for help.

"Do you really want it?" The priest sounded aggravated. R'lyeh could tell this hadn't gone the way he planned it would. "Or do you want to see heaven with your son?"

Ms. Louisa's eyes shone with salvation. She nodded and let go of her son. Jeremiah's spasmodic corpse ground its way up her body and pressed its gaping mouth to her own. He swallowed her apologies and prayers and proceeded to fill her with heaven.

Thin, vibrant, vermillion veins burst out of Jeremiah's mouth, like a thick trunk of earthworms. Forming a writhing bridge between him and her, they pumped themselves into her mouth and down her throat, into her belly and jerking appendages.

When she died, if she'd died, Jeremiah collapsed upon his mother's corpse and went back to being dead himself. Tiny holes opened up along the boy's body. From them, more vermillion veins poured. Slowly, they wrapped around mother and son until, after a few minutes, they were completely cocooned. They looked like oversized seeds themselves. R'lyeh was fairly certain where this new batch was going to be planted.

"Goddamn it," the priest said, at last. Looking down at the red cocoon, he jammed his thumbs into his temples. "This is more art than science. I'm sick of it."

He marched to the back of the church, grabbed a long metal rod with a hook at its end, and then went to the ball of veins. He dug it into the cocoon and started dragging it down the middle aisle to the backdoor, which led out to a gated path and, eventually, the cemetery.

"Grave's not big enough for the both of them. Too goddamn hot to dig anymore today." He stopped, mopped his brow with his sleeve. Right under R'lyeh, he mumbled, "Father Francis is going to laugh at me. Can't wait to hear—"

The rafter creaked beneath R'lyeh's weight. Her body went stiff as the priest looked up, confused. He squinted, grabbed a candle, and held it outward. She squeezed the handle of Vrana's ax.

"What's that?" The priest unhooked the rod from the cocoon and pointed it to the ceiling. "What's there?"

R'lyeh's vision dimmed. A torrent of nervousness flushed into her brain. Like a creature trapped in a cage, common sense disintegrated to the need for survival.

She dropped from the rafters, swinging the ax downward with her plummet. It caught on the metal rod and knocked it aside. The ax blade tore through the priest's hand, down his leg, and split his foot, forking it, like a snake's tongue. A geyser of blood exploded from the gory ravine that ran down his body and the sputtering stump he held.

"Time to meet your Maker," R'lyeh said, grinning behind her mask. *Snappy,* she thought, *but kind of stupid.* Then she swung the ax into his neck.

She hadn't been strong enough to cut through his flesh, but the force of the impact sent him spinning into the pews. He broke his fall on the floorboards. When he did so, the ax, still buried in his neck, ripped free and, with a thump, fell over onto the blood-soaked ground.

R'lyeh took a deep breath and grabbed the ax. What just happened? She knew what happened. She had so much hate in her heart for Penance that she didn't mind sharing some with Disciples of the Deep, too. If she hadn't struck first, then he might have killed her, or stuck one of those seeds inside her. Besides, she'd gotten all the information the Marrow Cabal needed. This would've been the Skeleton's next orders, anyway.

"Yeah," R'lyeh said, convinced. She exhaled and pushed aside thoughts of Geharra's pit. "It's fine."

R'lyeh went to the side of the church and started throwing the candles there onto the cocoon and the priest's corpse. The vermillion veins and his scratchy robes caught fire immediately. She moved through the church, gathering up anything she could use for kindling. There were quite a few of the Disciple's scriptures—*The Disciples of the Deep* by Amon Ashcroft—and she hurled them into the blaze.

When the smoke became too much to breathe in, R'lyeh ran to the front of the church. She undid the lock and flung back the doors. Thick clouds of smoke exploded past her and washed over the crowd of Bedlamites who had gathered outside.

Did she still have her mask on? She did. Raising her ax to the group of concerned citizens, R'lyeh rumbled, "Let it burn, or you will," and hurried down the steps as fast as she could to the riverside, where Will waited on horseback, looking as confused as she expected him to be.

"What the hell, Real'yuh?" he shouted, making room in the saddle for her.

R'lyeh, you idiot. Damn kid never got her name right. The crowd shouted behind her. She looked back. A few were coming after her. Night Terrors weren't all that terrible in the full light of day.

R'lyeh pounded down the shore. A foot from the horse, she jumped onto it and screamed, "Go!" into Will's ear.

The Skeleton's son snapped the reins. The horse took off. Chunks of mud from the ground flew up around them as its heavy hooves pounded the earth. R'lyeh straightened herself out in the saddle and held onto Will's waist so that she wouldn't fall.

"What happened?" he asked, Bedlam blurring around them as they hoofed it toward the bridge on the outskirts of town.

"I killed the priest. He saw me."

R'lyeh twisted around, ax out, ready to chop down anyone alongside them. But there was no one. Her pursuers had returned to the church to douse the flames that now engulfed it.

Will faced her and said, "Real'yuh, Dad's going to be pissed."

But R'lyeh wasn't listening to him. As she turned to look at him, her heart seized in her chest. Ahead, on the bridge that spanned the river they rode along, she spotted a blonde woman standing there, watching them. She wore a large leather hat, and a long leather coat covered in belts and buckles and makeshift pockets. In the woman's left hand, she held bandages, and in her right, a shepherd's crook.

She pointed to the shepherd and cried, "Will."

He spun around, sputtered out a string of nonsense. He cracked the reins and kicked the sides of the horse into a full gallop. They passed under the bridge, under the watchful eye of the shepherd. And when they came out on the other side, they both turned around and found that the shepherd was gone.

"D-Don't tell him," Will pleaded. "It wasn't what you think."

R'lyeh looked over her shoulder, Bedlam proper shrinking with every passing second. Great plumes of smoke wound into the sky, the scent of heaven burning in the autumn air. She searched what she could of the streets for signs of the shepherd, but it had vanished. Vanished, just like the Skeleton had warned it would.

"Hey." Will grabbed her arm, bringing her attention back to him. "Don't tell him. He won't let me work for the Marrow Cabal anymore if he finds out."

R'lyeh took off her mask and secured it in her lap. "Are you kidding me?"

Trees and bushes whipped past them as the horse plunged into the forest surrounding Bedlam.

"That's the dumbest fucking idea." R'lyeh shook her head. "He told me." She clenched her teeth. "Do you want to go back to the Membrane?"

Will opened his mouth to argue, but instead, he turned around and took control of the horse.

Don't tell the Skeleton? It made her sick with anger that he would ask. *I'm not losing anyone else. I don't care if you hate me for it.*

She closed her eyes and held on tighter to Will. Tight enough to keep him from the shepherd should it show up again. If she lost Will, then she'd lose the Skeleton. And if she lost him, she'd lose Vrana for good.

CHAPTER II

Aeson had just started kindergarten when he found his parents hanging from a tree outside Caldera. From six years old to today's sunrise, he had hated them for leaving him in the most selfish way anyone ever could. But now, as he stood below that tree, looking up at the branch Bjørn had cut his parents down from, he found himself empathizing with their suicide.

Because Vrana, his best friend, his only love and lover, was gone. He didn't know if she was dead or alive, but according to R'lyeh's letter, the Witch had taken Vrana to the Void, which meant she was probably both.

Killing himself made sense. In every piece of rope and sharpened blade, he saw sinister invitations to a place his feelings couldn't follow. The loss of his parents had been one thing, but losing Vrana? It was as if all the bones had been broken in his body, and all the blood in his veins had been replaced with sand. His heart hurt, too. He had thought the sentiment was just poetry, but there was truth to it. It was as if his heart had been turned into a pincushion, and every day a new needle was jammed into one of its failing chambers.

Aeson went beneath the bough that had helped snap his parents' necks. The splintery culprit, unpunished all these years later, was now bent, and the bark chalky and soft. If he placed any weight upon that beckoning arm or the other branches around it, they would surely break. The tree had been good for two deaths, and two deaths alone. If he were going to die, it wouldn't be here.

He took off his skull mask and dropped to his knees. Falling back on his heels, he groaned and said, "I'm an idiot."

"Aye, but you're our idiot, so that makes you special."

He looked over his shoulder. Bjørn stood behind him, his eyes winking in the dark maw of his bear mask. He was drenched in sweat. A few new fly friends buzzed around him, entranced by the big man's stench.

Aeson slid the Corrupted skull back on and jumped to his feet. "Uh, hey."

"Howdy partner." Bjørn put his hands on his hips. "This is where your parents died."

A hot nail of rage bore itself into Aeson's brain. Cheek quivering, he mumbled, "Oh? Oh, shit. It is, isn't it?" He laughed, clapped his hands together. "I didn't even realize!"

"Yeah, that's why I pointed out the fact."

Kistvaen shook behind them, shedding sheets of rock the same way a snake would skin. Whether or not the mountain's recent rumblings had to do with the spellweavers who made it vanish or its history as a volcano, Aeson couldn't say. But if lava were to burst from Kistvaen's peak and smote this mother fucker off the face of the Earth, he would've been just fine with that.

"Appreciate the sympathy," Aeson said finally, his face several shades darker.

"What?" Bjørn shook his head. "What do you want? To tell me how you've been sulking around Caldera for the last few months? Go on, tell me about how much you miss Vrana. Tell me about all the things you could've done differently. Or how about you tell me how you plan to kill yourself?"

Air caught in Aeson's throat. "What is—"

"Here? Was this to be the place?" Bjørn covered the bear mask's mouth, shocked. "Did I interrupt you? I know being an Archivist runs in the family, but I didn't realize cowardice did, too."

Aeson's knuckles were clenched so tightly that his nails dug into the heels of his palms. Where was this coming from? They were hardly friends. In the months following Vrana's departure and disappearance, Aeson had actually grown closer to Adelyn, her mother, than Bjørn. This right here was just some insensitive, overgrown man-child mouthing off to someone who he thought wouldn't say anything back.

Stepping up to Bjørn to prove him wrong, Aeson said, "I don't know what you think this is between us, but you don't speak to—"

"I'll speak to you however I like. And you know why?"

"Enlighten me."

"Because our Vrana is missing." Bjørn paused. He shook, the same way Kistvaen shook, as if he were unburdening himself of the heavy things not even his huge frame could sustain. "She's gone, but not for good. Can we agree on that?"

"I... I don't know." He clamped his eyes shut until the tears retreated. "Yeah. Agreed."

Bjørn shoved his finger into Aeson's chest. "You. Need. To. Get. Her. Back. No one wants to hear your tale of woe. No one is interested in that shit. We all know what's coming, so let's get to it.

"You're our Archivist and Vrana's boyfriend. You owe it to damn near everyone to save her from that Witch bitch. That's why I get to talk to you the way that I am. Same way I get to chew out a warrior for not fighting. And that's why you're going to listen, too. Because you know I'm right.

"I don't really believe you intend to kill yourself. Loner like yourself, down there, underground, in the Inner Sanctum, I would have thought you would have done it already. But you haven't. Like I said, no one cares about that shit. So what's the problem?"

Aeson cried, "What the hell do you expect me to do?"

"The same thing she would have done had this happened to you!"

Bjørn paced back and forth in front of the tree. Occasionally, he glanced toward Caldera where the harvesters' sickles flashed metallic smiles in the sunlight. He was frantic, Aeson could see that now. This big outburst wasn't some sporadic projection of his own unresolved bullshit. No, the Bear was desperate, just like him. But why? Had something happened back in the village?

Aeson drew a deep breath. "You don't think I don't want to help her?"

"Unless you've been formulating some master plan these last few months, then I don't know, Aeson. I don't know."

"I'm an Archivist." He directed his attention to the house of the elders. "The only one we have in Caldera. I'm not one of your warriors. And they—" he pointed to Faolan and Nuctea, who had just emerged from the garden behind the house, "—won't let me leave."

"How old are you?" Bjørn asked flatly.

Nineteen, Aeson thought but didn't say.

"You don't need to be a warrior." Bjørn crossed his arms and headed back toward Caldera. "I'll do all the killing. You just need to get us to where we need to go."

"What?" Aeson started after him.

Bjørn stopped, looked over his shoulder. Sweat drooled from the bear mask's discolored teeth. "I know you've been biding your time. I know you haven't ever left the village, except through all those books you have down in the Sanctum. But I also know you love her. I understand the confusion. It's easier to say you can't, that they won't let you. But you know what's even easier?"

Aeson didn't know.

"Me saying you will. You will get her back. They won't let you leave? Well, I won't let you stay. So figure it out, what needs to be done, because when we leave here, we're leaving together."

Bjørn nodded, as if an agreement had already been made between two of them, and headed back into Caldera.

His parents had committed suicide. That was a well-known fact amongst those who lived in Caldera. No one questioned it, especially not Aeson. Like his responsibility to continue the work they had started as Archivists, he accepted the cause of death and seldom entertained other possibilities. For a man whose entire purpose was to dissect the past, such willful myopia didn't make any damn sense. And now it was happening again with Vrana, just like Bjørn had said.

Aeson went to the tree and rested his head against the trunk. Digging his toes into the soil, he recalled R'lyeh's letter. It had arrived one month after she and Vrana would have reached Lacuna. Aeson and the elders couldn't figure out how she had managed to get it to Caldera, because the raven that delivered it wasn't from any Night Terror villages. The parchment was strange, too. It was coarse, and the paper had a purplish hue to it. If Aeson stared at the words written there for more than a minute, his eyes would go out of focus and his head would start to hurt. Anguis suggested Mara may have spellweaved the letter, but both Faolan and Nuctea agreed she was nowhere near powerful enough to do so.

"It sleeps again," Aeson mumbled, reciting the letter. "And the Children have left. But Vrana is in the Void. The Witch used her, used us all. Belief powers her. Now I'm going to get Vrana back."

That was it. That was all the letter had said. They had succeeded in putting the Blue Worm to rest, which scouts near the Widening Gyre could confirm. When Aeson pressed the elders on what R'lyeh meant by "the Children," they explained to him Lacuna's fertility project, where Night Terrors and Corrupted, with the help of the Blue Worm, were bred together to repopulate the Night Terrors' dwindling numbers.

"How many flesh fiends did you end up with?" Aeson had asked Anguis that day. He was already well aware of what happened when Night Terrors and Corrupted mated.

"Enough to feed the Blue Worm for years," Anguis had said. "Those Night Terrors and Corrupted who did not turn into flesh fiends were shipped off to the mainland, it seems. We will have our people in Traesk, as well as the Heartland, reconnect with them."

If not for the circumstances, he would have been floored by the notion of having hundreds of Night Terrors with the potential to practice telepathy. At that moment, Aeson didn't care about these mutant offspring the elders had consented to creating. All he had wanted to know was this: "How do I get into the Void? You told Vrana there may be a way in through Nachtla. And the Witch used her? What did R'lyeh mean?"

And all Anguis could tell him was: "I don't know, Aeson. Keep searching for us. Vrana is strong. If she's alive, she—"

Aeson smashed his second skull, his stolen skull, against the tree, bludgeoning the memory until it went away. It was bad enough that Anguis was clearly lying to him. But the fact Aeson had taken his word as gospel was ridiculous. After that, just like with his parents' death, he accepted the hand he was dealt, and instead of doing anything about it, he went through the same pathetic motions he had gotten good at for the last thirteen years.

There were stacks of books in his room about Old World folklore. If it had even the most tenuous connection to witches, he had plucked it from the Archive's shelves and brought it down to the Sanctum. The most relevant works tended to come from Connor Prendergast and Herbert North, two old-school supernatural investigators who had recorded their cases in a series of books called *Black Occult Macabre*. In the two and a half volumes Aeson possessed, there were numerous references to a woman who had to be the Witch, or the Maiden of Pain, as well as another woman, a sister, called Joy, the Maiden of Joy. They often mentioned that the women had a kind of otherworldly hideout, a Void, but they had never been successful in locating it. At the end of the day, it seemed the Witch would only appear when she wanted to. When she did, she did so at the height of her power. And until then, she used others to carry out her bidding, which Aeson figured was exactly what she had done to Vrana, up until the moment she had snatched her from this world.

In their writings, Connor and Herbert had made mention of ancient, occult weapons known as Red Death weapons. They were said to be created by Death Itself, and engraved with runes that could annihilate any creature, living or dead. Aeson had heard of such an object being held up in Eldrus, in Ghostgrave, that fitted the description, but with everything going on with the Disciples of the Deep, going there seemed out of the question. For a moment, he had considered asking Death to forge one anew, but that would mean taking the ferry to—

Aeson punched the tree. He reared back, eyes following along the bough that had caused his parents to spill their bowels. What the hell was the point of knowing everything if he couldn't do anything with it? If he had found a way into the Void from one of the books, what would he have done? Sent someone else to get his best friend back? Probably. And if he had one of those Red Death weapons? Assign someone else to carry out the mission? Definitely.

And that's where the myopia came in. When something had to be done that extended beyond his duties as Archivist, he suddenly became stupid. A doe-eyed dumbass who couldn't do more than two things at once, because it was easier being what he was supposed to be, than being something else.

He turned and headed towards Caldera, to the training yard, where children sparred with one another under Bjørn's cruel tutelage. At the moment, the yard was empty because the children were at school, sparring with their teachers instead.

Keeping out sight, to keep out of conversations with others, Aeson wheeled around the enclosure until he found where the gate sagged and hopped it. A muddy puddle broke his fall. He shook off the slough and skirted the gate to the shed where many Bjørn-forged training weapons waited.

He already knew what he wanted and where it was. The ax sat at the back of the shed, somewhat forgotten, like the kid who gets picked last for games.

"Figures you would use an ax," Aeson said, as if Vrana were there beside him. He took it in his hands and got a measure of its weight. "You blunt, brutal, beautiful love of mine." He laughed, thought of her, and then left the yard.

Aeson returned to the tree where his parents had died and swung the ax into its side. The blade was dull, but his will couldn't have been any sharper. Two deaths, this tree had been good for two deaths. If he let it stay here any longer, its roots would spread and claim a third. And it wouldn't be his ghost that hung from its boughs, but Vrana's—the noose around her neck his terrified reluctance.

He buried the ax deeper into the trunk. White shavings seeped out of the widening crack. He brought it back and swung in again. Crack. The tree braced itself against the impact. Old as it was, it wasn't going down without a fight. For thirteen years, he had been cultivating the very thing he should have been killing.

"Well, isn't this symbolic?" Aeson said in Bjørn's mocking drawl.

After ten minutes or so, a crowd began to gather behind him. It wasn't every day that they saw their Archivist engaging in manual labor, let alone severing the sore that had sickened his soul for more than half his life. He didn't speak to them, and they were wise enough not to interrupt. Their presence only made him hack harder, until his arms were heavy and numb, and the sounds of the ax were finally louder than the blood in his ears.

Two hours later, the tree's trunk had been whittled down to a small, bare spine of wood. Aeson stopped, almost as drenched in sweat as Bjørn had been, and gave long-delayed inevitability a chance to catch up and close out this outstanding account. At first, the tree stood unyielding, but with a little help from the wind off Kistvaen, it started to shake. Then, its spine started to break. And with a ghastly howl, his parents' makeshift gallows gave and snapped in half.

Aeson took a deep breath. He wiped his brow, but didn't drop the ax. For now, it was a part of him, just as much as Vrana's ax had been a part of her. He turned, half-cocked, to see how much of an audience still remained. Much to his surprise, there was only one.

"It was time," Anguis said, arms folded across his chest. His snake skull mask had smaller snakes slithering in and out of its openings.

"Yeah," Aeson said, panting.

"Will you walk with me?"

Aeson and Anguis went together in silence from the felled tree to the house of the elders. They climbed the steps, crossed the porch, and slipped into the dim domicile of Caldera's three most respected individuals.

Aeson already knew where Anguis was taking him, so he took the lead. On the threshold, he immediately turned left and walked down the dark hallway where glowing yellow eyes lined the walls. At its end, he turned left again and pulled back the sliding door there.

He stepped into the room. Anguis quietly followed after. To call it a room would be a lie, but there was no other way to describe it. It was completely overrun with mushrooms and the opalescent sprites that tended to them. There were no walls, and the ceiling was a black stretch of seamless night. Yet if someone tried to walk beyond the actual bounds of the house, the room would swallow them up and spit them out somewhere near the Den of the Unkindness.

"Want me to do it?" Anguis asked, shutting the door behind them.

Aeson ignored him. He crossed the room, through the transparent grass, and went to the large obsidian boulder at the edge of the edgeless room. Kneeling beside the boulder, he splayed his fingers and pressed them into the five invisible grooves on top of it. He waited five seconds, let go. With the tips of his fingers now stained black, he plunged his hand into the pond and let the color run off until the water turned black, like the boulder.

"Eil'en'kul," Aeson whispered as the pond's surface hardened over, like lava cooling into a black crust. He returned to the boulder, pressed all ten fingers to the ten hidden points along its craggy surface, and uttered, "Nyxannul."

This time, when he took his hands off the obsidian boulder, they weren't stained. If they had been, he wouldn't have been able to attempt the ritual again for another month.

"I did not mean to insult you when I asked if you wanted me to do it," Anguis said. "The heart of the mountain is difficult to read."

"Ready?" Aeson stepped onto the pond. A crack shot across the charcoal-colored surface, but it held.

Anguis nodded and stepped onto the surface of the pond with him. The orange and red snakes coiling around his body faded into his flesh until they were merely tattoos.

"Nyxannul," Aeson repeated. He balled his fists and spit on the pond. "Nyxannul."

Finally, the surface broke, and Aeson and Anguis fell through, straight down, until seconds later, they were standing upright again, upon the top of the same black pond; except the transparent grass was gone and so, too, were the mushrooms, sprites, and the ceiling of sky. Now, they were no longer in the house of the elders, but a mile outside the village, deep inside the mountain, Kistvaen.

Aeson gathered himself and stepped off the black pond into the cavern it had taken them to. Great, jagged walls of prismatic stone came together across the cavern, forming eerily perfect archways and steep, unreachable walkways. The ground itself was a hilly span of square-cut rocks that jutted out of the ground, as if they had melted into it a millennium ago.

But it was the place beyond here for which they had come. The place beyond the streaked arches, at the bottom of the hilly span, where the spellweavers lived. Where they spoke to the mountain and listened to its rocks and weaved the spell that made it invisible to those who lived outside Caldera.

"Before we go in," Anguis said.

Aeson stopped and stared at the Snake. He took off his skull mask because the heat inside the mountain was too much to keep it on. "What's wrong?

"The three spellweavers have been in contact with the other villages."

Anguis paused. He never paused. He never hesitated, not even when he had something awful to say.

"Something has happened to the Children of Lacuna."

Aeson furrowed his eyebrows and said, "The ones that left when the Blue Worm was sealed away?"

"No. The others. The ones we created and sent out into the world. There's… hundreds of them, Corrupted and Night Terror alike."

"What's happened?" Aeson felt himself growing impatient. "Did sealing the Blue Worm cause—"

"We keep losing contact with the Children. They are defecting. Those that we have been able to track down and speak with, they keep telling us the same thing."

Aeson's stomach sank. "What?"

"It does not matter how far apart the town or village is. Be it in Nora, Bedlam, Cathedra, or even Eldrus, the story is always the same. The Children say that a woman with the body of a raven forces her way into their minds. They say her eyes sparkle like blue gems, and that her mouth is full of bruise-colored worms. They say that when she speaks, their skulls burn hot and they lose control of themselves. They say her name is Vrana, and that she is calling them."

"C-calling them for what?"

Anguis sighed and looked the other way. "The Cult… the Cult of the Worm."

CHAPTER III

R'lyeh liked Hex, but she didn't need to be her best friend to know there was something wrong with her. A few minutes out of Bedlam and Hex came bounding through the forest on horseback. Unbeknownst to Will and R'lyeh, the Marrow Cabal's second-in-command had been watching them the whole way.

Yet that wasn't the weird part. The weird part was Hex's eyes, and the way they glowed as she rode them down through the trees. The light coming from them was a bright, crystalline blue; it guttered like torch flames around her sockets. As soon as she was beside them, the light vanished. But R'lyeh had seen it. She was sure of it.

"What's got you spooked?" Hex asked Will, her voice bobbing up and down with the rhythm of the horse.

Will pulled back on the reins of his horse and stopped it not far from where Adelaide's Deceit started. He leaned over, exasperated. If he were trying to hide the fact that he was freaking out, he wasn't doing a very good job of it.

But if R'lyeh were being honest with herself, she kind of liked the sight. The boy had been dead not minutes before they were formally introduced, back when the Skeleton slaughtered the Red Worm and pulled Clementine and Will from the Membrane. It was nice to know he still had some life within him, because lately, R'lyeh hadn't been so sure. Both he and his mother had an emptiness to them, a kind of lost look that reminded her of Geharra and the pit and—

"Alright." Hex wheeled the horse around and hopped off it. Her sword bounced against her leg in its scabbard. "Whose bright idea was it to burn down the church?"

"Mine," R'lyeh confessed immediately. After all the lies she had told to Vrana about her dead parents, R'lyeh had given up the stuff completely. "I did it."

Hex's blue braids bobbed beside her face, like tiny, frozen tornados. "Yeah?" Her hand shot out and grabbed R'lyeh's pant leg. "How come?"

Her eyes, she thought, staring into Hex's face. There were pricks of light flaring in her pupils, like gateways. "Well, I—"

Hex threw up her hand, cutting her off. "Save it for Bone Daddy." The nickname made her smile. She tapped R'lyeh's ax and said, "Keeping it safe for me?"

Grinning, R'lyeh chirped, "Keeping it sharp for you. Go find your own."

Hex's eyes fluttered, as if she were struggling to stay awake. She let go of R'lyeh and said to Will, "You look peaked."

"I'm f-fine." Will smiled, forced out a laugh. "R'lyeh back there—" he pointed at her, as if she were invisible, "—scared the hell out of me."

"Yeah, she's a spitfire," Hex said. Her eyes, now finally dimming, darted back and forth between the two adolescents. "It's a good thing I came to chaperone this here date you two went on."

Date? R'lyeh didn't care if she sounded mean. She took off her mask and started laughing. Yes, she and Will were the same age, but the attraction wasn't there. That part of them, whatever mechanism in their minds that might be, was broken. Maybe even beyond repair.

"I got no problem saying it," Will said, rearing up, looking cheerier. "I love this horse." He rubbed its back, hugged its neck. "R'lyeh's just my wingman, so Mom and Dad don't suspect."

Hex rolled her eyes, said, "You're not right in the head," and mounted her horse.

R'lyeh smiled at Will, put her mask back on. *I shouldn't assume he's like me,* she thought, as Hex took off.

"Ready?" Will asked.

Before she could answer, he kicked the horse into a gallop and followed after Hex.

Sitting there, the blood of the priest baking onto her skin, R'lyeh sank into herself. It happened like that sometimes. All of a sudden. Out of nowhere. Like stepping into quicksand.

I shouldn't assume he's like me, she thought again, and that was true. Because Will wasn't like her. Nobody was. She thought they were. After all, that was half the reason she had joined the Marrow Cabal. When she saw that motley crew of murderers—the Skeleton, Hex, Clementine, Will, James, Warren, Elizabeth, Miranda, Herbert North, and Mr. Haemo—she saw people—Mr. Haemo withstanding—covered in stitches. People who had wounds too big to heal, so they tried to seal themselves up the best they could with whatever they had on hand. She liked that. It was good company to be in, until she got her best friend back.

Nowadays, her dad would have said she just had a bad batch of woe-is-mearrhea, but it wasn't that. As far as she was concerned, the actual difference between her and the rest of the Marrow Cabal was that they seemed to be getting better, stitching be damned, while she seemed to be only getting worse. She couldn't afford to be an outcast amongst outcasts. She couldn't afford to be alone. Forty minutes by herself in a church and she had killed the priest and burned the place down. It would be easy enough to excuse herself by pointing to the traditions of her people—and she would, if she needed to—but the fact of the matter was this: There wasn't just something wrong with Hex; there was something wrong with R'lyeh, too.

They rode hard into the evening hours, until the wind turned red and the taste of blood soured their mouths. It was by these foul comforts Hex, Will, and R'lyeh knew they had made it safely home.

Farther on, the town of Gallows sat, its mile-wide lake of blood murmuring under the waning moon. Over the lake, a constant stream of countless mosquitoes flowed, to deposit blood from across the continent into their master's massive well. Around the perimeter of the Red Worm's resting place, elevated platforms had been constructed, to hold the barracks and buildings that housed and supplied the members of the Skeleton's Marrow Cabal.

Hex stopped her horse in front of R'lyeh and Will's and said, "Hang on."

They were on the outskirts, about a half a mile out from the town, where the marshy land thrived on the human mulch the Red Worm had left here. There were still bones lodged in the ground, and bodies, too. R'lyeh didn't mind being inside Gallows, but being out here, in this bloody backwash, she started to get anxious. It was too much like Geharra's pit, and the fact there was even a fraction of a chance she might stumble upon her parents' corpses—

"Get your stories straight," Hex warned. Her eyes flared. She grabbed her head and shrieked. "Ah, hell. Ah, shit."

"Hey." Will hopped off his horse. "Hey, what's wrong? Hex, what's the matter?"

Hex tore the sword out of its scabbard. "Stop!"

Will went stiff. His knees locked in place. The moon was bright tonight, but Hex's eyes were brighter. She crept forward, the tip of her sword moving closer and closer to Will's neck. Gems of blue light poured out of her eyes. Although her mouth was moving, she didn't seem to be saying anything.

"Hex, don't." R'lyeh dropped off the horse. She took the ax in both hands and ran in between Will and Hex. "A-are you sick?"

Hex stopped. She lowered her sword. A shadow passed through her eyes. Not across them, but through them, as if there were a cruel conductor inside her skull, controlling her every movement. She mumbled something that sounded like "pilgrimage" and started to cough.

"I-I'm sorry, you two," Hex said, rubbing her eyes until the light left them. "If I get like that again, leave me be. It's for the best."

Will's joints loosened. He took a step after Hex, who was already back on her horse, and said, "Dad said that's when you send your thoughts out."

R'lyeh kept quiet. She'd heard Hex had been capable of such a thing, but never had she seen it happen before. When the Skeleton had introduced her to the members of the Marrow Cabal, he told R'lyeh that Hex was from Lacuna herself, and that she was a telepath. When R'lyeh asked her if she could try to reach Vrana, Hex told her she could only communicate with other children of Lacuna, but she'd keep an ear out, just in case.

Hopping back onto the horse, R'lyeh asked, "Who's going on a pilgrimage?"

Hex shook her head. "You and your friend really messed things up putting that Blue Worm to sleep." She groaned. "The thoughts are re-goddamn-diculous, now. Barely enough room in my head for my own."

"Why'd you draw your sword for?" Will got back on his horse.

"Reflex, I expect. Don't mean nothing. Bone Man's going to want to know: Did you see a shepherd while you two arsonists were out?"

Will shook his head.

R'lyeh pretended not to hear.

"Alright, then." She rubbed her temple and said, "Let's get to it, love-birds."

Guard towers sat against the night sky. Their black, wiry silhouettes reminded R'lyeh of the dead bugs that littered the barracks. Hex took the vanguard, held up two fingers, and shouted to the sentries, "It's Hex, Will, and R'lyeh, and we've brought the same old, same old." The same old, same old was the passphrase for entry today. If anyone forgot it, they got about thirty arrows in their neck to remind them.

The horses cantered past the guard towers and onto the dock that circled the blood lake. There, torches burned across the wooden plat-form, as well as on the second level above. Together, they created a dirty cloud of smoke that drifted across the lake, leaving most of what was happening at its center obscured. But something definitely was happen-ing. There were ripples in the lake, as if something were churning in it, and sounds, too, in the air; incomprehensible whispers in Mr. Haemo's grating whine.

"The Bag of Bones must have him up to something tonight," Hex said. She turned her horse towards the ramp that led to the second level of the platform. "Stay indoors tonight, if you can help it."

Will and R'lyeh nodded. They followed Hex up the ramp, past a few passing cabalists, who quickly saluted Hex as she trotted by. Looking around Gallows, R'lyeh realized there weren't many people out. Most of the windows had candles in them, but the Marrow Cabal's soldiers were mostly absent. She couldn't figure out if the Skeleton's claims about their growing ranks were wrong—he boasted fifty here, two hundred or more elsewhere—or if they also had been given Hex's advice about staying indoors. It was strange, but when it came to Mr. Haemo, they treated him like a necessary evil. A lunatic lodger they all hated but couldn't be rid of. Like they owed him something.

"So." Hex stopped her horse in front of the large building designated as Operations. "Who wants to talk to the Skeleton first?"

Before Will could answer, R'lyeh was already on the ground, one arm leaning against her ax, the other high in the air. "I'm your girl."

"Alright." Hex wheeled her horse alongside Will's and told him, "Let's put these beasts to bed." And then, to R'lyeh: "After you're done with Bag of Bones, get to bed yourself."

She nodded. Her attention wandered over to Operations, and she wondered aloud, "Shouldn't there be guards?"

Hex snorted. "Why? So someone doesn't try to kill him?"

Will laughed uncomfortably. "Yeah," he said. He focused his eyes on R'lyeh and bore his thoughts through her orange octopus mask. *Don't tell him,* he seemed to say. *Don't you dare tell him about the shepherd.*

R'lyeh waved Will and Hex off and then entered Operations. She opened the door slowly; her breath caught in her throat. Over the last few months, she had spoken to the Skeleton on numerous occasions, but the journey to Bedlam had been the first mission he had sent her on. The last thing she wanted was to disappoint him.

Operations was one large, open, and well-kept room. Across it, several long tables ran, upon which stacks of maps, documents, field reports, and artifacts were kept. The walls were dedicated to the two religions currently battling for control of the continent. On the left wall, The Disciples of the Deep, and the right, The Holy Order of Penance. Both walls contained a timeline of events relevant to each religion's creation, as well as data about the number of followers each possessed in every major village, town, and city. There were piles of books, too, beside the walls. Mandatory reading for all members of the Marrow Cabal. For the Disciples of the Deep, they had to study *The Disciples of the Deep* by Amon Ashcroft. For The Holy Order of Penance, they had to read not only *Helminth's Way* by the Prophet Helminth and Mother Abbess Lillian, but the newly released and revised holy text entitled *The Sinner and the Shadows* by The Holy Child Felix and Mother Abbess Justine.

But, as interesting as all that was, it was nothing compared to the boney beast that inhabited this building on an almost constant basis. The Bag of Bones, as Hex so lovingly put it, was sitting in the back at his desk, shrouded in a cloak and surrounded by candles, poring over the papers in front of him.

"R'lyeh," the Skeleton said, his voice dry and high, his pronunciation slow. "Good to see you."

She stopped, saluted him. "Sir."

The Skeleton waved her off. "What'd I tell you about all that 'sir' business?"

R'lyeh lowered hand and dropped her head.

"Sit with me." He gestured to the seat in front of his desk. "Tell me 'bout Bedlam."

R'lyeh crossed the room. The Skeleton in his tattered cloak and rusty breastplate watched her the whole way. She could feel his hard, swollen, bloodshot eyes sizing her up, searching for the story she was about to tell. He lifted his hands, knitted his fingers together, and rested his chin against them. Other than the tone of his voice, there was no telling what the Skeleton was thinking or feeling, because he was nothing but bone.

R'lyeh smiled and took a seat in front of the Skeleton. She peered over the desk and saw that he had been reading a map of Bedlam. There were red marks all over it, in the town and outside it as well.

The Skeleton's fat, black tongue flopped around inside his jaw. His bones creaked and cracked as he straightened up. His robe started to drift, revealing a portion of his ribs where the breastplate didn't protect. The bones were covered in a black moss.

Quickly pulling back his robe, he said, "What'd we learn?"

R'lyeh filed the sight away. It was a necessity. She had a whole drawer inside her head marked 'madness.'

"The church was a church for the Disciples of the Deep. The priest had vermillion veins inside his head, but it seemed like he could control them. A woman came in. She brought her dead son with her. The priest said he had a 'seed of heaven' and fed it to her son. He was going to have her bury her son with it in him, but then the dead son started... transforming. And vermillion veins came out and killed her. The priest made it sound like that wasn't supposed to happen."

The Skeleton nodded. He took out a pen and made another circle on the map near the riverbanks, where the church would have been.

R'lyeh tried to stop herself, but the confession was already coming out. "I... lost control."

He set the pen down and cocked his skull. "What happened?"

"The priest heard me. I... killed him."

"Fair enough."

"And then I burned the church down."

"Oh." The Skeleton's insane eyes ground against their sockets. "Damn."

"I got scared." R'lyeh took off her mask and rested it in her lap. Fiddling with its tentacles, she added, "And the woman and her son had turned into this big, veiny... thing. Seemed like a bad idea to leave that there."

"How'd you escape?"

"Horseback. Will was waiting outside."

The Skeleton clicked his fingers against his cheekbone. "How'd he do?"

"He got us out of there quick." R'lyeh rubbed the scar that ran along her scalp. She did that sometimes, when she was nervous. "He was good."

The Skeleton leaned in closer. "Anything else?"

"On… on our w-way out." R'lyeh shook her head. "On our w-way out, we saw a… a shepherd."

At that, the Skeleton sank into his chair. The hood on the cloak slid down his face. He sat there a moment, his only gloved hand over where his heart had once been.

R'lyeh shrank under his wicked gaze. Without lids or lips, the Skeleton's stare and horrible grin made her feel like she was facing Death Itself. However, as they sat there in silence, she realized he wasn't looking at her, but listening to something. The way he turned his head, the way he leaned down and to the left, it was if there were someone else in the room, whispering dark paranoias into the Skeleton's shadow-drenched skull.

"It's good you told me first," he said, at last. "I'm sure he asked you not to say anything. Makes me wonder if he's seen them before."

R'lyeh shrugged. "I-I don't know."

"Thank you, R'lyeh. Been through a lot to get my family back. Don't plan on losing them again."

Lucky you, she thought but didn't say.

"So." The Skeleton came forward, clutching his cloak to hide the black moss growing over his ribs. "So, how are you, my resident Night Terror?"

"Oh, uh. I'm… good." She nodded, smiled, and then quickly changed the subject. "What's going on with Eldrus and Penance?"

The Skeleton saw right through her misdirection. He laughed at it. Even pointed his sharp finger at her to let her know he'd caught her.

But instead of acknowledging this, he pointed to the walls and said, "A lot. Penance is losing some favor with its followers. There are rumors they're throwing together an army. Eldrus, on the other hand, not so bad. Disciples keep springing up churches here and there. They're trying to summon something with all them vermillion veins they keep planting in the ground. They were at it before, a few years back, and now they're at it again. Or maybe they never stopped. Lost years when I went into the Nameless Forest. Hard to say."

The Red Worm writhed in her mind's eye. She said, "Are they trying to summon another Worm? Is that their God?"

And he answered, "Might be. The vermillion veins and Eldrus' new religion go hand-in-hand. A little girl, Gemma—a worldly thing like yourself—told me they're summoning what caused the Trauma years back."

"And we're going to stop them?"

The Skeleton stared at her a moment, like he had forgotten the purpose of the Marrow Cabal. Then, he said, "A lot of forces seem to be converging nowadays."

She raised an eyebrow. What did that mean?

The door to Operations swung back. R'lyeh jumped in her chair. In the doorway, the Skeleton's wife, Clementine, stood. Her red hair, redder than the blood lake behind her, whipped across her pale, tired face.

"Hi there, R'lyeh," she said, looking a little lost.

R'lyeh held up her hand, said, "Hi."

Clementine smiled and to the Skeleton said, "Husband."

"Wife," he chirped back. He didn't have lips or muscles, but R'lyeh was pretty sure he was smiling.

"Work day is over." Clementine leaned to one side, her soft, yellow dress shifting with her motion. "Bed time."

The Skeleton nodded. "Be there in a minute my sweet, lily-white princess."

Clementine scoffed, gave him the finger. As she closed the door to Operations, she said to R'lyeh, "Goodnight, dear. Stay indoors, whatever you hear."

With that warning, Clementine was gone. R'lyeh turned to the Skeleton, her next question written all over her face.

"Mr. Haemo is doing some blood work for me," the Skeleton said. "Helping me track a lead. Your next mission, if it pans out. Blood work gets greedy. Lashes out like a leech. Don't want to be near the lake is all."

R'lyeh nodded and then asked her follow-up: "You sleep?"

"Ha." The Skeleton sighed and stood. The ratty cloak fell around him like a hungry wraith. Flexing his gloved hand, he said, "Not no more I don't. It's a waste of my unlimited time. No, it just calms Clementine if I lay in bed with her 'til she's out. It's the little things that make us human. Or, in your case—" he laughed, "—whatever your kind is."

R'lyeh hopped to her feet as the Skeleton came around the desk. "You're going to send me on another mission? After I fucked the last one up?"

"You learned enough from what you accomplished and what you fucked up. You've held your own, and I still plan on holding up my end of our bargain. About finding your friend."

"Vrana."

"Yeah." The Skeleton touched her shoulder and—

Skyscrapers. Green gas and busted tubes. A grandfather clock.

Letters impaled upon tree branches. Mushroom clouds stretching over a garden of bones. Naked nuns in a convent questing for—

—and then he pulled away. R'lyeh gasped and stumbled backward, against the chair she had sat in. Hot, boiling bubbles of pain bobbed along her brain in a sweeping, pendulum-like flow. She held her neck until the foreign images ran like mucus down the back of her throat.

"I just saw—"

The Skeleton cut her off. "Your next mission will take you to Rime."

"That's one of our villages." *Damn it. What did he just do to me?*

"Yes, it is." The Skeleton opened the door. Over his shoulder, he said, "I need you to convince your people to release one of their prisoners to our cause."

"What?" R'lyeh threw up her hands. "Wait, I'm not anyone special. They're not going to—"

"They're holding Audra of Eldrus. King Edgar's sister. Turns out she's not dead at all. Get her to me, and I'll scour the Membrane myself to find your friend."

R'lyeh stared at him, dumbfounded. *Are you fucking kidding me?* she thought.

"Oh." He stopped, the door almost shut. "Would you mind blowing out those candles for me? Don't have no breath left to breathe."

CHAPTER IV

"The Cult of the Worm?" Aeson repeated, as Kistvaen trembled around them.

Anguis nodded. He slipped past Aeson and headed down the hilly span of square-cut rocks that protruded like teeth from the mountain's innards. Where the elder's feet landed, bursts of color exploded across the floor, as if the pressure from his weight were causing chemical reactions within the stone.

Aeson followed after him. The prismatic archways narrowed as they closed in towards the bottom of the hill.

"Stop," Aeson said, reaching out for the elder's arm.

Before his hand could touch him, the Snake sped up. "We need to speak with the spellweavers."

Is he going to let me use them to find her? Aeson wondered. He licked his lips. The sour taste of hope prickled his mouth.

"Okay," he said, quickly reverting back to the diligent lapdog everyone accused him of being. "Yeah, sure. Okay."

At the bottom of the hill, where the ceiling of the cavern and the archways were low enough to touch, they were stopped by the eighty-foot wall there. Several capillary-like tunnels had been bored through it. Faint lights winked inside the winding shafts from the wisps within. On the wind, Aeson could hear words being constantly spoken in scratchy, spit-slicked syllables. Supposedly, they could take any tunnel to reach the spellweavers, but he knew better than to test that theory, because when it came to the elders, nothing was ever that simple.

"Leftmost," Anguis said, going to the farthest passage on the left.

"What do the spellweavers have to do with Vrana?" Aeson asked. He leaned into the tunnel; the smoky darkness inside was almost gelatinous.

"She seems to be somehow channeling the Blue Worm's powers," Anguis said.

Aeson's mouth dropped open. "What? But didn't she seal it away?"

"She did." Anguis cleared his throat. "Come now. No more delays."

Aeson followed him into the tunnel. The smoke moved towards them, its clouds tightening into languid limbs. It reached forward, took Aeson's chin, and shoved its roiling digits into his mouth and nose. He closed his eyes, held his breath; waited until gray murk swept across the back of his lids. Then, when he could smell nothing but ash and taste nothing but earth, he opened his eyes and took a step forward into another location entirely.

Gone were the prismatic stones and the smoke-choked tunnels; they had been repurposed and replaced by what the spellweavers so lovingly called their lair. The chamber was a rough, disk-shaped room with angular walls and narrow trenches meant to resemble the image of a pentacle. Twenty meters across and thirty meters high, the lair, despite its size and few occupants, was stuffed to the stones with gaudy decorations and unnecessary adornments. Large, heavy curtains were drawn across segments of the lair. Plush couches and embroidered chairs sat scattered here and there, covered in dust from disuse. Carpets and rugs, from Old World mansions and museums, blanketed the floor, each of their cultural styles clashing against one another's. Between the rocky balconies above the main floor, a chandelier had been installed; on it, fifty candles burned constantly, never losing shape or intensity. And in spherical alcoves on the outskirts, black flames wavered, their searing tongues like liquefied obsidian.

For a place inside a volcano, it was one hell of a fire hazard.

But most of it was pure window-dressing; nothing more than a soulless recreation by something that itself lacked a soul. The fanciful and once-expensive décor wasn't meant to comfort its owners, but soothe the guilt of their masters. The spellweavers who benefited from all of this never used it. No, they stayed where they almost always stayed, which was where they stood now: in the center of the lair, at the heart of the pentacle, naked and convulsing, giving every ounce of their existence to maintain the illusion that made Kistvaen disappear.

There were three spellweavers altogether. The youngest was Enaar, the twenty-four-year-old who had been brought in from Traesk after the

Witch murdered his predecessor during her attack on Caldera. Enaar's responsibility was to support the other spellweavers, be it through channeling his powers into them or cooking them breakfast, lunch, and dinner. He rarely spoke, and every time Aeson saw him, he always looked as if he had been crying.

The second spellweaver, and most powerful amongst the three, was Gisela. At eighty-four years old, she was the oldest known living spellweaver. Gisela was blind, and had once chewed through half her hand to boost a spell through the energy of pain. She had a good sense of humor, but she had to be kept shackled and separated from the rest, because after she bit through her hand, she developed an unquenchable taste for flesh.

The final spellweaver was the one Aeson and Anguis communicated with the most. His name was Verat, and at forty-two, he had yet to succumb to the insanity most spellweavers, like Gisela, were known to contract halfway into their lifespans. When he wasn't making Kistvaen invisible to those outside Caldera, he spent most of his time walking around the lair for exercise.

"Verat," Anguis called, as he headed toward the center of the room.

Aeson stepped over the trenches that divided the room into a respectable attempt at a pentagram. They were filled with piss and shit, and the subterranean insects that inhaled the stench and consumed the waste here. Despite the elders' best efforts to dress the place up, there was always a depraved reminder to dispel the lie.

The spellweavers were a sick secret of their people. Every Night Terror village had a small group of spellweavers, and like Aeson, they were forced through the notion of purpose to dedicate their every waking moment to their craft. Until today, he used to hate coming here for those reasons, but now that he knew they might be able to help him find Vrana, there wasn't anywhere else he wanted to be.

Anguis stopped outside the center of the pentacle. Enaar nodded at him, but Gisela continued to chant, indifferent to the new flesh in the room.

Kistvaen shook; a curtain unhooked from the wall and crumpled into one of the shit creeks.

Verat's quivering body went stiff. Eyes darting back and forth in their sockets, he said, "Anguis." He nodded at the obsidian flames in the surrounding alcoves. "All is well."

"What's wrong with the mountain?" Aeson asked. The elders measured its health through the obsidian flames here, as well as the obsidian boulders they kept in the house and the garden of the elders. "It's an active volcano again, isn't it?"

Verat bit his lip. His bloodshot eyes shot over to Anguis, as if he were asking for help out of this conversation. The spellweaver started to scratch his forearm. Verat was forty-two, but his skin was so scarred from self-harm he looked twice his age.

"It is," Anguis said.

Aeson threw up his hand. "Well, what the—"

"It has always been active," Anguis added.

Aeson tightened his gaze on the elder. "What?"

Anguis nodded at Verat to go back to his work. Then, to Aeson, he said, "Tell me about Marcus Proust."

Oh, go to hell. Aeson's face somehow got hotter than it already was. He let his attention wander about the lair to hide the anger mounting inside him. Anguis always did this, always asked him questions the same way a teacher would a student. At first, Aeson didn't mind, but as the years went on, each question and confrontation made him feel more and more uncomfortable. Lately, it didn't seem like Anguis was looking for gaps in Aeson's knowledge; instead, the Snake seemed to be looking for moments to remind Aeson that, despite his best efforts, he would never be as smart as him.

Aeson slipped on his skull mask. It gave him the confidence he needed to stand up to this intellectual bully. "Marcus Proust was a zealot from Whiteshire, a town in the snowy wasteland outside Penance. About eighty years ago, he gained enough followers and support to ride across the Divide and attack Caldera. He wanted to eradicate the Night Terrors, because he thought our people were responsible for all the sin in the world."

He cleared his throat, fumbled for his words. "They made camp in what's now the Den of the Unkindness. While they attacked Caldera over the span of a month, they overworked that part of the forest and almost killed it. Eventually, we defeated Marcus' people. There were a lot more of us back then. Years later, his son vowed to get revenge but that never—"

"That's mostly correct," Anguis interrupted.

Rage knotted across Aeson's forehead. "That's exactly what you told me. What does this have to do with Kistvaen?"

"We did not beat back Marcus Proust because of our numbers. Not entirely," Anguis said. "Eighty years ago, our people were much more vicious, much less interested in sustaining a culture. When Caldera was settled at the foot of Kistvaen, it was done so knowing the mountain was an active volcano. The Night Terrors of the time were so radical in their idea of 'keeping the balance' that they deliberately placed themselves here, in harm's way. They believed that once the Night Terrors had killed enough Corrupted, Kistvaen would erupt and burn away the Night Terrors for good because they were no longer needed by the Earth.

"That suicidal fervor lasted a long time. Some Night Terrors even believed they were immortal. They lived so close to Death, they believed they had somehow bought favor with It. But then Marcus Proust arrived with hundreds of soldiers, and every time a battle was fought in these forests, more Night Terrors fell than did Corrupted."

Verat stepped forward, digging his nails into his dense pubic hair. "And then Kistvaen started rumbling." He stopped, sat in an oversized chair covered in paisley print. "Our people were losing the fight and, uh, the mountain was looking like it was going to erupt. That didn't make any sense to the Night Terrors. Marcus Proust saw the signs, too, so he backed off. Didn't want his own men getting melted."

The spellweaver puffed out his cheeks, bulged out his eyes. Talking to others in the common tongue wasn't something he was used to. "And at the, uh, same time, we were a few years into our work with the Blue Worm on Lacuna. No fertility project, yet. Just, uh, you know, our people trying to make sense of the creature."

"The Blue Worm had the power to understand and bestow ancient knowledge," Anguis said. "It knew what was happening in Caldera, and it knew what would happen if Caldera fell. The Worm still wanted to use us, and wanted us to use it. We were not stupid. We knew this. But we were also desperate."

Verat chanted something; the black liquid flames exploded in their alcoves. As if this was nothing to be alarmed about, he continued. "The Blue Worm's first gift had been telepathy. It opened up some of our spellweavers' minds."

Anguis took over. "Then the Blue Worm told us it could teach us how to calm Kistvaen. So, with its help, in the dead of night, the spellweavers used that ancient knowledge to calm the volcano. But with the mountain silenced, the Calderans were worried Marcus would use the lull to strike a final blow."

"The Blue Worm told the Night Terrors not to worry," Verat said. He jumped to his feet, wandered back over to his chanting brethren. "The Blue Worm told the elders at the time to wait until morning to see what their weaving had sewn."

"Kistvaen was still dormant in the morning," Anguis said, lowering his voice. "And Marcus Proust and his followers were defeated."

Aeson blinked the deluge of sweat out of his eyes. "How? What... happened?"

"The spell had not only calmed Kistvaen, but created an illusion around it, making it invisible to those outside Caldera." Anguis sighed. "But in order to do so, it had drained the life out of most of Marcus' men and the surrounding land."

Verat said, "It's... it's one thing settling a volcano. But making it d-disappear?" He laughed and rubbed his hands together.

"When news spread that the Calderans had killed Marcus' men in a single night, that was the end of it," Anguis said. "Because of the blight the spell left on the forest, the Corrupted thought the Night Terrors were in possession of some powerful pestilence. Afterwards, Corrupted seldom traveled into the south unless it was absolutely necessary."

Aeson shook his head. "The Den of the Unkindness. Marcus didn't kill that part of the forest. We did. And it won't get any better, because you keep having them—" he pointed to Enaar, Gisela, and Verat, "—cast that same spell over and over, every single day, to keep the mountain hidden, to keep it from going off. So what is it now? The Blue Worm is gone, right? Is the spell not working anymore?"

"Spell is fine," Gisela said, speaking in-between guttural groans. "Better than ever, baby."

Verat nodded. "A lot of life in the land, nowadays." He wiggled his hips and then jumped to his feet out of the chair. A black stain had spread outward from where he had been sitting.

"It's your girlfriend." Gisela stopped, tugged on her naked, wrinkled flesh, as if testing its elasticity. "She's doing things only the Worm was supposed to be able to do."

Aeson's eyes darted back and forth between Anguis and the spell-weavers. He stumbled over his feet. Words of protest lodged in his tightening throat. What was this? What were they saying? He dug his knuckle into the side of his mask. Only in times of stress did he remember how unnaturally large it was. Of course, it had to be to fit on his head, but the Corrupted the skull was taken from had to have some genetic defect or—

He gritted his teeth. *Focus,* he told himself. *Focus.* Aeson waved off the elder and the spellweavers. He hopped over a trench of piss-soaked shit and headed toward one of the spherical alcoves where the black flames flared.

They want something from me. He peered into the hot obsidian tongues. The smoke that came off them traveled up the alcove; it smelled of spices, like something a healer might burn to cure the sick. *Don't be an idiot. Don't let them trick you into saying something you shouldn't. They're trying to make Vrana out to be the—*

Kistvaen rumbled. A crack split across the lair's jagged ceiling. Something hissed inside the fissure. Aeson backed away from the black flames. He turned around and found Enaar, Gisela, Verat, and Anguis staring at him.

"Telepathy," Aeson blurted out, before he had a chance to fully process the revelation. "The Children of Lacuna. They're telepaths. Vrana is somehow tapping into that."

"Yes." Anguis waved his hand; the spellweavers scattered across the lair to their individual haunts. "The Witch has Vrana reaching out to the Children of Lacuna, using the power of the Blue Worm to manipulate them to whatever nefarious goal the Maiden of Pain has in mind. The Children of Lacuna all possess the gift of telepathy; it was a boon given to them by the Blue Worm, and given to us to control them. It need only be unlocked to be made use of."

Anguis stepped towards him. "I have no doubt in my mind that Vrana has no control over her situation. But if she has access to even a fraction of the Worm's powers, then we must act. If the creature had the knowledge to make mountains disappear, or for Night Terrors to procreate with Corrupted, can we not agree it surely had access to even more horrible spells?

"We both met the Witch, Aeson. We both know she will use those spells, once she discovers how to do so."

Aeson mumbled, "I... I... what do you want me to do?"

The Snake strolled forward with a slithery gait. The serpentine tattoos on his taut flesh flickered with life. "I want you to find her, reach out to her. It sounds as if the Witch has done terrible things to Vrana, but if she sees you, you may be able to save her. You have to remind her of who she is, who she was. She may be able to turn the Blue Worm's power on the Witch and free herself from the Void."

"How?" That was the only question that mattered; the one it seemed

Anguis was about to answer. "How am I going to do this?"

"We keep a registry of all the Children of Lacuna. Until recently, they were our eyes and ears into the affairs of the Corrupted. For those whose telepathic abilities had been unlocked, they would check in with us monthly to update us through an heir. We have lost contact with them, but I doubt they have gone far. I want you to use the registry and track down these Children. I want you to interrogate them. I want you to use everything you have ever learned about psychology and social interactions to break into their minds.

"The few Children we have been able to track down, the few that haven't killed themselves when captured, always mention the same thing."

"What?" Aeson asked.

"A pilgrimage." Anguis went to Aeson and put his hand on his shoulder. "Vrana is reaching out to the Children of Lacuna, and she is calling them somewhere. The Witch is planning to use our people. I do not want it to come to that. I hope that you can save Vrana before then. But if you cannot, then you may be able to find where the Children are going."

"The Cult of the Worm." Aeson shook off the elder's hand. "The Witch is building a cult, a new following. If they're going somewhere, then… then there may be a chance they could lead me to a way into the Void. The Witch may even step out of it for a moment."

Anguis nodded. "Enaar keeps the registry. He will conjure it for you. Do you have a companion in mind for your journey?"

I do, Aeson thought but didn't say. Instead, he said, "But I'm Caldera's Archivist."

"We have learned enough, Aeson. All of it will be for naught if we are undone by the choices of our ancestors decades ago. We were foolish to continue using the Blue Worm, but without it, you and I may not be standing here today. Nevertheless, the choice was made, and now we must deal with the consequences."

Simultaneously, as if called by some internal clockwork, the spellweavers rose from their places of rest and returned to the center of the lair. Enaar and Verat kept their distance from the cannibal Gisela, and then, all together, they started chanting once more.

Aeson took off his mask. He didn't need its bulk anymore to hide behind. "When I save Vrana," he said, "will you let me use the spellweavers to undo what the Witch has done to her?"

"Of course," Anguis said.

"And what about those that won't talk? Aren't they still a threat?"

"Kill them," Anguis said, "unless you have the means to transport them to one of our villages. They are a liability."

Telepathy, Aeson thought, the sudden realization overtaking the severity of the elder's order. *The Children of Lacuna are telepaths.* He stared at the spellweavers, watching their grotesque gyrations.

"What is it?" Anguis asked.

"The Witch contacted Vrana through her dreams. R'lyeh's letter said the Witch was using Vrana." Aeson scratched his face until it went red. "Now, the Witch is using Vrana to control the Children of Lacuna. You say Vrana's using the Blue Worm's powers, but if that was the Witch's goal, then why didn't she reach out to Mara? Or another Child of Lacuna? Vrana's just a warrior. She's not a spellweaver or—"

"We believe Vrana is in possession of the silver necklace that is used to summon the Blue Worm," Anguis admitted. "It, in combination with the Witch's power, may allow her to form some sort of connection with the Worm." He sighed and then said, "But you are right. It was not a coincidence that the Witch let Vrana live as long she did. She saw a potential in her not yet realized. The necklace appears to be amplifying that potential."

"What?" Aeson cocked his head. "What do you mean?"

"How much do you know about Vrana's parents?"

"Her father, Quentin, died looking into the causes of the Black Hour, and Adelyn is—" Aeson paused. His eyes widened. "Wait a minute. Wait. 'Amplifying her potential'? You sent her to Lacuna on purpose. It wasn't just because she knew about the Red Worm." He grabbed Anguis' robes and spat, "Where the hell was Vrana born?"

CHAPTER V

Vrana crouched atop the little girl's headboard, waiting for her to wake. She outstretched her wings and closed them like curtains around the child's bed. Gripping the frame with her talons, she leaned in closer until her beak was barely touching the little girl's nose. Vrana breathed her in. She smelled soft and sweet, like the warm cookies her mother had baked a few hours earlier. It was a shame the nine-year-old had to die, but at least she would die with food in her belly and love in her heart.

The floor creaked outside the little girl's room. Vrana tightened her gaze on the gap beneath the closed door, watching for shadows and shuffling feet. Though some part of Vrana was still a Night Terror, she took no pleasure in killing Corrupted for the Witches, so she tried to keep unnecessary casualties, like the rest of this little girl's family, to a minimum.

Vrana pulled away and sat upright on her weakening perch. She turned her head and stared at the moonlight coming through the little girl's bedside window. She preferred it this way, carrying out the Witches' cruel commands in the dead of night. Most of the time, her victims were asleep at this hour. When they woke, she imagined they told themselves they were still sleeping, and that the winged horror that stood over them was no more than a nightmare. Most people wanted to die in their sleep, but if they were awake and didn't realize it, wouldn't that be the next best thing?

The little girl coughed, turned on her side. She fussed over something, rolled onto her back again. A heavy sigh slipped past her puffy lips, and sleep took its hold on her once more.

Vrana had killed thirty men, twenty-two women, and forty-seven children in the last few months. The Witch hated children. Of late, she had Vrana terrorizing the backwoods settlements deep within the Heartland. These unmapped hamlets had more ignorance and children than they knew what to do with, but according to the Witch, she had just the plan to see those precious resources weren't wasted.

A low wheeze rattled inside the little girl's chest. She coughed. Whether it was allergies or illness, Vrana couldn't be sure. But the child looked cold, so she took the blanket in her claw and pulled it up gently to the little girl's chin.

As for the Children of Lacuna, Vrana wasn't sure how many she had made contact with. The process was exhausting, and painful. Somehow, it made her brain hurt. It was as if there was a separate organ inside it, and every time she used the Blue Worm's silver necklace, the organ was stretched beyond its limit. The worst part of it all was the memories. At first, she had thought they were the experiences of the Children she was invading, but the memories were too familiar, too intimate to be anybody else's but her own. And yet that was impossible, too. How could she remember being a baby, let alone through someone else's eyes? Why would Mara be standing over her in a field of rust-colored grass? Something was trying to—

The little girl's eyes were open. Beads of fear glistened on her brow. The color drained out of her face, so that she wasn't much paler than her pillow. She opened her mouth. A scream welled in her throat, like a bubble a few heartbeats away from popping. As if to wake from this terrible nightmare, she clenched her fists and closed her eyes and started to moan.

The Witch's will twisted like a hot wire inside Vrana's skull. With all her strength, she tightened her neck and stabbed downward, driving her beak through the little girl's chest. Fat tongues of sleep-warmed blood splashed like milk against Vrana's mouth. She gored the little girl deeper, until the tip of her beak broke through the child's back and pierced her bed.

Vrana reared back, flinging steamy, stringy entrails across the little girl's room. Making every effort not to look at the crumpled corpse, Vrana dismounted from the headboard. Her talons clicked as she landed on the floor. Quickly, she went to the scattered intestines and shredded organs she'd flung and gathered them like flowers against her feathered breast. She had to finish quickly, or others would suffer the Witches' wrath.

She went to the farthest wall. With a bloody palette in her palm, she dipped her finger in the thick red paint and began to write upon the wall. Voices traveled down the hall outside the little girl's room. There were footsteps, too, most likely from the child's mother and father. Vrana had studied the house for two hours before breaking into it. She had a minute and a half at best before the parents barged in and put themselves in peril.

Vrana squeezed a section of the little girl's intestines and smattered the thick digestion onto the wall. The footsteps drew closer. She took the child's stomach and squeezed it like a sponge. The voices grew louder. Frantically, she dragged her talons over the wall, creating bloody Ws and dripping Ss, while making sure to sop up the pinkish run-off to avoid ruining her morbid message.

"I'm sure it's nothing," a woman's voice said with assurance outside the little girl's room.

Vrana slapped the stomach against the wall, putting a putrid period at the end of her warning, which read:

THE MAIDEN OF PAIN LIVES AGAIN

"Flora, sweetie," the mother said. The doorknob started to turn.

Vrana lumbered to the window, her oily, black feathers standing on end. "Get me out," she hissed.

From the Void, the Witch whispered into Vrana's skull, "No."

The Witch's will reached inside Vrana and turned her around to face the opening door. "Kill them both."

Flora's father was the first to enter. Shirtless and half-asleep, he plodded into the room and stopped at the foot of his daughter's bed.

Flora's mother crept up beside him. Her hair was bunched up on one side, looking like a brunette landslide. She grabbed her husband's arm, opened her mouth to say something, but a yawn came out instead.

It wasn't until their eyes adjusted to the dark of the room did the screaming start.

Flora's father fell forward. His hands latched onto his daughter's ankles. He pulled her towards him. Flora's body, now with a gaping hole in the nine-year-old's gut, twisted unnaturally as he wrenched her into his arms.

Flora's mother, with one trembling finger pointing at Vrana, shrieked.

She cowered behind her husband and beat her fists against his back, each sweaty, meaty smack drawing only his ire rather than his attention.

"It killed her! It killed her!" Flora's mother screamed.

Flora's father looked up from his little girl's ragged corpse. Vrana's eyes met his. She fought every spell and incantation the Witch was pumping into her mind, but the Witch was stronger. Even from the Void, an immeasurable distance of death and despair between them, the Witch was stronger.

Vrana's restraint snapped. She ran forward, her winged arms outstretched. Flora's father struggled to his feet, and that was all he did. Vrana raked her claws across his face. His flesh peeled away in four seething strips. Then she drove her talons into his left armpit and scrambled the muscle and arteries inside. He gasped, shook, and then slumped to the ground, blood pumping out of his fatal wound.

Flora's mother spit in Vrana's face and went sideways out of the room. She crashed into the hallway and slipped into the thick darkness that filled it. Vrana stalked after, her vision unimpeded.

Flora's mother's feet, sticky with her husband's blood, slipped on the hardwood floor. "Please," she cried, tripping and landing with a crack onto her knees. "Please don't."

Vrana wanted to stop. She wanted to stop more than anything else in the world. But what she wanted was not what was willed. Her wants were the Witches' wants, and her needs non-existent. For as long as Pain and Joy were more powerful than her, she would be enslaved to them and their cruel campaign. She had ideas, but ideas were dangerous when the sisters were awake; ideas could be intercepted and dissected and turned against Vrana. Now was not the time for ideas, or for stopping. Now was the time for killing, and for going home.

So Vrana took the woman's head in her claws and bit it in half until it broke like ripe fruit in her mouth. The taste made her sick, but like her daughter's death, it had been a quick one, and until Vrana was more powerful, a quick death was the best that she could do for these sad subjects of the Maidens' rule.

"The neighbors will have a field day tomorrow morning," Joy said behind Vrana.

Vrana spit out the rest of Flora's mother and turned. The Witch's sister stood there in her white satin dress, one hand on her hip, the other pressed to her mouth, as if she were somehow appalled by the scene. A puddle of water was spreading out from under Joy's bare feet. The Witch and her sister used large bodies of water as a means of entering Earth. Unfortunately for Flora's family, their village had been built around a lake.

"Let's go," Joy said, holding out her hand, "before the baby wakes up."

It was three in the morning, and the village was already awake for the day. As Joy and Vrana went hand-in-hand from the woods and towards the lake, the villagers poured out of their homes behind them. They converged upon one another, shouting in incomplete sentences about screams and where they might have come from. While Vrana didn't want to die, she had hoped that someone would see her and Joy. Like the Witch herself, Joy was significantly weakened outside the Void. Vrana couldn't lay a hand on her, not with the Witch watching and controlling her every action, but maybe if enough people overwhelmed them—

Joy stopped, the lakeshore in view, and flicked her hand. As if slammed into by an invisible wave, Vrana flew off her feet and through the air. She skidded through bushes, bashed against trees; she rolled over, across the ground, a blur of black feathers like an overgrown tumbleweed, until the grass gave way to dirt, and the dirt to water.

Vrana reared back in the lake's shallows. Joy was still fifteen feet away, casually strolling toward her, flicking her hand this way and that, parting the foliage so that it didn't sully her dress.

"Slowpoke," Joy said, smiling. Her hair, a faint yellow fading into white, swished around her face as she accentuated the movement of her hips and chest. Unlike the Witch, who might have been attractive once, Joy was still beautiful, and she knew it. Her problem was the hole between her legs, and the things she tended to push out of it.

Vrana ran the green, moon-infused water over herself, and the lake turned red around her. The village took their drinking water from here; tomorrow, they would be drinking a part of their friends and not even know it.

Joy stepped onto the shore. The water before her began to change, the moonlight it held turning gray and then black. The lakebed, visible here in the shallows, started to breathe. It heaved up and down like an asthmatic chest. Vrana held out her arms to keep her balance. Thick clouds of hot smoke poured out of the vents around her feet. When they reached the surface of the lake, the bubbles popped, leaving behind a foul patch of decay in their wake.

Joy crossed her arms. "Do you think I should go back for the baby? I hate to see it left alone."

The patches of decay gravitated towards one another. Once touching, they stitched themselves together, forming a dark purple, almost black, net around Vrana's thighs.

"No," Vrana said. "You know what Pain will do."

Joy said, "Yeah, you're right," and then finally stepped off the shore. Her white satin dress shot in front of her, creating a path for her feet on which to step. "Our family is growing enough here as it is, isn't it? I shouldn't be selfish."

The decay climbed up Vrana's leg, getting in between her feathers, filling in her pores. Back on the other side of the lake, torches and tempers flared—the angry accusations loud enough to hear even from the lake. "The Maiden of Pain. Who is the Maiden of Pain?" Such and such had heard this and that. Then self-proclaimed experts would eventually spout nonsense disguised as knowledge; while Doomsayers weighed the scales and salivated at the profits of this new misfortune. Vrana sighed. It was always the same. Promises of revenge, followed by debates on appropriate rituals and tributes. Fear devolving into devotion.

"Sister has more work for you to do back home," Joy said.

The white fabric slithered forward and then upward until it began to wrap around both Vrana and Joy, like a cocoon. The dress tightened, brought Joy in closer, until her nose was touching Vrana's beak.

The dark purple decay stopped spreading at Vrana's stomach. It hardened into a wax. Sinewy strands of light, like a jellyfish's tentacles, wriggled out of the patches and immediately shot out and into Joy's body. The Witch and her sister were more than capable of entering and exiting the world on their own, but Vrana needed assistance, and an escort.

Joy sighed as the sinewy strands sucked on her flesh and channeled some of herself into Vrana. "Have you ever breastfed a baby before?" She reached out and squeezed Vrana's nipple, of which there was little left. "One day, I'm sure," she said, letting go. "Perhaps you could be our milk maid. Our family will be so large we'll need all the help we can get." Joy smiled. "Let's go, my pet."

The strands slipped out of Joy. They retracted into the patches of decay on Vrana. When they returned, her body temperature spiked. Her vision began to flicker; with every other flash, the cocoon and the lake gave way to black nothingness and gray Void.

The decay shot up her body to her torso and shoulders. Joy squeezed her fists. The cocoon constricted. The sinewy strands pushed out of the decay into her skin. Now infused with Joy's power and drawing from a place called the Membrane, the flailing appendages surged forward and turned Vrana inside out.

The lake vanished, and so did Joy. The sinewy light pierced her like spears and carried her off this earthly plane. A moment later, Vrana saw a tunnel of flesh and a yawning Abyss, but she paid them no attention, for she had seen them so many times before. They meant nothing to her, and she meant nothing to them. She was merely passing through to the Void behind it all; that unreachable and unknowable place, forgotten and forlorn.

Wet and raw, her innards exposed, Vrana flew forward until she met gray gloom. The Void swallowed her whole, body and mind, and when it seemed things couldn't get darker—

—Vrana woke in the Witch's house, at the foot of the fireplace. Her flesh and feathers were back where they belonged, on the outside rather than in. The silver necklace hung from the mantelpiece, its gem casting a blue light into the hearth. Blue tentacles flailed in the fireplace, feeding off the bones there like flames would a log. Dense, bruise-colored smoke poured off the writhing appendages and filled the crooked chimney above.

Joy had been right. The Witch did have more work for her to do.

Vrana dragged herself across the floorboards to Pain's bone-forged rocking chair. Using the light from the candles burning in the windows, she searched the house for signs of the sisters.

They weren't at the table; that long, splintery slab of black wood which was set with dirty plates covered in fuzzy, Void-grown food. Nor were they in the kitchen where cold, hard sheets of flesh hung like laundry left out to dry.

She turned around, looked the opposite way, where the house stretched down a dilapidated hall to unused guest rooms. A few ravens were there, sleeping on the corpse piles that congested the hall. The ravens were the Witch's new sentries; after Vrana had taken the Ashen Man's place, the Witch had the millions of flies here replaced with birds, instead. For all her supposed carelessness, the Witch did appear to have some need for consistency. She had even redecorated parts of the Void to make them match the new species scheme, by making the landscape darker, more jagged, like feathers and beaks.

Vrana pushed herself off the ground and came to her feet. She went to the front door, which was closed but unlocked. It rattled in its frame, the wind of the Void rocking the door like it meant to tear it off the hinges. Vrana pressed against the door, slid over to the adjacent wall, and leaned over to look out the nearest window.

The windows were filthy, caked in soot and wax and Joy's excrement. Vrana spit into her claw and palmed the glass until she had a clean spot to see through. The Void waited on the other side, an island of miseries in a sea of shadows. Her eyes darted back and forth between the black hills and gray mountains, the solid rivers and the boiling lakes. Where were they? She looked to the bands of ravens roaming the lowlands, and to the thorny gardens that choked the highlands. Even the plains, that desolate stretch of pale grass and broken pillars, were empty. Where were—

An angry shout shot like a missile across the Void. Vrana's trauma-trained eyes zeroed-in on the source. There, near the valley, where the Witch kept a visual record of her victims and followers, Pain and Joy floated. They were yelling at one another. Joy had a child in her arms, a baby, most likely the one from Flora's house. She had gone back for it.

Vrana turned away from the window and scampered over to the fire-place. In the Void, the Witch seldom kept control over Vrana's mind. Even though she was at the height of her powers in this place, it was still too difficult to maintain dominance over Vrana on a constant basis. And besides, what could Vrana do? There was nowhere to run to, and if she did manage to kill the sisters, they would only be resurrected seconds later. It simply wasn't worth the hassle.

Vrana went down on her hands and knees. She pressed her head into the fireplace, so that the blue tentacles were inches away from touching her beak. The Witch had finished the ritual of tapping into the Blue Worm's power, but, without Vrana, she wasn't able to go any farther. The Witch was capable of entering some people's minds, but the network that connected the Children of Lacuna was closed to her.

"But not to me," Vrana whispered. The bruise-colored smoke made her eyes water. "I want to know why that is."

Vrana shoved her head into the tentacles. They wrapped around her and yanked her downward into the bones they grew out of. She lost her sight, and her thoughts went blank. At this point, she usually let the neck-lace guide her to a random Lacunan, but not today. Today, she had some-one in mind.

Herself.

Show me, she thought. The secret organ in her brain swelled. A grip of agonizing pain closed around her skull. Slow, unfocused images played out across her mindscape. Whether the memories were hers or something else's, she couldn't be sure. But there was a reason only she was able to contact the Children, and she had to know why.

A hot spike drove through Vrana's mind, impaling the new thoughts forming there. The Witch had begun to impose her will on Vrana once more. Any other time, Vrana would have stopped what she was doing immediately, but this was different. She was using the Blue Worm's abilities to peer inside herself, to control herself. It was a force far greater than the Witch's. Was this her means to escape? If she could just—

A memory finally came into focus. It was the image she always saw, right before she delved into a Lacunan's mind. In it, there was a baby girl, Vrana, lying in a field of rust-colored grass, and standing over her was her father, Quentin, in his iguana mask, and her mother, Adelyn, in her raven mask. Mara was there, too, standing next to someone in the shadows; a large person who smelled and kept grunting, as if they were mad about something.

"We were wondering when you would get curious," a strange voice whispered into her thoughts.

Vrana tried to move the memory, to see who was addressing her, but the memory wasn't hers to manipulate. Instead, the memory moved on its own. The person's eyes through which she was experiencing the scene looked down at their feet. There, a mass of blue tentacles throbbed and flopped over one another. Then, the person looked at their hands, which were the color of space—black and pricked with dying light. The memory wasn't hers at all, but the Blue Worm's.

"You were too young to remember, so I put this in your head for you to find later," the Blue Worm said. It lowered its arms and gazed upon baby Vrana. "Did you ever wonder why you would have such strange dreams? Visions of things you couldn't possibly know? That's what they were, Vrana. They were visions, from your brothers and sisters and… myself."

The Blue Worm turned its head, so that it was looking at Vrana's father. "Your father's seed was strong."

An image ripped through the memory like a knife. In a brief, breath-taking second, Vrana saw her father descending naked into a milky pool, while the Blue Worm above him stretched its tentacles outward like a tree.

The image vanished. The Blue Worm then turned to Vrana's mother and said, "Her eggs were not."

A second scene forced itself upon the memory. In it, Vrana saw her mother in an empty shack, her legs spread open, pushing a screaming, worm-covered infant out of her vagina. Vrana's father stood beside her, holding her hand, telling her something that sounded like, "It's going to be alright. It's going to be alright."

The image vanished. The Blue Worm returned its attention to baby Vrana in the red grass. "It was good to see you again. I always liked you." It laughed. "Did you ever find out what happened to your father?"

Vrana didn't answer, not in thought or speech. The Witch's will was driving through her subconscious, trying desperately to shake her from the memory and the Worm's recollection. She could feel Pain's hands on her shoulders now, too, tearing out her fathers and bashing the back of her head. Any moment now and she would lose an audience with her creator.

"I'll show you," the Blue Worm said, smugly. "It's not what you were led to believe."

The memory of baby Vrana in the field dissolved into gray nothingness. Then a third image formed upon that dismal stage, piece by piece, sound by sound. First, there were trees, then the sound of water, the ocean, breaking on a shore. A cliff appeared, followed by the sky. Vrana could hear leaves rustling, and… snarls.

The image wavered. Then Vrana's father appeared. He was hunched over, drenched in blood; his iguana mask was torn apart and covered in strips of flesh. He howled—was it in pain or ecstasy? She couldn't be sure—and crumpled to the ground, a massive gout of blood exploding from his back. Then behind him, a second person faded into the scene.

It was Bjørn. He was panting, just as filthy as her father had been. In his hand, he held an ax, the very same he had given Vrana so long ago. A hunk of meat hung off its blade, from the place it had opened Vrana's father.

Bjørn stepped over her father and raised the ax over his head.

The Witch's will flayed the scene from Vrana's memory. In an instant, she was back in the Witch's home, facedown beside the fireplace, bawling.

"The girl who keeps on giving finally gave too much, eh?" Pain said, grabbing Vrana by the scruff of her neck. "Teach you to disobey me." She shoved Vrana's face back into the blue tentacles. "I saw your friend

R'lyeh when you delved into Hex, yesterday. Do it again," she screamed. "Kill R'lyeh, then we'll see if you disobey me again."

CHAPTER VI

R'lyeh had a secret she hadn't shared with anyone yet. It was an experiment that had started a few months ago, after Vrana had been taken, and before R'lyeh had wandered into Gallows for her reunion with the Red Worm. She had spent two weeks in the woods, and during that time, she had accidentally eaten a poisonous plant and been bitten by two venomous snakes. The plants were a deadly strain known as Deathshade, and the snakes a pair of malingas. Either the plant itself or the snakes' venom should have been enough to kill her, but instead, she just had a bad case of the sweats and a quick, fiery bout of diarrhea.

After that, curiosity crept stranger things into her daily diet. She started to seek out plants and animals to test the limits of her natural immunities. Prior to arriving at Gallows, she put down several blight beetles, a handful of poisonbite berries, and let a few more malingas nibble on her, for good measure. Sweats and shits and maybe a minor hallucination were the only result of this otherwise ill-advised bender.

Now it was dawn, and the barracks were already empty. R'lyeh was free to wake and roam as she willed until called upon; so, she woke and roamed her way through the barracks to the staircase that led up to the attic, her hideout. She climbed the steps, while hunger pangs sank their fangs into her growling stomach. The first floor's stretch of beds and bad smells shrank out of sight. She carried on past the second floor, which was an empty space, one window, and a whole lot of dead mosquitoes. Then, finally, she reached the attic door.

It was supposed to be locked, but Clementine had given her the key. The Skeleton's wife said a girl like R'lyeh needed a quiet place of her own away from all the men.

She took the key out of her pocket, unlocked the door, and pushed it open. The unfailing smell of must and rat droppings greeted her. Beyond, the attic sat filled with bottles, broken beds, dirtied sheets, and a whole mess of Old World artifacts everyone seemed to have forgotten about. They were things the Marrow Cabal had gutted out of the lower floors back when it was Poe's tavern.

R'lyeh shut and locked the door behind her. Just like back home in Alluvia, she was easily forgotten, but still, she didn't want anyone walking in on her during an experiment. And now that she was thinking about Alluvia—most of the time she tried not to—she realized that was where the secret had started. When Derleth the Eel had given her a piece of the Crossbreed, and she helped him plant it in the village's well to impress him. If the damn plant had just worked on her like it had everyone else, all that had happened, and where she was now… it could have all been ignored… or stopped… or have never happened at—

"Nope, nope, nope," R'lyeh said to herself. "We're having a good day today."

R'lyeh crept through the attic. She kept most of her personal belong-ings at the back inside a fort made out of Old World umbrellas, computer towers, and a desk covered in dick drawings. Today, her poison of choice was a thick, gritty liquid known as Thanatos. According to her teachers, Thanatos was found in the discharge of the maggots that roamed the Ossuary, the gigantic desert that swallowed up most of the southern por-tion of the continent. Thanatos was rare, and Thanatos was deadly; as soon as it came into contact with someone's bloodstream, they had sec-onds at best before the poison killed them cold.

R'lyeh had taken the vial of Thanatos from the Skeleton two weeks ago. He had left her alone in Operations one afternoon. She had seen it sitting on his desk amongst a bunch notes from Herbert North. She waited two weeks to use it, thinking he might make a big stink about it having gone missing. He didn't, and she never did figure out why he, someone who couldn't die, had it in the first place.

R'lyeh opened a drawer in the desk. The drawer was stuffed with greasy diaries that the previous owner, Poe, must have pored over. R'lyeh had gone through the diaries a few times. Most of them were from girls, teenagers like herself, and they talked a lot about friends, parents, school, and things called "sports." It made R'lyeh feel uneasy reading these Old World recollections, not because she couldn't connect with the kids, but because she could. They all wanted the same things she wanted, but what had stood in their ways couldn't have compared to what stood in R'lyeh's. Maybe it was all a matter of perspective, but here she was, alone with a bunch of mercenaries, living on a lake of blood; her parents were dead and her best friend was missing; and all she could do to pass the time was drink poison and kill people. It wasn't that she thought she was better than those Old World girls, but could they top that? Hell, could anyone?

R'lyeh smiled, her suffering becoming her strength, and reached past the diaries to the vial of Thanatos stowed behind them. She held the vial up to the light creeping in through the gaps in the attic's roof. It looked curdled, almost like a crunchy, black spread. She undid the stopper. A strong, putrescent smell—ear wax and body melt—poured out of it.

"H-Holy Child," R'lyeh wheezed. If the poison didn't kill her, then the smell of it would. "That's fucking f-foul."

What am I doing? She put the stopper back in the vial, the smell a wake-up call. *Everyone has their limits.* She swished the chunky, death-like discharge. Deathshade ingestion and malinga envenomation had cures; blight beetles and poisonbite berries probably weren't as bad as everyone made them out to be. Yes, she was immune to the Crossbreed, but what was she doing? Was she looking to die? Or looking for a reason not to?

R'lyeh bit her lip. She wanted to be good at something, and she knew you didn't get good at something by talking about it all the time. It would have been a hell of a lot easier if someone were up here with her, watching her, validating her.

But she was on her own, with no one to stop her, so she said, "Bottoms up," and popped out the stopper. The Thanatos moved like sludge inside the vial. "Here we go." She pressed the vial to her lips, death now a distant thought. "Here we—"

A loud crash came clanging up the staircase outside the attic. Her lips immediately went numb from the fumes wafting off the Thanatos. She stopped up the vial and slipped it in her pocket. *What the hell was that?*

She heard a table get flipped, and a bed kicked out of the way. Heels were being dragged across the ground in some sort of limp-legged waltz. It sounded like someone was drunk, pissed off, or both. R'lyeh crept over to the attic door, braced her body against it. She put her eye to the keyhole, held her breath.

The staircase was a straight shot from the first floor to the attic. R'lyeh couldn't see everything, but she could definitely see if someone were coming her way.

"I can't... hold... on," the intruder whispered, out of sight.

R'lyeh listened closely. Her eyeball hurt from being pressed so hard against the keyhole.

"Can't make... do it."

I know that voice, R'lyeh thought. *Who is that?*

There was silence for a moment, and then a shape passed in front of the staircase. Surprised, R'lyeh fell back on her palms. The attic floorboards creaked under her weight. She held her breath, held the Thanatos through her pocket. Had they heard her? She plodded forward on her hands like an infant and put her eye to the keyhole.

Hex was standing at the bottom of the stairs, bleeding blue light from the corners of her eyes. Her face was twisted into a maniacal grin; and her braids were moving around her head, as if she were caught in a windstorm. One hand was holding the bridge of her nose, while the other was behind her back, tightly gripping something.

"She's fighting... me," Hex said, but it wasn't in her voice that she spoke, not entirely. It sounded as if someone were speaking through her.

Whose voice is that? R'lyeh swallowed hard. *What's that behind her—*

Hex brought her hand out from behind her back. In it, she held a large, rusty machete. Her eyes focused in on the keyhole of the attic door. She smiled. With tears of light pouring down her face, she said, "Kill her."

Hex started to climb the stairs. Her arms and legs jerked wildly, as if she were fighting against herself. "R'lyeh," she said, dragging the machete against the wall. "R'lyeh."

Hex went slowly, as if she were trying to tease the terror from R'lyeh to savor every morsel. Spit foamed at the sides of her mouth; she was rabid with rage.

R'lyeh backed away from the door. *What the fuck is wrong with her?* She looked around the attic. There had to be a weapon up here, or something she could turn into one. She sprinted across the space, a trail of creaks and cracks following behind her. It didn't matter. Somehow, Hex already knew she was here.

R'lyeh went to the fort of Old World crap and tore it apart. How could she be so stupid as to not have a weapon on her at all times? She riffled through the desk, emptying out drawer after drawer. Behind her, Hex's footsteps grew louder, more forceful, and she could hear the machete skipping across the wall, grinding into the stone.

"You need to pick better… friends," Hex said, now on the other side of the attic door. She rattled the doorknob. "I know you're… up here. I was watching you sleep."

"Hex," R'lyeh finally said, "I don't know what is going on with you, but if the Skeleton—"

"I like… the lake. Too bad it's not… water." Hex laughed. She threw herself into the door. It held, but only barely. "Hey, R'lyeh." She stopped. Through the door, she said, "Do you think they'll notice you're gone?"

R'lyeh pawed inside the desk. She ripped out the metal track one of the drawers slid on. It was better than nothing, but not by much.

"I don't think they will," Hex said.

She yelled and rammed her shoulder into the door. She stumbled into the attic. Immediately, her eyes shot over to R'lyeh in the back. Hex waved, and then she barreled through the attic, the machete held out at her side, slicing through the air.

"Hex, don't!" R'lyeh took off. She went sideways through the attic, keeping the crossbeams between her and Hex. She waved the metal track feebly and cried, "Stop, please. Stop!"

Hex blinked against the light of her eyes. She shook her head—no, she wasn't going to stop—and then ran full-speed at R'lyeh.

R'lyeh swung the metal track. Hex slashed the machete downward and tore it out of R'lyeh's hand. She spat in R'lyeh's terrified eyes.

"Fuck," R'lyeh said, temporarily blinded. She stumbled, and then all the air blew out of her lungs as Hex's fist pummeled her gut. R'lyeh reeled and fell on her ass. Threads of pain weaved through her stomach until it was unbearably tight. She gasped. A noise, a voice maybe, came from downstairs, but R'lyeh couldn't move herself to speak. Instead, she lay there looking up at Hex. They were both crying now.

"I need you to die slowly." Hex took the machete in both hands and pointed it at R'lyeh's chest. "But you've been doing that since Geharra, so I know you won't let us down."

Hex drove the machete through the air. R'lyeh screamed. She put her forearms out. The floorboards rumbled, and then instead of impaling her, the machete slid along her arms, cutting her superficially from elbow to wrist. Hex yelled something and then tripped over R'lyeh's legs, as if she had been pushed.

Shock-numbed, R'lyeh scooted away. Behind Hex, Elizabeth stood, looking almost as scared as R'lyeh felt.

Hex got her bearings and whipped around, swinging the machete as if it were an extension of her arm. Elizabeth went sideways, dodged the blow. Then she balled her fist and broke it on Hex's snarling mouth.

"I'm s-sorry," Hex said, her busted lip bleeding profusely.

Elizabeth wrenched the machete out of Hex's now limp hand. And then, for good measure, or maybe because she had always wanted to, she socked the blue-haired telepath in the eye and knocked her out cold.

"You're okay, yeah?" Elizabeth said, panting.

R'lyeh sat up. The gash on her arm was long and bleeding, but it wasn't anything that wouldn't heal within a few weeks.

Elizabeth extended her hand, and R'lyeh took it. "Don't tell anyone what happened here."

R'lyeh held the gash; blood seeped through the gaps between her fingers. "What? What the hell? What the hell is wrong with Hex?"

Elizabeth bent down and took the machete. She trained it on Hex, who was still unconscious. "Bone Man wants you."

"The hell?" R'lyeh held out her arm; a few drops of red got onto Elizabeth's shirt. "Have you all gone crazy?"

Elizabeth looked at her coyly. "You throw a fit about that, you think Bone Man isn't going to let you go on the mission, yeah?" She chewed on her lip. "Don't tell anyone about Hex, okay? Miranda's downstairs. She'll patch you up."

R'lyeh's cheek quivered. "You're not telling me something."

Elizabeth nodded. "Obviously. Hex is second-in-command, yeah? If people know what she did here, well, that's not good for anyone, yeah?"

"Yeah."

"I'm sorry about your booboo, but get out of here, please."

R'lyeh scoffed. She let go of the wound and wiped her bloody hand down Elizabeth's side.

"Yeah, I deserve that." Elizabeth crouched and prodded Hex with the tip of the machete. "Go now. King Bones will fill you in on everything else, alright?"

R'lyeh started across the attic. Halfway to the door Hex had broken through, she turned and said, "How'd you know what was going on? I'd be dead if you hadn't showed up."

Elizabeth looked back. "Came to get you for Our Fleshless Leader. Clementine said sometimes you hang back. Then I heard the screaming. Thank god for coincidences, right?"

R'lyeh nodded. The vial of Thanatos suddenly felt very heavy in her pocket. "Right."

Mornings in Gallows were always a grim affair. Today, just like any other day, the sky was a gray mire in which both the sun and moon had been caught. At this time torches burned brighter than any light coming in from the heavens above. A heavy fog sat at the outskirts of town, as if waiting for an invitation to come in.

To R'lyeh, it was the blood lake that seemed most changed in these small hours. While Miranda stitched up her arm, she stared at the crimson waters through one of the barracks' windows. Every morning, something seemed different about the blood. Whether the lake was spreading outward or it was getting deeper, R'lyeh couldn't say for sure. But something was definitely happening inside Mr. Haemo's blood well. She couldn't have been the only one to have noticed it, right?

"There you go," Miranda said, snipping off the stitch. She turned R'lyeh's arm over and held her hand. "Not good as new, but not as bad as before, either."

Everyone liked to call Miranda a bitch, but R'lyeh had taken a liking to her. She wasn't a bitch. She just did her own thing. Miranda spent most of her time in Gallows due to her left arm, which was left dead due to nerve damage from a battle. The Skeleton had assigned Miranda to keeping an eye on Clementine and Will, which she did as if their lives depended upon it… which they did.

"I'm going to go check on Elizabeth," Miranda said, getting up. She put her left hand in her pocket, so it wouldn't hang limply at her side. That seemed to embarrass her. "You have your orders."

R'lyeh nodded. She ran her fingers over the stitches in her forearm. They tugged on her flesh; it felt like tens of ants were biting her skin.

"Bring your mask and your weapons."

R'lyeh slid her chair away from the table. Stomach aching, she said, "Why?"

"You're leaving today."

R'lyeh stomped across the docks, ax in hand, Cruel Mother's talons at her side. The leather armor she wore—a chest piece and bracers—were tight and irritated her stitching and stomach, but she didn't care. She pulled the octopus mask down harder on her head. Things were starting to spiral out of her control again, and she wasn't about to stand for that shit.

The blood lake gurgled beside her. Flashes of Geharra's pit flooded her mind. She quickly turned her thoughts to Hex's attack, which no one seemed to care about. Okay, she got it; Hex was second-in-command, but she'd just tried to cut her up with a freaking machete. And what the hell had she been saying? It was like someone was talking through her. And her voice? R'lyeh knew she knew that voice. It made her heart hurt when she heard it. It couldn't have been Vrana's, could—

R'lyeh ran into a passing cabalist. She bounced off his bulk and caught herself against the dock's railing. He kept going, never turning back, and she went ahead, never apologizing to him. She was a Night Terror, and he a Corrupted. That was the way of things, even here, amongst supposed allies.

Several more cabalists came down the ramp to the second level as R'lyeh went up it. They laughed under their breaths while they passed. Was she being sensitive? Or were they being shitheads?

She growled and quickened her pace to Operations. More specifically, was she upset because of what had happened with Hex? Or was it because of what hadn't happened with Hex? She held Vrana's ax in both hands. Things could have gone differently if she had been armed. Elizabeth wouldn't have had to have rescued her. *'You and your friend really messed things up putting that Blue Worm to sleep,'* she remembered Hex telling her, that night she and Will came back from Bedlam. *No shit,* she now thought. *But why me? What'd I ever do to her?*

Lost in thought, R'lyeh had wandered past Operations. She stopped, turned around, and headed back the way she had come. She noticed Will on the first level, walking with Clementine, and waved to them. Clementine waved a few seconds later, her movements all wrong, like she was drugged. Will, on the other hand, refused to recognize R'lyeh at all.

"Guess Bone Daddy grounded you because of the shepherd," R'lyeh said, watching them disappear into the general store. "Guess I can't get anything right, anymore."

R'lyeh headed into Operations. The Skeleton was seated at his desk. Herbert North was standing beside him, leaning over his shoulder, pointing to the papers laid out before them.

Herbert North looked up. His old eyes, dull and covered in cataracts, still managed to shine with a faint, joyful light. Leaning away from the Skeleton, he cried, "Iä! Iä! R'lyeh fhtagn!"

R'lyeh blushed. He was the only person she had ever met who had read the book from which she had chosen her name. Of course, that shouldn't have come as much of a surprise. The Skeleton had plucked

Herbert from the Membrane; he had been there a long time, and in the Old World, he used to be a supernatural investigator. Of all the people the Skeleton spent time with nowadays, he spent most of it with Herbert.

"I think I finally figured out the difference between Night Terrors teenagers and human teenagers," Herbert said. He patted the Skeleton on the shoulder, then shivered. Recovering quickly, he added, "Night Terror teenagers actually wake up before lunchtime." He stretched his face into a smile. "Ba-dump tsh," he said.

Neither the Skeleton nor R'lyeh caught the reference.

"Bah." Herbert waved them off. "Let me get out of your hair." He looked at the Skeleton's bald dome and cringed. "I mean yours," he said to R'lyeh. "Looks nice, by the way."

Did it? Without thinking, she touched it. Her hair was longer than she usually kept it. It was almost at her shoulders, now, just the way Mom always asked her to wear it.

"Whoa, R'lyeh. Hey." Herbert shuffled toward her and took her arm. "This is recent." His touch was tender, much needed. "Are you okay?"

R'lyeh looked past Herbert to the Skeleton, who was leaning forward, elbows digging into the desk, watching her. "I'm good." She smiled. "It's nothing."

Herbert twisted his mouth; he wasn't buying it, but he was in no position to have it refunded, either. "I'll leave you two to it." He gave R'lyeh a short hug, and then bowed cordially to the Skeleton. "Think about it," he told him. "It's better than the alternative."

Herbert North excused himself out of Operations.

The Skeleton quickly came to his feet. R'lyeh, wanting to see what Herbert had been getting at, went straight for the desk and took a peek at the papers scattered there. They were pages that had been ripped out of a journal of illustrations, the ink still wet on a few of them. They were pictures of buildings, skyscrapers from the Old World, and what looked like weapons. She recognized some of them—in Alluvia, the elders had a busted handgun and a rifle—but for the others, she wasn't sure what she was looking at. They were long tubes, pointed, kind of like arrows, while others were small, fat packages with wires coming out of them. The inscription beside the illustration read 'Bomb.'

"Déjà vu," the Skeleton said. Casually, he scooped up the papers and put them inside the desk. "Who you been scuffling with?"

"Hex," R'lyeh said, matter-of-factly. "She tried to kill me."

The Skeleton stopped, the statement hitting him hard. "Where is she?"

"Barracks, with Elizabeth and Miranda. Elizabeth saved me."

"Hex isn't right in the head, anymore. I'm sorry this happened."

"She came specifically for me," R'lyeh said.

The Skeleton walked past her, and she followed after.

"This isn't the only time I've seen her act weird."

"All kinds of things are coming to her now that the Blue Worm is gone," the Skeleton said.

"It sounded like she was talking to me, like, personally. It sounded like someone was using her to get to me."

"Might be." The Skeleton pulled his cloak shut, careful as always not to expose the black moss on his ribcage. "You're one of the few survivors of Geharra. Might be someone out there doesn't want you to talk."

"I don't think that's—"

The Skeleton walked to the doors of Operations and pulled them open. "You coming?"

R'lyeh shrugged.

"You got your gear on." The Skeleton growled. "Guessing Elizabeth didn't fill you in."

"No. She didn't." *What's wrong with him?* she wondered. "She said I'm leaving today. I'm guessing to Rime to get Audra."

The Skeleton cocked his head. "What?"

"I'm guessing—"

But it wasn't R'lyeh to whom he was speaking. He picked at his glassy, vein-choked eyes and said, "Yeah, that's right. Mr. Haemo didn't have much of Audra's blood, but all signs say she's up in Rime. You, Elizabeth, and Miranda are going to go up to Rime and get her back. It's best you all travel in a small group."

"And you want me to go now?"

The Skeleton looked at her as if he was bored with the conversation. It was the same look he always seemed to have. You couldn't see it, on account of him being only bone, but it was there. When it came to the Marrow Cabal, it was like he was going through the motions. His heart just wasn't in it, literally and otherwise.

"Come here," the Skeleton said, stepping outside onto the dock. "I want to learn you something."

There was a part of Gallows that was rarely ever used. It was a narrow boardwalk that extended from the first level of the dock into the heart of the lake itself. Because of the constant, bloody mist that sat over that part of the lake, you couldn't go much farther than ten or twelve feet without disappearing, along with the boardwalk, out of the sight of others. New recruits into the Marrow Cabal would sometimes dare one another to go out onto the boardwalk at night to see how far they could make it before chickening out.

Most of the time, people just assumed those new recruits made it all the way, because they never came back.

"It's going to rain today," the Skeleton said as he and R'lyeh went down a level and toward that very boardwalk. "I can feel it in my bones."

R'lyeh couldn't, but what she could feel were all the eyes of the cabalists on her as she and the Skeleton passed. To be walking with their leader was one thing, but to be walking with him to the boardwalk that led to Mr. Haemo's Haunt was another matter entirely. To them, she must have either looked incredibly privileged or incredibly damned.

The nearer they came to the boardwalk, the slicker, more blood encrusted that part of Gallows became. Because people seldom went to this part of the town, it seldom saw any care. It was here that the blood level of the lake was highest, far past the supports which held up the town. Strange plants grew here, too, out of the human corpses left by the Red Worm that formed the town's rancid beach. The foliage overwhelmed this part of the dock, creating a jungle of corpse-born flowers and weeds that, according to James, were most likely carnivorous and from the Adelaide line.

At the foot of the boardwalk, alone and away from Gallows proper, and surrounded by blood and the things that prosper from it, R'lyeh thought for one terrible moment that the Skeleton was going to kill her. It was the perfect place, wasn't it? And Hex had just tried to kill her like thirty minutes ago, which no one seemed all that alarmed about. Was it because she had botched the Bedlam mission? Or did they finally see what she really was and what she was capable of doing? Could murderers be made sick by other murders?

"R'lyeh," the Skeleton said. A cold wind blasted across the lake, causing his heavy, black cloak to whip around him. "What do you want?"

She cocked her head. "I'm not sure what… you mean."

"Everyone has a part to play in this here Marrow Cabal. I want to be sure what I see for you is what you want for yourself."

"I wanted to find Vrana. I mean, I still do, but… I don't know." She rubbed at her stitching. "I want to be good at something."

"Good at something, or good for something?"

Raindrops started to patter on the sanguine surface of the lake. Distant thunder boomed, but lightning was nowhere to be seen.

R'lyeh hesitated and then said, "Both, I guess. I, uh—" She dug into her pocket, took out the vial of Thanatos, and handed it to him. "Sorry."

The Skeleton took the vial. He opened his cloak—hints of the black moss, now denser than before, across his ribs—and stowed it. "What'd you want that for?"

"Don't know," R'lyeh lied.

"You're mad no one's making a big fuss about Hex and you." The Skeleton started down the boardwalk.

R'lyeh followed after, saying, "Wouldn't you be if it was the other way around?"

"Don't know," the Skeleton said, mimicking her. "You got to remember, though, that you're a Night Terror. Asking others to feel bad for you is like asking someone to feel bad for a snake because the rat fought back."

The bloody mist began to close around them. R'lyeh stopped.

The Skeleton stopped, too, and turned to face her; blood dotted his white bones, and the kicking wind made it smear. "Smart," he said. "You know when to follow, and when not to."

"I haven't seen Mr. Haemo for months."

"Consider yourself lucky, then."

"What's he doing?"

The Skeleton laughed. "That's top secret. Get to the center, and you're welcome to find out."

Something splashed in the blood beside R'lyeh. She leaned out and saw a strange reflection in the lake. It was a skyscraper that was almost identical to the illustration Herbert North left for the Skeleton. A raindrop rippled the scene, and when the blood was calm again, the image was gone.

"I'm going to be straight with you," the Skeleton said. "These days, I find myself relating more to monsters than men. You're young, but you're not human, and so that don't bother me as much as it should when I have you out there in the field, risking life and limb.

"I see some of myself in you. Someone doing something they don't really want to do for the sake of someone else. I have to use you. I'm sorry about that. But you're using me, too, to find your friend, so I figure fair's fair."

"Makes sense," R'lyeh said.

The sound of wings traveled through the air. Something was flying farther ahead in the impenetrable pink mist.

The Skeleton flung the hood of his cloak over his head. "Let's elaborate on our meeting yesterday. The Disciples of the Deep are gaining ground. King Edgar's soldiers are cutting through the Heartland, kindly forcing the conversion of the towns and villages. The vermillion veins are now part of the Disciples' holy rite. There's no uprooting them now. The Heartland is infested with the things. We have to stop what they're raising, instead.

"Penance has an army. The Mother Abbess and Holy Child are leading it personally. There's rumors the army even has angels in it, but I don't believe that myself. I know you hate Penance, but if we have to choose, they might be our best bet.

"Anyways, it may come to war, and the Marrow Cabal can't fight no war. We have a few hundred at best, but our weapon is information; subterfuge and shit. If the two cities come to blows, it's going to be in the Heartland, which means Penance or Eldrus are going to sweep over Gallows here like an unstoppable wave.

"But that's not all. The Nameless Forest isn't right, anymore. Monsters pour out of it every day, and spellweavers, I hear, are popping up all over. And that desert, the Ossuary, down south, might actually have something living in it. People are fighting like children over whose god can beat up the others', but I expect the real battle is the one going on behind it all; the one no one is paying much attention to. I admire that, and us Marrow Cabal need to be like that, if we're going to make a difference.

"So, you're going to go to Rime, and you're going to sweet-talk King Edgar's sister out of their custody. Get your people to join us, if you can, but bring Audra back. Her entire family was murdered. You can bet she has something to say about it and who might've done it. We're not the only one tracking her. The Winnowers' Chapter from Penance has been hot on her heels, supposedly. Few of our people brought back some of their flyers from the area."

"That's fine," R'lyeh said, plainly.

"I like Herbert's theory about the difference between Night Terrors and Corrupted." The Skeleton ran his fat, black tongue over his teeth. "But I got my own. Care to hear it?"

R'lyeh nodded.

"Difference between yours and my kind is that you all like killing.

Hell, it's what you live your life by. You ever known a Night Terror to be squeamish about cutting someone's throat?"

"I don't… know." R'lyeh thought back to Alluvia, to Caldera. "Not everyone fights."

"But they would, I bet, just like waking up in the morning. Have to, even if you don't want to." The Skeleton stepped forward, his boney hand outstretched. "Can't say that about humans. Some don't have the disposition. Show me a pacifist Night Terror, and I'll say that I'm wrong, but I bet you can't."

"Deal," R'lyeh reached out, as if to shake his hand on the matter, but stopped herself. The last time she had touched him, he had filled her head with awful things. His touch was poison—the kind no one, not even herself, could be immune to.

The Skeleton laughed, retracted his hand. "Elizabeth and Miranda are going with you because they do like killing, and they do it real well. That, and I don't want them around when my guests show up in a few weeks. I'm afraid they won't behave."

"Guests?"

The Skeleton ignored her. "Got any questions? They're ready to head out, it looks like."

R'lyeh turned around. At the end of the boardwalk, where the corpse-plants swayed, Elizabeth and Miranda waited on horseback, with a third horse behind them. In that dampening mist, they looked like bloody ghosts risen from the grave, ready go out again for that battle they'd been fighting forever.

"A couple," R'lyeh said, facing the Skeleton.

But he was already ahead of her, going farther down the boardwalk. She had seconds at best before he would be gone, out of reach to anything with blood in its veins.

"What's that growing on your ribs?" R'lyeh belted.

The Skeleton, not stopping, said, "Time."

What the hell does that mean? She took a few steps forward, shouted, "What will you do with Hex?"

Now, he was half there; a faint image of a shambling beast bumbling down the boardwalk. "Whatever I want. Now that she's out of the way, we'll be… doing things our way."

"What? What do you mean?" R'lyeh didn't dare take another step forward. "Haven't we been?"

The Skeleton laughed and slipped into the mist. "No," he said. "Have you?"

And with that, the Skeleton was gone.

R'lyeh's head was swimming with questions that had never been given a chance to surface. What's really growing on your ribs? What about Hex? She had a chance to ask the leader of the Marrow Cabal anything, and that's what she decided on? She should have asked why he chose her, why he really chose her. She should have asked about Vrana, and how he was really going to get her back. Because she was beginning to think he didn't care, or that he didn't have a way to save her from the Witch.

But she didn't ask, did she? R'lyeh turned back towards Gallows and headed down the boardwalk to Elizabeth and Miranda. She'd had months to do something about Vrana, and all she did instead was whatever the Marrow Cabal told her to do. She wanted to save her, she did, but did she have to be the one to? Something told R'lyeh Vrana wouldn't approve of the Marrow Cabal; she probably wouldn't let her keep killing Corrupted, either. Here, she could be good at something, good for something; back in Caldera, she'd just be another thirteen-year-old Night Terror, underestimated and underused.

R'lyeh didn't like the way she was thinking, so she thought about something else, instead. A swarm of mosquitoes cut across the boardwalk and wound into the sky, as if they were doing their best impersonation of a flock of birds. She waved to Elizabeth and Miranda, and they waved back enthusiastically. Maybe to them this was just any old mission, but to R'lyeh this was something more.

"Wouldn't have picked me if I wasn't a Night Terror," she mumbled, minding the slick spots on the boardwalk. "Need to stop forgetting I am one."

R'lyeh stopped at the end of the boardwalk. Elizabeth and Miranda parted to let the third horse pass in between them. It came right up to R'lyeh and lowered its head into her shoulder.

"Have a way with horses, yeah?" Elizabeth said.

R'lyeh nodded and petted the horse. It reminded her of the one that used to visit her in Alluvia, and the horses she and Vrana rode back home from Geharra.

"We'll be gone a month and a half, maybe more," Miranda said. "If you need anything done, I hope you did it yesterday."

R'lyeh's thoughts lingered on Vrana. "No," she said, bitter betrayal constricting her throat. "No, I'm ready."

R'lyeh handed the ax to Elizabeth to hold and mounted the horse.

Taking the reins in her hand, she thought: *Vrana will be okay. What was her boyfriend's name? A-Aeson? He'll save her if I can't. Probably already has.*

CHAPTER VII

Autumn-colored leaves washed across Caldera, the wind they rode in on cool and constant. In the fields, harvesters worked at the dwindling crops; their scythes and sickles slickly slicing through the tall, browning stalks. At the village center, children prowled and scowled and said their goodbyes, for the workday was done and evening had come. Out of the wilds and the haze of routine, Night Terrors poured; from the artisan tents to the Archive itself came a veritable ark of animal-headed people, some worn-down or others hyped-up, but all eager to go back home. There were still traces of the Witch's attack on the village; parts of the ground were still tainted, and some houses were still scorched from the flames, but the Calderans didn't pay these reminders much mind. They were a forward-thinking people, and to them, time was mostly mulch.

So Aeson thought, and so Aeson knew, as he stood outside the house of the elders, watching the village wind down for the night. With every passing week, fewer and fewer villagers had shown any concern about Vrana's return. Aeson knew that regardless of what she had done for them, the village, hell, the whole world, she, just like anything else, would be forgotten, too. Forgotten, just like the elders had probably hoped to forget how Vrana had been born.

Aeson clenched his fists and moved at a brisk pace away from the house. He was damn sure Vrana had no idea about the circumstances of her own birth. How could they keep that from her? He moved past house after house after house, banging his hand against the sides of them. He always knew the elders hid things from him, but they had gone too far this time. If Vrana had telepathic potential, then of course the Witch would've taken interest in her. They could have done something, but instead they ran her across the continent like their little lab-grown lapdog.

"Fuck," Aeson whispered under his breath. He felt sick to his stomach. It wasn't just the rage that made him nauseous. It was the question he kept asking himself, the one that made him cringe; the one he worried would come between him and her if they were ever together again.

What exactly was Vrana? How many parts Worm?

And from here until she was in his arms again, how many times would he pick her apart, oddity by oddity, searching for every seam the Blue Worm had used to stitch his love together?

Aeson spit and again: "Fuck."

Bjørn was banging away on his anvil; first to rise, last to quit, the Bear always seemed to be in a perpetual state of blacksmithing. His workshop of late had become increasingly crowded and cut off from the rest of Caldera. The stone hut was stuffed with more weapons and armor than the village knew what to do with, and the creations were arranged in such a way that they formed an almost impenetrable wall of leather and blades. Things had been that way ever since R'lyeh's letter arrived. Bjørn and Aeson had very little in common, but the same couldn't be said for their grief. They both wanted to hurt those they couldn't keep out.

Aeson stopped outside the workshop. He slipped his hand into his pocket to make sure the registry from Enaar containing the names of those born on Lacuna was still there. Anguis had told Aeson he had one more thing for him, a book, but he would deliver it later, after Aeson had made arrangements to leave. Despite wanting to save Vrana, Aeson almost fought with Anguis about whether or not he would even be allowed to stay, but he didn't. He knew they wouldn't let him stay. He knew too much already, and now that he was beginning to truly understand his people, he was a liability. The only way to gain their trust again would be to do everything they asked of him and not die in the process.

With a throaty belch, Bjørn slammed his hammer into the piece of metal laid out across the anvil. He reared back, brought the hammer down again. The metal flattened; a harsh chime shivered out of the steel and pierced the air. Bjørn straightened up, dropped the hammer. His old muscles tented and tightened over his quivering frame. He sighed, gripped the side of his mask, took it off, and placed it on the anvil. His hands groped at nothing in particular.

"I see you standing there," Bjørn said. He ran his fingers through his long, dirty, white hair until his infamous mullet fell into place. "Watched you walk off with the Snake. You looked pissed. What did he tell you?"

Aeson stepped up to the workshop, a wall of spears between him and Bjørn. "You were there, weren't you?"

Bjørn raised an eyebrow.

"You've always watched out for her." Aeson growled. "On Lacuna, you were on Lacuna with Adelyn and Quentin. You knew."

"What's that have to do with saving Vrana?" Bjørn asked, gripping the bear mask.

"It's everything, I think."

"Yeah." Bjørn wheeled and rummaged through the workshop. At last, he found his drink and pressed it to his lips. Sniffing the vapors, he said, "If we talk about this, then we have to leave Caldera."

"I want to talk to Adelyn." Aeson stepped away, turned himself in the direction of Vrana's house.

Bjørn shook his head. He guzzled the drink, slipped on his mask, and started smashing through his workshop, trying to get after Aeson. "No, don't you dare, Skull Boy. That's the last thing she wants to talk about right now."

"You were right. You and I are going to get Vrana back."

Aeson started across the village, Bjørn bumbling behind him.

"But if we're going to do that, I need to know everything."

"She can't talk about it," Bjørn whispered back. "You're going to get her kicked—"

Bjørn never finished his sentence. Aeson suspected it was because the Bear wanted to have this conversation just as much as he did. With Vrana's house pushing through the trees and surrounding buildings ahead, Aeson suddenly felt the cold touch of doubt in his gut. The whole reason he had moved so quickly out of Kistvaen was to avoid it, yet here it was, as it always had been, to make him second guess himself and his capabilities.

Could he kill someone? Aeson's skull wasn't something he'd earned through senseless slaughter. Like all Archivist masks, the skull he wore had been handed down to him. It was larger than a normal Corrupted skull, but since it was Victor Mors', the last true expert of the Worms of the Earth, its size made some sense. Like Aeson's dad had once supposedly said, to have gone into the Membrane the way that he did, Victor had to have had a head as large as his balls.

Bjørn picked up the pace behind Aeson. They hurried past the Archive; Gul and Lyre, librarians, were locking the place up as they did so.

Overhead, storm clouds knitted together in the sky; behind that tenuous fabric, thunderous rumbles sounded.

Could he protect himself? Aeson could rattle off every state and country that once existed on this continent and the other one supposedly on the other side of the world. He knew about the Dread Clock and the homunculi and the rebellion Geharra had funded in the Heartland years back. If someone was able to find all the parts, he could probably build a pretty decent car, a generator, or some semblance of a gun. Yet if Bjørn put a sword in his hand—and at this point, that was inevitable—he stood a better chance of stabbing himself with it than someone else.

Aeson and Bjørn hurried past Svaya's house, where he and the village's messenger birds nested. Ahead, clear across the northern path, there was Adelyn's. The home stood out amongst those that surrounded it because Vrana's mother had let her garden, both above ground and underground, go. Plants, poisonous and pleasing, wrapped around the property; they had grown over the walls, across the roof; windows were nearly covered, and there were holes in the yard from where the roots in the basement had burst through. Like Aeson and Bjørn, she had closed herself off from the rest of the world with things that could hurt others as much as they could hurt her.

As they approached the front door, doubt's last question forced itself into Aeson's mind. Could he save Vrana? It wasn't a matter of whether or not it was possible to save her. He had to believe that it could be done. It was a matter of whether or not he was right person to do it. And if he wasn't, what the hell kind of a boyfriend did that make him? Could he even admit if he wasn't? What would she think if—

The front door crept open. Adelyn stepped out from behind it. She was unmasked. Her hair was the color of dead leaves, and her ends had curled in the humidity. She was wearing the apron she always wore when she worked with potions. Now that Aeson was thinking about it, he couldn't remember the last time he had seen her dressed in anything else. Adelyn's eyes were red, too, but again, he couldn't remember the last time they hadn't been.

"Do my eyes deceive me?" Adelyn's chapped lips worked themselves into a small smile. "What are you two doing here darkening my doorstep?"

"Can we talk inside?" Aeson asked. He reached into his pocket to make sure the birth registry was still there.

Adelyn scrutinized Aeson, said, "Sure," and stepped aside.

Aeson and Bjørn filed into the house. Immediately, they were greeted by a heavy smell of various mixtures and concoctions. Adelyn's house—it was easier to call it Adelyn's than it was to call it Vrana's—wasn't large. There was a dining room, a living room, and two bedrooms—hers and Vrana's. In the past, Adelyn did her work under the house, but now that she was alone, it seemed she had given up on that. Now, she was making potions and growing plants in every room; every room except for Vrana's, which she kept sealed shut, as if it were some ancient tomb filled with priceless treasures.

"Here," Adelyn said, guiding them into the dining room.

Aeson stopped in the doorway of the dining room and exchanged glances with Bjørn. The table and the shelves were completely covered in flower petals and roots. The pantry had been raided, too; where there had once been food, there were now pots and rows of multi-colored vials.

"There's still a bit of Reprieve and Starry-Eye lingering in the air." Adelyn pulled out the chairs around the table and gestured for them to sit. "So if you get high while you're here, you're welcome."

"Great," Bjørn said, taking a seat; the chair squealed under his weight.

Aeson's gaze lingered on his chair. The back of it was covered in the thorns from the Bite bush Adelyn had planted underneath the table.

"Oh, sorry," she said, pulling out another chair. "Need to trim that bush back. Keeps spreading like it owns the place."

Aeson nodded, said, "Thanks," and took a seat.

"So—" Adelyn plopped down into a chair, "—what's up, men?"

Aeson took a deep breath, filled his lungs with what was left of the Reprieve and Starry-Eye in the air, and slipped off his mask. He laid the skull on the table and opened his mouth to say—

"He knows," Bjørn said, gruffly. "Elders told him about Vrana and Lacuna."

Adelyn took the news like a punch to the gut. Her neck snapped back. She curled over and dug her elbows into the tops of her legs. Her hair swayed across her mouth; she bit on its tips and sucked them.

Aeson felt like an asshole; he didn't want to see Adelyn this way. "I'm… I'm sorry."

She waved off his apology. "No, no. You're our Archivist, and you meant… mean so much to her. You should know. You should have known. Why did they tell you now?"

"Anguis took me to the spellweavers. The Witch is using Vrana—"

Adelyn's eyes grew wide and wet.

"—to contact the other Children of Lacuna. I'm sorry."

Adelyn wiped her face. "Keep going."

"Vrana has the necklace from the Blue Worm. The Witch must be using that and Vrana's ability to contact those who were born on the island. It sounds like the Witch is trying to gather the Children for something."

Bjørn slammed his fist into the table. He ripped off his bear mask and dropped it on the floor. His face was so twisted with rage that it almost looked permanent.

"The elders are sending me to get her back," Aeson said, trying to sound brave. "I have a registry of some of the Children and their last known locations. I think that if I find enough of them, I can somehow get to Vrana; somehow figure out where she is and how to get her back. Bjørn's coming with me, too."

This being the first he had heard of it, the Bear stared at Aeson, dumbstruck. He nodded; a little of the anger left his scarred face.

Adelyn closed her eyes. Her hand stretched across the table, through the roots and leaves, and closed on his. She squeezed it every time a tear slid down her cheek.

"I just... I need to know more. The Witch chose her because she knew what Vrana could do. Anything, Adelyn, will help."

"Okay," she said. "Yeah." She squeezed his hand. "Holy Child, it's been so—"

"Anointed One," Bjørn corrected. "He's the real 'Holy Child' now, Adi."

Adelyn smiled and ignored him. "It's been so long since I've talked about this. Give me a minute to get my bearings. But, Aeson?"

"Hmm?"

"You have to promise me you'll still love her. And us."

"Of course. Nothing could stop that."

Bjørn rubbed Adelyn's shoulder.

Adelyn sighed and kissed his fingers. "I wasn't always like this," she started, "Caldera-bound, I mean. Before... Vrana, I was an explorer. I went everywhere. If it had a name on a map, I was there, and if it didn't, well, even better. For the longest time, Mara was my partner-in-crime. She was obsessed with the Corrupted and trying to fit in with them. So as soon as I was initiated, the both of us took off. We would write the elders, let them know when tasks and missions were completed, but basically, we were—" she laughed, "—on our own. Which, if you knew us back then, was a terrible idea. We were stupid. So stupid. Bjørn can attest to that."

Bjørn nodded. "I had never seen two women come through Caldera as beat-up as they had been back then. You would have thought they lost every fight they got into. And the guys they chose? You're a twig, Skull Boy, but you got brains. Adelyn, here, wasn't big on brains but what was in between—"

Adelyn blushed, wiped her nose. "Being a young Night Terror back then, before all this shit with Eldrus and Penance and the Worms, you felt immortal. Took what you want. Went where you wanted. Killed who you wanted."

Aeson felt a pang of hurt in his heart as he watched Adelyn dreamily reminisce about her past. The life she had now wasn't the one she clearly wanted.

"I'm sorry." She cleared her throat, sat up in her seat. "I've had to dance around the topic so long that I don't even know how to begin."

"With Quentin," Bjørn said.

"Quentin. Vrana's father. I met him when I was twenty. He was from Traesk. Mara and I were in the area, and we stopped in the village for the night. Quentin was... Quentin was a lot like you, Aeson."

"A dweeb, a nerd. A twiggy bookworm," Bjørn said, grinning.

"Sounds like the perfect guy," Aeson snapped back.

"He was," Adelyn said. "He was an herbalist. Everything I ever learned about healing, I learned from him. Anyways, Mara and I came strolling into Traesk one evening, and there he was, in the fields, trying to talk to a few wisps about why they always helped the harvester grow the crops."

Aeson leaned forward. "Like the ones downstairs in your garden?"

"Exact same ones," Adelyn said. "They followed us here after... He never did manage to figure how to talk to them, but they must have liked him, since they pretty much followed him everywhere he went.

"So anyways, Mara and I were acting like asses, harassing people for a place to stay. Quentin comes over and offers us his place. So we stayed there the night. Mara tried to sleep with him to pay him back—that's how she handled her business, usually—but he told her no thank you and stayed outside the whole night, instead."

"And that's when she knew she loved him,' Bjørn said.

"Hey, yeah, kind of." Adelyn sighed. "I mean, he didn't do anything out of the ordinary, but he seemed so calm and sure of himself, but not in a cocky way like this brute over here."

Bjørn shrugged and started to scratch his ass.

"We left the next day, but every time Mara and I were in the area, I made an effort to visit him. After a while, the visits got more frequent, and I stayed longer than I planned. After a few months, we were together, and after a year and a half, we wanted a child.

"We tried for a long time. Back then, the Night Terrors knew about the fertility issues, but it was one of those things that happened to everyone else, but not you, you know?"

Aeson nodded. "Was that about the time Mara took over operations on Lacuna?"

"No, that was more recently. At the time, she just worked there. Anyways, the more I saw of Quentin, the less I saw of her. I didn't realize just how much favor she had with the elders; that is, until she showed up in Traesk one day while I was with Quentin, and I told her about our pregnancy problem.

"Quentin didn't necessarily calm me down, but I wasn't so stupid when I was around him. He let me be me, and I let him be him. I think... yeah, I think he wanted a child more than I did." She let out a slow exhale, and then said, "I can't believe I just said that. What the hell kind of a mother am I?"

"A good one," Bjørn said.

Adelyn ignored him and continued. "Mara was happy for us. Even though she would never admit it, I think she wanted what we had, too. So out of nowhere, against probably every warning and threat the elders gave her, she told us about Lacuna and what they were doing on the island."

"Everything?" Aeson asked.

She shivered. "Well, no, not everything. She left out some of the... grittier details. But here was an island I had no idea even existed, and here was a way to give Quentin a child."

Chewing on his lip, Bjørn said, "Too good to be true."

"Was it?" Adelyn shrugged. "I don't know if it was. I think it was exactly what it was, and nothing more. But we thought about Mara's offer for a few weeks, and then when she came back to Traesk, we told her yes.

"On our way to Nachtla, we ran into Bjørn. I think Mara always had a crush on him—"

"Who doesn't?" Bjørn chirped.

"—because she invited him onto the island, too."

"What were you doing up there?" Aeson asked.

"Fighting on the Divide," Bjørn said. "Penance was smuggling spies across the river into the Heartland. I was on my way back to Caldera. First time I ever met Adi's squeeze. Then Mara told me they were going across the Widening Gyre to an island hidden inside it. Tried to talk them out of it, then Adelyn told me the circumstances, and their trip didn't sound so stupid anymore."

"It's good that you came with us," Adelyn said, darkly.

Bjørn grunted. He looked into his lap and went silent.

"There was a passage outside Nachtla the spellweavers had created that transported us from the beach and onto the island. I was so overwhelmed by the place I had almost forgotten why we were there.

"We got to the village, Lacuna, and everything changed. Faolan and Nuctea were there. Quentin and I still hadn't fully decided what we were going to do, but Mara freaked out. She thought the elders were going to kill her for bringing us there. And I think they were going to. Before they had even said hello, Faolan and Nuctea had their knives out and were bearing down on us. But then Mara told them she had brought us there for the fertility project. And we went along with it, Quentin, Bjørn, and I, because what else could we do?"

"They would have killed us," Bjørn said, still staring into his lap. "I have no doubt in my mind. They would have killed us."

"Quentin and I stayed up that whole night talking about what we should do, but in the end, it didn't matter. He wanted a child. And I did, too. I did. I know it sounds like I didn't. Maybe not as much as him, but... Anyways, it was our best chance to get pregnant, and like Bjørn said, we didn't really have a choice at that point."

Aeson swallowed hard and asked, "When did... you find out about the B-Blue Worm?"

"Mara, Faolan, and Nuctea led Quentin and I deep into the island. They said there was a creature on the island they mined resources from, and as long as I was near it, the creature, I would be able to have a child. Of course, Quentin, being the herbalist, was asking every question he could about what this 'resource' was, but the elders wouldn't tell him anything. We were there doing things we weren't supposed to be doing, seeing things we weren't supposed to be seeing. No one owed us any explanation.

"They left us in this huge cave inside the island. It hurt to be there. There was this immense pressure, and the cave was covered in this kind of rust-colored grass. There were other people down there, too. They kept coming out of these shacks."

Aeson cocked his head.

"Yeah. Shacks. Tons of them. All across the cave. Four walls, no roof, dirt floor. And there were all these people. Night Terrors. Corrupted. All these people were down there in those shacks having sex. It was mechanical, like they were clocking in for work. Between all the pressure and the constant moaning, I thought I was going to go insane. But Mara said this was how it was, and Quentin seemed determine to see it through.

"We got our shack and our poor excuse for a bed inside. There was a—" Adelyn laughed, "—pool of water in the floor of the shack. It looked creamy, milky; and the way it smelled… I can't even describe it. Makes my mouth tense up just thinking about it."

"It's alright, Adi," Bjørn said, "if you need a break."

She shook her head. "We made it work, our accommodations. I kept telling myself I had been in worse situations, but that was bullshit. I've never done something so… just dirty. Degrading, really.

"I'll spare you the details, but we did what we had to do. They asked us to bathe in that 'milk' every few hours, so we did that, too. You know about the flesh fiends, right? Well, they were there, too. We could hear them being born in the cave. From the moment they were born until they were taken away or killed, all they did was scream.

"Somehow, we did fall asleep. I woke up a few hours later. And I… oh, how do I put it? There was something wet between my legs. Then I saw that the bed was covered in that milky water, and it ran from the bed to the pool in the ground.

"Before I could wake Quentin, I passed out. When I woke up again, Mara was there, talking to him. She told him we had to stay down there for three days. We had to… try as hard as we could. She brought us food and water and then locked us in. We probably could have busted down the door, but I trusted Mara, more than anyone else, and I knew we were tempting fate being there with the elders nearby. And Quentin was so determined… so we stayed, and we tried… as hard as we could.

"The last night. Oh, the last night." Adelyn crossed her arms and held herself tightly. "I'm only telling you this because I don't want the one thing I leave out to be the one thing you need to bring my baby back."

Aeson nodded, prepared himself for what was to come.

"Quentin and I were exhausted. There was nothing left in us. Three days is a long time to… Anyways, that night. That night I woke up again because, again, I felt something wet between my legs. And there was a pressure, too. I thought maybe it was Quentin, thought maybe he had one last go in him before Mara let us out. Might as well make it count, right?

"It wasn't Quentin. It wasn't him at all. There were tentacles inside me. Blue, slimy, fucking disgusting tentacles. They had come out of the pool in the floor, and they were feeding something inside me. I screamed, Aeson. I fucking screamed. You don't understand, but as a woman, seeing that, knowing… But as soon as Quentin woke up, they ripped out of me and slipped back into the pool. He didn't see them, but he believed me. And that's when we broke down that fucking door.

"Bjørn was waiting for us in the village. When he saw us come stumbling into Lacuna, I thought he was going to kill someone."

"God, how I wanted to," Bjørn said. "Might be one of my biggest regrets, letting Faolan and Nuctea live."

"Faolan and Nuctea pulled us into Mara's house, which wasn't much better than the shacks, and told us what was going to happen next," Adelyn said. "The creature told them I would be with child, so they had to keep us there until I gave birth. The child would be ours to raise, they said, but theirs to use. The child would be different, gifted, maybe. They told us it would be an honor to have a Child of Lacuna. We were one of the few of our people who had one. Most, you see, of the Children came from Night Terrors mating with Corrupted, and most ended up Corrupted in some way, so we were special." Adelyn laughed, cursed under her breath. "We were special, which meant we should have been grateful."

Adelyn scooted her chair back from the table. She came to her feet and walked over to a jug of water sitting on the floor. Meant for the plants around her, she drank from it instead, spilling the excess down her front.

"I stayed with them the whole time," Bjørn said, watching Adelyn. "Wanted to kill Mara, too. Whatever good reason had brought them to that cursed place didn't seem worth it anymore."

"It didn't," Adelyn said, "until four months later, when Vrana was born." She dropped the empty jug and leaned against the Chrism-covered wall. "She's beautiful now, Aeson, you know that, but oh my god, after everything, I didn't expect her to look the way she did. She was perfect, Aeson. Fat cheeks, fat feet. Had that baby smell. Almost immediately, I forgot about the shack and the tentacles and… she was ours, our baby. She looked like us. Had that little deviant smile of mine, that quietness of Quentin's. She was ours, and she looked okay. She looked normal. Regardless of the methods, Mara had come through for Quentin and me.

"We stayed there another month while I recovered. Watched a lot of flesh fiends get born there. Faolan and Nuctea said we could go back to Caldera together, the three of us. They reminded me Vrana would be different, and it took me years to piece it all together. You have to admit that Vrana is remarkable, Aeson."

"She is," he agreed, tears welling in his eyes.

Bjørn chimed in: "Fights like hell. Takes a beating like no other. Smart as a whip, and doesn't know when to quit. She went from Geharra straight to Lacuna, one Worm after the other, while a Witch messed with her mind. I've never met someone so unshakeable."

"And the dreams," Adelyn added. "Not the Witch's, I mean. Vrana had so many strange dreams and terrible nightmares growing up. Eventually, she stopped telling me about them, and I think that's because she just figured it was normal for her to have them. When she told me about the Witch, I didn't think much of it at first, because I figured it was just like the visions she used to have as a kid."

"That's what they were, weren't they?" Aeson asked. "Visions. Her connection to the other Children, and the Blue Worm."

Adelyn said, "Yes," and came away from the wall. She took a seat at the table again. "The elders made sure she grew up a ruthless fighter. They made sure Bjørn trained her constantly; it was part of the price he had to pay for knowing about Lacuna."

Bjørn rolled his eyes.

"But they never unlocked her telepathy. It still worked, obviously, but it wasn't used. Not until that fucking Witch got ahold of her." Adelyn made a fist; her nails dug into the heel of her palm and drew blood. "You know what pisses me off more than anything else?"

Aeson didn't.

"Myself. How I handled it."

Bjørn moved to interrupt, but didn't.

"I should have told her everything. I almost did. When she left for her second trial, I damn near went after her. I saw what the elders were setting her up for. But the elders stopped me, reminded me what they could do if I told Vrana anything. I thought they would take her away from me, turn her into some puppet, like the spellweavers in Kistvaen. So I kept my mouth shut. I let them run her all over the place. She would figure it all out eventually, I thought. Like Bjørn said, Vrana's smart. But everything escalated so quickly. When she told me she was going to Lacuna, I almost threw up. But then I thought that maybe she would learn everything there. That Mara would tell her. I don't know if she did. But she shouldn't have heard it from Mara or anyone else. It should have been me. Or Quentin if he were… still here."

"I'm sorry to ask," Aeson said, "but did Quentin really get lost in the Black Hour?"

"No, he didn't. He died on Lacuna." She said this without any emotion in her voice.

"But Vrana remembers him. She's told me about him."

"Vrana remembered only what we told her about him," Bjørn said. "Might be the Worm put the memories there, too."

"She could never remember Quentin's mask," Adelyn said, a sad smile on her face. "Every time she talked about it, the mask would be the skull of a different animal. She was making things up, I think, to make sense of him being gone."

Aeson pressed on. "H-How did he die?"

Bjørn faced Aeson and said, "I killed him."

"What?"

"I killed him." Bjørn stood up and headed out of the room. "You tell him, Adi," he said, on his way out of the house. "I can't."

Aeson's gaze met Adelyn's. "What is he talking about?"

"After Vrana was born, something happened to Quentin." She picked at her nails. "He changed. It happened so fast. One minute, he would be kissing me; the next, he'd be pacing the room, sniffing the air, like a dog. He stopped talking, and when he did, his words didn't make any sense. He never stayed with me and Vrana in the house. He kept going outside. The villagers on Lacuna said he was following people, stalking them. I thought it was some side-effect from being in the cave, what with all the pressure and what the Worm had put into the pool. I asked Mara, but she didn't know what was going on. And the elders just kept telling me to keep my distance from him.

"In that last week before we left, Quentin became violent. Wearing only his iguana mask, he rushed out of the house and chased down a bunch of kids who were playing outside. He kept picking them up and putting them down. Eventually, Bjørn stepped in. When he did, Quentin pushed Bjørn and came back inside the house. After that, he sat in the chair beside my bed and watched Vrana and me for hours. He didn't say a word.

"The morning before we left, Quentin sat down beside me and watched me breastfeed Vrana. Then, when I was finished, he ripped her away from me and ran out of the house. Bjørn was just outside. He heard me screaming, so he took off after Quentin.

"I caught up with them in the field outside Lacuna. Quentin had slaughtered a cow. He had torn open its stomach and shoved our baby, our Vrana, inside it. And he was trying to feed her with an udder he had ripped off the animal.

"Bjørn was screaming at Quentin, swinging his ax this way and that, telling him to stop, to get away from Vrana. Quentin kept hissing, spitting. He kept grabbing hunks of the cow's innards and rubbing them all over himself.

"I didn't know what to say. I didn't... I didn't say anything. That wasn't my Quentin. I didn't recognize him. I didn't know him. I didn't... I didn't want him. Maybe I could have talked him down, but I was so... I just stood there. I just stood there.

"Bjørn stopped trying to talk Quentin down and ran after him. Vrana started crying. God, she was covered in blood. And then Quentin lunged at me, like a wild animal. Bjørn didn't hesitate. He didn't know Quentin like I did. Bjørn, he was just trying to protect me.

"One swing, and the love of my life was cut down and left dead at my feet. I don't blame Bjørn for killing him. For a while, I thought maybe he did it because he hated Quentin, but he didn't. Bjørn has always liked me, but he wouldn't do that. I had made a stupid choice, going there, having a child with the help of that Worm. I was so stupid, and like always, Bjørn was there to save my ass at the last minute."

Adelyn was shaking. "I don't know what happened to Quentin. I don't know if the Blue Worm turned him into something else, or if, somehow, something was passed onto him. I don't know. But I hope it wasn't something like that. Not something genetic. Because I've seen a violence in Vrana that scares me. Bjørn said she's unshakeable, but sometimes I think it's more than that. She's ruthless. So far it has been for good, but goddamn it, if she finds all this out, will it stay that way? Now that she's with that Witch, I don't know what she'll become to survive. I love her so much, but I don't know her, not like I should, not like a mother should. She has part of me, but also Quentin and—"

"The Blue Worm."

"Yeah. It's not her fault. Not at all. But if the Witch is feeding into that part of her... Aeson." Adelyn stared into his eyes, pleadingly. "If anyone can save my daughter, it's you. Whatever she is, she needs you to make her more. You have to keep loving her, even if you see her do something that makes you not want to. Do you understand?"

"I do, Adelyn."

She nodded and wiped her nose. "Good, that's good. She wasn't always supposed to have the aspect of a raven, you know?"

"I didn't," Aeson said.

"No, the elders wanted her to be something else, but I fought them tooth and nail on it."

"What did they want her to be?"

Adelyn laughed and looked away. "A vulture. Subtlety has never been the elders' strong suit."

After Adelyn's confession, Aeson spent the rest of the night alone in the Archive, surrounded by the thousands of books and documents kept there. Hundreds of shelves containing information on any topic or genre ran across the building in a web-like layout. For bookworms, it was a buffet, and for him, it was one of the few places other than at Vrana's side that he truly felt comfortable and at peace. The smell of the books brought him back to a better time, when his mother and father were still alive, and words were worlds of mystery to be solved, not to be catalogued and quantified.

He had laid out the registry of Lacuna's Children on one of the long tables in the Archive and was now standing over and reading it by candlelight. There were thirty names on the registry. The list seemed several hundred short, but if he had to guess, Anguis and Enaar had only added those Children who would be the easiest to track down, or the most likely to be of any help. Beside each name was the person's birth date, a brief description, and their last known place of residence. The names were ordered not by proximity but importance; that is, where the most Witch-related activity appeared to be happening. The top of the list consisted of four people in the belt of backwoods farm country inside the Dires.

"The Dires, huh," Aeson said, running his fingers over the four names. He hadn't been there before, but then again, he hadn't been anywhere.

Charlotte Breckin, Aeson thought as he read the first few names on the registry. *Erin…* and then his thoughts were elsewhere. He imagined himself on Lacuna, and tried to put together the scene of Bjørn killing Quentin while Vrana watched from inside the carcass of a cow. But something Adelyn had said kept dispelling the scene. "You have to keep loving her," she had told him, "even if you see her do something that makes you not want to." He knew Vrana better than most, but why the hell was her mother making her out to be some sort of monster?

"Aeson."

His head snapped up. A frightened yelp escaped his lips. Aeson gripped his chest like an old man having a heart attack and shouted, "Who the hell is there?"

Out of the shadows, Anguis emerged. He was wearing a white toga that was covered in small, scale-like embroidery. The snake skull was on his head, like usual, but tonight he had a black cloth draped over it, as if he had just returned from a funeral. Aeson had never seen the elder dressed in such a way before. But what interested him more than anything else was the large book Anguis was holding against his chest.

"Whew, sorry," Aeson said, laughing out the last of his shock. "What… what time is it?"

"Three in the morning. You spoke with Bjørn and Adelyn?"

How the hell does he already know that?

"We are not upset with them. You were right to speak with them about the circumstances of Vrana's birth."

"Okay," Aeson said, suddenly very aware of how alone they were in the Archive. "What's going on? Is everything okay?"

Anguis took the book he held and laid it on the table. "Everything is fine. I wanted to give you this before you leave in the next few hours."

"The next few hours?" Aeson eyed the book.

"We can waste no more time, and Bjørn is already preparing. I passed his workshop on my way here. As for the book, it is yours. You were initiated at fourteen, and have done great work in your position. At twenty, you were to receive this book, but as I said, we can waste no more time. We will need you at your sharpest when you return with Vrana."

What was the book? Aeson leaned forward, out of his seat. The cover was blank, and so was the spine. It was thick; the page edges were rough, frayed, as if they had been recently cut and bound to the book. He had seen a million unmarked texts like this before, and yet there was something about it that told Aeson this one was different. Like R'lyeh's letter, it emanated a force all its own. He couldn't touch, taste, or smell it, but it was there, warping the air around it, activating senses he didn't know he possessed.

Anguis continued on. "What you will learn in here may help you in your journey. And when you return, it will guide your duties as our Archivist.

"This book is a record of our people. It is an Archivist's duty to chronicle our history. This history is history, and nothing more. No revisions or embellishments. Every Archivist has added to it, and now it is time for you to do the same. Adelyn and I have been keeping it up to date until you were of age. If you have not already guessed, we place great faith in Adelyn. If one of us elders were to be killed, she would be an immediate, but temporary, replacement. With everything she has experienced, I am sure you understand why.

"But before you make your first entry, you must read the chronicle in its entirety and understand its contents. The last Archivists to write in the book were your mother and father. Now that you are old enough, and wise enough, it is your time to record our accomplishments, as well as our failures."

Mom and Dad? Aeson reached for the book. Half-expecting Anguis to stop him, he paused, his fingers just barely touching the bare cover. But the elder didn't stop him; instead, he nodded at him, practically urged him to take the book into his care.

"As you can see—"

Aeson opened the book to the first page. There were two blocks of text written in gibberish and what looked like safety symbols from the Old World.

"—it is encoded. Each entry is encoded, and you must read each entry, beginning with the most recent, to uncover the cipher for the previous entry. In essence, reading it will take you back in time to our beginnings."

"Backwards?" Aeson flipped to the end of the book. There, the text, written in a muddy, chunky ink, was so strange and garbled it made him go cross-eyed looking at it. "Why?"

"To protect the secrets of our past. Very few know them, and it should be kept that way."

Going back to the first page in the book, Aeson said, "But I don't know the cipher for the most recent entry."

"It's there in the text. When you and Bjørn are on the road, you will figure it out. You have much on your mind at the moment. Now is not the time for code-breaking."

What the hell am I looking at? Aeson turned through the book once more. If he had to guess, there were about fifty pages. Some of the pages were covered in encrypted messages, while others only contained a single entry or sentence. The last thirty or so pages appeared to have been written by an Archivist who might have been insane. Because as he had seen before, the text was garbled and frantically laid out across the page. But this time, now that he was looking at it more closely, he realized that the ink used on these oldest entries wasn't ink at all. It was blood.

"The Trauma was a trying time for our forefathers," Anguis said.

Aeson closed the book and planted his hands on the table. "Why did they write it in blood?"

"It must have seemed like a good idea," Anguis said, smugly. He bowed to Aeson. "Follow the registry as it is laid out. Stay away from the East Coast. You will be tempted to go to Gallows because of the Red Worm having died there, but between Eldrus, Penance, and this… Marrow Cabal in the area, the danger will not be worth the risk."

"Does this book have anything to do with the Children of Lacuna?"

"Yes, it does."

"Does it have to do with where we came from?"

"Oh, yes."

Confused, Aeson asked, "Why should that be a secret?"

Anguis shoved his hands into the toga. "I am not sure that it is anymore." He turned on his heels and started to walk away. "I have to go now, and so do you, soon."

"Anguis," he said, stopping the Snake. "Why are you only sending Bjørn and me to get her back? This is too much ground to cover for just two people."

Anguis paused, the darkness of the Archive closing around him. Looking over his shoulder, he said, "There will be others tracking the Children—Deimos and Lucan were the first—but we must divide the bulk of our efforts between the Disciples of the Deep and the Ossuary."

The Ossuary? Aeson clenched his jaw as he belted out, "The desert? What? Why? There's nothing down there."

"We thought so, too," Anguis said, slithering into the shadows. "King

Edgar begs to differ."

CHAPTER VIII

R'lyeh slipped off her boots and took a seat beside the Divide. Her feet, hot and calloused, bobbed up and down in the river's weedy shallows. Elizabeth and Miranda had warned her not to stray too far from camp, but after several days' worth of riding, R'lyeh's mind was about as muddy as these waters. Besides, it wasn't like anyone was going to notice her this early in the morning; at least, not while Penance's army was stretched out across the eastern bank.

The massive river and the massive army upon it were almost too much to take in at once. She had never seen such things before, and both were equally terrifying and awe-inspiring. The Divide was miles long and wide; someone who didn't know better might even mistake it for the ocean. The river divided Eldrus' Heartland from Penance's peninsula. To R'lyeh, it looked like the Divide not only separated the areas, but had drawn inspiration from them as well. In the west, the Divide was lush, vibrant; an overgrown expanse that might as well have been some submerged forest the world had more or less forgotten about. In the east, it was cold, lifeless; a pale wasteland of ghostly grass caught in some unbreakable haze, like an image seen through an icicle. R'lyeh wasn't even that far from the Divide, merely on the outer banks north of Gallows, and even she could see the difference. Good and evil seemed like the obvious symbolism between the two parts, but for R'lyeh, measuring Eldrus' side against Penance's was like measuring the merits of puke versus diarrhea.

The Divide was cool, but Penance's army was better. There was a rush to seeing it, a nervous excitement that was one-part sadness, two-parts bloodlust. On the eastern shore, row after row of pale white tents had been raised. If she had to guess, there were hundreds, maybe even a thousand, of them. Guard posts and watch towers had been constructed, too, though they looked rickety, like they might fall over as quickly as they had been put up. There were boats in the water, twenty or thirty, and that was just what she could see. They weren't very large, and couldn't have been anything more than the boats Penance usually used to make trades on the river. What R'lyeh couldn't figure out was why the city-state had made their stand here. With the river being so wide and the boats being so small, how did Penance think they would get all their soldiers across? Better yet, how did Penance get all this here in the first place? Was it here all along?

R'lyeh's heart started to pound. She began to repeatedly swallow the spit in her mouth. Her temples throbbed, and then her vision blurred. Was the world getting larger? Darker? She took off her octopus mask. Leaning forward, she splashed the river water onto her face, baptized herself in its war-warmed waters. A cold shock shot through her body. Then a trickling sensation, as if the stress were melting from the inside of her chest. Her heart slowed, her vision cleared. But the world was still dark and larger than it should've been. Everything towered over her, and she over nothing.

Early morning mist rolled off the eastern bank. The lush, vibrant plant life was still there, but now that the air had cleared, there was something else, too. There were no soldiers, no guard posts, or watch towers. If Eldrus or some Heartland army were here, then they were somewhere else. No, behind the bank, a little farther inland, the ground shone, winked, as if a million tiny rubies had been spilt in the grass. And as the ground blinked in the light of the rising sun, it also throbbed; breathed almost, as if, like the rest of world at this hour, it was waking, too.

R'lyeh's breath caught in her throat. In the waters of the Divide, she saw the pit of Geharra filled to its bloody brim. She jumped to her feet, hurried into the woods behind her. Bravery would only get her so far; stupidity would take her to a place she had no intention of going. Elizabeth and Miranda were right; she should have stayed in the camp. And Mom and Dad had been right, too; she should have never left the house while they were gone. She wouldn't be here, and she wouldn't be alive. It was hard to tell whether that was a good thing or not, but she knew well enough the idea shouldn't have felt as good as it did.

"I need something," R'lyeh said. She scanned the woods and its leaf-choked ground for a snack to snack on. "Come on, damn it."

In five seconds flat, R'lyeh found something strong enough to kill her. Growing from the base of a nearby tree was a patch of gloom cap mushrooms. She hurried over to the green and gray fungi and quickly ripped a handful out of the soil. One would make her sick; two would make her sicker; and a third would deliver her to Death, gift wrapped in dirt and sweat.

Tough and terse, the gloom caps had to be eaten one at a time. R'lyeh took the first mushroom and pushed it shakily into her mouth. Sharp, intense spikes of earthy flavor stabbed into her gums and tongue. As she chewed and swallowed the first gloom cap, she noticed a pair of darkslick frogs hopping through the grass; they were poisonous, too, except she would only need one of them to kill herself.

Impatience often made her impractical, so R'lyeh took the last two gloom caps, crushed them the best she could, and crammed them into her already deadened mouth. Chewing both of them at the same time was like trying to chew through a leather belt, but she kept at it. And while she did, she spotted another source that could give her a certain demise: Death's Dilemma.

"Holy crap," R'lyeh mumbled, the suicidal mouthful getting in the way of her words.

She stumbled forward and knelt before the flower. Death's Dilemma was supposed to have been one of the rarest plants known to exist in the world. They had bone-white petals that hid shyly beneath their ice-blue stalks. Supposedly, each flower represented a love of Death's who had dared to love Death and let Death love them in return. Each flower, then, was unique; imbued, in a way, with the ecstasy and sorrow of an impossible union. R'lyeh had heard that those who picked or ate the flower were immediately killed. It wasn't like the Thanatos she stole from the Skeleton; that destroyed the system. It was said Death's Dilemma was like using scissors to snip someone's soul. It was immediate, irrevocable, and personal.

R'lyeh fell, narrowly missing the plant. The gloom caps in her gut had started to go to work on her. Some shouting came in from the Divide, and then what sounded like boat hulls hammering into one another. She pried her eyes open with her fingers, tried to get to her feet, but the pain blossoming around her belly was breathtaking.

Nose first into the leafy dirt, R'lyeh found herself staring at Death's Dilemma, and found her dilemma, too. She clenched her teeth, squeezed her legs together. She started to think about how easy it was to find poisonous things in the wild, and wondered if the Earth was trying to tell her something.

"Okay, okay." R'lyeh rolled over. She pushed her hands against the top of her pelvis. "I got this. I can do this."

A hot light flashed across the insides of her eyes. She dug her jaw into the top of her chest to stop it from quivering. Gaseous bubbles popped and hissed throughout her body, like they might in one of Adelyn's beakers. On her back, she trained her eyes on the canopy above. The trees were bare, their limbs skeletal; she imagined they were the Skeleton's limbs, and then imagined them hugging her.

By the time the poison had passed, she had pissed herself, but R'lyeh was still alive. Winded and wracked with hunger, she rolled over and came to her trembling feet. Facing the Divide again, she found that the tens of ships, hundreds of tents, and thousands of unseen soldiers were easier to deal with.

"Back in our day, we just cut our wrists when we wanted to hurt ourselves."

R'lyeh turned around. Behind her, Miranda stood; and behind her, Elizabeth was farther back, her hands in the air, as if she were asking R'lyeh just what the hell she was doing.

"I, uh." R'lyeh wiped her mouth. "I didn't—"

"Don't lie to me," Miranda said.

R'lyeh nodded and blushed behind her mask.

"Anyone see you?"

R'lyeh shook her head.

"You see anything worth mentioning?"

"Just," R'lyeh started, "the, uh, army in general."

"Yeah, that's interesting." Miranda turned away. "Come back to camp. Sun will be up soon."

Camp was one small tent a quarter of a mile from the Divide. It sat at the center of four old, sap-soaked trees that were almost bound to one another by the razor nettle running between them. When they had arrived last night after the Black Hour, Elizabeth had had to cut her way through to the middle in almost complete darkness. She had told R'lyeh cutting through the razor nettle was like cutting through barbed wire. R'lyeh didn't know what barbed wire was, but at that point, Elizabeth had lost a lot of blood trying to get in, so she took her word for it.

Now, Elizabeth was in better shape, but her bracers and gloves were still covered in dried blood. She was ahead of R'lyeh and Miranda, humming something to herself—a nursery rhyme, maybe, or a church song. It was hard to tell. To R'lyeh, who hated Penance so much it was damn near becoming a profession, there wasn't much of a difference between the two.

Miranda broke the silence by saying, "Were those gloom caps you ate?"

"Yeah," R'lyeh said, her stomach rumbling in confirmation.

"You should be dead."

Elizabeth looked over her shoulder, but didn't say anything.

"Yeah." R'lyeh cleared her throat. "I don't know how long I've been able to do it, but I can eat poisonous stuff or get bitten by venemous animals and not have it affect me. Well, I mean, not kill me." She shrugged. "It still sucks."

Miranda's eyes tightened on R'lyeh, who felt so small beside her. Miranda was at least six feet tall, though given that she looked like a squirrel—puffy cheeks, brown hair and eyes, and a short face—it would have made more sense for her to have been smaller.

"You sure King Boner didn't have anything to do with that ability?" Miranda asked.

King Boner? R'lyeh laughed, said, "No, I just happened upon it one day."

The wind stole past R'lyeh and Miranda, and a trail of leaves like begging children followed after. Shafts of sunlight beamed through the trees, like holy boons meant to bring life to this dying place. Fall was R'lyeh's favorite time of the year. The grayness of the sky, the darkness of the ground; the biting air and bending trees—she liked seeing the world in a different way, in an honest way, as her dad had once put it.

"So why did those gloom caps happen upon your mouth?" Miranda persisted.

Leaves crunched under their feet. They turned through the rows of scraggly trees. Ahead, a crumbling hill sat like a squished toad, and atop it, camp waited.

"I try to test myself whenever I find something new to—"

Still a few feet in front of them, Elizabeth let out a fake cough and said, "That wasn't it, yeah?"

"No, I don't think so," Miranda agreed.

"I, uh—" R'lyeh looked back at the Divide, which had shrunk to nothing more than a small lake at this distance, "—sometimes, I, uh... I don't know. I get anxious."

Elizabeth stopped at the bottom of the hill. "What made you anxious?"

Miranda stopped, too, and stood by Elizabeth's side. They weren't threatening, but they definitely weren't going to let her pass until she spilled her guts.

"The Divide," R'lyeh started. Then, begrudgingly, she said, "Penance."

Elizabeth tilted her head. A portion of the bat tattoo on her clavicle snuck out from underneath her armor. "And gulping down gloom caps made you feel better?"

They think I'm an idiot.

"You know what makes me feel better?" Miranda asked.

R'lyeh shook her head.

"Getting laid. There are a lot of men back in Gallows, aren't there?"

Confused, R'lyeh said, "Yeah, I guess."

"Do you know when the last time I got laid was?"

R'lyeh started to laugh.

"Two years ago. What I'm saying is that just because you can, doesn't mean you should. There's probably some higher quality stress relief techniques out there that don't involve destroying your body."

Feeling lectured, R'lyeh blurted out, "Like what?"

"Oh, I don't know." Miranda and Elizabeth started up the crumbling hill. "Talking seems to do the trick."

After they were back in camp, Elizabeth, their designated cook, started a fire and began on breakfast. While she did this, Miranda headed into the woods again; this time, to explore the western bank of the Divide and determine if Eldrus did have some sort of army waiting in the mist.

"I think I saw the vermillion veins on the western bank," R'lyeh told Elizabeth.

"Don't get any ideas about eating them," Miranda shouted, as she plodded down the hill.

"I wouldn't." R'lyeh had considered telling them about the Thanatos and the Death's Dilemma, and how she hadn't eaten those, but stopped herself. She figured they wouldn't have believed her anyways.

With Miranda gone and Elizabeth's face in the fire, R'lyeh went over to their horses to see how they fared. They weren't tethered, and they were nothing special; just skinny, brown beasts that had taken their sweet time getting them this far.

"You're good with them," Elizabeth said, not looking away from the fire.

R'lyeh ran her hands along her horse's coat, picking out the bugs that had made a home there. "Thanks. Elizabeth?"

"Yeah?"

"Why do you all call the Skeleton those names? Bag of Bones, King Boner, Bone Man."

Elizabeth snickered. She reached into one of the bags beside her and took out a few eggs. "Makes it easier not to be scared of him."

R'lyeh patted the horse, and then joined Elizabeth at the fire. A warm, itchy feeling spread across her cheeks as its heat washed over.

"He's a walking, talking, immortal skeleton," Elizabeth said, "who is carrying the heart of the Black Hour. If that's not freaky, then I don't know what is."

"I've seen his rib cage. There's this weird black moss growing all over it. That's where he keeps the heart, isn't it?"

Elizabeth took out an ancient skillet and cracked the eggs against it; she poured the yolk out onto it and held the warped piece of metal over the fire. "Definitely. You don't keep something like that anywhere else but on you at all times."

"You think it's getting to him?"

"I don't think the Skeleton was ever really right in the head." Elizabeth handed the skillet to R'lyeh, then fished out some bread and oats from the bag. "It's mostly Hex's show, anyways."

R'lyeh's stomach started growling again, but this time, it was for all the right reasons. The breakfast, even in its early stages, smelled fantastic.

"But since she tried to kill you, we'll have to see what happens next, yeah?"

"Yeah."

"I think the Skeleton would do anything to give up on the Marrow Cabal, but things are so bad now that he can't." Elizabeth took the skillet back from R'lyeh. "Leading the Marrow Cabal might be the only thing keeping him sane. The heart talks to him, you know? I've seen it happen before, yeah? I feel bad for Dusty Bones. I don't see how this will end well for him. If the shepherds ever snatch his wife and son again..." Elizabeth shook her head. "After all those gloom caps, are you still hungry?"

R'lyeh laughed and finally took off her octopus mask. "I'm starving." She set the mask on the ground, close to Elizabeth.

"I like that about you Night Terrors, the whole mask thing." Elizabeth took the eggs out of the fire and tilted the skillet until they poured off into R'lyeh's bowls. "I have twenty-eight tattoos, but I think I'd trade most of them for one sweet-looking mask."

"I could make you an honorary Night Terror," R'lyeh said, smiling.

"Well, yeah, why not? I've killed plenty of 'Corrupted,'" Elizabeth said with a snort. "I think I would fit right in. I bet you if I finished covering my Corruption in tattoos, you Night Terrors wouldn't even notice I wasn't one of you."

"Yeah, probably not," R'lyeh said, watching Elizabeth go to work on making the porridge.

"People always debate whether Night Terrors are really all that different from humans, but you know what?"

"What?"

"I wonder if people have it all wrong. Maybe it's not whether Night Terrors and humans are all that different. Maybe it's if Night Terrors are all that different from something else. Might be we're making you guys out to be something you're not."

Even though Elizabeth had the best of intentions, R'lyeh was beginning to feel as if she were being picked apart. So she said, "You might be right," and then didn't say anything else until breakfast was ready.

Miranda must have had one hell of a nose, because by the time breakfast was being divvied up into the bowls, she was back from her patrol, licking her lips and rubbing her stomach as she practically skipped up the hill to camp.

"Smells delicious, Liz," Miranda said. "It might actually give us away, because the Divide is rank today."

Elizabeth handed a bowl to Miranda as she passed behind her and R'lyeh. "What did you find?"

"Vermillion veins on the western bank." She took off her sword, laid it on the ground, and then loosened her armor some. "The rebellion didn't do a thing to stop Edgar from planting them everywhere." She sat down beside R'lyeh, so that the Octopus was sandwiched between her and Elizabeth. "I didn't see an army, but like we saw with Bone Daddy back at Carpenter Plantation, those things can be weapons themselves."

R'lyeh, with a handful of eggs and mouthful of porridge, said, "Huh?"

"Some of the veins explode outward, impaling anything in their path." Elizabeth took a drink out of her flask and then burped. "I guess you don't need an army when you've got the whole edge of the Heartland booby trapped."

Miranda nodded, chomped into her bread.

"In Bedlam, when I was with Will, I saw a priest put a 'seed of Heaven' in someone. It did that. Made the vermillion veins explode out of the person," R'lyeh said.

Miranda said, "I guess if all else fails with the Disciples of the Deep, King Edgar can always turn his followers into suicide bombers."

Bombs? R'lyeh remembered the piece of parchment she had seen on the Skeleton's desk before she left Gallows. Aside from the drawings of Old World buildings on it, the word 'bomb' had been written. Was that what he had been getting at? The vermillion veins as weapons?

"Penance has a whole mess of people on the eastern bank, and ships, too," Miranda said. "It might just be for intimidation. Most of the soldiers looked like regular citizens who had been conscripted on the way here."

Elizabeth, two egg-covered fingers in her mouth, said, "They'll still fight like hell, yeah?"

"Of course." Miranda slurped up some porridge.

R'lyeh was the first to finish off her breakfast. She literally licked the bowl clean. As she sat there watching the other two women stuff their faces, she cleared her throat and said, "Do you think there's really two gods out there?"

Miranda shook her head immediately; the answer to the question probably as obvious as the color of the sky.

But Elizabeth hesitated. Taking off her chest piece, so that she was down to her ratty, long-sleeved shirt, she said, "I don't know, R'lyeh. What do you think?"

Shit, she thought. She liked it better when she got to ask questions rather than answer them. Fiddling with the Cruel Mother's talons at her waist, she mumbled, "No. I think the Disciples and the Holy Order are both liars."

"Just because it's a god, doesn't mean it deserves to be worshipped, yeah?" Elizabeth removed her bracers; her forearms had long-since stopped bleeding, but they were covered in slashes from the razor nettle. "Gods have to be held up to standards, too, you know?"

Miranda said, "That's right," and set her bowl down. "If King Edgar came up to you right now, R'lyeh, and punched you in the face, would you let it slide because he was king?"

"Hell no."

"Then the same should go for any god. And if they don't like it, then tough shit. They're gods. If they can't take a little criticism, then they aren't worth our time."

R'lyeh smiled as she nodded in agreement. She stretched out her legs and fell back on her palms. She could feel the fire in the balls of her feet, working its way into her bones. *This is nice.*

"Liz, I did see some very thick spider webs not far from here," Miranda said.

"Arachne?" Elizabeth asked.

"Looks like it."

"Rattle Bones did say something like that might happen." Elizabeth turned to R'lyeh. "Ever been to the Nameless Forest?"

R'lyeh sat up. "I've seen it from a distance, I think. Have you?"

Miranda moved her paralyzed arm onto her lap and said, "We lived there."

The hell? R'lyeh brought her knees to her chest. "Seriously?"

"Our Ladies of Sorrow academy," Elizabeth answered. "Yup. It was an orphanage. We grew up there. Surprised, yeah?"

"Uh, yeah." R'lyeh couldn't believe what she was hearing. Did anyone else know about this? Was this something they were sharing with her in confidence? It had to be, right?

Elizabeth continued on. "Yup, lived there until we were fifteen, then we left about fifty years later, when we turned sixteen."

R'lyeh started to laugh. Then, when she realized Elizabeth wasn't joking, she said, "Wait, what?"

"Do you know what vampyres are?" Miranda asked.

No, they're screwing with me. But instead of saying that, she said, "They're bloodsuckers. Bite people's necks to turn people into them. They do everything at night, because they can't go out in the sun. Some of the kids back… home used to say the Frozen North was full of them, but… you're not saying you're vampyres are you?"

"Not anymore," Miranda said.

"Not anymore," Elizabeth repeated.

"Please, guys, don't mess with—"

"We grew up in the Orphanage. We weren't born there, but mothers in the Nameless Forest sometimes leave the children at the academy to keep the vampyres living there happy," Miranda explained. "Mine and Liz's mothers left us there. Nowadays, all vampyres are children."

"Or teenagers," Elizabeth added.

"Vampyres don't bite necks. The mouths they use to bite are in their palms." Miranda flexed her hands, and for the first time, R'lyeh noticed the faint vertical lines on her palms. "The sun weakens them, but it won't kill them. They can't spread the disease, either. They have to bring initiates to their master, Camazotz, for that."

R'lyeh's hair blew in front of her face. She quickly pawed it out of her eyes. "Camazotz?"

"The massive bat they have suspended in the academy. They have to feed on its blood to keep their immortality. If they stop feeding, they will eventually start to age again."

"At fifteen, the headmistress, Gemma, said that me, Miranda, and our friends Jessie and Emily, were ready to become vampyres."

Mouth hanging open, R'lyeh said in disbelief, "You really drank the bat's blood?"

Elizabeth and Miranda nodded.

"Did you get mouths in your hands?"

Again, they nodded, and they both showed the scars on their palms.

"Holy shit. I had no... but you said after fifty years you started aging again?"

"We did. We stopped feeding. We didn't agree with Gemma and the way she was handling things at the academy," Miranda said.

"And then the Bad Woman came," Elizabeth said.

R'lyeh raised an eyebrow.

"Her." Elizabeth raised her shirt and showed the tattoo on her lower back. It was of a demon-faced nun who held *Helminth's Way* in one hand, and a rosary made out of teeth and eyeballs in the other. There were four stones—red, white, pink, and purple—at the nun's feet. "The Bad Woman."

"No adults had been allowed into the academy ever since the Trauma," Miranda said. "That's what we had been told."

"But that little shit, Gemma, let the Bad Woman in and she took over. She promised to rejuvenate Camazotz; said if she did that, the vampyres could escape the Nameless Forest. She lied." Elizabeth lowered her shirt. "She tortured all of us, and made that rosary you saw her holding out of Emily's teeth and eyeballs. Miranda, Jessie, and I knew we had to get out of there, so we ran away. After a few weeks, the hands in our mouths healed and the disease disappeared."

"We stayed in Threadbare for a few years, another village in the Nameless Forest. This lady there, Lotus, took us in," Miranda said.

"Then we found a spellweaver and went back to Our Ladies of Sorrow academy."

R'lyeh leaned forward and whispered, "Why?"

"Sweet revenge, of course," Elizabeth said. "We went back and beat the shit out the Bad Woman while Gemma was away. We dragged her ass back to Threadbare, and the spellweaver wove her into my skin."

"W-wove her?" R'lyeh asked.

"Bitch was my first tattoo. She feels everything I do to her," Elizabeth said, "and she's not going anywhere." She poked the spot where the tattoo was through her shirt. "She isn't a part of me. She's just hitching a ride. So when we caught you eating gloom caps, I understood, because you know what I do when I get anxious?"

R'lyeh shook her head.

Elizabeth took a knife out of her belt and pressed it to her lower back. "I always end up cutting too deep and go past her into myself. But it's worth it, yeah?"

Miranda nodded, said, "Yeah."

R'lyeh covered her mouth. She blinked her eyes hard and had a look around to remind herself they were still in the woods outside the Divide. The sun was high in the sky now, and wildlife was scurrying and flying all about them. It had to have been eight or nine in the morning, but after everything so far, R'lyeh was ready to go back to bed.

"We will wait until nightfall to cross," Miranda said, standing up.

Elizabeth held out her hand, and Miranda took it to help her up. "East bank or west?"

"East," Miranda said, offering her hand to R'lyeh, who took it, too, and came to her feet. "Penance isn't so close to the Divide that we can't sneak by. I'm not risking walking through a field of vermillion veins."

Elizabeth and Miranda nodded and went their separate ways; Elizabeth to the tent, and Miranda to the woods to relieve herself.

R'lyeh, feeling left out again, then said, "What would you guys do if you saw Gemma again?"

Both women stopped what they were doing, but they didn't answer. Their silence said it all.

At nightfall, they broke down their camp, loaded their belongings onto the horses, and rode the beasts to the Divide. To the east, the bank was aglow with torches from Penance's encampment. There were voices coming from that area, but they were outnumbered and overwhelmed by the songs that were being sung from the makeshift masses that had cropped up around the base. There were a lot of people out tonight, R'lyeh thought, but if they had their heads in heaven for the next hour or so, then she, Elizabeth, and Miranda just might slip by.

Using the light of the moon as their guide, they followed along the edge of the Divide. Often, the horses would go off-course and start walking through the water. It wasn't quite pitch-black, but it was close enough that they were practically riding blind through the night.

Halfway to Penance's encampment, R'lyeh started to hear something move through the woods beside them. Using her ears, because her eyes were all but useless, she followed the noises. Whatever was out there, they were quick, agile, and were using the trees to get around, rather than the ground. The air smelled bad, too; like a mouth full of rotting teeth.

"What's that?" R'lyeh whispered.

Someone, probably, hopefully, Miranda, shushed her.

R'lyeh focused on the darkness beside her, using the moonlight to solve its mysteries. The trees creaked and moaned, and a branch suddenly snapped and plummeted into the shadows. There was a groan, maybe a hiss; and then the noises were closer. Whatever it was, it was just out of sight, and it was going where they were going.

Once they were close enough to Penance's encampment that the torchlight could give them away, Elizabeth, Miranda, and R'lyeh steered their horses into the shallows of the Divide and cantered very slowly down the river. The encampment was built on a steep embankment, and as long as they kept close to it, not even the sentry towers would see them.

R'lyeh tightened her grip on Vrana's ax as they fully entered the encampment. Above them, only the tips of the nearest tents could be seen. Torches flared, and so did the sounds from the Masses. Shadows moved back and forth along the rim of the embankment.

They rode in silence until Miranda halted the procession and whispered, "Stop."

A rush of anxiety wracked R'lyeh's body so hard she thought she might curl up like a spider and fall off her horse. Stop? Stop for what? There were thousands of soldiers just over the embankment. All it would take was one of them to see them, to round them up, to march them through the encampment and make them—

"Ah, that's what I'm talking about," a man's voice said ahead.

R'lyeh squinted. Two shapes were standing on the embankment a few feet ahead. They had their dicks out, and they were pissing into the wind.

"I was about to explode," the second man added. He shook himself a bit, and then wiped his hands on his trousers.

The first man grunted in agreement. Still pissing, he said, "Ragtag group of soldiers they got here."

"Yeah, but feels kind of like a big family get-together," the second man said. He started away from the embankment, then turned, so that he was directly facing R'lyeh and the others.

Fuck, oh fuck, oh fuck, she thought. *He's going to see us.* She pressed herself against her horse. Elizabeth and Miranda did the same.

"Everyone from everywhere. Seen a lot of faces I haven't seen in forever," the second man continued.

"Ah, you know why everyone's here." The first man finally put his dick away. "I mean, how often do you get a chance to actually see the Mother Abbess and the Holy Child?"

"Never. Once in a lifetime." The second man clapped his hand on the first man's shoulder. "Think they'll be here soon?"

The first man said, "I hope so," and walked with his companion back into camp.

But before they had gone completely, R'lyeh heard one of them say, "Can't wait to see the Mother Abbess turn into an angel. Once she does that, all those Disciples will come crawling back. You'll see."

CHAPTER IX

One day into the Dires, and already Aeson wasn't a fan. North of Caldera and east of Geharra, the Dires was all red rock and yellow earth; a flat, dusty territory that, without sand and scorching heat, seemed to be nothing more than a poor man's desert. The place had a haunting quality to it. With it being so empty and vast, every brittle field and trembling wood suddenly became homes for horrors unseen. Aeson tried not to let his imagination get the better of him, but after hours riding beside Bjørn and not seeing another soul, it was hard not to. A place even as boring and inhospitable as the Dires couldn't possibly be this empty; the only solution was that they were being watched, followed, and measured up for some forthcoming massacre.

Aeson told Bjørn his concerns, and Bjørn laughed at him and told him he was being paranoid.

"You've never been this far outside of Caldera," the Bear went on, bobbing up and down in his horse's saddle. "It's alright to be scared."

"Yeah, yeah," Aeson said. "Damn, these horses are uncomfortable."

The two horses they rode were conjurations the elders had created for them from what was left of Caldera's fields. Made up of rock, wood, soil, and whatever unfortunate creatures had been in the field during the ritual, the horses were incredibly fast and impervious to exhaustion. Their time, however, was temporary. Aeson's and Bjørn's horses each had about three hours left before they would fall apart and return to the earth that had spawned them. After that, they'd have to find their own rides.

They rode for another two hours in silence, and then the Dires decided to do something different. The unending expanse of dead fields and dry thickets started to become healthier, fuller. Out of the unnaturally even earth, hills like fat, melted candles formed. Farther on, parts of the sky sat low to the ground, as if the clouds in it were weighing it down. The path they had been following once ran in every direction, but as the land sloped, it funneled them into a steep ravine.

"What do you think?" Bjørn asked, taking the vanguard.

"I feel like something bad is about to happen," Aeson admitted.

The walls of the ravine shivered rocks around them, as if something were tracking their movements from above. Aeson's eyes darted back and forth, searching for signs of a stalker.

Bjørn, undisturbed by this, corrected himself. "I mean being out of Caldera."

Aeson's horse let out a grunt. The spit it spat as it sneered wasn't spit at all, but small seeds that whistled in the wind.

Bjørn shifted in his saddle. "You're holding your own."

"Oh, thanks."

Aeson still couldn't believe he was here, hundreds of miles away from home. It had all happened so quickly, so easily, that it made him wonder if it would have happened sooner if only he had asked for it. How much of his isolation had been self-inflicted? The elders had nurtured it, but he had been the one to impose it. Like the tree his parents had hanged themselves from, it was easier to let things be than to have them be anything else.

"It's great," Aeson said, catching up and riding beside Bjørn.

"What is?"

"Being out of Caldera." Aeson smiled behind his mask. "We've been on the road for weeks now. A little late to ask, don't you think?"

"Now we're deep in it, that's why. You can't turn back," Bjørn said. He stopped his horse as the ravine branched off into several different directions. "Which way, Skull Boy?"

"Northeast should take us to the Dismal Sticks," Aeson said. Then, jokingly, he added, "Papa Bear."

As if struck by lightning, Bjørn sat straight up in his saddle. Slowly, he turned his head and stared Aeson down.

"Do you mind if I call you that from now on?" Aeson asked, doing his best not to laugh.

"Do you mind riding the rest of the way with my boot in your ass?"

Aeson shrugged. "Can I get back to you on that one?"

"Take your time," Bjørn said. He kicked his horse and took the ravine's northeastern passage.

Words must have been a limited resource for Bjørn, Aeson thought, watching the big man brute-force his way through the ravine. He could get Bjørn to speak for a few minutes at best, and then he would go quiet. The strange thing about Bjørn was that he was the one who usually started the conversations, here and back in Caldera. It was like he wanted company and companionship, and then, when he got a hint of either, he hid.

By the time they emerged from the ravine into the woods beyond, the horses were literally on their last legs. Quickly, Aeson and Bjørn dismounted, removed all their belongings—bags, books, and swords—and gave the beasts a wide berth.

The horses wandered in circles around the woods, pieces of their earthy, makeshift bodies dropping off them in melted chunks. They slammed against the trees, neighing pathetically, as if they were experiencing pain they couldn't possibly feel.

Aeson and Bjørn backed up; the horses kept trying to return to them, either for comfort or because these two men were all they had known.

"Don't let them touch you," Aeson said.

His horse plodded forward toward him. Its knees buckled and broke, sending it face-first into the ground.

"Anguis said that while they're dying, if they touch you, they'll sap some of your life force."

"Why wouldn't they do that earlier?" Bjørn went sideways as his horse clumsily charged toward him. It crashed into a tree, the impact liquefying its head and splitting its body like a wishbone.

"Most things don't think about living until they're dying."

Both horses had one more go at trying to reach their masters. They made it about two feet before their bodies separated into the substances of their making. Like the threads they were, all the rocks, roots, bones, branches, crops, and animals that bound the horses together broke, and the beasts were instantly reduced to piles of stinking muck.

"They can call them whatever they like," Bjørn said, "but those things aren't what the elders said they were."

Aeson nodded, took up his bags. He tightened the scabbard at his waist. He turned away from the steaming conjurations and set his sights on the woods they were now stranded in. They still had all the telltale signs of the Dires—dusty earth and a dearth of life—but there appeared to be some sort of drop-off ahead, right past where the trees were at their thickest.

Bjørn had seen it first, and because he was Bjørn, he went first. Bastard sword out, fist tightly balled, he barreled through the woods, breaking on his body any branches that got in his way. Aeson trailed after him, the bags and his sword already making him short of breath. He had been training with the Bear every chance he could get, but the fact of the matter was he was still one hundred and forty pounds of skin and bone. He had a few measly muscles to show for the effort, but they were so sore all they did was slow him down.

Reaching the thicket before the drop-off, Bjørn said, "Is that it?"

"Is... what... it?" Aeson panted, several feet back. He stopped, bent over, and shook his head, embarrassed. "What the hell is wrong with me?"

Bjørn doubled-back. Straightening Aeson up, he said, "You look like one of those horses."

Aeson laughed, wiped the sweat out from under his skull mask. "What do you think Vrana would say if she saw us like this?"

"Probably yell at me for being an asshole. Probably make fun of you for being a wimp." Bjørn turned toward the drop-off. "Come on. Think I saw the Dismal Sticks just over this ridge."

Aeson pulled himself together and pushed onward. They were at the top of a chain of hills that loomed over the shadowy valley beneath them. Carved out of the wilderness at the valley's center sat their destination, the Dismal Sticks.

The Dismal Sticks was a backwoods farming community that ran diagonally across the valley's floor. The so-called "state" was divided equally into six "counties," with each county represented by one of the six families settled there. To the northern side went the counties of Misery, Gloom, and Ache; directly across from them, separated by the large lake between them, sat Grief, Woe, and Stitch. The Dismal Sticks was the only known community thriving in the Dires. According to the records Aeson had read, they took pride in their ability to weather the suffering of their surroundings. They wanted others to know the misery, gloom, grief, and woe they felt on a day-to-day basis; they wanted others to feel the ache in their hearts, the stitch in their sides. But most importantly, and Aeson was beginning to realize why the Dires made him so uncomfortable now, these farmers wanted others to know they were better than everyone else, because they had taken torment like a tonic for so long they had developed a taste for it.

"You pick a person?" Bjørn mumbled.

Aeson had heard him, but not really. He was too busy watching the Corrupted move across the six farms, in and out of the corn fields. There were so many, and many of them he probably couldn't even see because of the growing dark. Other than the odd prisoner here and there, he had never really seen a Corrupted before, and never up close. And those from the Dismal Sticks were a brutal bunch. They could try to sneak through the "counties," but Bjørn didn't strike him as the sneaking type. If they got caught—

"Skull Boy."

Aeson snapped out of it, said, "Sorry," and then: "Person?"

"From your–" Bjørn snapped his fingers, trying to think of the word, "registry. The Children of Lacuna."

"Oh, yeah." Aeson swung his bag in front of him and removed the registry. Reading from it: "Charlotte Breckin, Ichor, Grant Erickson, Erick Grantson—"

Bjørn laughed. "The hell?"

"Hey, it's the country." He shook his head, smirking. "That's all of them; all of the Children in the Dismal Sticks. Charlotte should be in Misery, Grant in Woe, and Erick in Stitch."

"Hmm." Bjørn leaned away from the ridge, clearly searching for a way down. "You've got your heart set on that Ichor character, don't you?"

"The description says Ichor has blue hair. And his name is Ichor. If anyone is going to help us, I'm guessing it's him." Aeson placed the registry back into the bag. Taking a deep breath, he added, "What's the plan?"

"This is a close-knit community out in the middle of bumfuck nowhere." Bjørn stuck the tip of his bastard sword into the soil. "So we'll wait until the sun sets and go in and give them some night terrors." His bared teeth glistened with spit inside his bear mask. "Sound good?"

No, no it doesn't, Bjørn, he thought, watching the giant man nimbly make his way down the side of the ridge. "We just need to get in and get ahold of Ichor. No one needs to die."

Bjørn stopped. His shoulders tensed. The falling sun framed his old musculature in a reddish, hazy glow. "You're a Night Terror, aren't you?" he asked, not turning to address Aeson.

"Yeah."

"They're Corrupted, aren't they?"

"I mean, other than the Children... yeah."

"Been a long time since some balancing has been brought out here." Bjørn lifted his bastard sword and rested its blade on his right shoulder pad. "Someone most certainly needs to die."

The ridge must have been used by the citizens of the Dismal Sticks at some point, because the farther Aeson and Bjørn went down it, the more hints they found of past expansions. Amongst the dead leaves and wild weeds, they found signs of steps built into the sides of the hills, and bridges, too. There were shacks as well – dilapidated, of course—and shallow caves that might have been meant for mining at some point. There were even half-finished observation decks protruding from the incline, some of which had been equipped with busted Old World telescopes. Bjørn ripped one off its post; the lens dirty and fractured but manageable.

Twenty or so feet from the valley's floor, Bjørn stopped in front of what was clearly the unfinished foundation of someone's house. They had built the beginnings of it into and against the hill, but hadn't gotten much farther than a few layers of brickwork. There were three skeletons at the center of the would-be home—two adults, and one child; each of their skulls had been bashed in with what must've been a hammer.

"About thirty years ago, some people from Dismal Sticks reportedly tried to move out of the valley," Aeson said.

Bjørn stepped over the foundation. He went to his knees and stared at the bones lying where beds could have been. "Something from the woods stop them?"

"Not exactly." Aeson turned to face the Dismal Sticks. "Friends and family killed them. They were afraid if too many people left, the community would die out."

Bjørn's hand hovered over the tiny skull of the dead child. "And they left all this here as a reminder for future generations, I take it?"

Aeson shrugged. "People who are one thing and one thing only don't know what to do when someone comes along and tells them they could have been something better. When you do that, you may as well be insulting their existence."

Bjørn said, "Yeah," came to his feet, and joined Aeson in surveying the Dismal Sticks. "You start reading that book Anguis gave you?"

The cool evening wind rolled over the hillside, teasing out goose bumps from Aeson's flesh. "Just the inscription, which I'm pretty sure is the title."

Bjørn slid his sword into its sheath and crossed his arms. "What is it?"

"*The Blood of Before.*"

"Hmm."

"Yeah. I don't know what that's about."

"You said your parents were the last to write in it?"

Aeson's body jerked. "Yeah, other than Adelyn. Hey, you see—"

"You afraid to read what they wrote?"

He closed his eyes, pressed his hand against the skull mask; a spider there skittered across the bone and onto his knuckle.

"You afraid you might find out why they killed themselves?"

Aeson's eyes snapped open. Without thinking, he shoved Bjørn as hard as he could. The Bear didn't move but an inch.

"I don't know, either," Bjørn said. "Just figured you might be getting tired of being one thing."

Aeson's arms tightened, but he resisted the urge to shove the son of a bitch again. "I'm here, aren't I? I'm here, trying to save Vrana with you. Where the hell do you get off—"

"Anguis gave you that book for a reason, Skull Boy. And it wasn't to haul it across the continent to see how much dust you could gather on it."

"I have been training with you. I have been doing my best to keep up with you every step of the way. We are here, outside the fucking Dismal Sticks, and I'm pretty sure you're going to make me fight and kill some Corrupted tonight. What's your problem with me? Quit—" This time, Aeson did shove him again, but it was like shoving a boulder. "Quit fucking with me. I'm terrified, alright? I don't know how we're going to pull this off. And yeah, I'm afraid to read the book. Alright? I barely remember my parents. If I start *The Blood of Before* and it's a recount of their last dark days before they killed themselves… I don't think I can—"

"You have to," Bjørn said. "I'm not insulting your existence, Aeson, but you need to be more if we're going to bring Vrana back."

"So just put myself through hell for the hell of it? I don't think you realize what it was like to live for years under Caldera—"

Bjørn, ignoring Aeson and pointing to the Dismal Sticks, said, "What's that?"

Aeson huffed, shook his head; he wanted to fight for the sake of fighting, even if it wasn't a fight he wanted to have to begin with. "What, Bjørn?" he said through his teeth.

"On the farmhouses; the icon of Penance."

It was getting almost too dark to see across the few mile stretch between here and the Dismal Sticks, but Bjørn was right. Taking the telescope from him, he saw painted on the roofs of Misery, Grief, and Woe were white circles inside which diamonds and crucifixes were held.

"Yeah, so?"

Pointing to the opposite end of the Sticks, Bjørn asked, "That's the Disciples of the Deep's calling card, right?"

It was harder to see the icons on the even farther away farmhouses of Pang and Stitch, but again, Bjørn had been correct. On their roofs, the icon of the Disciples of the Deep—an eye crowned with a crescent moon, and a wreath of tentacles—had been rendered in purple, almost phosphorescent, paint.

"I'm guessing the Sticks is a god-fearing place," Bjørn said. "I'm guessing they didn't feel the need to start announcing holy devotions until the Disciples moved into town. We might have come at the right time. They'll be so busy one-upping each other's god, they may not even notice us. Which house does Ichor belong to?"

"That one," Aeson said, his voice shaking as he directed the telescope to the farmhouse that sat in the middle of the Sticks, between Misery and Pang, and across from Woe.

"What's that one called? Gloom?"

"Yeah."

"I can't tell—" Bjørn sounded strained; he took the telescope and leaned forward, "—but I don't see any anything painted on Gloom. What do you think that's about?" He laughed. "The Sticks' first atheistic family?"

"Ichor's a Child of Lacuna," Aeson said, shaking his head. "And there is an icon. See it? On the front door?"

Bjørn started to say, "No," and then: "Oh, yeah. Yeah. Looks like it was written in blood. But I don't recognize the symbol, Skull Boy."

The icon was splattered across the front door of Gloom. It was simple, crude; a stick figure with four arms and four legs, with two heads from which long, crooked lines ran. Aeson had never seen it before in his life, and he was grateful for this, because every second he spent staring at it, it felt as if nails were being driven into his eyes. And yet, despite the pain, it was almost even more painful to tear himself away from the savage imagery.

"If I had to guess," Aeson said, tearing his gaze away from the agonizing gateway, "I'd say that's the Cult of the Worm."

"A lot of gods running around these days," Bjørn said, unsheathing his sword. "Did the Night Terrors ever follow a religion?"

"Yeah, for a while after the Trauma, I heard. They used to worship the Lord animals."

Bjørn ran his fingers along the bastard sword's edge, cutting them. "And now we wear their heads."

"Yes, we do." Aeson paused, and then added, "I'd like to wear the Witch's head."

Bjørn nodded, clamped his hand down on Aeson's shoulder. "I think Vrana may have dibs on it. How about her guts?"

"Those'll do, too."

The plan was to wait until nightfall, but by the time they made it into the valley, they saw an opening that was too good to ignore. They had come down from the hills behind Grief, Woe, and Stitch; to reach Gloom, they would have to pass through the corn fields behind the farms and find a way around or across the lake that sat in the middle of the Dismal Sticks. But as they crept through the corn fields at the back of Stitch, several Corrupted emerged from the farmhouse with lanterns in their hands. They spread out across the property, and kept pointing to a series of smaller houses that lined the lakefront.

"What's going on?" Aeson asked, he and Bjørn slowly pushing through the field. "Can you make out what they're saying?"

Bjørn kept running his hands against the stalks, as if the sensation calmed him.

"It looks like a lynch mob," Aeson said, heart pounding so hard in his chest he could hear it in his ears.

Bjørn brought out the telescope, said, "There's seven of them; hard to tell this deep in the field," and stowed it back in his bag. "Let's go."

Aeson took a few deep, controlled breaths, and then, with Bjørn's silent insistence, he took the lead. He waded forward, parting the dry stalks and taking them into the thinner part of the field. As he went, he noticed a cold green hue started to form like a film over the Dismal Sticks. Looking past Woe Farmhouse, he noticed that the light was lifting off the surface of the lake, as if it were being extracted from the waters by the moon above.

It was no wonder that the Dismal Sticks thrived in the Dires; it had been built on the grounds of a luna lake. The lakes were extremely rare, so much so that they weren't but a few tall-tales away from pure myth.

Whereas Echoes were believed to be the Earth's dreams of the past recollected in real time, luna lakes were said to be distilled reveries from the Earth's hope for a better future. Anything planted in the vicinity of a luna lake was guaranteed to prosper, and anyone who drank from it was rumored to be gifted an extended life and increased fertility.

"This is their secret," Aeson whispered.

They stopped a few feet from the end of the corn field. Aside from what was blocked by the back of the three-story Woe Farmhouse, they had a pretty good view of the Sticks from here.

"That's how they've lived out here so long. You'd have to be an idiot not to prosper next to a luna lake."

The seven Corrupted swung their lanterns back and forth in heated debate. Three broke from the pack and headed for Stitch Farmhouse, which was about a quarter of a mile east of Woe. The other four kicked some dirt around, and then followed after.

"There's more coming," Bjørn said, nodding to the west, where a group of ten was pouring out of the Grief estate.

In a matter of minutes, the light from the lake had grown exponentially. It was now radiating outward in every direction, blanketing the Dismal Sticks in a dim, miserable wash that left all lighter tones green and all darker tones black. To Aeson, it looked somewhat like one of the day-for-night film scenes he'd seen in the movie reels stored in the Inner Sanctum. It gave to the Dires a kind of natural camouflage that might have been, in some ways, better than darkness itself.

Apparently, Bjørn felt the same way. "This is good," he said, admiring the way his body and the cornstalks seemed to blend into one another. "I see boats up by the shore, past the lake houses. If we could steal—"

Half a mile west, twelve lanterns flared on the property of Grief estate. The light from the lanterns was so severe the farmers may have been carrying fragments from fallen stars. Like those from Woe, these twelve of Grief took off toward Stitch, but instead of going by foot, they went by horseback.

Nervously, Aeson asked, "What's going on?"

The twelve horses thundered past Woe. Aeson's legs trembled with each rumbling gallop. Immediately, he went for the hilt of his sword, but his sweaty hand was doing him no favors.

"Stop," Bjørn said, grabbing his wrist. "They're gone."

Aeson nodded, let go of the sword. "We can't take on that many."

"We're not going to. Something has this place spooked."

"You think they know we're here?"

Bjørn pushed forward a few feet and stuck his face out of the fields. "No," he said, scanning the area. "More coming from across the lake. Come up here. No one's going to see you."

How the hell do you know that? Aeson thought but kept to himself. Carefully, dead crops crunching under his feet, he went to the end of the field and cast his gaze across the misting lake.

What was going on? The mist across the lake was quickly thickening into a fog, but even so Aeson could tell that there were more people gathered on the other side of the Dismal Sticks at farmhouse Pang. They were moving too fast to be on anything but horseback, and like those from Woe and Grief, they were headed toward Stitch. At the head of the procession, someone was ringing a bell.

Bjørn slipped out of the corn fields and into the open. He unsheathed his sword and skirted the side of Woe farmhouse. He waved Aeson over, and when Aeson went to follow, his legs locked up and a chunk of fear lodged itself in his throat.

"I can't," Aeson whispered, shaking his head. He kept looking back and forth between the lake houses and the farmhouse, waiting for someone to open a door or window and spot them.

Bjørn twitched. He stormed over to the corn field and wrenched Aeson out of it. Dragging him by the straps of his breastplate, Bjørn hauled him to Woe and flung him against the side of the farmhouse.

"God damn it," Aeson hissed, his shoulder cracking against the brickwork. "Have you ever done anything gently in your life?"

Bjørn lifted up his bear mask. Flashing his glistening face, he said, "No," and then nodded eastward at Stich. "How many people live out here in the Sticks?"

Rubbing his shoulder, Aeson said, "There's not really a clear consensus. Maybe sixty or seventy?"

"Looks to be about twenty or thirty over at Stitch."

"Yeah," Aeson said, those from Pang having finally joined the throng of people outside Stitch's fields. Thirty, it was closer to thirty the number of people there, congregating and cussing and moping about with their hands shoved deep in their pockets.

"Those are the bigwigs," Bjørn said. "Place like this, only they get to ride out big and fancy at night. Notice how nobody came out of Gloom?"

"Yeah," Aeson said. He tried to look across the lake at the farmhouse where Ichor lived, but with the fog, it was impossible to see that far anymore. "No lights on there, either."

"Three houses sworn to the Holy Order of Penance, and two to the Disciples of the Deep. They should be fighting, and yet they're all gathered together tonight."

"Except for people from house Gloom. House Cult of the Worm."

"Maybe." Bjørn walked to the edge of Woe farmhouse. "If Ichor's not there, we'll catch him when he gets back. If he is—"

"We'll get him alone before everyone returns," Aeson finished.

Bjørn took off for the lake houses. Aeson, not wanting to be left behind, even though that's exactly what he wanted, bit his lip and, with a burst of speed, sprinted after him. Out in the open and the thick of the Sticks, he could get a better bearing on their surroundings. The luna lake ran east to west; all long stretches and hard curves, he imagined it must have looked something like a diamond from space. The lake houses that ran along it were more like huts, and there seemed to be about nine of them in total between Woe and Grief. Two of them had a dock and rickety rowboats, and that's where Bjørn was headed now.

The Bear hoofed it between two lake huts and onto the small, fog-covered dock. Aeson, bent over to avoid passing in front of windows, followed after him. He could hear people in the huts beside him; quiet murmurs following indistinct questionings. A part of him wanted to stand, to look through the glass and see what sat on the other side of the sill. But he was a chickenshit, so he slid through the grass like a simpering snake and ambled clumsily onto the dock.

"Get in," Bjørn said, standing near the rowboat.

Aeson did as he was told. The boat rocked back and forth as he stepped into it and sat. Small ripples of icy light broke across the water beside him. He leaned over the rowboat, peered into the depths of the luna lake. Petals of light bloomed in that emerald darkness, folding and unfolding, living and dying for the glory of the great moon above.

"Ever been in a boat before?" Bjørn asked. He sat down in it, and the whole thing almost capsized.

"You know—" Aeson hung onto the sides as Bjørn situated himself. "You know I haven't."

Bjørn took up one oar, and handed the other to Aeson. "Bet you've done a lot of things I haven't."

"Are you trying to get on my good side after treating me like shit all night?" Aeson dipped the oar into the water. "Am I doing it right?"

Bjørn snorted, started to row. Aeson mimicked his every movement, albeit much more slowly, and far less gracefully.

"You disappointed we haven't killed anyone yet?" Aeson asked, not letting his voice rise much higher than a whisper. They were out in the lake now, under the cover of the cotton-like fog, but even still, they had to be careful. Who knew what waited for them on the other side?

"There's still time for killing," Bjørn said, muscles bulging, as if he were trying to murder the lake itself with the oar. "Try not to freeze up again."

The lake gurgled. Tiny bubbles rose to the surface and popped, expelling a fetid odor.

Cringing from the smell, Aeson said, "Trust me, I'm not doing it on purpose. If things could just keep going this way the whole way, what with people rushing off to secret meetings and—"

"They won't." Bjørn rowed faster; they had reached what must have been the middle of the lake. "Be ready for that."

"Why are you so determined to see me kill?" Aeson twitched; something had scratched against the bottom of the boat.

The fog rolled over the boat, and in it, Bjørn disappeared for a moment. "You need to know you can," he said, nothing more than a disembodied voice. And then, reappearing: "If you wait until the Witch to do it, you won't."

Again, more scratching from underneath the boat. Aeson moved his legs away from the center, afraid something might burst through.

"You saw her when she attacked Caldera, didn't you?" Bjørn asked.

"Yeah." The question took him back, took him back to the heat, to the screams; to the Maiden of Pain staring him down, Caldera burning behind her; her claws splayed, her mouth open, a sick, clucking laughter coming out of her throat as if it were stuffed with bones. "She could have killed me. She just laughed, instead."

"She ran that night," Bjørn said.

"Back to the Void, I guess," Aeson said.

"We have to keep her away from it to kill her?"

"From what I've read from those who have gone toe-to-toe with her, yeah, I think so."

Bjørn scratched his neck. "Keep her away from it? Or cut her off from it?"

"I don't know," Aeson said, shrugging. "I hope it's not the latter. We're not prepared for anything like that. I think there's a way—"

"What?" Bjørn interrupted.

"I was thinking we could slip her some Death's Dilemma, but that's not going to happen."

"No. What else?"

"A Red Death weapon," Aeson said.

Bjørn let out a mocking laugh. "You plan on calling in a favor with Death?"

"No, but you could. Didn't you run into Death once?"

"Once was enough," Bjørn said, not backing down from what most had agreed was a bullshit story. "Think of another way."

Aeson, biting his lip, said, "I'm just... thinking aloud, Bjørn. Look at me. I can barely handle sneaking into the Sticks. I don't want to see Death, either. It was just an idea, that's—"

"Think of another way," Bjørn said.

"You really met Death?" Aeson couldn't believe how scared the Bear sounded.

"I don't want to talk about it," Bjørn said. He wrapped his arms around himself. "Not now. Not until this is over."

"The Sticks?"

"All of it. I'm not testing my luck."

"What?"

Bjørn grunted, and that was the end of that.

The boat drifted for another minute or two, and then the fog finally broke, and they found themselves a few feet out from the shore. Beyond, across the road, Gloom stood, a haunted house if Aeson had ever seen one. The farmhouse was two stories of black wood and cobwebbed glass; the porch, which wrapped around the estate, was in pieces; where it wasn't splintered, it was warped, and where it wasn't warped, weeds had taken over. A rotted apple orchard twisted out from behind the house and wrapped around the back of it like hair. In the front, the house had all the features of a face; windows like eyes, a chimney like a nose; four small doors, each of which was covered in the bloody symbol of the Cult, formed the building's lurid teeth. But the resemblance to a face was a resemblance to a face after a stroke, after a terrible shock; it was the face of a place calling out for help, because it knew its owners no longer could.

As the boat began to make landfall, an infant cried out from the gloom around Gloom. Aeson turned. This time, when he reached for his sword, Bjørn let him draw it.

A man with nothing on but a silk nightgown shuffled out of the shadows and went straight for the shore. In his arms, he held a newborn still wet and steaming with afterbirth. Everything was green in the Dismal Sticks, but by the man's age and striped Corruption, it had to have been Ichor.

Not seeing them there, or not caring, Ichor knelt down beside the lake. He lifted the baby up to his face, inspected it. Its shrill, shaking cries set Aeson on edge. He looked back at Bjørn, and then heard something go into the water.

Aeson whipped around. Ichor was still kneeling on the shore, except the baby was now under the water, kicking and screaming and filling its tiny lungs with that drowning light. Aeson moved forward, ready to lunge out of the boat, but again, Bjørn grabbed his wrist.

"I do not enjoy this one bit," Ichor said, sinking the dying baby deeper into the lake. He moved one hand off its chest and pressed it against the baby's face. "Sometimes I wonder if there is a better way, but it isn't our place to wonder, is it?" He cocked his head, having seen something Aeson and Bjørn hadn't. "Ah, here we go."

Ichor jerked his hands out of the water. The baby lay there in the shallows, its movements sluggish, pained. Tiny bubbles crowded around it; when they popped, a patch of decay, like a trampled bed of roses, formed, coating the surface in a sticky residue. A hand, pale with long fingers, shot out of the water, the near-dead baby in its clammy grasp. There was a giggle, a kind of deviant glee, which rose out of the waters from something below.

The hand held the child there a moment, as it coughed up lake water and fought to live. And then, when it seemed it would come to, the hand took the baby back into the water, back into the dark depths from which the creature had come.

"Whew," Ichor said, "glad that's over." He struggled to his feet, and then waved at Aeson and Bjørn. "Night Terrors? In the Dismal Sticks? My prayers have been answered. Please, please come ashore."

Aeson looked back at Bjørn, but the Bear kept his gaze fixed on Ichor. "Okay," he said, taking the rope and tossing it to the Child of Lacuna.

Ichor smiled, started to tug them in. Silk nightgown aside, the man was deranged. His blue hair had been chopped into, as if by some barbarous barber with blunt tools instead of knives. Dark circles, which were made darker by the luna lake's light, crept beneath his eyes, like two black holes. Both of his arms were caked in grime, from the tips of his fingers to the ends of his elbows; and his legs were wiry twigs covered in scabs and bruises. He had seen better days, but when, probably no one could be sure.

Ichor pulled the boat as hard as he could. It slid through the patch of decay, where the hand and the baby had been, and then lodged itself with a thump into the shore.

"I've been trying to reach out to the elders up in Eld for help here," Ichor said. He dropped the rope and offered a hand for Aeson to take.

Aeson gathered up his bags and quickly moved past Ichor.

"The locals have been patient so far, but I'm not sure how much longer that'll last." Ichor offered his other hand to Bjørn.

Bjørn ignored the man. He drew his sword and stepped out of the boat.

A scream broke across the front lawn from somewhere deep inside Gloom. The wind kicked up; a cold front washed over them, making sure that all three of them were shivering by the time it passed. Across the lake, the numerous lanterns began to extinguish; either the meeting was over, or the night work had just begun.

"What's... going... on?" Aeson asked, looking back at Bjørn with every word he spoke.

Ichor clapped his hands together, those filthy, long-nailed, root-like appendages. "Well, they saw you coming. I think they thought you were here to kill me." Ichor laughed, went to nudge Aeson, and missed. "Also, a little girl and her mom and dad were sacrificed over in Stitch a few weeks back. They're still a little sore about that. Hey—" he started for Gloom, "—let's head inside fellas. I want to show you around."

"Ichor," Aeson said, staying still.

"Yeah?"

"We're here for the Cult of... the Worm." Aeson could feel the heat pouring off Bjørn now; the tiny explosions that accompany a proper bloodlust.

"Yeah? Yeah, I know." Ichor smirked. "That's why I'm happy to see some friendly faces. Well, I'm sure they're friendly beneath your masks. Ha. Anyways, where did you say you're from? Eld?"

Aeson started: "Cal—"

And Bjørn finished: "Yeah."

I'm not going in there, Aeson thought.

A candle flickered to life behind one of the first-floor windows.

I'm not going in there. Behind the house, the dead orchard rattled, the wailing wind serving up a buffet of fetid apple and wet manure for them to sample.

Was that her? Was that the Witch's hand? I'm not going—

Ichor stopped at the bottom of the porch and turned around. His ass and cock were pasted to the nightgown now, both of which looked like old meat behind the silk. "Hey, weird question, but any chance you've heard about my sister?"

Bjørn asked, "Who's that?"

"Hex. She has Corruption on both her arms. It's just... last I heard she was with the Marrow Cabal, but since the Worm network went down, I don't..." He smiled; a few of his teeth were missing. "So she's not around?"

Aeson shook his head.

"Oh, well—" Ichor started up the porch, stepping on every splinter he could find, "—that's good. Good. She's always looking for me, trying to kill me. I thought coming out here in the Sticks would get me away from... Hey, never mind all that. Come inside. We're good company."

Aeson dug his feet into the ground. "We?"

"Yeah." Ichor stopped, leaned against the porch's railing. "The Choir." He snorted, waved them off. "Shit, they really do keep us Night Terrors in the dark, don't they?"

"You're Corrupted," Bjørn said, pointing to Ichor's arm, which, like everything else, was green; nevertheless, the crimson defect was still there.

"Ah, yeah." He rubbed the back of his head. "But only on the outside. Really, though, you should come in. If the rest of the families see us out here conversing, then they might just attack. Let's not give them a reason to, you know? I'm running out of excuses to keep them at bay." He went across the porch to the front door; the blood-writ icon of the Cult glowed as he touched the knob. "You coming?"

Aeson stared at the Child of Lacuna, while a thousand questions raced through his mind. Was that the Witch's hand? Where is Vrana? Have you seen Vrana? Where will the pilgrimage take place, and will Vrana be there? What the hell are you doing inside the house? Where is Vrana? Have you seen her? Is she okay?

Bjørn walked toward the house, his sword arm tensed, his focus fixed on Ichor. "What just happened there in the lake?"

Ichor opened the front door halfway, and then turned. A pathetic laugh left his lips. "Ah, uh, yeah, I guess you wouldn't know about that."

Aeson readjusted the bags at his waist and over his shoulder. For being leather, the armor he wore may as well have been stone. It was starting to suffocate him, weigh him down. The stress spreading throughout his body had him so tense he hurt, like tiny drops of acid had been dribbled onto his muscles. *Ignore it*, he told himself, but he couldn't. Not with Bjørn holding his sword like that. Not with Ichor grinning on the porch like that. Something bad was about to happen. And who was that in the doorway? What was that thing in the doorway, in the shadows? This was a trap. This was too easy. Why didn't Bjørn see that?

"That was Joy," Ichor said. "The defective go to her. That's what they did on Lacuna, right? Fed the defective to the Blue Worm?"

"You're… breeding Night Terrors and Corrupted?" Aeson asked, going to the bottom of the porch. "You mean Pain, right? The Maiden of Pain?"

"Pain? Oh no, no. She doesn't come around much. She leaves the Dismal Sticks to her sister most of the time. I guess the messages weren't clear, Worm Network being down and all." Ichor slapped his forehead, screwed up his face. "Yeah, guys, we're keeping the good work going here and elsewhere."

She's real? The Maiden of Pain has a mother fucking sister? Aeson looked at Bjørn, and Bjørn's wild eyes seemed to say he was thinking the same thing.

The thing in the doorway behind Ichor moved; the floorboards creaked, and a shadow lengthened across the porch.

"For the Cult?" Aeson asked.

"Everything for the Cult," Ichor said.

"You fed a flesh fiend to the Witch's sister," Bjørn said.

"No, of course not. I fed her a human. What's more defective than a human? And not really fed. I don't know what she does with them. We keep the flesh fiends. They're our angels. They're our Choir. You can't hear them. They're locked up right now, but they're inside, singing beautiful songs to God. We don't choose a side, you see. Holy Order, Disciples of the Deep. Doesn't matter. Pain and Joy are God's servants. They just want to make God feel welcome when It finally comes. A song brightens everyone's day. We're going to have songs being sung everywhere soon.

"Come in, please, come in. I'll show you. You have to see it for yourself."

Aeson and Bjørn headed up the porch and stopped at the front door.

Several more candles ignited in the windows. Now that the door was open, and they were close enough to the threshold, they could hear something coming from inside the house. Something sorrowful, something wracked with anguish; a haunting chorus that befitted this haunted house. It was screaming, there was no doubt in Aeson's mind about that, but the way the pained cries came together, they formed a kind of unholy union that turned those terrible notes into something melodic, into something that, like Ichor had promised, sounded like music.

The Witches are parasites, Aeson thought, as Ichor flung back the front door. *Attaching themselves to the major religions to build a following of their own. Fuck. But why flesh fiends? You can't control—*

A creature limped across the threshold. A flesh fiend. It was dressed in an Old World suit, something that a man might wear to a dance or a prom, with scuffed-up shoes on its feet and dirty white gloves on its hands. But it was the fiend's face that Aeson couldn't tear himself away from. The flesh fiend's head was grotesque; a pink, encephalitic swell that housed two white eyes and a mouth so torn apart the beast's diet for the last two weeks had to have been nothing more than bone and glass. It had no hair, but that's not to say it didn't make an effort; across its scalp, long, stringy tendons had been nailed into place; they ran from the flesh fiend's cracked cranium to its crooked neck, and were still wet from the blood of the poor creature they had been stolen from.

"This is Ezra," Ichor said.

The flesh fiend bowed its head to Aeson and Bjørn. Like an animal sick with rabies, thick slobber poured from its mouth, and left foam across its lips.

"He and Belia will show you to your rooms. Where is Belia?"

Ezra shook its head. The tendons whipped back and forth, slinging bloody specks.

"You... you said a little girl and her mom and dad had been killed here?" Aeson asked, giving everything he had to hide his repulsion. "Did... one of your... Choir escape?"

"No, no." He snapped his fingers, and Ezra turned and went back inside Gloom. "Pain and Joy wanted to show the Sticks the power God had given to them. They sent their weapon down, and well, I think they got the hint. I mean, here I am, still alive!"

Bjørn was trembling, had been ever since the flesh fiend showed up. He grabbed onto Aeson for support. "Weapon?" he said.

"Yeah, Vrana."

Aeson's heart stopped. "V-Vrana?"

"Yeah, you got it. Listen, guys, I'll tell you more later. I really want to show you the place. Besides, Joy will probably be back soon. So if you don't mind the Choir singing all night—they have a lot of practice to do—you can ask her anything you'd like. She's very sweet. Feels like one big, happy family with her around. Better than Lacuna ever turned out.

"So what room do you want to see first? The feeding pit or the fuck pens?" Ichor snorted like a pig, wiped a tear from his eyes. "I'm just joking. They're the same thing."

CHAPTER X

For a man who was all bones, the Skeleton wasn't much when it came to boning. It was midnight, and he and Clementine were in bed. Fleshless digits between her legs, he was using every trick in the book to make her feel anything other than the repulsion she must have felt right now with this dead thing inside her. He wanted to stop, but he knew she'd throw a fit if he tried. It wasn't right to be touching her like this; it wasn't right to be touching her at all. He had the power of the Black Hour in his fingertips, and here he was, putting death deep in her cradle of life.

Clementine let out a moan. It sounded genuine, but the Skeleton didn't have any ears anymore, so the jury was still out on that. He leaned in closer, his lidless eyes beaming down on his wife's glistening neck. She wrapped her hands around the back of his skull and pressed his face to her flesh. He knew what she wanted, so he opened his sneering mouth and let his black tongue loose over her breast. She let out another moan. It would be over soon, like it always was, and in the end, everything would be the same.

The Skeleton lifted his head away from Clementine's chest. She was staring at him, a smile a small crack in her otherwise frigid face. Her eyes were dull, distant; still set on some sick sight back in the Membrane. The Skeleton cupped her face, ran his fingers over her lips. She bit at them playfully, but only because she knew that was what he was expecting her to do, and what she would have done before she died years ago.

"Are you sure there's nothing I can do for you?" Clementine asked, rubbing his spinal column.

"Being with you is enough." The Skeleton climbed off her and settled into his spot on the other side of the bed. "Clem?"

She wiped herself off with a sheet—hygiene wasn't exactly something she got hung up on anymore—and rested her head against his ribcage. A few inches above her head, the Black Hour's heart sat in a cocoon of the very same black moss that had spread to some of his ribs. He tried to shift her away from the foul growth, but like with most things, Clementine would not be moved.

"Yes?" she said, pulling the blanket up to her neck.

"What do you see when I touch you?"

Clementine groaned. She flicked a rib with her finger and shook her head. "Enough. Ask me something else. We've talked that topic to death."

The Skeleton's bloodshot eyes wandered around the room. Red waves, sanguine refractions from Gallows' blood lake outside, were coming through the window and washing along the walls. There was a bookshelf and a desk; some rug they had wrung a fraction of the Red Worm out of, and a chest of drawers that was filled with Clementine's clothes, on account of the Skeleton not needing clothes himself. It had been Clementine's idea to make the room look like their room back home, but she gave up that ghost about a week into the project. She said she didn't have the time, but the Skeleton knew it wasn't time she was lacking. The woman had all the time in the world. It was memories she had a shortage of. Her body had come back from the Membrane, but not much else.

"Will's still raw about me grounding him," the Skeleton said.

Clementine sighed. She threw an arm around him and held onto his bones tightly. "I think—" she yawned, "—he's a little more upset with R'lyeh than anyone else."

"He just can't go on anymore missions. He likes her, don't he?"

"Will likes any pretty little thing that shows him an ounce of attention. Don't you like her? You sent her out on something important. Can she fight that good?"

There was a commotion on Gallows' platform. It sounded like several of the cabalists were getting into it about something. The Skeleton had half a mind to break it up, but this wasn't the farmhouse; this wasn't home.

"Don't know. She's a Night Terror, though. The only one we got. If she can snag Audra, then we'll be in good shape."

"Yeah. How you plan on using her?"

"Don't know. This was mostly Hex's idea. If King Edgar catches wind of his sister here, he's going to rain hell down on us."

"How is she?"

The Black Hour's heart twitched. Instinctively, he clutched his chest, as if the thing were giving him a heart attack. The damn thing wanted to speak to him, but this was his time with his wife. Like everything else, it would have to wait.

"Don't know—"

Clementine snorted. Looking up at him, she said, "Don't know, don't know, don't know. Is that all you know how to say?"

"Don't know."

"Bah." She nestled her head harder against him. "She isn't right. Hex, I mean."

The Skeleton pulled Clementine into a hug and held her there. "Don't I know it."

"It's been weeks now. People follow you, Atticus, but I think they're getting antsy wondering where Hex is at. Most sicknesses would've passed by now. You need a new excuse."

A new excuse? The Skeleton wondered to himself what excuse would fly if he started flaying Hex. Their relationship was a complicated one; one that swayed back and forth between cross-eyed hate and begrudging tolerance. Hex wasn't a bad woman; what she wanted was just, and what she had created with the Marrow Cabal was commendable. But she had taken advantage of the Skeleton. She had seen him for the monster he was and the bloodlusts he possessed, and used this knowledge against him every chance she had. The Skeleton was too valuable to cut loose, and he understood that. Their connection had been built upon using one another. Now, she was useless to him, and she had infinite uses for him, the Skeleton, their undead lord and savior.

"You're doing good," Clementine went on, speaking in the syllables of sleep. "You're doing... good."

The Skeleton waited a minute until his wife was out; and then he moved her off him and onto her side. Clementine slept a lot these days. She used most of her energy on tiny tasks that didn't amount to much. It was only when she was asleep that the Skeleton could really get a look at her. He could see the texture of her skin, the thoughts coming out as creases across her brow. He could smell her to make sure she wasn't rotting or that something wasn't growing inside her. Sometimes, Clementine would speak in her sleep, and the Skeleton would listen to those dream-driven ramblings, for in them were unguarded truths.

His wife assured him every day that nothing was wrong with her, but he knew better. You didn't go to bed with a pile of bones and the Black Hour itself and come out unchanged. Not a day had gone by that the Skeleton hadn't considered leaving Clementine and Will, but what he couldn't figure was what would hurt them more. Staying with them? Or abandoning them for good? Sometimes he wondered if they could die, and if they couldn't, sometimes he wondered if he would love them more for it.

"I got to go," the Skeleton whispered an hour later, when Clementine was good and comatose. He kissed her cheek with his sneering teeth.

"Check on Will," Clementine said, from somewhere deep inside a dream.

The Skeleton threw on his tattered cloak, fastened it, and slipped out of the bedroom. Outside, in the hall, a lantern was suspended from the ceiling, the candle inside it all but gone out. This "home" of theirs had been made out of the remains of the town hall. It was the largest building in Gallows, and even though they shared it with Hex, it was still by far the emptiest place in town. The Skeleton and his clan had their own corner, and the blue-haired Lacunan had hers; the rest was for the bugs and the cobwebs that caught them. It wasn't a place meant for roots; they wouldn't take.

Atticus stopped outside Will's room. The door was shut, but there was a little light coming out from underneath it. He reached for the doorknob and—

Bound and gagged, Hex is yours for the taking. Bleed her until she's yours, or until she won't bleed anymore.

"Quiet," The Skeleton snarled to the Black Hour inside him.

He turned the doorknob and let himself into his son's room. The fourteen-year-old was sleeping fitfully in his bed. Holding onto his pillow, with the sheets snaking between his legs, Will shivered and said nonsensical things under his breath. He was sweating badly. Every few seconds, he would reach out to the wall beside his bed and beat his fist against it. Three slow thuds. Thump, thump, thump. A pause, and then three more. Thump, thump, thump—the same sound the shepherds would make every time they had banged their crooks on the ground.

"Hey," the Skeleton said, going to the side of his son's bed.

Will jerked awake. His eyes fought to blink out the crust at their edges. With a shout, he pressed himself against the wall, because even now, the sight of the Skeleton was still too much of a shock.

"Dad?" Will let out a nervous laugh. "What… what's wrong?"

The Skeleton shook his head. He did a once-over of Will's room. It had no windows, nor closets; just four bare walls with an empty floor in between. The only thing Will had to call his own was his bed and his clothes, which he kept under it. Like the Skeleton and Clementine, he had brought nothing here. Everything they'd ever had, it was still back at the farmhouse, in the kitchen where they'd died.

"About to head-off," the Skeleton finally said.

Will yawned, scratched at the stubble on his face. "To work? You're always working."

"Yeah." The Skeleton sat on the edge of Will's bed. "Can't sleep, even if I wanted to."

"Mom wants you with her at night."

"Too much going on to stay in bed with your mother. She understands."

Will nodded, even though it was obvious by the look on his face he didn't agree with his dad. He opened his mouth to speak, but nothing came out. That happened a lot these days to him; efforts undone by the slightest unseen thing. The Skeleton had the Black Hour whispering insanity to him most of the time, that's what distracted him. What distracted Will, though? What did he hear whispering in his mind?

"You, uh, dream about shepherds a lot?" the Skeleton asked.

Will's jaw slightly dropped. He glanced around the room, as if he were trying to find something by which he could change the subject. He yawned, rubbed his feet together, but quickly gave up the tired act when he clearly realized the Skeleton wasn't having it.

"You dream about the Black Hour a lot?" Will shot back, living up to his current curse of adolescence.

The Skeleton ignored him. "How long you been having these dreams?"

A lie: "I don't know." And then: "Since you got us out of the Membrane."

"What're the shepherds doing in your dream?"

Will laughed uncomfortably. "They watch me. Like, they, uh, look right at me. Like they can see me through the dream. We're in some hot place in the dream. I've never seen it. The sky is really gray, almost black. There isn't a lot around. Just me and the shepherd."

"Just the one?"

"One, yeah."

The Skeleton scratched his ribcage like an ape. "You seen another shepherd since Bedlam with R'lyeh?"

Will tightened his mouth. He puffed out his chest, as if preparing himself for a beating. He didn't say anything else, but he didn't need to.

"Where Will?" the Skeleton went on. "When and where?"

"Outside Gallows." He swallowed hard. "I… saw Mom talking to one once."

The Skeleton shot out his hand and took Will by the arm. He squeezed him so tightly he left bone prints on the boy's pale skin. These two were—

Clementine and Will came back wrong, and on the wrong side. They are the shepherds' crooks now, and while your back is turned, they are going to ground you into dust.

"God damn it," the Skeleton said, letting go of his son.

Will rubbed his arm as tears welled on his eyelids. He shook off scenes from the Black Hour.

"What do you mean… talking to one?"

"I… that's what it looked like. I don't know. I didn't… I just saw the two of them out of the corner of my eye. When I turned around, it was gone."

The Skeleton felt a heat in his bones. Ever since he'd started housing the Black Hour's heart in his chest, it seemed as if new flesh were forming over him; invisible flesh fitted with invisible veins and arteries that throbbed with time and all the Black Hour's putrid permutations.

"What did your mom do? What did she look like?" The Skeleton got to his feet, so Will was out of his reach.

"It was a few weeks ago. I don't know. It was only for a—" Will dropped his head. "It looked like she was laughing."

I can't do this. The Skeleton turned away from Will, wished him goodnight, and headed through the doorway.

Halfway into the hall, Will cried, "When are you going to let me out of here?"

Laughing, the Skeleton turned around and said, "Boy, you must be joking. After what you just told me? Why you want to tempt fate?"

"The hell are you going to do with us? Keep us chained to you forever?"

"You don't understand—"

"I don't care!" Will gritted his teeth. "None of us are living. Hell, you can't, so I'll cut you some slack."

"You'll cut me some slack?"

He has the Membrane inside him. He is a carrier.

Will leaned over the side of his bed, to where the candle sat beside it. He gave the Skeleton the cruelest look he could muster and then blew out the flame.

The Skeleton stood there in the hallway, the after image of his son's hatred hot in his brain. It should've hurt, but it didn't, not even when he pretended that it did. Pain wasn't something he experienced much anymore; like a man in a desert looking for water, he had to work for it. But like a desert is dry, the Skeleton's scarring was deep. Sooner or later, the well was going to run out.

He had Hex held up in her room, which in the last two weeks had been repurposed into a cell. There was one way into the room, and it was double-locked and double-guarded by the Marrow Cabal's finest. She hadn't said much of anything these last few weeks; she'd come down with a bad case of guilt, and like a bookworm, it had chewed up most of her words.

The Skeleton skirted through the house like a wraith. Cobwebs and corners, that's all the place had going for it. It was two stories of nothingness; a brightly lit warehouse that held a few bodies and bated breaths. Part of it was their condition, this emptiness, and part of it was his strategy. When building it, they had chosen the creakiest wood and noisiest doors; everything was an alarm. There were no hiding places, nor was there anything to become attached to. Their home was a cage meant to catch shepherds. It never really occurred to the Skeleton until now that he was using his family and himself as bait.

He passed through the foyer—two guards outside the front door, as ordered—went down the hall that led to Hex's side of the house. The rooms attached to the hall were shut, locked up tight.

Hex has a lot of skeletons in her closet. How long will it take until you join them?

The Skeleton rounded the corner. He shook off the Black Hour's threats. About a month back, it had stopped showing him disjointed images and started speaking in full sentences. It had developed a consciousness, or maybe it had borrowed a little of the Skeleton's. He couldn't say.

The Skeleton stopped. Hex's room, or rather Hex's jail cell, sat behind the double-locked door ahead. Except the door wasn't double-locked. It was open. And the two of the Marrow Cabal's finest? They were gone, too. And there was something else.

The Skeleton took a step forward and strained his non-existent ears. There was someone in the room with Hex, talking with her. He broke into a sprint, his fingers outstretched, clawed. He didn't need a weapon to kill a thing anymore. His hands were better for it, anyway; a sword could only split a soul; with his hands, he could grab it whole.

The Skeleton burst into the room. A mountain of wasting muscle barred his path between him and Hex's bars. It was Warren, and he was looking at the Skeleton as if he were offended he was here.

"What are you doing?" the Skeleton asked, planting his feet to stop himself from pouncing.

Hex lingered behind the bars of her cell. The strands of her blue hair were pasted to her forehead, because sickness made the best adhesive. She looked better than before, but not by much. There was a glow to her eyes, too; specks of sapphire that burned like embers. They hadn't gone out since she'd tried to kill R'lyeh.

"Keeping watch, Bone Daddy," Warren said. He smiled, stepped out of the Skeleton's way. "I'm going to get some sleep."

The Skeleton put his hand on the big man's chest.

As if stabbed through that spot with a sword, Warren immediately stopped. His face contorted. Air caught in his throat. A seed of chaos from the Black Hour's heart had buried itself into the big man's brain.

"Atticus," he said, shaking.

The Skeleton let go of Warren. Behind him, Hex backed away from the cells, so she, too, couldn't be touched by him.

"Goodnight, Warren," he said, having so successfully reduced the mountain of muscle to nothing more than a whimpering puddle.

Warren looked back at Hex. She gave him a half-hearted shrug and waved him on.

"I'll be fine," Hex said, her throat somewhere between sore and dehydrated. "Can't do no worse to me."

Warren nodded. He moved as if to intimidate the Skeleton, then moved past him, instead.

The Skeleton waited until they were alone. When it was clear that the coast was clear, he went to the corner of the room, grabbed a stool, and took a seat in front of Hex's cell. King Edgar had done the same to him once, when he was locked up underneath Ghostgrave, before he let loose the flesh fiend. It felt good to be on the other side of the bars for once.

"Warren said you sent R'lyeh away," Hex mumbled. She wandered around the cell and then sat on the edge of her bed. "That was smart."

"Best hope we have getting Audra to come to our side," the Skeleton said.

"Something's taken over new management of the Children of Lacuna." Hex leaned forward onto her knees. "It wanted me to kill her. I think it might be the same thing that took her friend—Vrana."

"Yeah, the girl being marked made it easier to send her away. That, and she's a Night Terror."

"You going to tell her it's the same Witch?"

"Maybe not." The Skeleton shrugged. "Not until we know it is."

Hex nodded, pinched the bridge of her nose. "What do you want, Gravedigger?"

Gravedigger? Haven't heard that in a while.

"Come in here acting tough with Warren, and now you want to be cordial? You got me locked up. Warren said you're saying I'm sick. What do you want?"

"See if you're still sick."

Cut her open, and you can find out for yourself.

The Skeleton shook off the suggestion.

Hex laughed. "Don't you like it this way? With me out of the way?" She leaned forward, pointed her finger at his heart. "Bet your ticker is happy. Bet you two are getting real chummy nowadays."

The Skeleton growled. He stood up, undid his cloak, and dropped it on the ground.

With a gasp, Hex said, "Atticus, it's getting—"

"Worse?" The right side of the Skeleton's torso, from his clavicle to the bottom of his sternum, was covered in a thick, black moss. The ribs there were gone, completely overtaken by the overgrowth. Where his heart had once been, the Black Hour's was now suspended, its beating being what kept it afloat; a machine of perpetual and perpetually polluted energy.

"Does Mr. Haemo know?" Hex asked

"He's not happy about it, but the blood keeps him quiet."

"For now."

"Until it's time."

"No." Hex waved her hand. "No. We are sticking to the plan with Audra. What you and Herbert and that fucking bug are up to—"

"Then get better. Let me and mine go. I'm done being your symbol."

"And if I don't? What're you going to do? Sabotage everything we've worked for?" Hex went to the bars, pushed her arms through them, as if daring the Skeleton to touch her. "Go, if you want to go. I can't stop you." She grabbed at him.

The Skeleton took a step back.

She smiled, dug her teeth into her lip. "You can't die, Atticus. Nobody's pulling your strings. You just like to pretend. Give you something to get good and bothered about. Hate me if you like, but when you're with me, you're right. When you were left alone?" She nodded at him. "You came back nothing but bones.

"Get that shit out of your chest." Hex hit the bars and backed away. "Keep me in here until the end of the week. I need to know I can trust myself. Are your friends here?"

The Skeleton picked his cloak up off the ground. Touching it, he still could hear Blythe dying in its threads. "Soon, I expect."

"How's your wife and son?"

The Skeleton shook his head and said, "Seeing shepherds everywhere they look."

"Ever figure out what they see when they see you?" Hex plopped down onto her bed. "Might be a shepherd yourself. Wouldn't that be a son of a bitch?"

The Skeleton slipped out of the house at 3:30 AM. The two guards stationed outside it gave their usual respects. This early in the morning, Gallows was dead. Those that weren't asleep in bed were most likely asleep at their posts. The blood lake, that final portrait of Geharra's and Alluvia's people, was quieted, too. All that was left were the beasts that hunted in the dark, the things they killed, and the Skeleton himself, who still couldn't figure where he fit into the fold.

On his way to Operations, he reviewed the state of things. The Disciples of the Deep were deeply entrenched in the Heartland. Reports from his scouts in the field stated that the Disciples were co-existing with members from the Holy Order of Penance. The takeover was taking its time, but it was taking; whereas the Holy Order demanded faith, the Disciples only asked that the people watch, and listen. Miracles were being performed on a daily basis across the Heartland, from the Blasted Woodland to the foothills of Kistvaen. Generally, the miracles were always the same; some sort of feat performed with the assistance of the vermillion veins. It was a show that should've gotten old, but it hadn't, because gods didn't dull.

The Holy Order of Penance had mobilized an army, and it was now currently stationed on the western banks of the Divide. There were reports that the Mother Abbess and Holy Child himself were headed to the frontline. Whereas the Disciples of the Deep were peacefully integrating into each town and village, the Holy Order was resorting to violence to force out the invader parasites. Last week, fifty people had been killed in Cathedra, most of whom were self-proclaimed Disciples. All signs seemed to point to war; a war Penance seemed desperate to start. Eldrus, on the other hand, wasn't interested in taking the bait. The city-state had an army of its own, and yet it was nowhere to be found.

The strangest thing the Skeleton had read reports of were the vermillion nests scattered across the continent. They were sometimes a mile long, and looked like deadfalls, except they were teeming with vermillion veins. At first, the Skeleton had thought it was King Edgar's new Nameless Forest coming to fruition, but the way the scouts described the scene, it sounded as if the veins weren't growing in these places, but rupturing out of the ground, as if something was being awoken.

The Skeleton crossed the wooden platform to Operations and tore off the lock from the door. He had forgotten the key and didn't want to go back home. Navigating the pitch-black building, bumping into what seemed like every table and chair, he finally made it to his desk at the back and dropped into his seat. He sat there a moment, gathered himself, and then lit the candle.

You can't stand her.

"Who? Hex?" The Skeleton rummaged through the drawers for the notes from Herbert North. He had read them a thousand times over, but even still, that wasn't enough. Everything needed to be accounted for. He wasn't smart enough. Not yet.

Hex hates her brother so much she tortures him. She's adopted you and yours for when he's not around.

"What's between her and Ichor has nothing to do with me." He stopped looking for the notes, buried his skull into his boney palms. "I can't be myself, not with you inside of me."

You're exactly what you've always been. Flesh makes fiends of us all.

The Skeleton ripped a dagger out of the drawer. "I'm going to cut you out."

Then how will you save them?

"I don't need you."

You did back then.

"Not anymore."

Not right now, you mean.

"You need me."

A nice thought, isn't it? Indulge, and I'll show you our intentions.

"No, you won't. You can't show me nothing." He pressed the dagger past his ribs, directly into the Black Hour's heart.

Don't be stupid. You could drop a nuclear bomb on us and we still wouldn't flinch.

"Don't know what that is." The Skeleton shoved the dagger into the Black Hour's heart, but it kept on beating.

You will, or something like it, when all else fails. Pillage the graves of cities, and see what you will see.

The doors to Operations flung open and snapped back against the walls. The Skeleton's eyes widened as dawn crept inside the building. In the doorway, four or five cabalists stood, their weapons drawn, their hands shaking.

"Sir?" one of them called out.

The Skeleton scratched his corneas. What time was it? How long had he been speaking to the heart? He stood and stepped out from behind his desk.

"What is it?"

"There's, uh, there's—"

A second soldier: "Something's coming."

And a third: "It's… it's—"

Finally, the fourth blurted out, "A giant bat, sir. We're under attack!"

The Skeleton stormed out of Operations and joined the crowd of cabalists at the edge of the platform. Across the lake, beyond the edge of Gallows and past the sentry towers, a gigantic, twenty-foot bat was tearing across the countryside, crawling on its hands at a rate of twenty or thirty miles per hour. On its back, hanging onto its blood-encrusted fur, were what appeared to be at least sixty or seventy children in school uniforms.

Over the cries of the cabalists, a buzzing could be heard. The Skeleton tore his gaze away from the sight of the feral bat and saw that Mr. Haemo was hovering above him, his skin cloak hanging looser than usual off its insect body.

"Don't see that every day," Mr. Haemo said. He landed beside the

Skeleton, and the rest of the cabalists ran to the lower level of the platform. "What? Do I stink or something?"

"That's Camazotz," the Skeleton said, pointing to the bat, which was now on the outskirts of town, navigating the bloody, body-choked swamp that surrounded it. "The vampyres from the Orphanage are here to help. Do you mind sharing your blood well with the bat?"

"Share with Cammie?" The mosquito laughed. "No, not at all. Don't think she'd give me a choice, anyway. Home girl and I go way back."

Camazotz barreled past the guard towers. The humungous, sore-swept bat went headfirst into the blood lake and waded forward, sending wave after wave of gore like bloody baptisms onto the children on its back.

"Must be nice to finally be out of the Nameless Forest," Mr. Haemo said.

"Must be," the Skeleton agreed.

Camazotz stopped directly below where the Skeleton and Mr. Haemo stood. A child amongst the tens of children on her head came to their feet, waving. She was wearing a green dress with a red collar, and the slits in both of her palms were gawping.

"Hi there," Gemma shouted to the Skeleton.

And the Skeleton nodded back.

"Nice place." She levitated upward, off Camazotz's head, until she was on the same level as the Skeleton. "Hope your men don't mind us." She extended her hand to shake the Skeleton's, and when he went for it, she pulled it back and said with a grin, "Too slow, Old Bones."

"Where's the Arachne?" the Skeleton asked.

Camazotz bucked in the blood. The Orphans on its back hopped off and disappeared into the sanguine waters.

"Yeah, bad news." Gemma floated down from the air and landed beside him and Mr. Haemo. "They went a different way."

"What do you mean?"

"Lotus convinced them to side with King Edgar. All three thousand of them."

"Gemma." The Skeleton made a fist. "Where are they now?"

"Good question." She smiled, shrugged. "Headed for the Heartland, I imagine."

CHAPTER XI

R'lyeh was literally freezing her ass off. Sitting there in the snowdrifts outside the Night Terror village of Rime, she could feel her butt cheeks hardening into two crystalline hunks. All it would take was one bad bump into something and they'd surely shatter. She looked to Elizabeth and Miranda for support, but they didn't so much as move; they were about an hour away themselves from turning into full-blown ice sculptures.

The razor-sharp wind cut across the drift, sending wave after wave of stinging snow at them. R'lyeh pulled her furs and faerie silk cloak closer. Overhead, the sun shone brightly through a cloudless sky, and yet not even a fraction of its warmth reached them. It was bullshit.

Rime was about a quarter of a mile from where they waited. The village was a wooden sprawl of coffin-shaped buildings that had been built on (or unearthed from) the desolate plains that surrounded it. Dozens upon dozens of people moved through and out of the village, into the rickety woods behind it, or toward the tundra further still. There was a storybook quality to it; be it the wood the buildings were made out of, the fires that blazed so closely to them, or even the damn snow glittering on every rooftop. Dream-like and comforting, it called to R'lyeh's mind the tales Mom and Dad used to read from the Old World children's books she had liked so much.

It was obvious that the place had no problems with its obviousness. Caldera had Kistvaen to protect it, and Alluvia had the Elys to shield it; Rime, on the other hand, had the elements, and the assumption no one would be stupid enough to risk hypothermia to come all the way up here and attack it. And yet here they were—R'lyeh, Elizabeth, and Miranda—

three women who took orders from a psychotic Lacunan and a walking, talking Skeleton.

When it comes to stupidity, R'lyeh thought, *we probably have it in spades.*

"You're g-g-good g-g-going in alone, y-y-yeah?" Elizabeth asked.

The morning sun's brightness flared; its light bounced off the snow and blinded them. Together, they moaned in pain and buried their heads into the crooks of their elbows.

"No, n-not really," R'lyeh said, peering out from behind her arm.

"L-l-listen, we would come, but I d-d-don't think we're g-g-g-g-g—"

"Going?" Elizabeth teased.

"Fuck you, it's c-cold," Miranda snapped back. "We're not g-g-g—"

Elizabeth snickered.

"—going to find two Lord animals nearby." Miranda shoved Elizabeth face-first into the snow. "Cold, yeah? Yeah?"

"Yeah," Elizabeth said, her face splotchy and red, the snow melting down it. "You'll do fine, R'lyeh. These are y-your people."

They are, aren't they? And yet to R'lyeh, it didn't feel that way. The snow crunched beneath her as she crawled back to the top of the snowdrift. Rime was a quarter of a mile away, but even from this distance she could say that, yeah, Elizabeth was right—these were her people. Here, a bear skull, there a seal skull; Night Terrors wearing the heads of foxes and wolves moved in packs around the woods, animals and the efforts of their foraging slung over their shoulders and across their backs. In the plains, Eels in heavy furs rooted through the snow, checking traps and for the still edible, frozen dead.

Yeah, these were her people; not people she knew, but people she was supposed to belong to. And she couldn't have been any less excited to join them.

R'lyeh said, "Y-you sure I should g-go alone?" and shook the snow off her octopus mask. The hollowed-out cephalopod had been coated and reinforced to prevent wear, but even the cold was taking its toll on it. "Why c-can't—" she checked the Cruel Mother's talons, took up Vrana's ax, "—you two sneak in? Knock s-someone out?"

Crouching low, Elizabeth and Miranda slipped and slid down the snowdrift.

"We're not Night Terrors," Miranda said, throwing the hood of her coat over her head. "If our c-cover is blown, they'll k-kill all of us."

Elizabeth joined Miranda at the bottom of the drift. Tightening her gloves and chewing on her lip piercing, she said, "We're Corrupted, yeah?"

R'lyeh nodded.

"I know you d-don't see it because we're so badass—"

R'lyeh smiled behind her mask.

"But—" Elizabeth rolled up her sleeve and showed her arm, "—we are Corrupted. They w-won't show us kindness—fuck it's cold—and if they f-find out you did, what do you think they'll do?"

"I don't know," R'lyeh said with a shrug.

"You do, you know." Miranda smiled. "If we come, you have to choose. Sometimes, it's best not to have any other options."

R'lyeh reached under her mask, wiped her dripping nose, and watched Elizabeth and Miranda head southward, one plunging lunge at a time, through the soft snow and layers of ice, toward the cave thirty minutes back—their hideout, and redoubt. She started after them and then stopped. They weren't abandoning her. The Skeleton didn't send them into the outskirts of Gelid territory to get rid of her. This was just a mission. This was just a mission, and she was the best person for the job. She had been through worse, and probably had worse to come.

R'lyeh shoved her shaking hand into a pocket and pulled out the last of the gloom caps she had brought from the Divide. Her jaw was too tight to chew, so she just swallowed the mushrooms whole. All the ice in her belly melted. The anxiety in her heart thawed. She had sworn off poisons to make Elizabeth and Miranda happy, but she needed them now more than ever. Because if she stayed in the shadow of Death, she would be invisible to It. The same had been true in Geharra, so what could possibly make Rime any different?

R'lyeh pulled the faerie silk cloak tight, stuffed the collar of it under her mouth, and bit into the fabric to stop her teeth from chattering. The plains were frozen over to the point that everything looked as if it had been caught in an eruption of ice. The rime, which was also the village's namesake, was thick, spindly, and grew off the rocks, bushes, and snow-pack like wild, white hairs. It crunched beneath R'lyeh's feet like glass, and like glass, it made it impossible to sneak. She could feel the gazes of four nearby Eels tightening on her, sizing her up to decide if she was worth a sword point or an arrow shaft.

Thirty feet from Rime, the wind howling in her ear like a wraith, the gloom caps went to work in her gut. As the Eels in the plains started to converge on her location, she stopped, dropped Vrana's ax in the snow, and held her stomach. Now wasn't the time for weakness; she needed confidence and courage; and yet the best she could manage was a warm trickle of piss and hot diarrhea down her leg.

"Fuck, fuck, fuck," R'lyeh said, the steam coming out of her pants. "I'm from Caldera," she recited, the Eels, looking absolutely feral in their furs, drawing closer. "I'm from Caldera and I'm here to—"

She groaned, bent over, lifted up her mask, and vomited into the snow. The pale splat of breakfast etched itself into the top layer of ice. Glancing up, she saw that the four Eels were only a few feet away. They stood next to one another, their spears at their sides, mumbling. They weren't threatened by her, but she sure was by them.

The Calderans were known for their savagery, but these people of Rime, with their heavy furs, thick leathers, and weatherworn masks, literally looked like animals themselves. Of all the Night Terrors R'lyeh had ever met, these four were the only ones who truly deserved the title. They were the way she imagined her people must have been years ago, before the Trauma had tortured them into being civilized.

"Who are you?" the Eel in the white furs asked. His voice was raspy, his words rounded; it sounded like two glaciers colliding. His mask was an eel's skull with three bloody smears running down the face of it. "You're not from here," he said, pointing his spear at her. "I am Ghelys. Who are you?"

R'lyeh exhaled. "R'lyeh of Alluvia." She yanked her ax out of the snow; the other Eels flinched, but Ghelys didn't. "The only survivor of the Red Worm and Geharra." Memories of the pit punctured her thoughts, but she kept it together. "I come from Caldera."

Ghelys chuckled. "Another?"

Another? Another what? Survivor? Or person from Caldera?

"You sick?" Ghelys moved toward, his head moving up and down, as if he were sniffing the air. "What's wrong with you?"

"Ate something bad." R'lyeh stared at the other three Eels; they were smaller in size, not as thickly dressed, and far less intimidating than Ghelys. They didn't speak. She figured they probably wouldn't unless Ghelys gave them permission to.

"I don't mean to be rude, but why you here?"

R'lyeh glanced back at the snowdrift, hoping that Elizabeth and Miranda were watching, waiting—preparing for an attack. But they weren't there. They were back at the cave, warm and cozy, and probably cackling around a crackling fire. And here she was, shit running down her leg, her life on a quickly fraying line.

Finally, she said, "I… I… I have a message for your elders."

Ghelys grunted. "Birds are better for delivering messages."

The wind kicked up and sliced like a scythe through R'lyeh's mask. "B-birds can be intercepted." And then, out of nowhere: "B-by Witches, or e-even the Marrow Cabal."

"Witches?" Ghelys ground his spear into the snow. "Hmm." He looked at the other three Eels, and they nodded at him, silently.

"What do you know of Witches?"

R'lyeh shrugged, thought: *Oh shit, is she here?*

He gestured for the other Eels to return to their duties in the plains. "You're small," he said, watching the three go crunching through the snow.

"Yeah," R'lyeh said, her heart beating faster.

Ghelys nodded and gave his spear the up-down.

"That's great," R'lyeh said. She brushed off her shoulder. "I get the point."

Ghelys snorted. "You just might."

R'lyeh took the lead, because with Ghelys at her back, his spear in her spine, she wasn't in any position to do anything else. The field fought her every chance it could get. If R'lyeh wasn't stumbling across the uneven terrain, then she was wrenching her legs out of the snow, breaking them free from the icy barbs that littered it, which seemed capable of freezing anything around them on contact. She glanced over her shoulder at Ghelys to see if he were struggling, too, but he might as well have been levitating he was walking so gracefully. These were her people, she realized, but this wasn't her place. The field knew she was foul, and it wanted her out.

Rime was ready for her; this much R'lyeh could tell now that they were only fifteen or so feet away from the village. Hulking Night Terrors draped in furs and animal skins started to gather outside the village—a sinister welcoming party of Oxen and Walruses that breathed fog as if it were fire. Past the demonic bulwark, R'lyeh noticed smaller, more agile Rimeans darting back and forth between the bonfires at the village's center and one of the coffin-shaped buildings. They were carrying rags and buckets, and heavy, lumpy sacks were slung over their backs. There was something else, too: the noises. It sounded as if whoever was in the building was tearing it apart from the inside, ripping up the floorboards, hammering through the walls.

R'lyeh dropped her voice to a whisper. "What's going on?" She stopped, the guard of Oxen and Walruses now toe-to-toe with her. She searched their masks for eyes, mouths—anything to convince her they weren't some grotesque parody of the creatures they resembled. But there was nothing. No eyes, no mouths. Just stolen flesh and pilfered bone, and the smell of blood on their steaming breaths.

"Another Calderan," Ghelys said, smugly. "I'll take her to him."

The Rimean brutes didn't budge. They weren't equipped with any weapons as far as R'lyeh could tell. But with arms like tree trunks, what did they really need weapons for?

"Real'yuh," Ghelys started.

She cringed underneath her mask.

"Show us your face and arm."

R'lyeh dropped the ax into the snow. She rolled up the sleeve on her right arm to show she wasn't Corrupted. Then, she tipped back her mask and revealed her clammy, wind-chafed face. Ghelys stood over her; he bent his knees and pushed his Eel skull against her forehead. It was then that she saw his eyes: two black pearls in the skull's sockets, wet and quivering.

"She's clean," Ghelys said, rearing up.

The Rimean brutes exchanged glances with one another, and then they broke apart, the Oxen going into the plains, while the Walruses headed into the village.

R'lyeh lowered the octopus over her head. "Clean?"

"Not sick." Ghelys gave her a nudge with the tip of his spear. "Go warm yourself by that fire. You have rime growing out of your skin."

R'lyeh pulled up her sleeve. He was right: on the underside of her forearm was a patch of thin, white needles protruding like hairs from out of her flesh. She freaked; with her other hand, she scraped the icy growths from out of her pores. They came out easily enough, but not before leaving behind a dull pain and a few droplets of blood.

She grabbed the ax out of the snow and hoofed it into Rime. Heading straight for the nearest bonfire, she tore off her gloves, stuffed them in her pockets, and pulled off her mask, too. Now that she knew about the growths, she could feel them all over; on her forehead, on her earlobes; along the edges of her neck; across the small of her back.

Rimeans stepped out of R'lyeh's way as she ran up to and dropped down in front of the roaring bonfire. A wagon rolled past; the chop, chop, chop of butchers' knives from some meat stall found her ears. Maybe it was the aftereffects of the gloom caps, but she couldn't handle this shit right now.

There was a pile of wood next to the fire. Quickly, she hauled a thick trunk out of it, dropped it in front of the fire, and sat on it. She unfastened and unbelted all her layers, and then let the heat get to healing her.

"Rime Rot," Ghelys said, coming up beside her. "Same family as Vein Rot, Mind Rot, and Morph Rot."

Was that sweat dripping down her brow? Or blood? She wiped it: blood. Little vortexes of pain opened across her body as the icy needles were pricked by the warmth from her flesh.

"Thought you s-said I was clean." R'lyeh leaned in closer to the fire. So cold, she had been so cold; she looked back just to make sure her ass was still there.

"The air in this part of the North is different." Ghelys pointed to the back of the village. There, the black woods, like a crude charcoal drawing, began. "In the heart of the wood, there is a lake. It is completely frozen, except for one, thin crack. At the bottom of the lake, Onibi waits, trapped in the ice. Onibi is a spirit of the dead; it takes the form of a burning headstone. The North once belonged to it, until it hid in the lake to escape the Trauma."

Ghelys nodded at the Rimeans rushing into the coffin-shaped house. "Now it stays down there forever, and the hateful breath it breathes through the crack is our wind. Onibi tries to kill us with the wind, to make our bodies frozen like its body, but we have lived here a long time. Like with many things, we Night Terrors are immune."

R'lyeh craned her neck. The coffin-shaped house had gone quiet. Now that she was in the village, she could get a better look at it. It was a two-story row house, and its appearance did a pretty good impression of the side of a ship. Wiping the fire out of her eyes, R'lyeh saw that the house was covered in symbols; they had been carved, painted, etched, and burned into the doors and walls. The symbols were simple, child-like; a stick figure with two heads, four arms, and four legs.

R'lyeh tore herself away from the sight. The symbols made her uneasy, like she had fingers inside her stomach trying to get out.

"Madness. Little bits of blue in the iris, like diamonds." Ghelys grabbed R'lyeh by the scruff of her armor and hauled her up with one hand. "Gibbering mouths. Talk about pilgrimages. Hallucinations." He spun her around to face him. "That's the sickness we seek."

That's what Hex had, R'lyeh thought. "W-what is it?"

Ghelys ignored her. "Don't have a lot of bodies up here in the North.

Everybody matters. You say you're here to see the elders? What for?"

"To… to—" R'lyeh's grip tightened on the ax, while her other hand slowly made its way for the Cruel Mother's talons.

Ghelys grabbed R'lyeh's wrist and twisted it a few centimeters away from a sprain.

"Ah!" she cried.

"I know you're a Night Terror. I've heard of you. But I don't know why you're here." The Eel's black eyes squirmed in the mask's sockets. "There is only one elder in Rime, and I'm it. Anguis, Faolan, or Nuctea would've told you that before they sent you here."

He dropped her wrist and, in a flash, drove the spear tip into her neck, just barely breaking the skin.

"S-stop," she begged.

"Those two Corrupted you were with—"

Oh, fuck. Elizabeth and Miranda. She turned toward Rime's entrance and saw that several more Rimeans were in the plains, headed toward the snowdrift they'd spied the village from.

"—you're not going to tell me they were Night Terrors, too, are you?"

R'lyeh shook her head as Ghelys twisted the spear into her esophagus.

"So, if you're not with the Cult, who are you with?"

R'lyeh didn't answer.

"Thought so." Ghelys tore the spear away and punched R'lyeh in the gut. As she was doubled-over, wheezing, he straightened her out and said, "But you're in luck. You have a fellow Calderan here who might be able to vouch for you. Come, R'lyeh of Alluvia—" he nudged her, "—before the Rime Rot ruins your perfectly good… skin."

Ghelys stripped R'lyeh of her ax and daggers and shoved her past the bonfire, deeper into Rime. The cold crept back into her bones, and paranoia gave life to the Rot probably eating away at them. As she plodded down the main thoroughfare, Ghelys' spear pushing against her back, the Rimeans there stopped to take notice of her. Bears and more Oxen; Foxes and Seals; jagged Ice Dweller skulls and pulpy Winter Wraith masks—with Rime being so spread out, it was hard to tell how many people lived here, but by R'lyeh's guess, it had to have been two or three hundred. They were all armed, mostly with spears, and they were all intensely interested in her, the Octopus, who was so far from home, she'd have to go back in time to find it again.

With so many eyes on her, and with Ghelys marching her through Rime like a prisoner, bad thoughts started to brew inside R'lyeh's brain.

Dark memories, like beads upon a necklace, began to form, began to come into focus. She tightened her gaze on the black woods beyond and considered Elizabeth and Miranda.

I hope they're okay. They are; they're okay. A sour taste like snot and gum plaque washed over the back of her mouth. *They're not stupid. They can handle themselves. But what're they going to do to—*

The snowy stretch of Rime thawed, and out of the melt, Geharra grew. The coffin-shaped buildings disappeared into a haze of cobblestone and buckling wood; the ice-slickened paths cracked and gave way to winding streets and gutted gardens. Gone were the Rimeans; gone were their horrid masks and musky furs. In their place, soldiers stood, the icon of Penance pinned to their breasts. Looking back, R'lyeh saw that Ghelys had vanished; where the one Night Terror should've been, there were now hundreds shuffling behind her, swaying to the saccharine spell of the Crossbreed's will. They were the people of Alluvia in all their bloodied, beaten, and bruised glory, and here they were once more, unearthed ghouls doomed to die again and again, day by day, in the graveyard of R'lyeh's mind.

She stopped, sweat and tears a stinging mixture in her eyes. The spear stabbed her skin, but the flashback's grip would not be broken. An invisible hand squeezed her breast; grimy fingers plunged into her pants. Sickened pleas sat in her throat, desperate to be let loose. She fumbled for weapons, but they had been taken from her. Like then, like now, everything had been taken from her.

"Move," Ghelys shouted with a shove.

But R'lyeh couldn't move. Maybe if she were still in Rime she could, but she wasn't, not anymore. Breathing deeply, she could smell the dead fish coming in from the Western District. Listening closely, she could hear the rattle of the Marketplace, all those pretty, overpriced things being bullied off their carts by the wind. Was she a fool to think she had ever left this place? There was only one way to leave Geharra, she knew that. She had watched everyone do it; watched them do it every way that they could.

R'lyeh's head went forward. Ghelys had slapped the back of it. Her vision blurred. Rime came into focus. There was a moment of relief; even the cold pricks of Rime Rot didn't bother her so badly. Then, she started to shake, and suddenly, everything was off balance. Her ankle twisted. Her arms went limp. She fell into the snow. When she thought the ground should've stopped her, she kept going, through the snow, darkening layer by darkening layer, until all that had been pure was tainted, and all that had been full was now hollow.

The pit of Geharra lay before her like a dish, the mutilated meals of its serving all along its blackened rim. At the center, naked children splashed in a pool of blood, the limbs of their elders held high above their heads.

"—are you doing to her?"

Something inside R'lyeh. That voice; she knew it. Had it been Alexander Blodworth's? A shadow stretched across the pit of Geharra; where it fell, intestines grew, like writhing roots; from the holes of those ragged organs, infants dropped, egg-like and mottled.

"R'lyeh? Can you hear me? R'lyeh?"

The voice was coming from somewhere else, somewhere outside of this place. R'lyeh's arm shot outward as someone grabbed it. Her mask fell off her head. Flashes of Rime broke across the pit, but they were fleeting. In them, she saw another Night Terror trying to help her up. His face was... strange, and his hands were soft. He kept saying her name, but he didn't expect her to hear him, did he?

R'lyeh's body left the ground, but her mind never left the pit. Someone was carrying her. She wrapped her arms around them, pressed her head to their chest. She told herself it was her dad, but then she remembered he had no arms at the end. So she told herself it was her mom, but then she realized she wouldn't be able to walk after what the soldiers had put inside her.

"Get out of the way. Move!" the voice commanded. A door was kicked open and then: "Hold on, R'lyeh. Hold on."

Wasn't that what she had been doing this whole time? Holding on? God forbid she should let go. And what if she did? What if she did? She was dead enough to be the Skeleton's daughter. Hadn't she heard he had one once?

R'lyeh's body was laid out on the ground. First, there was heat—a wave of it; scorching, purifying—and then cold—a stinging splash; jarring, rectifying. Her eyes snapped open. Before her, a fireplace, roaring, blazing, and in its flames, Blodworth's image wavered, lingered; his likeness immortalized in fire, from here to hell.

"No!" R'lyeh scooted across the ground and twisted around to get a measure of the place. It was a small room—a study, or a private library, most likely. There was a desk, a chair, and several shelves filled with books behind what appeared to be ice standing in for glass. The floor had been fashioned out of pale wood, but there were fresh scratches and deep gouges along the boards, as if a fight had broken out recently. There was only one door to the room, on the farthest wall. It was closed, and beside it, a painting hung; done in oils, covered in wood pulp, it depicted a field of yellow, dirty and distressed, with a single word scratched into the center: Want.

Mind finally clearing, R'lyeh noticed her mask on the desk. She came to her feet, grabbed it, and put it on. She stood there a moment, taking long, deep, controlled breaths. The pit was still inside her, like a rotting piece of food stuck in her bowels, but the sick sensations it served were subsiding. She breathed in—*one, two, three, four, five*—and exhaled—*one, two, three, four, five*. She breathed in—*one, two, three, four, five*—and remembered there was still some Canticle at the bottom of her pocket.

"Screw deep breathing," she said, exhaling. R'lyeh reached into her pocket, pulled out the cubes of Canticle that had been in there for Holy Child knows how long. They were tiny rocks, almost like sugar cubes, and were a vibrant emerald green. She had found a ton of them when she and Will were on their way to Bedlam. Cults used to use them to assist their members into suicide, so that they could go to heaven and give praise directly to god. R'lyeh, on the other hand, had popped so many of the rocks, the most they did for her anymore was make her fingertips tingle.

She ate the last of the Canticle. Before it could even possibly take effect, she already started to feel better. These days, it was becoming less about the poison itself, and more about the gesture, the routine. R'lyeh really didn't know what to make of that, so she didn't make—

The door to the private library opened and a Night Terror walked through. Of all the people R'lyeh had seen in Rime, this one was the worst. His mask... his mask. She covered her mouth, started backward to cower in the corner. The Night Terror's mask was a mangled patchwork of fur and stitching; a grotesque head that had chewed-up ears and one of the dead animal's eyes still in its socket.

"Get back!" R'lyeh cried.

The Night Terror had her ax in one gloved hand, the Cruel Mother's talons in the other. The mask... the mask. What the hell was it? The fur was encrusted with blood, and it smelled of shit and piss. It wasn't any animal she'd ever seen before.

"R'lyeh, please, calm down," the Night Terror spoke.

That voice; that had been the voice she'd heard earlier. The voice of the man who had swept her up and carried her out of Geharra.

"Take a deep breath," he said.

The mask sat like a tumor on the Night Terror's shoulders; something parasitic that wasn't meant to be or be there. Maybe she had spent too much time away from her own people, but standing there now, R'lyeh realized how wrong they looked, how out of place they seemed, like creatures that should've died out years ago, and yet through sheer stubbornness kept on living.

"Get away," R'lyeh belted. "I'm here from Caldera. That's all."

The Night Terror nodded and laid her weapons on the desk. "It's me," he said. "It's me. It's Deimos."

R'lyeh cocked her head. "W-what?"

"New mask. I have not made it back to Geharra for my old one. It's a bat—" he touched the side of the mask, "—and I made it out of the skulls of smaller bats, like my old one. But since I lost my mask, I have to start over. I have to earn the bone again."

"Deimos?" R'lyeh remembered Deimos and Lucan marching through the marsh outside Geharra. They had set off to meet the soldiers of Penance, who were headed toward the city to investigate what had happened there. But even if Deimos showed her his face, that wouldn't be proof enough. She didn't know what he looked like. He had to be tested.

R'lyeh cleared her throat. "Where did we meet?"

"In Geharra, in the prison cells outside the pit. It was me, Lucan, Serra and… Vrana. After the Red Worm was born, I split the group up. Lucan and I went to Penance. Serra stayed behind to destroy the Crossbreed. You and Vrana went to Caldera. R'lyeh, I don't know if you know, but something has happened to Vrana."

"I know," R'lyeh said, trying not to cry. "I was there when the Witch took her."

Deimos closed the door behind him and took a few steps closer to R'lyeh. "I am so sorry. She is still alive, though. I am certain."

"She is? How do… how do you know?"

"Lucan and I went to Penance and met the Holy Child. Vrana had been trying to contact him. They had crossed paths once. The elders had sent us there to find out more about the Red Worm, and then they told us we had to kill the Lacunans there. The Cult of the Worm. Did you see the building on your way in with the strange symbols?"

R'lyeh nodded.

"It's the Witch. She is using Vrana to contact the Lacunans. The Witch is drawing them together, using them to create chaos. It's happening in all the villages. Here in Rime, they have quarantined the Lacunans in that building… and also their… offspring. They were trying to get to Angheuawl."

"Wait… offspring?"

Deimos ignored her. "R'lyeh, how are you here? Ghelys asked me to look at you, to see if I recognized you; otherwise, he was going to kill you. The elders in Caldera have been strange lately, but they would not have sent you. What are you doing here?"

"I, uh, I'm here to… to…"

It's Deimos, she thought. *Tell him. He's the only friend I have up here, besides Elizabeth and Miranda… oh god, Elizabeth and Miranda.*

"Who are those two women you were with?" Deimos asked, as if he had read her mind.

R'lyeh crept closer to the fire, in need of its warmth to clear away the Bat's growing chill. "I don't know."

"They are bringing them into the village now."

Outside, on cue, two women shouted and screamed, until they were cut short by fists and chains.

"No, stop!" R'lyeh ran for the door, but Deimos stood in her way.

"I cannot help them if you do not tell me who they are." He held out his arms. R'lyeh backed away. "Who sent you here?"

In a flash, R'lyeh ripped the ax off the desk and swung her arm back, to cut Deimos down.

But Deimos didn't move.

"The Marrow Cabal," R'lyeh cried, the ax still cocked back. "They're my friends." She dropped her arms, teared up. "Please."

"The Marrow Cabal sent you?"

R'lyeh nodded. "Yes."

"Why?"

"To get—" she punched the side of the desk, "—to get Audra of Eldrus."

"She is here," Deimos said, surprised. "I would not lie to you. I brought her here after Lucan and I left Penance."

"We need her to fight King Edgar," R'lyeh said. "The Skeleton wants the same thing we do."

"The Skeleton?" Deimos shook his head. "Oh, R'lyeh, I have met that man once, and I have heard what he has become."

"He killed the Red Worm." Again, more screams from outside. "He killed it! And he has the Black Hour. And he can't die. He has a lot of men, and... he can't die. He can do anything."

"If he can do anything, why did he send a thirteen-year-old hundreds of miles north to bring back one of the most important people currently living?"

R'lyeh growled. "You're not listening."

"I have seen what Audra can do," Deimos said, "and she should not be in the hands of someone like the Skeleton."

"That's not up to you!"

"You are right. It is up to her." Deimos turned his head toward the door, as he heard footsteps approaching the room. "R'lyeh, do not tell anyone else why you are here." He sounded panicked, scared. "I will do all the talking. If they find out—"

The door flung open, and Ghelys stood on the other side, the front of his furs drenched in blood.

R'lyeh screamed.

Deimos put himself between her and the Eel and said, "What's happened?"

"The little bitch. The little bitch!" Ghelys drove his spear into Deimos' chest and said, "How many did she bring here?"

"I don't know."

"Two," R'lyeh said. "Two! Please, don't hurt them."

"Two?" Ghelys scoffed. "Two? Two? Who the hell is Isla Taggart?"

Deimos whispered, "What?"

"You know her?" Ghelys lowered the spear and took Deimos by the throat. "I took you in. I gave Lucan all our best medicines, and still he died on us all the same. Are you working with this little bitch?"

"Why... did you say... Isla Taggart?" Deimos rasped.

"Because she's out there right now. Sixty men on horseback surround our village. They call themselves the Winnowers' Chapter."

"What... do... they want?"

"You tell me, little bitch," Ghelys said to R'lyeh.

She shook her head, tightened her killing arm.

Ghelys pressed his mask to Deimos' and whispered, "They want her. They want Audra. And after I kill you and this little bitch, I'm going to give them her."

CHAPTER XII

Rfc Mqqsypw qfmsjb lmr zc fcpc. Mjb Umpjb kynq fytc am-
ldgpkcb rfgq dyar, rgkc ylb rgkc yeygl, zsr rfc bcqrpsargtc
nmucp md rfc Rpysky fyq kybc kylw qafmjypq mtcpjmmi rfc
bcqcpr'q caaclrpgagrgcq. Pcaclr pcnmprq qseecqr rfyr rfc
Mqqsypw gq lmr y bcqcpr gl rfc rpybgrgmlyj qclqc, dmp gr gq
lmr amknpgqcb md qylb zsr zmlc. Dmp rfgq rm zc rfc ayqc,
zgjjgmlq snml zgjjgmlq umsjb fytc rm fytc zccl bcagkyrcb gl
rfyr uyqrc. Rfgq umsjb qseecqr rfyr rfc Rpysky kyw fytc
qryprcb rfcpc, pyrfcp rfyl rfc Lykcjcqq Dmpcqr; fmuctcp, rfgq
gq sljgicjw.

Rfc Mqqsypw qfmsjb lmr zc fcpc, zcaysqc gr bmcq lmr zcjmle
fcpc. Qamsrq fytc pcnmprcb bgqrspzylacq gl rfc bcqcprq, zsr
mljw bspgle rfc Zjyai Fmsp, ufgaf qseecqrq rfc njyac ylb rfc
ctclr ypc qmkcfmu amllcarcb. Rfc Bpcyb Ajmai asppclrjw
pcqgbcq gl rfc Lykcjcqq Dmpcqr; gd rfcpc gq y amllcargml
zcruccl rfc Mqqsypw ylb rfc Zjyai Fmsp, rfyr kyw kcyl rfyr rfcpc
gq y amllcargml zcruccl rfc Lykcjcqq Dmpcqr ylb rfc Mqqsypw,
bcqngrc rfc kylw kgjcq rfyr qrylb zcruccl rfc rum njyacq.

Rfc Lykcjcqq Dmpcqr epcu msr md rfc Rpysky. Rfc Mqqsypw
ynncypcb mljw ydrcp rfc Rpysky fyb clbcb. Rfc bcqcpr gq lmr
rfc clb md rfgq amlrglclr, yq uc fytc qm jmle zcjgctcb, zsr rfc
dpmlrgcp rm ylmrfcp. Ufcl mlc bmmp ajmqcq, ylmrfcp mnclq.

Aeson lifted his eyes away from *The Blood of Before* and, much to his dismay, found that nothing had changed. In the past, books had been his escape from those things he refused to let overcome him. At the Inner Sanctum, his subterranean home, books had been his shield, and words his sword; they were weapons anyone could wield, and if wielded well, they were weapons more fearsome than most. But he wasn't at the Inner Sanctum anymore, and words wouldn't get him far; not here, in the Dismal Sticks, at house Gloom, where downstairs, in the basement, thirty flesh fiends fed and fucked in filth and squalor, while the madman Ichor urged them on, desperate to draw from his quickly growing Choir every ounce of suffering needed to see the witches satisfied. No, this was no place for books or words; this was a place for no one, nothing; a place out of time, in a season of perpetual depravity—beyond books, beyond words; susceptible only to the one thing that had birthed it: heartless, horrendous brutality.

Ichor had set Aeson and Bjørn up in a room on the third floor of the farmhouse. With the two small beds inside it and the toys beneath each of them, it was obvious to Aeson the room had once been a room shared by siblings. When he asked Ichor where the children had gone, Ichor smiled and told him they had beautiful voices.

Bjørn was sitting on one of those beds now, his height and size making him look like an absolute giant against it. Bastard sword over his lap, he sat there in rigid silence as he sharpened the blade. For the last hour, his attention had been fixed on the door to the room, as if he were waiting for the moment for something to come crawling in. They were on the third floor of the house, but even up here, the sounds of the Choir had such a clarity to them they were impossible to ignore. Ichor had the flesh fiends singing a universal song, one that was sung everywhere, endlessly.

Aeson, too, sat in silence on the second bed, but only because he knew that, if he started speaking, it wouldn't be long until Bjørn was shaking the insanity out of him. With the help of Ezra and Belia, Gloom's flesh fiend servants, Ichor had given them a grand tour of the estate. In his studies, Aeson had read about hell more times than he could count; it was a constant across most Corrupted cultures. But in no way had his studies, nor Vrana's recount of Geharra, prepared him for what waited in the basement. All five senses had been put to use. Each one had been decimated in a matter of seconds. There was being numb, and then there was being in a coma. Currently, he was in the twilight between the two—

this book, *The Blood of Before*, the only shield he had to stop from himself from slipping into a maddening sleep.

It was easier for Aeson to act smarter when he was scared; his brain was the only muscle he could flex.

"You know what that mess says?" Bjørn asked, eyes never leaving the door.

"Yeah."

Ignoring the screams coming from outside the room, Aeson grabbed a piece of parchment, quill, and ink out of his bag and started deciphering the text.

"It's a Caesar cipher. It's simple; barely even encrypts the text. The letters are swapped, A to Z; in this case, A to Y, B to X—that kind of thing."

"Why do it then?"

"This was… Mom and Dad's last entry." He stopped decrypting the text and sighed. "Think they knew if they made it too difficult, the next writer would struggle. I don't know. There were a few entries before this one from Adelyn. They were simple, too."

Bjørn stopped sharpening and huffed.

"I didn't say she was simple. I—" he paused, the tortured songs of the Choir drawing out images of the basement from his mind, "—can't do this. I know this sounds naïve, especially coming from me, but how can something be so evil?"

Bjørn pressed him: "What did the other entries say?"

"Nothing we don't know. The Blue Worm, the Red Worm, the attack on Caldera by the Witch; the rebellion in the Heartland, and our support of Geharra funding it; the death of King Edgar's family and—"

"That one there is the first one you've read by your parents?"

"Yeah."

"What's it say?"

Aeson nodded and focused all of his efforts on the cipher. He didn't process what he wrote; he just wrote, absorbing the information with machine-like indifference. If only he could have done the same for the birthing chamber downstairs.

When he finished deciphering the text, he realized that the reason the cipher had been so simple wasn't so others wouldn't be too confused, but so that he, Aeson, wouldn't be too confused. His parents had expected him to pick up in the book where they had left off. It was a childish cipher meant for a child; a withheld legacy left to gather dust in the hands of others.

Aeson looked over at his sword at the foot of the bed. Suddenly its steel didn't seem so intimidating. Bad thoughts bringing him back to Gloom's basement, he returned to the parchment and read aloud to Bjørn:

"The Ossuary should not be here. Old World maps have confirmed this fact, time and time again, but the destructive power of the Trauma has made many scholars overlook the desert's eccentricities. Recent reports suggest that the Ossuary is not a desert in the traditional sense, for it is not comprised of sand but bone. For this to be the case, billions upon billions would have to have been decimated in the waste. This would suggest that the Trauma may have started there, rather than the Nameless Forest; however, this is unlikely.

"The Ossuary should not be here, because it does not belong here. Scouts have reported disturbances in the deserts, but only during the Black Hour, which suggests the place and the event are somehow connected. The Dread Clock currently resides in the Nameless Forest; if there is a connection between the Ossuary and the Black Hour, that may mean that there is a connection between the Nameless Forest and the Ossuary, despite the many miles that stand between the Nameless Forest and the Ossuary.

"The Ossuary appeared only after the Trauma had ended. The desert is not the end of this continent, as we have so long believed, but the frontier to another.

"When one door closes, another opens."

Now, Bjørn did take his attention off the door. "When did they write that? Twelve years ago?"

"Son of a bitch," Aeson said, returning to the top of the text to read it over silently once more. "Son of a bitch."

"What?"

"Practically the last thing Anguis said to me before we left was that King Edgar thought there was something in the Ossuary. Something for the Disciples of the Deep."

"What is their Vermillion God? A Worm?" Bjørn asked.

"Probably, yeah, I think so. I don't know. But twelve years ago, they knew something was in that desert and…"

Bjørn took the bastard sword off his lap and placed it between his legs, letting its blade fall against him. "What? What's wrong?"

"You think that's why they killed themselves?"

"Listen, I don't—"

Aeson's hand, still holding the quill, started to shake so badly, it splattered ink across the bed. He dropped the quill, sat on his hand; red speckles of embarrassment dotted across cheeks. His eyes went huge, and he looked at Bjørn through the tears pouring out of them. He smiled, laughed at nothing in particular, and then pressed his face into his other palm. In the humid darkness of his flesh, he saw the tree that had killed his parents, and there was sand amongst its roots.

More screams came up from the floorboards; guttural groans of ecstasy moved like rats through the walls. Wave after wave of sin and sorrow crashed into the door. The Choir hit an orgiastic crescendo, and then the notes of discord were stripped away, one cry for help at a time, until all that was left was an agonizing aria that closed in on the room, like mourners closing in on a casket, desperate to see Death in any way that they could.

"I can't do this," Aeson cried. He stood and went to the small window. "I have to get the fuck out of here." And then, staring through the window: "Shit. We have to go. We can't stay here."

The light from the luna lake was gone, but it was no matter: there were now twenty-five farmers on the front yard of house Gloom, lanterns and torches burning brightly in their hands. Standing there, they looked scarecrows, and like scarecrows, it was clear they meant to scare Ichor and his Choir away, through whatever means possible.

"That's good," Bjørn said, leaning in over Aeson's shoulder. "Better than we could have hoped for."

Aeson twisted around, his body practically pinned by the Bear's to the wall. "No, it's not. They're going to tear this place apart. Flesh fiends in the basement, those hillbillies in the front yard... We need to get out of here before Ichor comes back."

Bjørn cleared his throat, backed off him. "You forget what we came here for?"

"No," Aeson said through his teeth. "You know I haven't."

"This isn't easy. It's not going to be clean. Ichor's insane, but if he's telling the truth and the Witch does show up, or hell, even if it's only her sister, that may be all we need to rescue Vrana. Let those yokels tear the house apart. Whatever they don't finish off of the flesh fiends, we'll take care of."

Aeson's mouth dropped open. "I... can't go back down there."

"I know you've read about flesh fiends, and I've seen what they can do." Bjørn pointed to the door, as if the creatures were behind it. "If they get out, if they start spreading, we aren't going to have to worry about some Worm coming out of the desert."

Aeson hated how right Bjørn was about all of this. He turned back to the window; outside, the farmers were still there, not having moved an inch. He fought his thoughts, but his thoughts were stronger; they had been reinforced by sight and sound, taste and smell. He started to feel the hot stench of the basement creep up on him and settle into his pores. He tried to close his eyes, but not even in darkness, especially not in darkness, could he find an escape, for there he saw it, the Choir's performance on its literal manmade stage.

He didn't know how long this had been going on here in the Dires, but the fact that the town's residents hadn't put it down immediately gave credence to Bjørn's claims. If these things were to escape, the Dires and the nearby Blasted Woodland would be the perfect environment for an outbreak of flesh fiends.

"The Witch needs to be separated from the Void, right?" Bjørn asked. He spun Aeson around to face him. "That's where she draws her power from, right?"

"Yeah. If we can do enough damage and stop her from getting back there, we might be able to make a bargain or, I don't know, break her spell over Vrana."

"What do you know about Joy?"

Aeson laughed pathetically. "The feeling, or Pain's sister?"

Bjørn didn't answer. Instead, he strolled over to Aeson's bed, picked up the sword, and came back and shoved it into his hands.

"About as much as I do about Pain. So… not much." He held the sword tightly, felt a little bit better with it in his grip. "Joy has been known to obsess about having a family, whereas Pain creates her own tortured playthings."

Donning his sword and mask, Bjørn asked, "So the flesh fiends are hers, then?"

"Could be."

"Every mother wants to protect her child in some way, no matter how foul it is. Joy's the witch we need. You can't hesitate, Aeson." He gave the bastard sword a swing. "They're spellweavers. They can kill us from a mile away."

"What if they do?" Aeson went to the bed and put on his own mask. "Then what? At least we tried?"

"Yeah? What else you want?"

"Better odds." He slipped *The Blood of Before* and the parchment into his bag.

"I don't want to hear about no Red Death weapons. We both dodged Death once. Once is enough."

We both dodged Death? Aeson stared at the Bear, and the Bear refused to make eye contact, for it was clear he'd said something he hadn't meant to. "Bjørn."

"What?"

"Why did my parents kill themselves? You know, don't you? Was it the Ossuary? Did they even kill themselves?"

"Thought you were decided on that matter."

"You have to tell me."

Bjørn drew a deep breath and held it. Aeson could hear him running his tongue over his teeth, as he often did in deliberation.

But before Bjørn could answer him, there were footsteps coming up the stairs outside the door. Aeson and Bjørn exchanged glances and then readied their weapons.

Three knocks upon the door, weak and slow. And then came a voice behind it, thin and clumsy, like the speaker's tongue couldn't figure out how to form its words right. It said, "Sirs, I… am… coming… in."

The door crept open jump scare slowly. A white hand, marbled with veins and bruises, gripped the side of it. Then, out of the shadows, Ezra, Ichor's flesh fiend servant, appeared. One eye had slipped out of its socket, a bundle of nerves the only thing keeping it in place. The corners of the flesh fiend's mouth were yellow and crusted over.

"Sirs…" Ezra went on, the inside of his mouth covered in weeping sores, "Master… Ichor… asked… me… to… retrieve… you." The flesh fiend continued to stand there, most of his body hidden behind the door, like a pervert peeking in on the unaware. "Dinner… is… ready. He… has… invited… friends." Ezra pointed one finger toward the window. "He… hopes… you… will… help… them… understand… our… work. Come."

Ezra turned around. Stabbed into the back of the flesh fiend's skull with glass and nails was a small pelvic bone. It sat on low on his head, like a fallen crown. "Come…" he said, disappearing into the shadows. "Come… before… Mother… returns."

If things had gone differently, or if Aeson had been a braver man, he might have found it funny to have a flesh fiend serving him a fat slab of raw meat for dinner. But Aeson was not a brave man, and at this moment, as Ezra and Belia wheeled cart after cart of fly-infested, maggot-filled meals to Ichor's dinner party, he was not even a man. He was a child on the edge of his seat, on the edge everything, held back only by the presence of Bjørn at his side.

I'm going to die here, he thought. *I'm going to die.*

Ichor's dinner party took place in Gloom's dilapidated dining room. To call it a shithole would be degrading to other shitholes. It was a huge room flanked by cobwebbed windows and cockroached curtains. Chairs lined the dining room; in them, blood splatters like shadows were seated. From the double doors that let out of the room, to the fireplace at its end, picture frames and portraits covered the floor; they had been slashed to pieces, and wiped with every kind of bodily fluid.

But none of that compared to the dinner table. Its surface was a cross between the bottom of a bird cage and an old, unemptied chamber pot. At first, Aeson had thought that parts of it were covered in candle wax, but upon touching it, found that it was grease, and hair. The table could easily sit thirty—enough for all the farmers outside, as well as those inside—but instead it sat eight. There was Aeson, Bjørn, and Ichor; and then there were those five who were the heads of their individual families here in the Dismal Sticks: Rustin Carr from Misery, Dalia Dark from Grief, Agnus Buckles from Woe, Jack Remy from Pang, and Big Scar Pedro from Stitch. The other twenty-two seats were occupied by the cockroaches and bones they lived in.

Their host, Ichor, hadn't bothered to change out of his nightgown. At this point, it was so dirty and wet that the fabric and the naked skin it was pasted to were indistinguishable from each other. A plate full of overcooked chicken before him, he sat between Rustin Carr, a Holy Order of Penance follower, and Jack Remy, a self-proclaimed Disciple of the Deep. Aeson figured he might have sat between the two men to avoid having them fight like children, but in actuality, Rustin and Jack had chosen those seats themselves—perhaps so one of them could hold Ichor down, while the other carved him up with the dinnerware.

On the opposite side of the able, two seats away from Aeson's right, sat Dalia Dark and Agnus Buckles—both of whom were rocking the icon of the Holy Order of Penance on their lapels. Down Bjørn's way, right next to the Bear, Big Scar Pedro was slouched, a tattoo with the Disciples of the Deep's symbol on the top of his hand.

They had been seated at the dinner table for fifteen minutes; no one, except for the cockroaches, had done much talking. Outside, the remaining twenty farmers, handfuls of which were from each family, shouted amongst themselves. To Aeson, the debate sounded like a decision between burning Gloom down, or high-tailing it for the hills.

Do what Bjørn said, Aeson told himself. *Let them talk. Let them tear each other apart. We're Night Terrors. We have the advantage. They're Corrupted, and we're better than them.*

Big Scar Pedro cleared his throat as Ezra and Belia wheeled around the dining table, leaving behind dishes and desserts like the droppings they resembled. Ezra kept bumping into the chairs, spilling his slobber on the shoulders of Dalia and Agnus, but it was Belia, the female flesh fiend servant, who was really struggling. Her left leg was shorter than her right, and her right arm had been bitten off at the elbow; and the dress Ichor had her wearing wasn't doing her any favors, either. The top half was a corset too large for her bust, and the bottom half a cage crinoline from which most of the fabric had been ripped off. Through the bulbous base, Aeson could see her skinny, scaled legs struggling to keep pace with Ezra.

"Goddamn it," Belia said, dropping her last plate—a fishbone platter—in front of Pedro. Unlike Ezra, who spoke in partial sentences, "Goddamn it" was about the best Belia could muster. For a member of the Choir meant to praise the glory of God, it was an odd choice of words.

Aeson's cheek quivered. Somewhere inside his chest, in that maelstrom of madness wreaking havoc on his system, he felt a need to laugh.

Again, Big Scar Pedro cleared his throat. He tongued the scar on his lip, which actually started farther up, at his hairline. "We appreciate what you've done for us, but I think I speak for everyone here—"

"I wish you wouldn't," Dalia Dark mumbled.

"Goddamn it," Belia said, bumbling toward the double doors.

"—when I say," Big Scar Pedro continued, "you're not an honest... man."

Big Scar Pedro eyed Bjørn, but Bjørn but didn't budge; he played dead—as dead as the bear whose head he now wore. That was part of the plan, too. The Corrupted would be looking for any kind of semblance of humanity in him and Bjørn, to connect with and to abuse. If they were going to get through, they had to live up to their people's infamy.

"I don't give a rat's ass what party you claim to represent," Agnus added. "Yeah, you did us a solid by knocking off Grandpa Gloom. The fat bastard's time was up. He just never had the sense to check the clock. But what you did to the family—"

Ichor held up his hand. "Have I not been honest with you? House Gloom was on its last legs. Grandpa Gloom was a rapist and a pederast. I killed him for you, like you asked. And I made something out of the scraps, like you asked." He laughed, shrugged, and shook his head, and then started digging into the rotting meat oozing on his plate.

Rustin covered his mouth to hold back his vomit.

Jack, one eye rolled back like he was having a seizure, said, "Those 'scraps' were children, and some of their parents were our friends."

"Listen, they're still here guys," Ichor said, "in the basement." He took a chunk of raw meat and choked it down. "I killed Grandpa Gloom, like you asked. I gave you free reign of the property and his fortune, like you asked."

"Goddamn it," Belia barked, as she walked in circles.

"I took care of the family members who weren't too keen on me killing Grandpa Gloom, like you asked."

Carefully, Dalia rested her hands on the table. She had to be in her seventies; her fingers looked like roots, twisted and gnarled. "We should have killed you years ago. First, you brought in that Disciples of the Deep nonsense—"

Both Jack and Pedro stirred, ready to take offense as if it were their favorite pastime.

"—and now this? Are you mocking us? Mocking our cordiality?"

Ichor snorted. He picked his nose; he seemed disappointed when nothing came out to eat. "You hypocrites. All of you. No one cared what happened here until Pain's pet killed that little girl."

"Flora!" Big Scar Pedro flew forward; his arms shot across the table to wring Ichor's neck, but fell short. "Her name was Flora!"

Pain's pet? Aeson's stomach sank. He turned toward Bjørn and noticed the man's fingers looped tightly around the straps in his armor.

"Flora? Fauna? Who gives a shit?" Ichor stood up, leaned in. "I gave you the closest connection with God all you shitkickers are ever going to get. Pedro, I saw your spies, heard about your plans to sabotage my house. I had to remind you about all the forces we are dealing with here."

Belia fell into the curtains, sending a shower of insects every-which-way. "Goddamn it, goddamn it, goddamn it," she moaned, as Ezra hurried over to help her out.

Ichor turned to the Holy Order of Penance's side of the table: "Dalia... Agnus... Rustin—you think God cares about you out here in the Sticks? Away from everything, no good to anyone? Stuck in your ways? Not even following the right path It's laid out?"

Rustin rubbed his temples. "The Holy Order is the oldest religion, and the true religion. God gave us the luna lake. We have survived because—"

Ichor spit on Rustin's plate. To the Disciples of the Deep's side of the table: "Big Scar Pedro... Jack... we're all new to the true God, but we have to do more than change the flag we fly. Holy Order or Disciples? It doesn't matter to Pain and Joy, and it shouldn't matter. Pain and Joy have come up from heaven to test our faith, to show us the way."

Jack Remy pulled his fork out of the maggot-ridden mutton. "We even gave you Charlotte Breckin, Grant Erickson, and Eric Grantson. I want to see them. You said they were sick, that the Sisters could heal them. I want to see them. Where are they?"

The other Children of Lacuna who live here, Aeson thought.

"With the Choir, where we all will be one day soon, I hope," Ichor said.

Pain's pet? The phrase reverberated through Aeson's skull. *Pain's pet killed the little girl?* Questions coagulated in his throat. *Was it Vrana? Did she look like a raven? Someone, say something!*

"If you want to kill me Dalia, then do it." Ichor sat back down. "You've had plenty of time to do it."

All at once, the heads of Misery, Grief, Woe, Pang, and Stitch looked at Aeson and Bjørn. And not a second later, Aeson's and Bjørn's hands were wrapped around the hilts of their sheathed swords. They had brought their weapons to dinner (and Aeson, *The Blood of Before*). In this part of the continent, no one seemed to mind much.

There was so much sweat in Aeson's mask, he was practically drowning in it. His eyes darted back and forth between Dalia, Agnus, and Rustin, and Jack and Pedro. If he had to kill someone, who would he kill first? The old women, Dalia and Agnus? Or one of the three men, who each had dark, diabetic splotches around their necks, like the rings of a tree. It would be easy. Ichor wouldn't stop him. Bjørn would only encourage him. Without thinking, he slid his sword slightly out of its sheathe. He didn't want to kill, didn't want to know if he could kill. But if they thought they had no choice but to attack...

"I told you Night Terrors would come, didn't I? I told you I had a connection with them, just like I have a connection with Eldrus."

Ichor clapped his hands together like a pompous aristocrat; Ezra and Belia went hobbling out of the room.

"Joy and Pain are powerful, I think even you can agree to that, Dalia."

Dalia Dark shook her head, most likely to spite him.

"I promised you more bodies to work the fields, and they're ready. You call them flesh fiends? Maybe so, but look at how we can control them. You can keep your way of life here in the Dismal Sticks, and you can keep worshiping God any way you choose. But the Sisters have demands, and we must meet them." Ichor smiled, going hard underneath his nightgown. To Aeson and Bjørn he said, "Right, guys?"

"Why are they here?" Big Scar Pedro asked, his voice shaking. He almost reached out to touch Bjørn's bicep.

"If it wasn't for the Night Terrors, we would have never made contact with the Sisters. They are our betters, aren't they? Uncorrupted and all that? Who better to guide us to the gates of heaven? And we needn't die! The Sisters know Death personally. Our ferries will be paid for in full."

Outside the dining room, Ezra and Belia were making a huge ruckus.

"Ah!" Ichor's eyes lit up. "Now, if no one is going to kill me, then let's get to the main course."

The dining room's double doors flung back. Ezra and Belia stood there on the threshold, a huge cart between the two of them. Ichor waved them in, and in they came, a ghoulish grin upon their faces. On the cart, the naked, bloated corpse of a five-hundred-pound man lay; his flesh was bruised, stiff; his stomach, a massive mound of swollen, pimpled flesh that gave him the appearance of being pregnant with a smaller, lighter, perhaps two-hundred-and-fifty-pound man. In the corpse's mouth, an apple, cleaned to the point that it glinted in the light, had been wedged. This was Grandpa Gloom, Aeson knew, and like a slaughtered pig, he was here for them to consume.

With the double doors still open, the Choir's songs were coming into the dining room at full volume. In combination with the grisly spectacle laid out before Ichor's guests, Aeson, beginning to laugh again, started to realize what the deranged Child of Lacuna was attempting to accomplish here.

It's a test—the food, the setting, all of it. He looked at Dalia Dark, Agnus Buckles, and Rustin Carr—the Holy Order of Penance followers, and then Big Scar Pedro and Jack Remy—the Disciples of the Deep adherents. These were hard people—walking calluses, really—who had lived in the Dismal Sticks all their lives, and would continue to live in the Dismal Sticks for as much time as their lives had left. History had shown them to be no strangers to killing their own if deemed necessary. And Ichor wasn't even one of their own.

It was a test, for both Ichor and for the heads of the families gathered here. A competition to see who could stomach the others the longest.

Can they beat the Witches? Aeson glanced around the room. Everyone here was armed. Dalia had a blade in her belt, Agnus an Old World flintlock pistol across her lap; Rustin's fingernails were so long they may have been knives, and Jack had a dagger in his boot. Big Scar Pedro kept eyeing Bjørn's bastard sword as if he had a mind to steal it, so that was always a possibility.

Pain's pet.

Ichor clapped his hands again.

Belia, mumbling, "Goddamn it, goddamn it," hurried over to him and handed him two gigantic butcher's knives.

Pain's pet. Aeson white-knuckled the hilt of his sword. *Let them kill each other, like Bjørn said. She'll come. Maybe they'll kill her or, at least, weaken her.* He swallowed hard; his throat constricted, and breathing became impossible for a moment. *Nothing is going to stop them from killing us.* He looked at Dalia, at Big Scar Pedro. *I'm going to have to fight.*

"We're all here because of Grandpa Gloom," Ichor said, handing one butcher knife to Rustin, the other to Jack. "I fled to the Sticks a stranger, and I brought you heaven and its two gatekeepers. All I'm saying is that I held up my end of the deal. It's time for you all to hold up yours. Ezra! Belia!"

Ezra and Belia slammed the cart into the end of the table. They then jumped onto the table, grabbed Grandpa Gloom's fat, mushy ankles, and started hauling him down it. His arms knocked the dinnerware out of the way; forks and knives got caught between his legs and the crack of his ass. Like ants lifting something far beyond their weight, Ezra and Belia backed down the dining table, past the guests, until Grandpa Gloom's bloated, five-hundred-pound corpse was splayed out in the middle of everything.

Ezra dropped off the table, his eyeball bouncing against his face.

"Goddamn it," Belia said, her stunted arm and leg giving her some trouble as she struggled down to the ground. "Goddamn it."

Bjørn came to his feet, because Grandpa Gloom's gigantic belly was too big to see over.

Aeson followed the Bear's example. His legs almost gave out as he stood up, they were shaking so badly.

"Good idea, my brothers," Ichor said. He ran his hands through his blue hair, slicking it back behind his ears. "Up, up, everyone."

Begrudgingly, Dalia and Agnus rose. Big Scar Pedro did the same, and then sidestepped away from Bjørn, now apparently not so interested in the Night Terror.

Rustin and Jack were the last to stand, the butcher knives in their hands sharp temptations they were struggling to not give in to.

"Our love for God is what brings us here tonight, isn't it?" Ichor said. His eyes started to glow bright blue. "The Choir is thirty strong, but that isn't enough for the Sisters. We need more for our pilgrimage to Angheu-awl, to open the way into the Void and heaven. The journey... it's going to be a long one. People will try to stop us, even our own Disciples. The Dismal Sticks—"

Grandpa Gloom's corpse shuddered. The flesh on his bulbous stomach ripped, as if several weeks' worth of gases were trying to get out.

"—could be a new Mecca. People will say that the Choir started here, and they will send their children to have them trained. And you greedy leeches can bleed their gullible parents for all they're worth. I don't care!" Ichor smiled, rotted meat wedged between his yellow teeth. "I just need ten children from each of your houses. The Choir downstairs is a little overzealous and they keep breaking the babies before they can get old enough... Ten. I just need ten. When we leave, House Gloom is yours. The Sisters will provide and—"

A rumble came from within Grandpa Gloom's distended gut. A squirt of blood suddenly shot out of his belly button.

Ichor held out his arms, his vibrant, blue eyes darting back and forth between his guests. "So, what do you say?"

"Where's Pain and Joy?" Rustin asked, setting the butcher knife down on the table.

Ichor bit his lip. Pointing to his eyes, he said, "We're watching everything."

With a shout, Jack dropped his butcher knife and punched the side of Ichor's head. Without missing a beat, Rustin grabbed a handful of Ichor's blue hair and drove his face into the table, breaking his nose.

"Anointed One!" Ichor cried, rearing back, holding his nose as blood seeped out from in between his fingers.

Rustin wrapped his arm around Ichor's neck, put his knee in his back.

"You'll get nothing from us, no more."

"Call them down. Call Pain and Joy. We got something for them, too," Jack said. He grabbed Ichor's jaw and pried open his mouth. "Don't worry about waiting for heaven. We'll take you there now."

Bjørn tore his bastard sword out of its scabbard.

Before Aeson could draw his, Agnus had her flintlock pistol trained on him.

"Don't do it, Night Terror," she said.

Jack reached into his pocket and pulled out a red, bristly, walnut-sized mass. He shoved the seed to Ichor's lips, but the Lacunan was laughing too maniacally for him to get it past his teeth.

"Sing," he said, biting Jack's fingers. "Sing!"

Rustin grabbed Ichor's balls through the nightgown. "I'll have you singing, you goddamn freak."

Ichor bent over, wailed. Jack shoved his entire fist into Ichor's mouth and deposited the seed personally into his throat. While Ichor tried to cough out the growth, Rustin twisted his scrotum, as if he were trying to tie it into a knot.

"Witches and Night Terrors, we've dealt with worse," Dalia said, drawing her knife. "And we've recruited worse. Should've just killed Ichor, Skull Boy and Bear Man. We might've let you go."

Does she know how to use that? Aeson wondered, his attention fixed on the flintlock pistol. *Hit her. Hit her. She'll never load it in—*

Ichor retched; his hands pawed at Rustin's and Jack's while they bent him over the table and held him there. He then stopped and stretched his arms forward, taking the meaty wrist of Grandpa Gloom and shaking it.

"Sing!" he commanded the corpse, while vermillion veins began to burst out of his mouth. "Sing!"

Grandpa Gloom's gigantic belly jerked to the left.

Silence fell over the dining room.

Oh no. Aeson took a step away from the table.

Grandpa Gloom's gigantic belly then jerked to the right.

Bjørn put his arm out in front of Aeson and corralled him even farther back.

Outside, something slammed into the ground, as if it had been dropped from a great height. Someone shrieked, and then a splash of flames washed over the outside of one of the dining room windows.

"Son of a bitch!" Pedro turned to the window. "I told them to—"

Grandpa Gloom's gut stretched upward and outward; hard objects from within the corpse's now bleeding stomach were pushing against it.

"Sing," Ichor whimpered, his face encased in vermillion veins. Rustin and Jack let the Lacunan go, and he hit the ground.

With a sickening snap, Grandpa Gloom's pregnant belly exploded, sending bloody chunks all across the gathered guests. Flaps of dead skin, rank muscle, and putrefying organs splattered the walls and lathered the table. The smell of shit and the thick, permeating musk of intestinal lining filled the room, and even sent the cockroaches running. Gurgling sounds, like an infant cooing, rose out of the corpse's stomach cavity.

Aeson leaned forward and saw that the worst had yet to come.

Inside Grandpa Gloom's blown-out stomach, five small flesh fiends, probably no older than seven or eight, sat, their naked, emaciated frames covered in a sludge of gore. Their beaming, bloodshot eyes roamed around in their skulls, going this way and that, while their tongues tasted the bloody body pudding on their lips.

Bjørn shouted, "Aeson, watch out!"

Agnus Buckles had taken out a pouch and was frantically pouring gun powder down the barrel.

Head pulsating, Aeson swung his sword and hit Agnus with the flat end of the blade. It smacked against her face, leaving two bloody inden-tations across her cheeks where the edge of the sword had dug in. She screamed, dropped the pistol, and fell back onto Dalia Dark.

Aeson smiled—the cold touch of relief washing over him—and then he flew backward as one of the boy flesh fiends leapt out of Grandpa Gloom and onto him.

"Get it off me!" he cried, the pale imp digging its tiny fingers into his neck.

He fell against the window that was burning on the outside, sending a crack across the glass. The flesh fiend swiped its sharp nails across his mask, knocking the skull sideways. Aeson grabbed the boy's thin arm, tried to break its grip on him. But the creature was ravenous, and it was stronger because of it.

"Kill it!" Bjørn shouted at him. Two flesh fiends on his chest and shoulders drove him out of sight.

"Get off me," Aeson said, shoving his forearm against the flesh fiend's chomping mouth. It was wet, too slick to hold; and its movements were erratic, as if it were being constantly electrified. But in truth, it was the face that kept stopping Aeson. The fiend had the face of a little boy.

Blue eyes, a small nose and mouth. Its body was scarred, tumorous, and twisted, but its face was untouched. Innocent. Maybe even mistakable for something other than monstrous.

The flesh fiend sank its teeth into Aeson's arm and tore away a hunk of flesh. Tears burst from Aeson's eyes. He elbowed the fiend, sending several teeth further into its purple gums. The flesh fiend spat out the blood like a snake would venom and then dragged its ass up Aeson's chest. It took hold of his mask and drove its fingers through its sockets.

Aeson grabbed the fiend's wrists and clamped his eyes shut. He could feel the creature's sharp nails grazing against his lids, getting caught in the corners of his eyes. The fiend ground itself harder against his chest, the texture of his armor amplifying the boy's excitement. It then stood up, wrists still held by Aeson, and started jumping up and down.

Aeson's eyes shot open as the flesh fiend knocked the wind out of his lungs. Holding the creature there, while it jumped gleefully on top of him—it felt like they were playing a game. And to the little boy, maybe they were. This was all the creature knew, all it had ever been promised. Aeson looked at the flesh fiend; at its wrung-out body covered in bite marks and scratches; its long hands and even longer fingers, bits of its siblings underneath its nails. He looked at its face, wrinkled and mischievous, and searched its jet-black pupils for any sign that it could stop, that it could be reasoned with. That it didn't have to die. That he didn't have to be the one to kill it.

Then Aeson heard something outside: wings.

He let go of the flesh fiend's wrists. The little boy lunged forward, thumbs going immediately for Aeson's eye sockets. And when it was close enough to grab, Aeson took the boy by the back of his head, flipped him over, and bashed his face into the ground, into the portraits and paintings that lined it; over and over again, he slammed the little boy's quickly softening skull into the artwork—not out of malice or sadism, but because the faster he killed him, the less he would feel.

When the boy's head was too slick to grip, Aeson let go, grabbed his sword, and stumbled to his feet. Dalia Dark rushed past him, drenched in blood, for the double doors. Across the table, Agnus Buckles was being stripped of her clothes by two of the little girl flesh fiends, who kept pausing to take bites out of her breasts and, in between chomps, would mumble about milk.

Where was Bjørn? Aeson looked at his bloody hands and felt sick at how Corrupted they looked. He reached for the curtains to wipe them off and saw that the entire outside of the house was engulfed in flames.

"Skull Boy!"

Bjørn rose off the ground on the opposite side of the dinner table. His breastplate had been torn off, and there were deep, seething gouges in his chest. The Bear's sword was bloodied up to the hilt.

Aeson grabbed *The Blood of Before* from underneath his chair and stuck it behind his breastplate. A few feet away, two flesh fiend children were doing their best to rape Big Scar Pedro.

Aeson climbed onto the dinner table and stepped over Grandpa Gloom's ravaged corpse. He was missing an arm; in the heat of the moment, someone had probably ripped it off to use as a club.

He dropped off the table, joined Bjørn on the other side. There, Jack Remy lay; his dead body had merged with the nest of vermillion veins still growing out of Ichor's corpse. Rustin Carr was gone, but given the tortured screams coming from deeper in the house, Aeson figured he wasn't far off.

"Got the book?" Bjørn asked, even though he could clearly see it.

"I heard her." Aeson paused, controlled his breathing. "I heard Vrana outside."

Bjørn nodded, looked at Aeson's bloodstained hands, and ran. They hurried through the dining room as smoke and flames wound their way in. Bjørn bashed through the double doors. He stumbled, Dalia Dark's dead body in the hall tripping him up.

"Goddamn it," Belia belted farther down the hall, where the front doors sat open. She was the one holding Grandpa Gloom's torn-off arm. "Goddamn it," she said, pointing at them. She ran out of the house.

"Vrana?" Bjørn straightened up as he heard the sounds of the bloody bacchanal coming out of the basement. "She's here?"

Tongues of flame licked around the edges of the front door. The fire was finally starting to work its way in. Outside, people were screaming, crying; they could hear people constantly running back and forth, and again, the sounds of something being dropped from high above.

Aeson nodded. "Yeah, I think so."

"Okay." Bjørn took his bastard sword into hands and raised it in front of him. "This is it."

Aeson grabbed the Bear by his straps. "What about the witches?"

"I'll… take care of them. You grab Vrana." Bjørn touched his chest where the flesh fiend had dug into his skin. "Can you kill?"

Smoke rolled between Aeson's legs; a carpet of cockroaches passed beneath it. "Yeah."

"The world isn't always like this. I'm sorry." Bjørn grabbed his shoulder, gave it a squeeze. "Okay. Let's go."

As soon as they had made it out of house Gloom, it took everything Aeson had not to turn back.

There were flesh fiends everywhere—thirty, maybe more—tearing through the Dismal Sticks, chasing down farmers and concerned citizens who'd been drawn by the noise from their homes. Flailing bodies were being thrown to the ground by groups of three and four flesh fiends, to be torn apart and fucked to pieces. Male flesh fiends set upon the women of the Sticks, impatiently spilling their seed anywhere they could, while female flesh fiends held the men of the Sticks down and let their sisters take turns on them. There were a few Corrupted children, too; those that weren't slaughtered immediately were being hauled off to the lake, where the waters had rotted over and sinewy tendrils of light waved like cancerous reeds.

The fire was burning dangerously close to Aeson, but he couldn't move. He had wandered into a mire of depravity, and only by depravity could he escape. Standing there on the porch, he watched torchlights flare to the east and the west, and across the lake, too. He waited for the screaming to start from those farmhouses, but the sloppy noise of rape here was drowning everything else out.

"Ah!"

Aeson's eyes looked up. From the sky, a man fell, his arms and legs reaching for purchase on the very fabric of night. He crashed into the ground, landed on his neck, and broke his head off from the spine. It was then that Aeson realized that the ground was littered with similar bodies. Bodies of broken men who, too, had been dropped to their deaths.

He looked up again and gasped. There she was. There she was; a feathery silhouette against the pockmarked moon. Vrana, his love, his best friend, soaring through the night, the blood of the men she had murdered falling like rain from her feathers.

"Get her," Bjørn said, shoving Aeson off the porch.

The Bear took off towards the lake, cutting down the flesh fiends that stood in his way.

Aeson followed after Vrana, his shadow in hers—where it belonged, and where he wanted it to be. Sword out, he navigated the tortured throngs of people and flesh fiends, doing his best not to draw attention to himself.

House Gloom groaned as the fire worked its way through the wood-work. The night wind rushed across the Dismal Sticks and blasted the front yard with the blaze's scorching heat. In places, the grass, despite the evening chill, caught fire. At the back of the house, the rotting or-chard erupted, the fruits of flame blooming all across the once-dead boughs. Even the air was on fire, leaving scorch marks with the gentlest of breezes. It was as if hell itself were passing through this plane, to smote from the Earth this desperate imitation.

"Vrana!" Aeson cried, pleadingly.

He got a response, but not from the shape of his love above. A flesh fiend a few feet away looked up. It was holding a still-dripping severed head, and it had been trying to shove the head down over its own, like a mask.

"Fuck, fuck, fuck." Aeson raised his sword, locked his arms to stop them from shaking. In his peripheral, another flesh fiend had taken no-tice of him. This one had a long strip of coarse black hair running from its neck down to its crotch, and in its hands, two broken ribs, like daggers.

"Vrana!" he screamed, spit flying out of his mouth.

The flesh fiend dropped the severed head, giggled, and rushed him. It got down on its hands and feet and bounded across the front yard like a dog. Aeson backpedaled, trying to keep the other flesh fiend who was watching him in sight.

By the lake, Bjørn had just suplexed a flesh fiend onto a boulder, breaking its back like a buckling ship.

I can do this, Aeson thought, remembering the little boy inside. He held the sword out and ran forward to meet the fiend in its death charge.

Blade inches from the dog-like fiend's chest, Aeson was suddenly thrown off his feet and pounced to the ground. From behind, a third flesh fiend had sprung. Aeson slid across the smoldering grass, the edges of his armor digging up dirt and fat earthworms. In less than a second, three full-sized flesh fiends were on top of him.

"Stop, stop," he begged, bucking his legs. One flesh fiend grabbed his knees and held them down, while another stretched Aeson's arms over his head and locked them into place. The third flesh fiend, which was female, crouched over his pelvis and started tearing through his pants.

Vrana, he thought, jerking his body to throw off the female flesh fiend. He could hear her wings overhead, and another body hitting the ground, exploding on impact. Did she know he was here? At this point, did she even care?

The female flesh fiend pulled down his pants. She shoved her blood-caked hand into her mouth. She shook, heaved, and vomited gore onto his cock. Wheezing out a laugh, she massaged the curdled lubricant into his flesh until he was hard.

A wave of repulsion rocked Aeson. His eyes rolled back into his head. As the fiend gripped him and worked herself onto him, he started to retch, started to cry. He gave one last shake, but with fiends as fetters, the fetters were too hard to break. He was helpless, hopeless. He had left home expecting pain, and he had gotten something worse, instead. His body wasn't his anymore. He didn't want it. It belonged now to the fiend who rode him, and those that would come later to wear his withered remains.

The female flesh fiend started to moan, to quiver. She grabbed Aeson's mask to steady herself. He said nothing, did nothing. He lay there, playing dead, preparing himself for the real thing. Something stirred inside him—not pleasure, but practicality. The sooner this ended, the sooner he could die. The sooner he would see his parents, and be able to finally ask them "Why?"

The flesh fiend arched back, braced itself for climax. Her thighs tightened. The fetid swamp of pubic hair and viscous desire puddled in the pockets of Aeson's bones. The flesh fiend clenched her muscles, twisted her nipple until it tore off, and—

The air snapped like tendons, and a black blur smashed into the fiend, ripping her off Aeson. The two flesh fiends holding him let go. He sat up, dazed.

A few feet away, Vrana stood, the female flesh fiend at her feet. She was everything the elders had warned him of, and more. Her body was narrow, severe; a malnourished monument of jagged feathers and rough, scaled skin. Her hands and feet had become claws, and her nails talons, like pieces of sharpened obsidian. She still had arms, but they were now attached to the massive, ragged wings that had grown out of her back.

He looked at Vrana's face, or what little was left of it. The raven skull had been stripped of feathers and fused directly into Vrana's own. The mask's beak was as big as it had ever been, but now it moved, because the Witch had grafted it to Vrana's mouth, and bones and tendons, so that she wouldn't be a raven in appearance only.

The only thing that kept Aeson from turning away from her in disgust and disbelief were her eyes. They were the only things he recognized, the only things he could point to and say were hers. They sat in the sockets of the raven skull, far back and surrounded by swollen skin. They were dark, distant; lidless eyes that never knew sleep and lost the sheen of sympathy. And yet when Aeson looked into her eyes, he saw a glimmer in their darkness; a pinprick of light, a spark of recognition; the smallest gem of hope in an otherwise excavated soul.

It was her, and he was hers, and now it was time to take her home. "I'm here," he said, quivering. "Vrana, I'm here."

Blue light burst out of Vrana's eyes. She sank her talons into the female flesh fiend and ripped her in two, flinging her torso toward Gloom, and her legs toward the orchard.

She then lifted off and flew over Aeson. He pulled up his pants, came to his feet, and faced the lake. At the center of it, on top of the rot, surrounded by strands of sinewy light, Pain stood, one arm outstretched, as if she meant for Vrana to land on it.

Aeson grabbed his sword off the ground and ran towards the lake. As he did so, ten more men on horseback riding out of Pang converged on the lake, torches in their hands, bows and quivers on their back.

"There she is!" the man at the front of the procession shouted. "Burn her to the ground!"

They fired tens of arrows into Pain, but still, she didn't budge. In twos and threes, they hurled their torches at her. She went up in flames, her silvery, spidery hair falling off her head in crackling clumps.

Aeson pushed himself harder. She had to be weakened, and she wouldn't see him coming. If anyone was going to kill her, it had to be him.

But as he made for the lakefront, Pain shrugged, and the flames slipped off her body like a cloak. She was charred, blackened to the bone, but it didn't seem to matter. She didn't seem to care. The men fired more arrows at her until she was riddled with shafts, but even then, she kept on breathing.

Pain rolled her eyes, raised one finger at the men on horseback, and sent Vrana after them. She swooped down from the sky and tore through their ranks.

"No, stop!" Aeson shouted, waving his hand at Vrana to get her attention.

But Vrana couldn't stop, wouldn't stop. In a flurry, she ripped the men and their horses to pieces.

"Leave a few," Pain told Vrana, laughing. "They're no good to us dead; at least, not yet."

Vrana grabbed a man and his horse off the ground and flung them into the wild blaze that was house Gloom. While she made her way back to the Witch, a wounded man crawled out of the carnage she had just created.

"Go on," Pain said to the man. Her scorched flesh was dropping off her in sheets, revealing new flesh underneath. "I'll give you one chance."

The man grabbed a machete off the ground and rushed the Witch. Instead of stepping into the rotten water, his feet moved along top of it; the crust of decay somehow able to support his weight.

Aeson stopped, and when he did, he noticed Bjørn, about ten feet across the yard, had done the same.

Wait and see, he thought, watching the man with the machete make his way to the Witch.

The Witch dropped her arms, her burnt flesh almost completely replaced now, and smiled. "Go on," she goaded, the man inches away from her. "Go on, and get it out of your system."

Vrana landed behind Pain, her tattered wings fully outstretched.

Aeson's grip tightened on his sword; under his breath, he muttered every prayer he could muster from every religion he had ever known.

The man lifted the machete, paused; the decay was climbing up his legs now, eating through his clothes, spreading to his flesh.

"This is for everyone!" he cried.

Pain rolled her eyes. "That's nice."

And then he swung the machete through Pain's neck.

And the blade passed right through, severing her head from her smoking body.

But there was no blood, and there was no wound. In a matter of seconds, Pain's head reattached itself to her neck, and she continued to stand there with a stupid smile on her haggard face.

"Shame," Pain said. "At least when you get to hell, you can tell everyone you tried."

Pain snapped her fingers. Vrana jumped over the Witch and bore her beak down through the man's gaping mouth, killing him instantly.

Oh no, Aeson thought, the sword in his hand no better than a branch. *Oh shit. Oh no. We're too late.*

He turned to Bjørn.

Bjørn was already sprinting towards him, waving his hand, screaming at him to run.

"Go!" Bjørn crashed into Aeson, spinning him like a top. "The other one is here, too." He grabbed Aeson. "There's nothing we can do."

Aeson shook off the Bear and looked back.

Vrana had taken to the sky again and was headed for Misery, while a pack of flesh fiends followed her from below, like rats let loose from a ship.

Out of Gloom, the Witch's sister, Joy, emerged with an armful of children, both dead and alive. Even more children, Corrupted and flesh fiend, clung to her white satin dress, which had escaped the inferno unscathed. Joy shivered with joy and glided towards the luna lake; she was so happy she could barely contain herself.

And then there was Pain, who was moving her hands over the surface of the lake, opening a portal to the Void. She kept touching her neck where the machete had passed through; she had healed it, but maybe not entirely.

"Hurry, Sister!" Pain howled. "Where's Ichor?"

Joy stopped, picked up a few babies she had accidentally dropped. "Incapacitated."

Pain growled. "Fetch Ezra and Belia. They'll do until the next town over."

"Seriously?" Joy huffed and dropped all of the children she was carrying. They hit the ground hard, and those that weren't dead started to cry.

Bjørn tugged on Aeson's shoulder. "Come on," he said.

They made it to the woods a few minutes later, and in the woods, they stayed, for it was dark and dense, and there was no flesh here, aside from their own, for the fiends to feast on.

"Are you okay?" Bjørn panted. He dropped his bastard sword. He dropped to the ground.

"No." Aeson tore off his mask. He found the nearest tree and banged his head against it. "No, I'm not."

"That was her," Bjørn said. He slipped off his mask, wiped the tears and snot off his face. "What did they do to her?"

Aeson balled his hands. He could still feel the flesh fiend gyrating on top of him, mining misery from his loins.

"There were... too many." Bjørn got choked up. "Did she talk to you?"

Aeson shook his head.

"Did she… recognize you?"

"Yeah, I… I think so."

Bjørn opened his mouth to speak, but stopped. He dug at the ground, rolled the dirt around in his hands.

"What if this wasn't a coincidence?"

Bjørn looked up at him. "What do you mean?"

"We can't stop them. I can't. You can't. No one has for thousands of years. They weren't killing her the right way. No one was." Aeson pulled away from the tree and knelt in front of Bjørn. "I know you don't want to do it, but we have to." He rolled his eyes, and tears swept across his face. The words clung to his throat, reluctant to go any farther, but go farther they did, and so he said: "We have to talk to Death."

CHAPTER XIII

R'lyeh ran her fingers over her fetters and wondered if she could get used to this. Like her poisons, if she were imprisoned long enough, could she become immune to the numbing horror of being at the mercy of something far worse than herself? She rubbed her shackles together and glanced at Deimos. He didn't look scared. He'd been through about as much as she had—probably more.

If she had nothing to give, then there wouldn't be anything to take. R'lyeh smiled at the thought, and wept at another. She had a birthday coming up.

R'lyeh stood outside, near the bonfire and the Cult house she had passed earlier. Elizabeth and Miranda were beside her and Deimos, shivering themselves deeper and deeper into the snow. Every few seconds, they would each rub their arms, legs, chests, and faces to stop the Rime Rot from breaking out across their skin. Ghelys had stripped them of their coats and weapons. If a spear didn't kill them, then the weather would.

At least twenty armed Rimeans were standing behind R'lyeh, Deimos, Elizabeth, and Miranda. The rest of the village was in attendance, too; they were farther back, on every stoop and porch, in every shop and stall. There was little fog on the air, because most everyone was holding their breaths, waiting for a response or reaction from the invaders at their gates.

Isla Taggart. Could anyone rock a name like that and not be an asshole? R'lyeh had never heard of or seen the woman before, but even so, it was easy enough to spot her. Isla Taggart was about ten feet away. She stood beside her horse, separate from the line of sixty riders she had brought to Rime. From her neck and down to her feet, Isla was covered in pieces of red leather that had been tailored to give the appearance of a flowing dress. She was short, a few months of bad meals away from being full-on stubby. The right side of her head was completely shaved, while the left side was a mess of blonde tendrils that twisted down to her waist. Small tattoos—eyes and moons—circled her neck, like a choker. She had weapons, too; in one hand, an obsidian sword, and in the other, the holy text, *The Disciples of the Deep*.

R'lyeh hated to admit it, but Isla Taggart did look kind of cool.

"Those tattoos are fake," Elizabeth said, lip curled.

"And that sword is bullshit," Miranda added. "First thing she hits, it'll shatter." She rattled her chains and said to Deimos, "Your people have her outnumbered. What the hell is this?"

Deimos turned; flakes of dried skin and tufts of hair drifted off his garish mask. "There used to be three elders in Rime."

At that moment, Ghelys shoved past R'lyeh, knocking her to the ground. The octopus slid off her head and flopped across the snow.

"No, no." R'lyeh grabbed it and, clumsily, threw it back on. Without the mask, she was just another member of the Marrow Cabal. Without the mask, she was just another prisoner, and Rime was just another pit.

"Where is Audra of Eldrus?" Isla boomed.

Deimos bent down and offered R'lyeh his bound hand. She smiled a smile he couldn't see and took it.

"Stand closer to the fire," he whispered.

R'lyeh did, but didn't need to. A half an hour at the village and already her body was immune to the Rime Rot. If only the same could have been said about the spears at her back.

Ghelys stopped a few feet away from Isla. He slammed the end of his spear down hard into the ground and puffed his chest out, as if he were challenging the whole of the sixty Winnowers gathered here.

From the west, snow blew in. It whipped across Rime in painterly swirls that were painful to the touch. Cold was still cold to R'lyeh, and this cold front was freezing. R'lyeh shuffled closer to Elizabeth and Miranda; they took her in and pressed their bodies against hers. They didn't have much warmth to offer, but in some ways, it was better than the bonfire's.

"Are you Night Terrors hard of hearing with t-those masks on?" Isla was shivering so badly R'lyeh thought she might shatter. "Bring h-her out."

"Should I know this woman?" Miranda asked.

"No," Deimos said. "She's no one."

Elizabeth threw her arms over R'lyeh and pulled her in closer. "She seems like someone, yeah?"

Deimos sighed. "She's trying."

Isla slipped the obsidian sword into its sheath. Taking the *Disciples of the Deep* in both hands, she started forward. "You are h-harboring an enemy of God. You are—" the thickening snowfall was taking its toll on her, "—are over-privileged, cultural-appropriating, f-fascist f-freaks. But God will forgive that f-for now. And so will the ghost of Lux."

"That's good," Ghelys said. "You had me worried."

"Where is—"

"You're from Penance. Aren't you used to the cold?" Ghelys held out his hand and caught snowflakes. "Or is this your first time out of Pyra?"

"I have a d-direct line with King Edgar. I am his r-representative on the Western f-f-front." Isla sniffed her nose and spit at Ghelys' feet. "Give me his sister, or I will burn your village to the f-fucking ground."

"He's stalling, yeah?" Elizabeth asked.

"No, he is going to give you three to her," Deimos said, while looking at the Cult house. "This storm isn't natural."

She's an idiot, R'lyeh realized, watching Isla open *The Disciples of the Deep* and furiously flip through its pages. *I have to kill her.* She flexed her hands; Vrana's ax, the faerie silk cloak, and the Cruel Mother's talons had been taken from her. It made her stomach turn thinking she might never get them back.

"'And God will rise from Its slumber and destroy those who do not bear Its red mark, for they are imposters. However, even beasts can be baptized, and those who cast their minds and hearts into the heaven below will be spared. Those who seek salvation need only ask, but those who seek it should ask soon; there is nothing pride can purchase on the day of reckoning but oblivion.'" Isla shut the holy text and smiled cruelly.

"We'll pass," Ghelys said, unimpressed. "The two women and the Octopus behind me. You know them?"

Isla's smile shrank into a frown. She stowed the holy text in a bag on her horse and drew the obsidian sword. Holding it like it was too heavy, she marched past Ghelys.

Collectively, Rime went tense. All around R'lyeh, she could hear grips tightening on handles, and arrows being nocked into bows. There were whispers, too; words of doubt that were as chilled as the wind itself. Ghelys wasn't following tradition, this much R'lyeh could tell; and if it came to blows, she wasn't sure who would fall first—him, or Isla.

Isla stepped up to R'lyeh, Elizabeth, Miranda, and Deimos and ran her tongue over her teeth. "Yeah, they're mine. If they had done their job, we wouldn't b-be standing out here, f-freezing to death. G-give them back or k-kill them—I don't c-care."

Isla lingered on Deimos. Gusts of snow swept across her face, wiping out the little color still left on her cheeks. "You s-should f-feel fortunate. You're a man, and right where you ought to be. Chained up, f-freezing your balls off, and indebted to me." She jabbed the tip of her obsidian sword into his side. "I'll t-take this o-one along with Audra."

Out of the coffin-shaped Cult house, there was a scream. Girlish and grating, it stabbed like icicles into R'lyeh's ears. All eyes had been on Isla, and now they were on that house.

The icon of the Cult of the Worm—that two-headed, eight-limbed stick figure—started to glow on the front door. Then the front door began to shake, as if a great pressure had built up behind it. The hinges whined, the wood buckled; light, black not blue, stretched out from underneath the door, like one long shadow cast from some monolithic source. Deimos had mentioned something about crazed Lacunans, their offspring, and the Witch. Was this it?

R'lyeh pressed herself harder into Miranda. She'd already had one major freak out, but she wasn't far off from another.

"Come on out, Audra," Isla said, taking her sword from Deimos' side. "It's time to go home."

Overhead, clouds had formed over Rime, and over Rime only. The ashen nimbuses churned out thunder and snow in equal doses. Occasionally, the clouds would flicker and pull apart, as if the wintry bindings that had brought them together were failing. Deimos was right: this storm wasn't natural. Someone had weaved it here.

And Isla knew it.

Pale as a corpse, and as rigid as one, too, she went up to Ghelys and barked into his eel mask, "Nice try," and then kept going, back to her horse. She mounted it, shouted, "Joseph, get the prisoners."

A man in black and fifteen soldiers broke away from the line of Winnowers and galloped forward. The man in black, Joseph, was ugly as sin; even in his armor, R'lyeh could tell he was all bone. His hair looked like it hadn't been washed since birth, and his face was so craggy a meteor must've hit it. If this was Isla's boyfriend, then they were perfect for each other. He looked like the kind of person who would do anything for anyone for an ounce of attention.

"Joseph Cleon?" Ghelys laughed as Joseph and his fifteen soldiers met up with Isla. "You escaped Pyra with your life and the Hydra's Demagogue? There must be more to you than your winning personality." He gave her the up-down.

She recoiled in offense.

Joseph drew his sword, which was steel, not obsidian. "She is not a piece of a meat to be ogled by your demonarchy. Your kind are ethnocentric, prejudiced, mansplaining monsters that have been oppressing the human minority for centuries. You should feel fortunate that Isla has given you an ounce of sympathy."

"Alright." Ghelys took his spear in both hands. "Now that I know how smart you all are, you can have your prisoners."

There's something wrong. R'lyeh nudged Deimos, and he put his hand on her shoulder.

The coffin-shaped house's front door flew open. The armed Rimeans behind R'lyeh and the others broke rank for a moment, and then quickly reformed. In the doorway, Audra of Eldrus stood, the butcher's gown she wore splattered with gore. From inside the house, streams of fresh blood poured past her feet, across the porch, and down the steps, before hissing to a freeze in the snow. She was unarmed, but unlike Isla Taggart, she didn't look like the kind of woman who needed a weapon or an army to get something done. Her face was hard, unflinching; a scar like war paint was slashed across her eyes. And there was a glow to her, too; very faint, like she was outlined by the shadow of herself.

"Great," Isla said through her teeth. She kicked her horse forward.

R'lyeh drifted toward Audra, as if called by her image.

Deimos grabbed her by the straps of her armor. "Stay."

"She should be g-guarded, yeah?" Elizabeth chattered.

"She was." Deimos stepped in front of R'lyeh. "Those are her guards pouring past her feet." Then, to Ghelys: "Ghelys, you are making a mistake!"

"Deimos," Ghelys said, "you are the one who put us in this mistake. Shut your mouth."

"Deimos?" Isla hummed. "I like that name. Ghelys, is it? I'll take the women, actually. God invites all creatures to dine at Its table. Now, come here, Audra."

Deimos started forward; the guard of twenty Rimeans quickly raised their spears, stopping him.

"Audra, don't move. Don't do anything," he pleaded.

A violent wind rocked Rime, staggering R'lyeh. She grabbed onto Miranda. Thunder bellowed from the frosted firmament, and all at once, a heavy snowfall like an avalanche fell upon the village. The temperature plummeted further; R'lyeh could feel it dropping in her spine—her bones like barometers. Any sensations she had before were gone; the cold had come to eat them all.

With the conditions close to a total whiteout, Isla Taggart gave up her game. Shouting over the pummeling wind, she said to Ghelys, "I just wanted to see how stupid your kind are. This is impressive—" she held out her hands in the near-blinding snow, "—but not enough. God is my shelter—"

Joseph Cleon and his band of fifteen each reached into their satchels and took something small out.

"—and Its roots my shield—"

The forty-five Winnowers started forward on their horses, closing in on Rime from almost every direction.

"—and I shall never know pain or sorrow—" Isla reached into a satchel and held out a red, bristly, grapefruit-sized mass.

A seed of heaven. R'lyeh's throat closed-up. *Just like in Gallows.* She turned to Elizabeth.

"—for God is everywhere—"

Isla threw the seed of heaven at Ghelys' feet.

"—always watching, always—"

And then Joseph and the fifteen soldiers threw their seeds.

"—waiting."

Audra screamed, "No!" and ran down the front steps of the Cult house. Where she had been, her shadow still stood.

Ghelys shouted, "Stop her!" and was thrown off his feet as the ground heaved and broke apart around him.

There was a moment of silence, like there might be at a memorial, and then there was terror: the ground opened up and the veins of God poured through. Long, thick stalks of vermillion veins exploded out of the snow and shot out across Rime in every direction. They weaved through the village like snakes seeking out prey, striking buildings and bodies with bone-shattering strength. In a matter of seconds, the vermillion veins had begun to create a ceiling over the village, as if to shield the

Winnowers from the weather.

R'lyeh took one look at Elizabeth and Miranda, and ran. Winnowers' horses thundering behind her, she broke through the armed Rimeans, toward the Cult house and toward Audra.

"Grab her!" R'lyeh said, Elizabeth and Miranda at her sides.

Deimos sprinted past R'lyeh into the worsening whiteout. He crashed against the Cult house, his bound arms doing him no favors.

Audra quickly regrouped with him.

"No," he panted to R'lyeh. "She cannot go back with you."

"She has to!" R'lyeh bounced off the Rimeans surging through Rime. A vermillion vein whipped past her face, impaling three Night Terrors at once. "We need her!"

Audra of Eldrus looked at the Winnowers charging toward them, and at Isla, who stood at the center of the vermillion storm, reading psychotically from *The Disciples of the Deep*. Then she trained her gaze on R'lyeh, Elizabeth, and Miranda.

"I'm sorry you came all this way," Audra said, "but no one is using me ever again."

She took Deimos' hand. Her shadow ran down the porch and joined them there. It dropped to the ground on its hands and knees and started to cough and wheeze and spit up an ephemeral fluid. The fluid bubbled and throbbed, and spread across the ground, built upon itself. Gray growths formed on Audra's shadow; its entire frame ballooned into something bulbous, like a four-foot grub.

Audra and Deimos mounted the shadowy grub. Twelve legs shot out of its rippling sides and lifted the creature's body off the ground.

"Go to Caldera," Deimos said. "You deserve better."

And with that, the shadowy grub ran up the front of the Cult house, onto the roof, and took Audra and Deimos into the impenetrable fog beyond.

Several vermillion veins slithered across the ground, snatching Night Terrors off their feet and hauling them like hooked fish into the air. The Winnowers rode back and forth through the village, cutting down Night Terrors caught by the veins. Rime was constricted, like a garden overrun with weeds.

"God is everywhere," Isla cried, somewhere inside the red chaos. "Rejoice, for though you did not know it, you have been living upon a most holy site! Repent, and you shall taste Its salvation!"

Elizabeth and Miranda took off in front of R'lyeh, and R'lyeh followed after. They tore through the village as fast as they could. What had been an open sprawl had now become a dense maze, as the vermillion veins continued to weave themselves around Rime. Night Terror after Night Terror ran into and past R'lyeh and her Corrupted friends, but no one stopped to stop them.

R'lyeh spotted an opening at the back of the village and hurried towards it. Her joints ached; rods of pain jammed their way through her arms, legs, and chest and did everything they could to make her stop. But she couldn't stop, wouldn't stop. R'lyeh was on the move. R'lyeh had to always be on the move. Even if she lost her toes to frostbite, she couldn't go anywhere but forward. The past was in everything but the future.

She bit her lip, licked the snot off her nose. The whiteout was worsening; she couldn't see but a foot in front of her. And then there was a ringing in her ears, and despite the cold, she suddenly felt very hot. Her vision went fuzzy. One leg stumbled, followed by the other.

R'lyeh was down on the ground before she knew it. Looking back, underneath her, in between her legs, she could see the shapes of Death coming for her. They were coming for her, and for her alone. She had cheated Death too many times. Maybe the Skeleton could get away with it, but not her. The clammy hands of delirium closed in on her head and held it there. Held it there to make her watch. To make her watch the shape of the vermillion Death spiraling towards her.

She looked forward. Vrana's ax, the Cruel Mother's daggers, and the faerie cloak lay not far from where she was, gathering snow like a mantle would dust. Ghelys had dropped them here as if they hadn't meant anything at all. Priceless treasures to her and her alone.

"Get. The. Fuck. Up." Elizabeth grabbed R'lyeh with her bound hands and hauled her off the ground. R'lyeh managed to grab the cloak and daggers, but not the ax.

Miranda bent down and rammed her shoulder into R'lyeh's stomach. With Elizabeth's help, she lifted R'lyeh up, over, and onto her shoulder.

"Go to sleep, little Octopus," Elizabeth said. "We tried."

R'lyeh forced her eyes open. Her body bobbed up and down as Miranda ran with her over her shoulder through the village. There was Rime Rot all over the back of Miranda's neck. Before R'lyeh passed out, she brushed a little of it off. After all, it was the least she could do. In fact, it was all she could do.

R'lyeh woke up two days later, seventy miles away from Rime, in a small cabin Elizabeth and Miranda had "borrowed" from an old man she never actually ended up meeting. R'lyeh had been asleep on the hearth, her head a few inches away from a small fire. A loud sound and a whimper had brought her out of her slumber. Her neck, forearms, legs, and feet were itchy and red, and dotted with hard, black blisters that were begging to be popped. Turning over to face the rest of the cabin, she found that she had sprained an ankle, and had also bled all over the ground at some point—but from where, she couldn't be sure.

Elizabeth and Miranda were sitting at the table, watching R'lyeh wake. Miranda looked sick, and her lips were still wet with vomit.

R'lyeh wanted to ask them what was wrong, but speaking was too difficult, so instead, she stood. Miranda was leaning forward, and she had her left arm, her paralyzed arm, laid out across the table. Except her hand wasn't connected to her left arm, anymore. It was in front of Elizabeth, beside a meat cleaver. Like R'lyeh's blisters, Miranda's hand was hard and black, and it looked like a hunk of wax. There was blood everywhere.

"Don't worry, little Octopus," Miranda said as Elizabeth began tying off the amputation. "I didn't need that hand anymore, anyways."

"Where are we?" R'lyeh croaked, unable to take her eyes off Miranda's severed hand.

"Safe," Elizabeth said, sounding as if she were about to cry. "Say, R'lyeh, do you have any drugs left?"

R'lyeh had failed the Skeleton twice. First, at Gallows, by killing the priest and burning down the church. And then again at Rime, where she hadn't managed to even speak to the woman she had been told to bring back. The Skeleton had promised to help her find Vrana, but why would he help her now? And Vrana's weapon? The ax? They were gone, too. How could she save someone so far out of her reach, if she couldn't even manage to save someone within her grasp?

R'lyeh took a deep breath, the smell of the distant Divide filling her nostrils, and set her sights on the woods ahead. She had to keep moving.

"You're quiet," Miranda said, slowing down.

R'lyeh had lagged behind the two women. She had spent most of the time back there staring at the nub on the end of Miranda's wrist.

"Thinking about everything," R'lyeh said, which was true, but not in the way Miranda probably thought.

"We did what we could, yeah?" Elizabeth said. She slowed down, too.

"Bone Daddy has a backup plan, I'm sure."

"She made vermillion veins come out of the ground." R'lyeh squinted; ahead, through the gaps in the woods, the Divide's water twinkled with drowning light. But even so, why was everything so white? Not just the river. The trees, too.

"And that's good to know. And it's good to know the Winnowers now have a base in the North. And it's good to know Audra is safe." Miranda looked at her left arm and what was left of it. "No offense to your kind, but it's nice to know there are a few hundred fewer Night Terrors running around, too."

"Fuck them," R'lyeh said, touching her mask. "I hope Deimos is okay."

"Me, too," Elizabeth said. "Hey, Real'yuh?"

She took off her mask, thought about throwing it. "Yeah?"

"How would you like to be inducted as an honorary member of the Deadly Beauties?"

Instead of putting the mask back on, she held it at her side. It was October, and though the wind was brisk, it was better than the new dark inside it.

"Uh, what's that?"

Miranda puffed out her squirrel cheeks. "She doesn't know?"

"Hey, go easy on the girl, yeah? She's only been traveling with us for months now."

"What is—" the Divide was definitely white, and where were all the ships? "—what?"

Elizabeth stopped, started putting a few piercings into her nose and lips. "When we lived at the Orphanage, before we were turned into vamypres—"

"Temporarily," Miranda added.

"—yeah, duh. Let me tell the story, alright?"

Miranda rolled her eyes and turned toward the sliver of water that was the Divide. "Huh?" She had noticed something strange about it, too.

But Elizabeth hadn't or didn't care, so she carried on. "When we lived at the Orphanage, before we were turned temporarily into vampyres, me, Miranda, and our two friends, Jessie and Emily, decided to form a club. We were the only few non-vampyres at the Orphanage and we thought we were a lot cooler than everyone else there. Prettier, too, you know, because they all had been alive for so long and were kind of gross. The Bad Woman said we were deadly, because we reminded the other kids of what it was like to be mortal. Too much of a temptation, yeah? And no matter what anyone could do to us, they couldn't keep us down."

"Hey, Liz," Miranda said, pawing for her attention.

"So, Jessie and Emily aren't with us now, and Miranda and I've been keeping a close eye on you."

R'lyeh covered her mouth, to hide the smile and how much she was blushing. Why the hell was she blushing?

"Deadly doesn't even describe you, girl," Elizabeth smirked. "Deadly with a blade; hell, even your blood is deadly from all that crap you eat. And look what we just went through. I don't even know how we survived. You're thirteen. I mean, you're a Night Terror, but still. Anyways, how about it?"

"I, uh, yeah!" R'lyeh threw on her mask.

"No, no. You have to let that pretty face breathe, yeah?" Elizabeth lifted the Octopus mask off her head. It might've been the only time she had ever touched it. "Now, there's no gold star for joining. But trust me, when you're a Deadly Beauty, people will know! And so will you. And that makes all the difference."

"Okay," R'lyeh said, grinning. "You guys are—"

"Liz," Miranda said.

Elizabeth handed the mask back to R'lyeh. "Damn, what?"

"Look at the Divide."

"Eh." Elizabeth bit her lip piercing and plodded forward. "It's just the... huh."

"What?" Maybe it was from their time in the North, but to R'lyeh, it really did look as if the river was covered in snow. The month wasn't exactly right for the weather, but she wasn't exactly from these parts, either. "Looks like snow," she said.

"No, wait." Elizabeth pointed at the river. "See it?"

R'lyeh went ahead and searched for the spot she had picked out. There was a white strand coming off the surface of the Divide, and it connected with the woods on the shore. Seeing that, R'lyeh then saw other strands running off the Divide, into the trees. And the surface of the river was strange, too. It could've been frozen, but the water was still moving beneath whatever covered the surface.

"That's not snow," Elizabeth said.

"Those are spider webs." Miranda twitched; something had just bolted through the woods ahead. "Son of a bitch. Those are Arachne webs. King Edgar has an army after all."

CHAPTER XIV

Every time Aeson looked away from *The Blood of Before*, Vrana was there, waiting for him, blood-drenched and blood-drunk, Worm-enriched and Witch-transformed. Every time Aeson stopped deciphering the text, the flesh fiend was on him again, slamming her lust into his crotch and sopping up his seed. To escape the present, he had to slip into the past. There was no place for him here, in this dark forest, under this dim moon; he needed to be a ghost amongst ghosts, until this skin was his again.

Bux wrfvhb ytfbuewwer lnv jlvnepl eihv okinflhl vg xuh fdarfiaw si Ølrzenuh'v pbltvweo. Wax lhqhumq aszxrfcyb arui iwhgh vqwllr. Fsfw si buxq jhvh agbpy fsqvrvxrg xr bux Qbnmwi ztgulrha. Sbzr rj wpr lgbxxv erki xlpomq pexlrj bux gehewcexw. Gki kwznrpxpl zryyfhh ww yxeih xkm uhwclxdt oxgnxwh buxc jhvh "lvlecsslvgxh vq akig pi udzh jrvszh."

Aeson could tell Bjørn was trying to get his attention, but he ignored him. Up until this point, every entry after Adelyn's that Aeson had read was by his father; this one, however, had been written by his mother. Discovering this was like discovering a small, forgotten wonder. It warmed him when nothing else could, and made him forget when nothing else would.

"We need to talk," Bjørn said. He had gathered kindling into a pile, but not the courage to make a fire out of it.

Intended, Aeson thought. He took out his quill and parchment and wrote the alphabet vertically and horizontally, and then wrote it again and again, creating more rows and columns until he had a table. In the previous entry, which had detailed the efforts in Eld to increase fertility amongst the Night Terrors, portions of it had been written in someone else's scrawl—his mother's. Together, the portions formed the word 'intended.' He hadn't spotted it at first, and had spent the last hour trying different decrypting measures as a result.

"It's a Vigenere Cipher," Aeson told Bjørn.

Bjørn sighed and buried his face in his hands.

"Across the top—" he flashed the table at him, "—is the Key letter row. Intended is the Key. This first column going up and down is the Plaintext, or, you know, what's written in the book. In the middle, you have to repeat the alphabet over and over again. So A, B, C… and then below that B, C, D… and then you start over if you need to."

Bjørn grumbled. "Just stop for—"

"You match the Key letter row with the Plaintext column and the letter they meet at in the table is the actual text." Aeson nodded, smiled. He started scribbling his decryption. "Make sense?"

Bjørn didn't say if it did or didn't. And that was fine. After a few minutes, it didn't matter, because Aeson had what he wanted.

He read: "The secret laboratory has finally been breached in the basement of Ødegaard's hospital. One hundred homunculi were found inside. Most of them were still connected to the Mokita machines. Five of the scouts were killed waking the creatures. The homunculi refused to leave the hospital because they were 'disappointed in what we have become.'

"See, it's hard to keep track of these events because the Archivists didn't date the entries," Aeson said. In a phantom flash, he felt the flesh fiend's run-off on his thighs. "So—" he choked, "—I don't know where this one fits, but—" and then he shook, "it's right before the entry about Eld and the fertility project."

Something howled in the woods. Something panicked in the trees. The dark lifted for a moment to the illuminating chemicals of dread. Aeson dropped the parchment, dropped the book; he grabbed his sword and stabbed the air, the image of the flesh fiend having just been there.

Bjørn stared at him from across the dead bonfire. They had run south for hours out of the Dismal Sticks; if something were hunting them, it would have hunted them already. It had to have been three or four in the morning; besides the moon, the only company they kept were the demons their minds kept propping up in all the shadows and trees.

"Homunculi," Bjørn started. He waited until he had Aeson's attention and then: "What are they?"

I know what you're doing.

Aeson let go of the sword, and it clanged against the ground. His eyes tightened as his mind narrowed in on the image of Vrana—his girlfriend, his best friend—mutated and mutilated. Would it have been easier if the Witch had changed her completely? If there had been nothing left to recognize, he could have lied to himself; he could have convinced himself it wasn't her, or that she was dead. The mask... her neck... the way she stood, so full of herself, even when she was full of someone else. But it was the eyes that got to Aeson now. He had seen those eyes almost every day of his life, in every state of happiness and hurt. He would know them anywhere, despite any masks that might cover them, or deeds that might darken them.

He pinched the bridge of his nose. Snot running down the back of his throat, he muttered, "They're from the Old World, before the Trauma."

He stopped; his words were wavering, and so was his strength. Even when he wasn't thinking about Vrana, he was thinking about Vrana; she was in his cells, in his subconscious—everywhere but in his arms.

Bjørn leaned forward. "Aeson?"

"Frederick Ødegaard is credited with discovering the homunculi, or creating them. The sources are contradictory."

Aeson smelled the musky heat of the female flesh fiend, and recoiled.

"They showed up about the same time the s-stories of the... flesh fiends did." He clenched his teeth. "Ødegaard is sometimes c-credited with discovering them, too."

Bjørn mumbled something that sounded like, "Screw it," and put his hands into the kindling. He started chipping at the starters he'd brought from Caldera, until, at last, a tiny flame was born in that dry, dead nest. "What the elders want the homunculi for?" he finally asked.

"They outlived the Trauma. They weren't supernatural, like a lot of the things that came out of it, but things made from science."

Aeson scooted closer to the fire; tiny ropes of orange and red shot through the kindling, creating smoke and heat where they went. Warmth and light grew out of the heart of the nest, and although it would attract attention, right now, even though Aeson's nerves said otherwise, it was worth it.

"*The Blood of Before* isn't an exact history. It's backwards. I have to read it from present to past to be able to break the ciphers. There's no reference to the previous entries, either, other than the hidden codes to crack them." Aeson saw the female flesh fiend at the corners of his eyes; he blinked her away. "It's like… our people are reluctant to write their history, so they only do the bare minimum. I think it was the homunculi who tried to tell us how to reproduce better."

A giant flame ripped through the kindling, setting the entire thing ablaze. Satisfied, Bjørn fell back on his hands and said, "Homunculi were disappointed. In us, or themselves?"

Aeson shrugged. "I… I don't know."

"Stories say the Night Terrors were much more violent and savage back in the day. Seems a strange thing to be disappointed about." Bjørn reached for one of his bags and took out a piece of dried meat. "I know you're disappointed in Vrana."

"Man, I… I can't… talk about that—"

"You stood here not an hour ago talking about Death and getting help from It. You need to talk." Suddenly, across the fire, Bjørn's massive frame seemed so much smaller, like that of a wild animal who had finally given in to a trap. Reluctantly, he muttered, "I need to, too."

The fire shivered embers into the cold night air. Throughout the woods, boughs creaked and branches broke, and the smallest, weakest things spoke in the loudest, most desperate voices. The wind kicked up, casting rattling waves across the crumpled canopy. Those that couldn't bear the change broke off and fell to the ground. And it was there they lay and decayed, in the faded grass, atop the hardened soil, waiting to be reduced, and dreaming of rebirth. It was the season of dying.

Aeson twitched; he could feel the silence between him and Bjørn reaching its crest. Soon, it would break, and he would break, too. *I don't want to talk about it,* he said. *You didn't see what it… did to me.* He stared at Bjørn blankly, as if the Bear could hear the conversation going on inside his head.

Vrana is a monster. He rolled his eyes, clenched them shut. His throat filled with saliva and sorrow.

She is a monster, he told himself, now whimpering. *She's gone.*

His teeth started to chatter as memory after memory of her hit him like a fist. He remembered the first time he had met her—it had been outside the garden of the elders, and Blix had crapped on her head—and the first time he had made love to her—in her room, the night before she left for Geharra; two minutes of action, forty minutes of warm sighs and comfortable silence. He remembered their future and saw that it had passed. He had wanted more than he had told her, and felt more than he had shown her. Marriage, children; warm sighs and comfortable silence; kisses that didn't mark departures like death sentences. He had wanted to himself, and to himself he now wanted.

"Seeing her like that tore me to pieces," Bjørn said, shivering in the fire's heat. "I swear to god, if you hadn't been there, I would've got myself killed."

"We shouldn't have run," Aeson whispered. "You ran because of me."

"I ran because we aren't any help to her dead."

Aeson's mouth was so full of spit he had to spit, but he swallowed it, instead. He knew what he looked like to Bjørn right now. He looked exactly like any Archivist would.

"I'm sorry," Bjørn said.

Aeson knew what was coming; apologies were apocalyptic in situations like these. He grabbed his sword and reached for his mask. No, he wasn't ready—

"I didn't realize what the flesh fiend was doing to you 'til it was too late."

Aeson stopped; the sword fell first, and then his head. He felt hands on his legs, hands on his wrists, and again, he was crumpled and reduced, in the faded grass, on the hardened ground.

"I'm no good at this kind of thing."

Aeson snapped. "That would be a first, wouldn't it?" He hurried to his feet. "You made me d-do this. You g-guilted me into this. Why didn't you take someone else?" He kicked dirt and leaves at Bjørn, but the fire caught them midway.

"You're scared."

"Fuck you."

"I brought you because—"

"Fuck you." Aeson picked up his mask and, holding it against his chest, said, "She's gone. And I'm not—" he dropped the mask as he tasted the female flesh fiend. "Fuck. Fuck!"

"She will still love you," Bjørn said.

Aeson stared at the Bear, his face not far from a snarl. The blood pumping in his ears was making it hard to hear anything, anymore.

"She still loves you." Bjørn rose to his feet, now much larger than he had been before. "She tore the flesh fiend apart, not you."

"I—" Aeson grabbed his chest, "—I... what the hell can I do?" He threw back his head, covered his face with his hands. "I can't stop seeing it. I can't stop seeing her. Every... fucking day... everything... it's always been out of my control." His face was tight, twisted—misery-chiseled. "I haven't even... cleaned it off." He laughed, coughed up phlegm, and dropped his mask. "Vrana saw everything. I was supposed to save her. Instead, she saved me. And then I fucking ran. I'm pathetic."

"Then what're you doing here?"

"Don't, Bjørn. I'm only here because of you. Alright?"

"All of us are somewhere because of someone." Bjørn stepped closer to him. "You don't go through shit like this alone."

"That means a lot coming from you."

Bjørn chewed on his lip. Twigs and branches snapped inside the fire; it caved in, but even then, there was still some life to it.

"I don't know why I thought I could be different," Aeson said. He exhaled slowly and looked around the woods. "I don't know what to do." Crying, shaking, he pleaded, "I don't know what to do. I just want her back. I'm so fucking scared." He dropped to his knees. "I'm so fucking stupid." And punched the ground. "What they've done to her..." He glanced at Bjørn, trembling. "Vrana... I can't... I can't..."

"I brought you, Aeson, because I knew you would do anything to get her back, and you'd stop me if I went too far." Heavy tears were pouring out of Bjørn's eyes. "I never meant for this to happen to you. I thought we could suffer through this together. It didn't seem right bringing anyone else. I will... never forgive myself for what happened to you, but I am... glad you are here. You saved me on the lake. I will kill myself every day for not... saving you. Always... too late with you."

Aeson lifted his head. Sniffling, he said, "Too late? What... what are you t-talking about?"

Bjørn stepped closer to Aeson until he was near enough to touch him, and then didn't. Instead, he sat beside him and focused his attention on the heart of the fire, where the dead gave life when they had none of their own.

"I met Death once," he started. "The story is true. I met Death once at midnight, on an empty road, on my way home to Caldera. I was thirty years old, and I haven't celebrated a birthday since.

"After I killed Quentin on Lacuna, Adelyn, Mara, and I left with Vrana. We stopped at Traesk on the way. Adelyn wasn't doing good. Quentin's death and giving birth to Vrana... it was too much for her. We were going to stay, wait until she got better, but then Anguis sent a letter, demanding we bring Vrana to Caldera immediately. He wanted to see her, start going to work on her. She was their very own Child of Lacuna. He was… excited." Bjørn spit in the fire. "He made threats, and Adelyn got scared. She didn't want to take any more risks. She didn't want to lose Vrana, too. So she asked me to take Vrana to Caldera, while Mara helped her get better.

"I love Adelyn. That's no surprise to no one. And when she asked me to take little Vrana home, I knew she loved me, too. Maybe not in the way I wanted, but it was a better way.

"We left Traesk the next day. I took the long way, the safe way. I changed her and fed her every chance I could get, because I wasn't taking no chances. She was perfect, Aeson. Fat, quiet little thing. Wouldn't have known she was there if not for the stink of her drawers. For all my boasting and battles, I've never felt more like a man than when I had her in my arms, and she had me wrapped around her damn tiny, fat, pink finger."

Bjørn cleared his throat and wiped his eyes. "We were outside Nachtla—this was before it was completely abandoned—and I got a bad feeling. Too much movement in the forest. Too many Corrupted nearby. I bundled up Vrana and broke down camp and started for home. I took the back roads. Didn't see a soul. Moon was bright; the light was good. And then there was Death, standing in the middle of the road, waiting for us.

"A man knows some things. It's instinctual, primal. I saw Death, and knew It was Death. Everything inside me sank. Would've lost hope, too, I have no doubt in my mind. But I had Vrana. I had to be better for her. Something so new doesn't know what it's like to end.

"I kept walking down that back road. I held Vrana as tight as I could and kept at it. I walked straight at Death. Either It was going to take us both, or It was going to get out of the way. I wasn't thinking. I wasn't feeling. It was instinctual, primal. Death is my god, but even god needs to know when it's time to give. So I walked straight at Death, and when we were about to touch, Death stepped aside.

"I don't know why It did, and I didn't stop to ask. I didn't stop at all. I walked for hours, in shock, and then I ran for days, in relief. I never stopped moving, not until we were home, in Caldera, and Death was days behind us.

"After a while, I got stupid again. I got jealous and selfish and did a shitload of self-loathing. I told my story about Death. Left Vrana out of it, of course. Did it, I think, to taunt Death. To see if It would change Its mind. You see Death enough, you start to miss It."

"Does anyone else know?" Aeson asked, his lips chapped and raw.

"Just Death." Bjørn sighed and shook his head. "I hate to lay this on you now, but I got to."

Aeson shifted uncomfortably. "W-what?"

"I stopped telling that story when you were six. When your parents killed themselves. When they tried to take you with them."

"What!" Aeson's eyes went wide and he grabbed Bjørn by the shirt. "What the hell are you—"

"Didn't know why they did it until tonight at Gloom when you read that book to me. Now it makes sense."

Aeson sat there in silence, hanging on his every word.

"I found your mother and father hanging from that tree. You know that. I cut them down. You were up there, too. Hanging. Choking. They hadn't tied your rope right. And you were hanging onto them, trying to stay alive.

"I cut you down before anyone else saw and hid you in my shack. Then I went back for your parents and cut them down, too. By that point, the village had heard what was going on."

"My d-dad's last entry in the book was about the Ossuary and how there was something in it and—"

"They knew what was coming," Bjørn said, "and they didn't want you to have to go through it. No one really knew your parents well. They were recluses because of their position. They were just... trying to save you the only way they knew how."

Bjørn closed his eyes and shook as he cried. "Two times I've taken a life from Death. And then you two end up together? You said we have to go to Death to stop the witches. I stopped taunting Death the day I saved you. I'm not looking to start it up again."

Aeson let go of Bjørn's shirt and fell back on his haunches. His whole body felt as if it were deflating. Digging his thumb into his temple, he said, "I... I... didn't know..."

"That's the way I would've liked to have kept it." Now, Bjørn turned and faced Aeson. "Tell me about the weapons."

"The Red Death weapons?" Aeson shook his head. "No, you're right. There h-has to be another—" *he saved me; they tried to kill me,* "—way. I don't know what I was saying earlier." *They tried to kill me; he saved me.*

"Tell me," Bjørn persisted.

"No, you're right."

"Tell me."

"They… fuck… they are said to be able to kill anything. Living or dead, it doesn't matter. Death forges them Itself. It's like a safeguard against things humans can't normally kill." *They tried to kill me; and he saved me.* "One was up in Eldrus, but the last story about anyone using it was… I don't know." *My parents tried to kill me.*

At the edges of the sky, there was light; soft and white, it rose slowly, as if the night were a curtain that had been cast over the Earth.

"There's no way we're going to find any unless we go straight to Death. There's the Ferry Woman outside Caldera to take us to Death. That's true. Everyone knows that." Aeson sighed. "But I don't think I want to. You're right."

Bjørn made fists; he squeezed his knuckles until they were white. "How many Night Terrors are left?"

"I… I don't know. Seven hundred? Maybe less?"

"How many Children of Lacuna are there?"

"Hundreds, I guess. Thousands? I don't know." Aeson's mind clicked. "The Dismal Sticks was our first stop. There's Lacunans in every town and village. What if this is happening everywhere? Or is about to? Most of the Night Terror population nowadays is from Lacuna. Just them building their Cult is going to wipe us out.

"And there's going to be an outbreak of flesh fiends, and I don't think anyone is prepared for that."

Bjørn nodded. "And Vrana."

Aeson's heart started to hurt again. "And Vrana?" Aeson squeezed his eyes shut; he started to cough; his breaths became shallow. "You saw what they did to her. What they were… making her do. She's going to get worse. It's all going to get worse, whatever they are planning."

"I don't want to see Death again." Bjørn stood, and pulled Aeson up with him by the hand. "And I don't want you or Vrana to see It again, either. But—" he paused, swallowed hard, "—we don't have any more options, and we're… out of time. They're headed for Angheuawl to finish their pilgrimage. We can meet them there or on the way, but we have to move now."

Aeson didn't mean to, but it happened, anyway. He leaned into Bjørn and dropped his head against the big man's chest. "I haven't gotten anything right so far. What if I'm wrong?"

"Vrana fought two Worms, and everything else those witch bitches have thrown at her so far. We owe her this." Bjørn took the back of Aeson's head and held it. "This is why I brought you, Skull Boy. To stop me from doing something stupid. And you're not stopping me. Besides, seeing Death again—" he held Aeson away and laughed, "—third time's a charm, right?"

CHAPTER XV

Felix was two peanut butter sandwiches deep when the Arachne had attacked the Divide. He was cutting the crust off a third sandwich when he heard Justine outside his tent, working her way through a sea of praises. She was coming to tell him it was time to make a choice about who was going to live and who was going to die. For most of the men and women they had conscripted on their way to the Divide, living was preferable, but death wasn't so bad, either. Those who fought for the Holy Order of Penance were told they would be automatically admitted into heaven, regardless of their sins. Felix didn't like that lie so much. Not because there wasn't actually a heaven to have them, but because it gave the bad people a good reason to keep on being bad. Justine had told him not worry about it; but the joke was on her: He worried about everything. He had to. That's what gods were supposed to do, wasn't it?

Hearing Justine just outside his tent, Felix took the sandwich in two hands and went to town on it. He could buy himself about forty-five seconds of silence if he got his mouth good and gooey. He would need that silence to think; otherwise, he'd just end up doing whatever she told him to do.

The tent flap flipped back and Justine came through. Instead of the warm, campfire smell that used to precede her, there came a soft breeze of her natural odor: Lilac and wine. The White Worm of the Earth no longer had the sealing stone in her breast that could force into her slumber; instead, it was now around Felix's neck, where it had always been ever since she had given it to him that night on top of Pyra. She had never asked for it back, and she had never treated him differently. They were partners-in-crime, she had told him back then, as the petrified Holy Children carried Deimos, Lucan, and Audra away. And since they were pretty much lying to everyone about the existence of god and heaven, partners-in-crime sounded about right.

"You're awake," Justine said, taking a seat at his table. She touched his face and added, "When was the last time you slept?"

Felix looked at Justine and wondered the same thing about her. Ever since they had arrived on the Divide two days ago, she had never changed out of her clothes. But were they clothes? Felix really couldn't tell. Both the dress she wore and leggings underneath it were variations of white, sometimes pinkish, sometimes grayish, but there didn't seem to be any seams or edges. And they didn't look like any fabric he had ever seen before; they were terse, almost glistening, like a carapace or a kidney. Justine used to wear the opposite of what she felt to remind herself how to act. Now, to Felix, it looked like Justine just wore herself, plus whatever the tendrils beneath her skin could conjure.

"You said—" Felix chomped through the peanut butter and bread in his mouth, "King Edgar wouldn't—" and then took a big swig of milk, "—attack." He swallowed the last of the sandwich and sat there as his stomach gave off nervous gurgles. "Are there as m-many spiders as they say?"

"Even more than they're saying." Justine smiled and took his hand from across the table. "Thousands."

Felix arched an eyebrow. "Why're you smiling?"

"Because this has worked out perfectly." Her eyes lingered on the chained sealing stone around his neck. Then: "It's happening just like you said it would to our people."

"Lucky guess."

Justine laughed. "Not at all. King Edgar couldn't help himself once he got ahold of the Nameless Forest. Instead of sending Eldrus' army to meet us, he's summoned an army of monsters."

"Yeah, but he's saying they are servants of God," Felix said.

"I've been playing this game a long time. Anything that makes people nervous is a 'servant of god,' or better yet, the 'will of god.'"

"They're going to lose a lot of faith in the Disciples if we beat them," Felix said, the red of hope returning to his cheeks.

"We will beat them," Justine corrected. "But if we're lucky, some of the Arachne will scatter into the Heartland and start killing people there."

Felix didn't like the sound of that, and he didn't like the way Justine's eyes shone when she said it; it was like she hadn't realized that was a possibility until now. So to distract her, Felix said, "King Edgar will just say it was the will of God."

"Eh, maybe." A thick cord rippled behind the skin on Justine's forehead, and then it was gone. "When God starts killing its own, suddenly, it doesn't seem so godly anymore. That's what the Vermillion God does, Felix. That's why we have to stop this madness, once and for all. If we crush the Disciples of the Deep in the days to come, then God is done."

Felix touched the pile of crusts, while his mind overworked itself to make sense of everything that was going on. "Why didn't the Trauma stop God before?"

"Because God threw a temper tantrum and went back to bed." Justine took one of the pieces of crust and ate it. Cringing, she said, "It left on Its own, and I was too stupid to make sure It couldn't come back. I—" she took his hands, "—we won't make that mistake again."

Sitting there, his hands in Justine's, Felix felt a longing for Penance and Pyra he hadn't realized was there before. The ride between home and here had been a blur; one unending arctic wasteland of hamlets, villages, and towns that had been almost completely emptied by the conscription. The peninsula, now called the Holy Land to spite the Disciples of the Deep, had a population of about eighteen thousand—twenty-one thousand, if you included Penance. The conscription had snatched about three-and-a-half thousand, two-thirds of which were still here; the others had fled, died, or simply disappeared. Penance's main army, Narcissus, was four thousand strong, and it was still many days away, simultaneously guarding the city, while also waiting for an opening at the Nameless Forest.

Because if the Vermillion God was going to wake up, it was going to wake up in the Nameless Forest, for that was where It had fallen into slumber so many years ago. With the Dread Clock taken from the Forest, all It needed now was enough belief to make Its waking worth the unfathomable effort required to do so. To make matters worse, there was reportedly a massive blood well at Gallows, where the Skeleton who stole the Black Hour resided. Between the Forest, the Disciples of the Deep, and a portal that was weakening the barrier between worlds, conditions were more or less crap. Justine had told them they needed to act fast. Felix, and he felt bad for doing it, was the one making them do everything slowly.

Because here he was, hundreds of miles away from home, surrounded by thousands of people ready to lay down their lives for him and Justine and their bullshit faith. To do anything but take it slowly didn't seem right.

"The people need to see you," Justine said, standing. "And you need to see the Arachne."

Felix gulped. He had heard stories of the Arachne at the camp's borders and across the Divide, but he had yet to actually lay eyes on the creatures himself. Justine wouldn't let him, and even though she didn't know it, he knew she had been spiking his food with a little bit of Null to keep his anxiety away. Any other day, he might've minded; but given that there were thousands of humanoid arachnids spinning webs on their doorstep, he could make an exception.

"The people need your strength," she added.

"I'm twelve," he said, his heart beating faster and faster at the thought of finally leaving the tent.

"Not to them." She motioned for him to get up. "Not anymore."

Felix stumbled to his feet. The sounds and smells from outside the tent flooded his senses as he was finally forced to acknowledge that they were there. He went to his bed and threw on the holy vestments strewn there. Ever since Avery and Mackenzie had been killed by the Cult of the Worm in Pyra, Felix's guards had become the statuesque Holy Children who'd preceded him. They didn't speak to him, they didn't prepare his clothes, food, or bath; they simply stalked him at all hours, and murdered anything that drew too close. There were no better guards to have, but in his darker moments, Felix often wondered if Justine had assigned the Holy Children to him as a reminder of what could still happen to him, if he didn't do his part in all of this.

"It was smart of you to suggest we not attack the Divide. The Lillians were always too aggressive." Justine watched as he stripped down to his underwear. "Our being here was enough to frighten Edgar into responding."

"Yeah, but he was supposed to send an army, not A-araka-"

"Arachne."

"—Arachne and vermillion veins."

"All the better." Justine came over to him and slipped his robe over his head.

"Because—" he wiggled the robe down his body, "—it makes him look bad."

"No. It makes him look bad when we defeat his monsters, and his justification for using them falls through. Then he'll have to use the very people he supposedly spared." Justine smiled, kissed his forehead; her affection felt acidic. "Edgar has everything to prove."

"And we've been here for untold years," Felix said, basically repeating the Mother Abbess' words verbatim.

"Exactly. Granted, we worshipped the same God back then, but no one needs to know that." She wrapped her arm around him; he could feel appendages inside it. "First we deal with the spiders. Then we'll treat with the Skeleton, if he isn't already on his way to ask for an alliance."

"Then the Nameless Forest," Felix said. He tied his sash and fixed his hood and went to consult the mirror that wasn't there. "What about the Heartland?"

Justine smirked. "We're already there. Religion is no different than anything else you can sell. When Edgar's product breaks, they'll come back to ours."

When she wasn't looking, Felix grabbed the contrition knife from under his pillow. The blue blade sang as he slipped it inside his clothes. "Yeah, but what about the followers we have now? They're going to die."

"They're going to die defending their faith, not spreading it. We want martyrs, not crusaders, right? That's what we both agreed to."

If this does or doesn't work, someone's going to say I messed it all up. Felix leaned to the side; just beyond the tent's entrance, he could see the star-shaped head of one of the Holy Children.

"It will look dire out there." Justine went to the tent flap and pulled it back. "But I promise you, our faith has weathered worse."

Felix nodded and stepped towards the entrance to the tent. The sunlight pouring through the opening made his eyes hurt. "Why did you make me stay in here?"

"Because once Edgar knows you're here, he's going to have to attack."

"So am I bait?"

"No." Justine sighed. "Not intentionally. Felix?"

Head swimming, stomach sick, and one foot outside the tent, he said through his teeth, "What?"

"I love you."

Felix blushed, mumbled a few vowels, and pushed past the Mother Abbess. Out of the tent, he wasn't really outside. Surrounding his tent and Justine's was a ten-foot stretch of incredibly sharp palisades. Beyond that, there were guards, and tents as far as his short self could see. He and Justine were so entrenched in the encampment that if they lost this battle, they might need a raven to deliver a letter telling them so. And the same was true for the Arachne. Here, at the heart of their god machine, everything looked fine, as everything often did. It wasn't until someone reminded him of the truth of reality that he let himself realize it wasn't.

When they realized he was there, the Holy Children guarding the high command's post turned to face him. There were forty of them. Forty grotesque, marble-like abominations draped in pale sheets with star-shaped heads. They came in all different shapes and sizes; some were skinny, some were overweight; some were muscular, while others were no more than bones. Regardless of their size, their strength, like their appearance, was unchanging. They didn't eat or drink or sleep; they watched, and they waited, and crushed things the way the stone they re-sembled crushed things—effortlessly, and without empathy. They were the Mother Abbess' angels, which meant they were now his angels, too. They were another lie he had to tell, because he was pretty sure angels weren't supposed to cry at night.

"Show him the Divide," Justine said, coming out of the tent. "I'll be there in a moment."

I love you. The confession caught up with him as Justine disappeared inside her tent. Twenty Holy Children converged on her tent, while twenty others converged on him. *Why did she say that?* The Holy Children encircled him—their star-shaped heads catching the sun and casting strange shadows onto the grass—and urged him forward. *Why didn't I say anything back?*

Justine liked to throw a lot on Felix at once, he knew that. Like the Null in his food, her telling him she loved him was a way to take his mind off what was to come. She was expecting him to fall apart, and that ticked him off. He had been through a lot this year. He wasn't a kid. Samuel Turov made sure of that. The Cult of the Worm made sure of that. And so did Justine. He could handle this. He had to, damn it.

With their pale, distended bodies, the Holy Children formed a phalanx around Felix. He sighed, held the contrition knife through his robes. This would be his second official appearance since arriving at the Divide. A lot of knees were about to be bent, and a lot of tears were about to be shed. He could already feel it, the change in the air; the rumors, the gos-sip; the whispers like lightning crackling through the camp. Sometimes, Felix wondered if there was something special about him, because he did seem to have a presence others could sense. He tried to not let it go to his head, but admittedly, the thought was pretty cool.

The wind kicked up and reminded him that winter wasn't far off. Felix hugged himself for warmth, and then let go as a tide of vapors twisted languidly into high command. He reached for them, like they were snow-flakes. Expecting them to evaporate, the vapors curled around his hands and lay in his palm like limp pieces of fabric.

"Spider web," he whispered to himself.

At first, his hand tingled, almost tickled; and then the webbing began to burn along his lifeline, like fire riding a wick. He flailed the web away and, dodging the hundreds of pieces of other loose Arachne webs, made his way for the tall tower outside high command.

Passing through the palisades, Felix found hundreds of soldiers wait-ing for him on the other side. Hundreds of faces he didn't recognize that looked back at him as if he were their closest friend. Some held swords, others *Helminth's Way* and *The Sinner and the Shadows.* Those who weren't star-struck formed a second guard in front of the Holy Children, to en-sure those who lurked farther back wouldn't try and fall into Felix's orbit. It was like this everywhere nowadays; he was a prized piece of work from god's great museum only to be seen, never to be touched. He missed the days of Pyra, of talking to the Exemplars, of meeting the common folk during his lunch hour. He had always been held above everyone else, but now they held him so high they didn't even see him for what he was anymore. They couldn't, but honestly, they probably never had.

Felix kept moving; his destination was the tower nearest high com-mand. More pieces of spider webs slipped and slithered through camp, but most didn't pay them any attention, and neither did he. The encamp-ment was a massive maze he had no interest in getting lost in.

"Over here, your Holiness," a woman called out to Felix.

Felix turned, slipped between several tents. The second guard dis-persed back to their duties. The ground sloped upward to the base of the tower; there, Commander Millicent waited, a couple of apple cores at her feet. She was in full plate armor, with the helm in her arms, against her side. Like Justine's armor, Millicent's didn't appear to be made out of any kind of metal; in a way, it almost looked like pearl. Millicent was a large woman, but even so, she wore the armor as if it weighed nothing at all; as if, like with Justine's armor, it was now a part of her.

Felix stomped up the hill and took out his contrition knife. Com-mander Millicent always gave him a compliment when he looked pre-pared, and Felix was one for compliments.

"Your Holiness." Millicent bowed; lice fell from her buzzed hair. "Do you plan on bleeding any sins today with that knife?"

"Put me in the front line," Felix joked awkwardly.

Millicent smiled her gap-toothed smile. "The Mother Abbess requested that I show you what we're up against. After that, we will move at your command."

Felix nodded, put the knife away. "Take me to the top."

He had climbed the tower before, that first night he and Justine and their huge armed-guard had ridden into the outskirts of the Divide. At that point, it had been dark, and though there were torches and fires everywhere, it didn't really give him a great sense of the encampment or the Divide itself. But now it was day, and there wasn't a cloud in the sky, and nothing could be hidden or obscured from his or heaven's eye.

Heading up the tower's winding ramp, Felix saw in quick succession the three things he would have to make a decision on.

First came the camp—that half-mile, labyrinthine sprawl of tents, stalls, and wagons; muddy pits and unfinished additions; and a constant stream of men and women, armed and armored, waiting for god to speak and give them a reason to make bloody their hands.

Then came the Divide—that three-mile-wide, sparkling sliver of... The tendons in Felix's neck went taut. He stepped back, bumping into Millicent. Reluctantly, as if she might lose her hands if she touched him, she stopped him and stood him up straight.

The Divide hadn't been much the night he rode in; just a sparkling sliver of black water, like a piece of obsidian pricking the side of the sky. Now, the Divide was more; it was everything he had feared and fought against on a daily basis, in his tent, in his dreams. The Divide wasn't black or blue, but spider web white. From the eastern shore to the edge of the western bank, innumerable webs had been spun across the river, creating crystalline bridges, glistening haunts, and nightmarish bulwarks. In between the dense lattices, boats and ships protruded, like wooden glaciers that had been caught in this winter of webs. He couldn't see any Arachne from where he stood, but he knew they were there. The countless threads shivered constantly, and occasionally, he would catch a glimpse of something—something jittery, and obscene.

Maybe it was his imagination, or maybe it was because he was about to crap his pants, but Felix swore he could hear the creatures, too; their clicking whispers, their clucking laughs. The Conscription had halted on the eastern banks because he ordered it. And now they had no choice but to turn back or go forward. The gates of heaven were different for everyone. Today, the gates of heaven were cobwebbed; and when the souls of the dead finally made it through, what would they do when they realized there was nothing there to greet them but darkness and Death?

Felix took his first breath in a long time and grabbed Millicent's forearm. *I'm the Holy Child. I'm the Holy Child.* Justine had told him once that if something was said enough, it could become true. *I'm the Holy Child. I'm the Holy Child.* He cast his gaze toward Millicent, but Millicent's rigid face looked back, neither disturbed nor concerned; she only wanted orders. Sympathy wasn't something anyone was supposed to have for one of god's chosen. They were above such things. Sympathy would've been an insult, like pointing out a flaw in perfection.

"Your Holiness?"

I'm the Holy Child. I'm the Holy Child. Felix forced himself to look at the Divide once more. How could something so dangerous be so beautiful? The countless silk strands gleamed and hummed and shed soft wisps like feathers into the air. But he knew if he sent the soldiers into that lovely hell, their flesh would burn and their lungs would seize, and the Arachne would spin them into sacs, where their bodies would be liquefied and their lives reduced to nothing more than snacks for beasts that should not be.

"We will have to fight them on our side of the river," Millicent said. "We cannot traverse the webs without heavy casualties."

If Felix listened closely enough, he could hear the god that didn't exist whispering in his ear. He knew Penance's god wasn't real; had probably known it even before Justine broke the news. But here god was again, and it said: *You can do this. She is always testing you. Be what she does not expect.*

Millicent went on. "There is a dense overgrowth of vermillion veins on the western bank. We have heard enough stories of the veins being manipulated into rudimentary attacks. The fight will be here."

She pointed ahead, where the encampment ended and the Divide began; it was a mile-wide stretch of dirt and driftwood, sand and shore. There were a few soldiers out there now, clearing the strands that had taken hold. They moved cautiously, their attention never leaving the gigantic web that still shivered not far from where they stood.

"King Edgar is mocking our reluctance to engage in combat." Millicent's armor made a squelching sound when she shifted, as if there was fluid in between each piece and plate. "He could have sent the Arachne to attack from another angle."

Felix cleared his throat and said, "Advise me, Commander."

"The Arachne are vicious. This marks the first time they have been out of the Nameless Forest since the Trauma. They are also known to be prideful. They are said to look at their webs the same way we look at holy relics and rarities from the Old World."

"We're going to have to tear this web down," Felix said. "Why build it in the middle of the battlefield?"

"To show off, and to attack with furious righteousness."

Felix squinted; it was difficult to tell if it was mist or web, but the western bank was shrouded in a ghostly veil. He could make out the vermillion veins, but it was the shapes that teemed behind them to which he drew his attention; the dark, brooding shapes that seemed to be standing there, much like the conscripted below, waiting for orders and the moment in which they would put blood in their mouths. There were thousands of them. God, there were thousands of them; and if they didn't kill every last one of them here, then it would only be a matter of time until they turned on the Heartland and killed everyone there.

"King Edgar wants them to die," Felix said.

Millicent hummed. "You see it, too?"

"They could have overtaken us from the rear. The Nameless Forest is behind us. I bet you there's... so many more Arachne still in the Forest. He's thinning their numbers."

"As long as they kill enough of our people, I do not think King Edgar will mind all that much if his spider army here is depleted." Millicent smiled and bowed again. "We are ready, Your Holiness. What does god say?"

Like a dog salivating at the sight of its meal, the gears in Felix's brain immediately went to work, pounding out phrase after phrase. What does god say? He used to think it was divine inspiration, but now he knew it was mostly just the Mother Abbess' subtle suggestions. But here he was, alone, all the right words falling into the right places; no one and nothing to stop him but himself.

He was the Holy Child, and now he had to be more. To prove everyone, including himself, wrong.

"They are aiding and abetting the Heretic of our time," Felix said, voice deep, like how it might sound when he was twenty or thirty. "They have built false idols to mock our beliefs. There is nothing god can do for them in life, so deep is their betrayal. Let us show them to death, where even the most wretched such as those before us can find forgiveness and salvation."

Felix's delivery had been so cheesy, Commander Millicent couldn't help but cover her face. "We will burn the Divide, then?"

"Yes," Felix said, still acting. "They're going to have to get used to hellfire, anyways."

Felix rushed back into his tent and collapsed upon his bed. Quickly, he turned over, hiked up his robes, and put the contrition knife to his thigh. There were all kinds of cuts there, from the Horror of the Lake and the Horror that that was Samuel Turov. Now, he had to make another. The contrition knife was for bleeding out sins, and with a few stupid sentences, he had just murdered thousands.

The tent flap flipped back and Justine came in. Immediately, the smell of lilac wafted over him. In a frenzy, he put the knife under his blankets and dropped his robe. Whether or not she had seen what he was about to do, she didn't say. Instead, she went to the side of his bed, held out her hands, and helped him to his feet.

"Commander Millicent informed me of our decision."

"I—"

"Any decision we make alone, we make together." Justine's hair touched his cheeks, tickling them. "The soldiers will begin assaulting the Divide in five hours."

Felix dropped Justine's hands. He needed to learn how to stand on his own.

"It's soon, I know," she said, "but it's necessary. Against such a threat, Felix, we must be proactive."

"Who is leading the spider army?" Felix asked.

"Lotus, King Edgar's warden of the Nameless Forest. I don't expect we will see her. She means too much to him." The White Worm of the Earth fingered the silver, white-gemmed necklace around her neck. "I have something for you. My most precious gift. Walk with me, Felix, and I will share it with you."

They emerged from the tent, the forty Holy Children quick to swarm around Justine and Felix. The Mother Abbess whispered something in a language he couldn't understand, and all at once, the statues dispersed back to their posts around high command.

"I know you feel bad about making the decision to attack."

Justine led them out of high command. Like ants at a picnic, the soldiers outside the palisade quickly formed a guard around her and Felix. So eager to please the Mother Abbess and the Holy Child, they didn't realize at first that Justine was shooing them off. And when they did, the fifty or so soldiers marched back to their tents and duties, disappointed and defeated.

Past the tower and the second palisade of what Felix's mind kept calling low command (high, low; whatever), he and Justine were now on the edge of the encampment proper. To ride through it at night or to see it from the tower was one thing, but to be in the thick of it was something else entirely. Penance had been here for weeks, and already they had made their place on the Divide something that, with a little redecorating, could have easily passed for a brand-new city entirely. People, food, animals; any kind of vehicle, and every kind of trade; there weren't just tents, but full-blown homes—cabins and decent looking shacks. The Lillians and their followers had been known to settle everywhere they went—always making homes in the most inhospitable places; after so many years later, it seemed their descendants hadn't lost that desperate trait.

"Whether they die here fighting, or at home cowering," Justine said, nodding at every dirty face that turned towards her, "they're going to die fighting Eldrus. It's better they should go on their own terms."

Felix wished he had the contrition knife, or even the Holy Children, because the soldiers around them were starting to look suspicious. He became aware of how muddy the ground was, and how hard it would be to run away. He started to wonder if their distant eyes had dimmed because they were thinking about hurting him. They were surrounded by people who loved them, sure, but did they all really love them? Justine had said it herself: there was no such thing as universal love. Some just hate for the sake of it.

"We don't need guards," Justine said, keeping on, driving them through the encampment, bringing them closer and closer to the Divide. "Only each other. You are the Word of god. I am god's sword and shield."

Felix left a gap between him and Justine. "Where're we going?"

"To the stage," she said with dramatic flair.

Felix smiled, waved; waved and smiled. The soldiers were going down to their knees; their praise was catching like cold; their faith intensely contagious. They had to weave through the encampment, because their followers were as rocks in their path—rigid and unmovable. Felix felt some tension leave his body. No one wanted to hurt him here, and those who did would be committing suicide if they tried.

"When we're finished with Eldrus, people will be this way every-where," Justine said. "I was wrong to isolate the Holy Order in Penance all these years. It made us strong, but it turned our religion into a matter of convenience. There was nothing better to believe, and there was no reason to stop believing. When we're finished, we will return to the Heartland, to Cathedra, and be where we should have always been."

Felix didn't say anything, but what was there he could say? The Mother Abbess had a very clear plan of what she wanted for the Holy Order, and he agreed with every step of it. The conscripted prostrated around them were happy, fulfilled; they believed in god so deeply they would die for it. But at the same time, he could taste the sin in the air, smell it on their breaths. The Exemplars always told Felix that isolation had made the Holy Order humble, and that the Lillians' quest for expansion was what had made them so unbearably entitled.

The Holy Child stopped. Slowly, he spun in place, surveying those who had fallen to the ground, most of whom would need some help getting up, because of how heavy their gear was. Those who hadn't dropped to their knees quickly did so when his eyes met theirs. A lot of these men and women were about to die, and a lot of them were here for the glory of conquest and the sin of excess. King Edgar had sent the Arachne here to fight and to thin their numbers, so that they could be more easily controlled. And Justine... Justine had deliberately called forth and conscripted the garbage of the Holy Land. Was she intending to do the same?

Justine touched Felix's shoulder and pointed ahead to a rounded hill where a platform had been built. There wasn't much to it but six pillars, one podium, and a large banner bearing the icon of the Holy Order of Penance.

"A stage," Felix said, shaking his head, finally having gotten her mean-ing. "You want me to give a speech."

"Just like in Pyra."

Felix grabbed the sealing stone around his neck.

Justine noticed, and her cheek quivered. She still had a hole in her chest from where she had once stored the sealing stone. It would never heal, and it would always hurt.

Felix cringed as he asked, "You said you... had a gift?"

Justine continued on, and Felix followed after. Their path was clear to the stage, and looking back, Felix saw that already hundreds of soldiers were gathering. The Holy Child was to give a speech, either now or in the next few hours; no one here was going to miss a word of it.

At the top of the hill, at the edge of the stage, the encampment below them, the Divide before them—webbed and writhing—Justine turned to Felix and told him this: "Every Worm of the Earth is capable of granting a boon. We do not grant a boon lightly, as it will often reveal us for what we are. Those who identify us as Worms will then destroy us, or enslave us. Either way, we will sleep, and many, many will die. I am different. You are, too. I trust you. I have given you my undoing—" she nodded at the sealing stone, "—and now I want to give you my power."

Felix made sure they were alone. With thousands of eyes upon them from the encampment below, he felt as if he were naked before the world, with every secret he had ever held on display. If anyone had heard a word of what she was saying…

"I have not forgotten your friend Vrana."

Felix gasped, because he had. Somehow, somewhere on the journey to the Divide, he had given up on helping her. Most of the time, he thought of Audra—Audra, and the silly, stupid, love he had for her. God, where was she? Was she okay? Was Vrana okay? Thousands in his care not far from where he stood, and all he could think about were the enemies he hardly knew.

"The Cult of the Worm has spread into the Holy Land. We have lost soldiers to the Cult, too. They defected and disappeared days ago. Word is that they are headed for Angheuawl."

Felix shook his head. "What is that?"

"Mining village in the foothills of Kistvaen. It's not on any map, but many say the lakes are absolutely stunning there." She sighed. "We can go to Gallows for the Skeleton, or we can go to Angheuawl. We'll send our soldiers to whatever you do not choose. If your friend is involved with the Cult, it's likely their base of operations is there. I keep my promises, Felix. I know that I am not human, but I am trying my best to be."

Jaw quivering, tearing up for no good, goddamn reason, Felix whispered, "Why?"

"For you. Everything I do, you must question because of what I am. I'm glad that you do. I want to be better. I want this to work. I love you. I hope that one day, you will love me, too, and not because you're scared of what may happen if you do not."

Felix swallowed all the spit in his mouth and nodded. He wiped his nose and eyes and straightened his back and became the Holy Child he was supposed to be. "What's the boon?"

"Language is the carrier of religion. Through language, we spread our beliefs, creating our doctrines, and build our rituals. Some would call it a virus, but I am not the Green Worm, so I cannot say for sure.

"Through the power of language, I have made this Holy Order. Through inspiration and faith, I have sustained it for hundreds of years. When you speak to people, Felix, they listen to you. They trust you, because you are giving them the word of god. They don't realize that this isn't the real word, because they never truly heard god speak.

"After the Trauma, I spoke as a god would speak. I put fires in the hearts of those who had gone cold. When you speak as a god, you can inspire someone to fight harder than they ever thought possible. King Edgar puts the seeds of heaven in his followers, but I say we should put the seed of heaven on their tongues, so that they can share it with everyone else, not take it to their graves.

"If I give you my boon, when you speak to these people, they will be in your command completely. They will do whatever it takes to further our cause. To defeat an enemy like the Arachne, this is the only way. And if we succeed… if we succeed, then no one will able to doubt that you speak for god, and that god works through us."

"You… want me to control their minds?" Felix said in disbelief.

"I want you to inspire them. To me, language is more of a drug than a virus; your words will only amplify what is already there. Those who want to fight will fight, but those who don't have it in them, they will stay behind. It's not mind control. I am not a Crossbreed."

Felix looked up at Justine, the Mother Abbess, the White Worm of the Earth, and searched for signs of a lie. But her face was one of many; there were more behind it, and each one had probably had this same conversation with the Holy Child of the time. She said she loved him, and he did love her; he really did. He could kill her at any minute, betray her at any second. She had spared Audra, Deimos, and Lucan, and she had given him free reign of the Holy Order. He did question every decision she made, but what else could they do? It was war, and this was not a religion of peace.

"I don't know what to say," Felix whispered, tufts of spider web blowing off the Divide, coating the encampment like snow. "To them, I mean."

"Yes, you do. You speak for god. You speak for us." Justine ushered Felix behind the banner strung up between the pillars and asked, "Will you accept my boon?"

Felix looked back. Most of the conscription was in attendance, from the foot of hill, all the way back to high command. No one spoke, let alone moved. They were bound to him, tethered like prisoners to the chain of their faith. In a way, they had always been, but now he could see it, and now it truly mattered.

"Will we lose if I don't accept your boon?" he asked.

"We may not," Justine said. She put her finger in her mouth. "But we will not win miraculously. King Edgar has worked many miracles. It would be nice if we could, too."

"Will it… be a good thing if a lot of our people die?"

Justine laughed, said, "That's for them to decide," and shoved her hand down her throat.

The White Worm of the Earth retched, and then yanked her hand out of her mouth. With it came a long piece of pearl-colored muscle that frayed at the end into tens of small, waving tendrils. At the end of each tendril were tiny balls of light, like those of an angler fish.

"Oh my god." Felix dug his nails into the heels of his palms. If he hesitated, he wouldn't do it. If he hesitated, someone might see something.

"What is a Worm?" he asked, stepping up to her.

"The soil it sleeps in," she said, her voice in his head.

I'm the Holy Child. I'm the Holy Child. And she loves me.

Felix closed his eyes, opened his mouth, and tipped his head back, and let the White Worm fill him with her blessed light.

CHAPTER XVI

R'lyeh's heart nearly stopped as a loud voice exploded in her ears from Penance's encampment. The voice broke across the land like thunder, and sank into her mind like rain. She looked to Elizabeth and Miranda; by their surprise she saw that they heard it, too. It was the voice of a child, and it was the most beautiful voice she had ever heard. It made her weep. Without realizing it, she started drifting forward to hear it more clearly.

"I'm the Holy Child," the voice started; it was so great, and yet at the same time, like a whisper in her ear. **"I'm the Holy Child. I have a message for you from god."**

Elizabeth screwed up her face. "What the hell is this?"

"That's some straight sorcery right there," Miranda said. She pointed to the eastern bank of the Divide. "We have the worst timing."

All along the eastern bank were several trebuchets that hadn't been there the last time the Beauties passed through. Beside each of them were numerous barrels and pots; and beside them were numerous soldiers with fat, blazing torches. Not far off from there, the web across the Divide was miles long; its strands blew in blizzards across the encampment. R'lyeh couldn't blame the soldiers; if she were them, she'd want to burn the damn thing down, too.

"God has spoken to me," the Holy Child said, **"and god has shown me what must be done. God has sacrificed much for us. Now, we must make a great sacrifice ourselves."**

R'lyeh, Elizabeth, and Miranda broke into a sprint. This side of the Divide was uneven—a lot of dunes, copses, gargling gulches. As long as

Penance kept their eyes on the Holy Child, they just might not see them coming.

"We have always been a religion of tolerance and acceptance. But what god cannot tolerate and accept any longer is the cancer destroying our faith and our land. This is not about the fate of the Holy Order, but the fate of the World."

Wait. R'lyeh stopped, the encampment a mile and a half away. She looked at the Deadly Beauties and said, "What the hell are we doing?"

"Going straight through, yeah?" Elizabeth went on, up a dune, and into a dense copse. "See them?"

R'lyeh followed after and muscled past Elizabeth. She jumped for the lowest bough and hoisted herself onto it.

"The Disciples of the Deep mean to eliminate anyone who disagrees with them. They mean to shape this world to their liking, regardless of the Trauma it will cause."

R'lyeh glanced down; Miranda was standing at the foot of the tree, holding her paralyzed arm, rubbing her wrist where her hand had been. She looked lost, without purpose; much like R'lyeh used to look, before the Marrow Cabal took her in.

"You need only look across the Divide to see what ruin Eldrus' 'God' will sow. It has filled their army with demons, and the King's head with devils. See the western bank and the vermillion veins that choke it! The Disciples claim these growths are the gateways to heaven. But why do they kill more than they save?"

In the tree, R'lyeh could see that the entire encampment was at attention; not one of the thousands of bodies that ran up and down its length dared to turn away. Everyone appeared as if they had stopped in the middle of something. Some were half-dressed, others completely naked; a few were still wrestling with carcasses they had brought in from the morning hunt. Most were stroking their swords. There seemed to be a low drone of gibbering in the air. Everyone was speaking in their own private language, or doing their damndest to learn God's.

Not since the pit of Geharra and the Crossbreed had R'lyeh seen such utter devotion. These soldiers weren't paralyzed by the presence of their lord's speaker; they were empowered; they were becoming.

"He's amazing," Miranda mumbled beneath the bough.

R'lyeh turned her gaze towards the stage from which the Holy Child preached. She had known he was young, but holy shit was he young. Like her age. He was small, too. Not frail, just not very intimidating. And yet here he was, writing what would certainly be history tomorrow. R'lyeh felt a pang of jealousy, and, begrudgingly, respect.

"Let us not forget that it was from the Nameless Forest King Edgar emerged years ago," the Holy Child boomed, his words literally rippling the air. **"And since then, what deeds has he done? He murdered his family, tried to take over the Heartland; he murdered Geharra and summoned the Red Worm. He has now overrun the Heartland with his vermillion veins, and has convinced his followers to consume the debilitating growths. This is not a religion he is building, but a weapon. It is a weapon meant to strike us down, so that he may take what he wants freely and shape this world as he sees fit. Does King Edgar sound like a man to anyone, anymore?"** The Holy Child shook his head, touching his Corruption while he did so. **"He is a demon, and he belongs in hell. Let us send him there, before he brings it here for all of us to burn in."**

Backed up like a dam, those gathered finally burst into a deafening applause.

Shit, R'lyeh thought, squeezing her eyes shut. A sudden sensation, sour and prickling, had pressed itself against her, into her. "Guys, do you feel—"

"She's beautiful, yeah?" Elizabeth said, tugging on R'lyeh's heel. "Statues don't do her justice."

R'lyeh shook off the strange sensation; it made her feel fuzzy inside, like a slick sickness telling her everything she wanted to hear. *Beautiful?* Who were they talking about? Again, she looked to the stage and—*Holy shit*—there she was, the Mother Abbess, standing beside the Holy Child. Had she been there the whole time?

"If the Disciples of the Deep are right about anything—"

The Mother Abbess of the Holy Order of Penance was beautiful. She was slender, and her skin was almost ephemeral; her hair was the color of pearl, and though there was no wind, each strand moved, as if it had a life of its own. There was an aura about her, too, like the ghost of something.

"—it is that we all carry heaven inside of us."

Now, the ghost was haunting the Holy Child, seeping its languid, multitudinous limbs through his back. A spasm rocked the boy's body—the power of this holy spirit apparently almost too much for the kid to handle.

"We have carried it with us from birth," the Holy Child said, recovering. **"God gave it to us to nurture, and to share. Heaven is inside all of us, at all times. Can you feel it? Touch your chest. Can you feel it inside you, blooming like a flower?"**

The Holy Child and the Mother Abbess touched their chests. Throughout the encampment, the soldiers did the same. Voices amongst those gathered began to grow louder; where once the people had stayed rooted, they now shifted, like slobbering beasts left too long in their pens. They stopped touching their chests and started beating them; like phlegm, heaven was apparently something that needed to be knocked loose.

Eyes wide, heart about to rip in half, R'lyeh looked down and said to Elizabeth, "What the hell is going on?"

Elizabeth ignored her and clambered into the tree and onto a different bough. "Get up here," she hollered at Miranda, but Miranda wouldn't budge; she seemed to be listening to something, the same way the Skeleton would listen to the Black Hour.

And when R'lyeh went to say something about this, she heard something, too: a cool, soothing voice that smelled of lilac and wine, speaking to her from all the dark corners of her skull.

Little girl, you hate the Holy Order of Penance for what it has done to Alluvia, but your hate is misplaced. Fight with us, so that you may truly strike back at the man responsible for your mother's and father's deaths.

R'lyeh's legs locked and she fell backward off the tree, babbling, "What the fuck, what the fuck, what the fuck?" She slammed into the ground, her mask cushioning the impact. She stumbled to her feet. Pulling out one of the Cruel Mother's talons, she spun around, swiping at the air.

Elizabeth dropped out of the tree, landing on her hands and knees rather than her head, like R'lyeh had done. A snake of spit on her lip, she groaned and played with her nose piercing.

Little girl, you hate the Holy Order of Penance—

"Ah!" R'lyeh pounded the side of her head. "Do you hear it?" she asked, bending over Elizabeth.

"Yeah, yeah." Elizabeth struggled to stand. "Straight sorcery, like Miranda... Hey, Miranda!"

Using her sword like a walking stick, Miranda had stab, stab, stabbed her way out of the copse and down the dune.

"Hey, lady, stop!" Elizabeth said, taking off after her.

Little girl, you hate the Holy Order—

How is he doing that? R'lyeh grabbed her mask and chased Elizabeth. *How the hell does he know that about me?*

Elizabeth caught Miranda before she made it down the dune. Grabbing her by her bum arm, she screamed in her face, "Stop! Those two idiots are spellweaving."

Miranda jerked away. Misty-eyed, she thrust her sword at Elizabeth, just barely missing her. "He knows," she said, nodding. And then she turned away and kept on towards the encampment.

Feeling vulnerable in the open, R'lyeh backed up the dune. "What did you hear?"

Elizabeth, caught between R'lyeh and Miranda, growled. "The Holy Child. He said—" she bit her lip piercing, "—god still remembers my prayers from the Orphanage. He said… Mom and Dad are waiting. It's fucking bullshit. Miranda!"

"I heard him tell me I could help fight those who killed my village," R'lyeh said. The pit of Geharra opened in her mind; with a lethal dose of hate, she promptly sealed it shut again. "What is she doing? I thought Miranda hated religion."

"No, she just pretends. Miranda, stop!" Elizabeth ran her hands over her dirty face. "She's a few bad habits away from a habit and becoming a full-blown nun. R'lyeh, please, help me bring her back."

As R'lyeh started back down the dune, the Holy Child bellowed from the stage, **"King Edgar has to grow his heaven to convince his followers it is there. You are heaven, each and every one of you. Go as god would go, and see the sinners through your gates!"**

A violent tremor shot through the webs over the Divide, causing them to buck and billow. Great, silken bridges and glassy, glittering towers caved-in and collapsed. Tangled highways bulged; womb-like funnels stretched. The waters of the Divide, agitated by the unseen agitation, rippled and churned, and flooded the lower levels of the crystalline city. The boats and ships still caught in the suffocating storm groaned and capsized; as they took on water, they let loose the desiccated bodies of sailors and traders from their impacted bowels.

The turmoil went even farther back than the river itself, though; on the western bank, in the fog and the vermillion jungles, trees were felled and blood-curdling shrieks were let loose, and things were gathering into masses, great and dark.

The spiders were coming.

"I saw stables at the back of the camp," Elizabeth said. "Miranda, we're going to grab some horses and go home. No one will notice us, I swear."

"I have to fight for my home," Miranda said. "I have to, or it won't be here tomorrow."

"No, listen, damn it," R'lyeh said, tugging on Miranda's shirt. "That woman and kid are spellweavers. This is just a—"

"They're not spellweavers," Elizabeth said, tapping R'lyeh's shoulder. "Oh, fuck. Spellweavers can't do that, can they?"

R'lyeh turned around, and almost swallowed her tongue. In a matter of seconds, it looked as if a windstorm had formed over Penance's encampment. The clouds had merged into a filthy sludge of whites and grays, like some kind of wintry runoff. Pouring from the clouds were what appeared to be tornados; numbering in the hundreds, or maybe even thousands, the segmented columns danced violently around the encampment. R'lyeh strained her eyes for signs of damage and debris, but no matter where the tornados went, everything was left untouched, as if they weren't truly there—as if they weren't tornados at all. Because they didn't really look like tornados, not with how they were segmented and how they moved; they looked more like…

Worms.

The Mother Abbess and the Holy Child were no longer on the stage, but floating above it; their heads were back and their arms outstretched. From their mouths and fingertips flowed phantasmal strands to which it appeared all the larger tornados were connected. Below them, the soldiers screamed, tore at their armor, and slammed into one another, all the while professing their faith at the top of their heaving lungs.

"For those of you who feel the presence of god in your hearts," the Holy Child said, jellyfish-like chandeliers of light emerging from his chest and into the sky, **"rejoice! For if you fight today, you and god shall be equals tomorrow."**

Wood bent. Rope snapped. There was a shout followed by raucous laughter. R'lyeh tore her gaze away from the Holy Child and saw the western bank aflame. In rapid succession, the trebuchets were loaded with pots and vases and great, leaking barrels. Worm tornados exploded out of the breasts of the soldiers there, but they went about their business all the same.

Someone shouted, "Fire!"

One by one, the trebuchets were let loose. The huge, wooden arms snapped forward, slinging their sinister payload into the web over the Divide. R'lyeh watched the pots, vases, and barrels tumble through the air, and instinctively took a step back when they started their descent onto the river.

At first, there was nothing. No explosion, no eruption of flames. The projectiles ripped through the web with their speed and weight. They broke apart somewhere inside the sparkling nest. R'lyeh reached for Elizabeth, but her grasp fell short as small, angry pricks of light began to blink from inside the web.

Elizabeth reached for R'lyeh and shouted in her face, "Run!"

At first, there was nothing. Then hell. A great, searing explosion erupted at the heart of the web and fire flooded the silken deathtrap. Like the creatures would that had created it, the web curled and hissed in the heat, losing its size and shape, meter by meter, second after second. Scorched became the highways, and immolated the towers. The silken bridges snapped; their flaming suspensions lashed across the Divide and set fire to the trees on western shore. For something so feared, to R'lyeh, it was almost a shame to see it so quickly undone.

The Arachne started pouring through the smoke.

The sentiment turned to salt in her throat.

The Arachne came in vast, writhing swarms—a spider-slide of legs and mandibles surrounded by a storm of silk and hair. The humanoid beasts broke through the vermillion roots on the western bank; by the thousands, they went willingly onto the Divide and the burning web. Meter by meter, second after second, the hissing battalions drew closer and closer, creating webs where there were none, or skirting across the water altogether. So dense were the arachnid packs that R'lyeh couldn't tell where most creatures began or ended; they were death and all its textures; a swathe cut from the great killer Itself laid out along the land, to remind those who might've forgotten the only afterlife that mattered.

R'lyeh was somewhere in the tunnels of Geharra when she turned on her heels and fled for Penance's encampment. She felt Miranda and Elizabeth behind her. That was good enough for now. Eyes watering, throat tightening, R'lyeh couldn't feel much but everything all at once. *I'm going to die,* she told herself, tearing towards the worm-ridden camp of her enemy. *I'm going to die. This is how I die.* She laughed, thought of when the soldiers had drugged her village, and laughed some more. She was seeking salvation from her slaughterers. Even at thirteen, the irony was not lost on her.

Every step she took brought her closer to the encampment and the heavily manned towers that surrounded it. All it would take was one order or one shaky hand to let loose a wave of arrows to pin her and her friends to the ground. Common sense should've told her to veer away, back to the dunes where she could've disappeared and waited this out. But she ate poison for fun, ran with murderers for friends; home was a lake of blood, and her boss was a Skeleton who sent her on suicide missions. The only common sense she had nowadays was the common sense that told her she needed more of it.

R'lyeh gulped as worm spirals swept back and forth through the encampment. It was so hazy inside that she really couldn't see the soldiers anymore, but that wasn't a problem; her imagination was more than happy to fill in the scene. Geharra was the weed that infested every piece of her and her world. If she dug long enough, she would always find it, destroying everything from the inside, turning everything into something it was never meant to be.

Anxiety coursed through her body, leaving itching rashes where it went. R'lyeh, running as hard as she could, reached into her pockets for poisons, but there were none there. She couldn't break down, not again, not like she had in Rime. If she stopped, she'd be stopped for good. She was a Deadly Beauty, and Deadly Beauties weren't weak; they weren't soft. Elizabeth never crumbled, and neither did Miranda, even though she kept falling apart. She was one of them now, not a Night Terror. So, taking a deep breath, she slowed down and, for the first time since Alluvia, let herself look back.

The Arachne had not only crossed the burning Divide, but overrun the eastern bank. The trebuchets and the soldiers who manned them had been swallowed by the spider swell. The ground was gone, replaced by the skittering carpet that choked it. The horizon had been transformed into dark, jagged mounds that moved with horrifying synchronicity. And the mounds weren't stopping. The great, clicking, spitting brood were headed straight for the encampment, and she, R'lyeh, the dumbass who had decided to stop, to look back, to face her fears for once, was right in the middle of the two.

Elizabeth, towing Miranda, grabbed R'lyeh by the front of her armor and screamed in her face, "Get out of the way!"

She snapped out of it. "Get out? What the hell—"

R'lyeh went sideways as a soldier slammed into her from behind. Elizabeth balanced her. As she pulled herself together, she saw more soldiers running past them, breaking around them like waves around rocks. It was Penance's army, all of them. They were tearing out of the encampment with wild abandon, their spears held high, their tongues wagging psychotically in their mouths. Gaseous, worm-shaped columns whipped across the frontline, giving those they passed through an angelic glow.

"Don't let go of me," R'lyeh cried.

Elizabeth shook her head. She wheeled Miranda in front of her and took R'lyeh's hand. Groups of soldiers marched past in an endless parade and parody of religious zealotry. The ground thrummed with movement. In the thick of the attack, this side of the Divide had grown hotter; all the hateful, faithful mouth-breathers having increased the temperature substantially.

Running through the army was like running through quicksand: despite how much they moved, it never seemed like they could get anywhere. An arm or a shoulder or an unbreaking wall of heavy, sweaty men kept throwing them off course. The worm-like dust devils weren't any help, either. They spun sporadically through the ranks by the tens and twenties, infecting everything they touched with their rabid blessings.

R'lyeh squeezed Elizabeth's hand hard enough to break it, and then squeezed harder. *It's almost over, it's almost over,* she told herself. But, Holy Child, was it? The encampment was drawing nearer, but the flood of soldiers wouldn't relent. She knew what thousands of people looked like—she'd seen it before, in Geharra—but this was somehow different. These people weren't being controlled. They knew exactly what they were doing.

"Almost there!" Elizabeth yelled back.

Miranda jerked away from Elizabeth, but she quickly caught her. "I have to fight," Miranda said, beating her nub for a hand against Elizabeth's side. "It's all I can do."

Behind R'lyeh, there was a massive crash of wood and steel that sounded like a building collapsing. Penance's soldiers had already been screaming, but now they were screaming in pain and unbelievable agony. She told herself not to look back, but being a girl of little self-restraint, she did it anyway.

The frontline and the Arachne had met a thousand yards back, and there everything was now red. The Arachne were crushing themselves to get to the soldiers. Severed arms and legs and crushed heads were being hurled at the living, to blind them with the blood of the dead. When the humanoid horrors weren't eviscerating the soldiers with their teeth and claws, they were pulling them into eight-legged embraces, where they would either break the soldiers' backs, or spit webs into their eyes, until the strands melted their faces into pink, bubbling cavities.

But for all their savage strength, the Arachne couldn't match the soldiers' sheer will. Dismembered or damn near dead, the men and women of Penance broke themselves by the tens and twenties on the Arachne menace. They hacked the spiders to bits, and gored them straight through. And those that glowed with the Worm's blessing were absolutely brutal in their assault. They tore through the Arachne with adrenaline-soaked strength. Spiders were cleaved in two, others stabbed into sputtering hunks of hairy, wheezing mush.

More soldiers surged past R'lyeh, while more Arachne swarmed in from the Divide. Every clash between the two came with a clap of blood that drenched the armies in every direction. She didn't need to be a military strategist to know which side would win; they matched each other in almost every way. By the end of this, there would be nothing left—just blood and guts and Nature doing its best to make the most out of all that fresh compost.

R'lyeh, Elizabeth, and Miranda found a breach in the warring bodies and slipped through it. They wound through the thinning ranks, until they were right outside the encampment. Overhead, flaming arrows ripped through the air from the sentry towers, but still no one noticed these three out of place women.

Breathing fire out of her burning lungs, R'lyeh dropped Elizabeth's hand and hurried past the wall and into the encampment. The ground was a muddy ruin from all the marching feet trampling it. She found the nearest tent, ripped off her octopus mask, and fell against the fabric. She wheezed; every breath she took was a fight, for the air, still hazy and thick here, seemed reluctant to give itself to her.

"Just… across from here," Elizabeth said, sweat pouring off her face. "The horses."

Miranda kept trying to wiggle out of Elizabeth's hold. Crying out to the soldiers, she said, "Please, sir. Take me with you. She won't let me fight!"

For the first time since all this started, one of the soldiers stopped and paid them some attention. He raised his spear, chewed on his lip.

"Fighting for god is the greatest thing a woman can do in this world!"

the soldier said, pressing forward, the tip of his spear trained on Elizabeth. "If you feel heaven in your heart, sister, you must share it!"

Miranda nodded, said, "Yes, yes, yes!" and started pounding her heart with her amputated wrist.

"Should I kill these heretics?" the soldier asked.

"Yes," Miranda said, while at the same time shaking her head. "Yes."

Elizabeth drew her sword and thrust the soldier's spear away. "Don't."

R'lyeh felt a change in the wind. Looking into the thick of the encampment, she saw several worm-like dust devils whirling through the remaining soldiers, jumping between them like bolts of lightning. But that wasn't it. There was something else.

At first, she saw them as shadows on the ground, moving across the encampment like clouds across the sun. They reminded her of the shadow Audra had conjured, the one she and Deimos rode out of Rime on. As Elizabeth cussed at Miranda and hacked at the soldier, R'lyeh went to one knee and touched the ground where the shadows moved.

Just shadows, she thought, realizing how stupid she was being. She struggled to her feet—that small moment of rest a near-death sentence—and then looked up to the sky. *Oh, crap.*

In the gray, cancerous murk above Penance's encampment, hundreds of large carrion birds wheeled; oily, black feathers falling from their gore-caked wings. Out of their torsos, long, intestine-like appendages whipped back and forth, showering from their mouths those below in gory regurgitations.

"What the hell are those?" R'lyeh shouted.

Elizabeth batted the soldier's spear again once more and pressed her advantage. She put him in a headlock and ran her sword through his stomach, back and forth, back and forth, until his godly fuel gave out and he died in her arms.

Letting the soldier fall to the ground, Elizabeth said, "They're from the Nameless Forest. Edgar's aerial force." She stared at the beasts a little while longer, memories clearly overtaking her, and grabbed Miranda again. "We have to hurry."

R'lyeh nodded and followed after Elizabeth and Miranda. As they worked their way through the camp towards the stables, the carrion birds drilled downwards through the air. One by one, they slammed into the soldiers around the encampment, tearing out their throats, or goring their chests. Bodies fell around them from those soldiers who had been taken off the ground and dropped to their deaths.

R'lyeh threw her mask back on, took out the Cruel Mother's talons, and readied herself for a fight she was certain would come. It had been too long since she had killed something. If not now, then never, and never didn't sit right with her, no matter what Elizabeth and Miranda thought.

Nearly at the stables, R'lyeh dug her heels into the ground and threw herself behind a tent. Elizabeth, dragging Miranda down with her, did the same. Between here and the horses were a bunch of weird looking statues. Twenty or more. They had cloaks on and star-shaped heads and—*what the hell?*—they were moving.

"He's here," Miranda said, giddily.

Elizabeth punched Miranda in the chest. "Shut up, goddamn it. I know it's not you, yeah? But shut up."

Miranda snarled. "I heard his voice. I hear him now."

"You hear a Worm. You hear only what you want to—"

Miranda shrieked and kicked Elizabeth's side. She hurried to her feet, kicked away Elizabeth's outstretched hand, and ran past R'lyeh.

"Miranda, stop, you idiot!" R'lyeh cried, catching the back of Miranda's shirt, but losing her hold on it. "Stop!"

Dead arm swinging limply at her side, Miranda approached the statues. "Your Holiness, I can hear you inside there. I'm sorry I didn't fight. I'm sorry I never fought."

The statues stopped their procession and turned to face Miranda. Cringing, R'lyeh lifted her head from the ground and saw that she was right. There was someone behind the statues, hidden there, protected there by this reanimated guard.

Miranda dropped to her knees, crying. "I turned away for so long. Let me see you, so that I know god isn't upset with me."

Someone murmured inside the statues.

R'lyeh crawled forward. Through the gaps between the stone creatures, she could see the outline of someone small. And beside it, something large, except it couldn't stop moving. *Is that the Holy Child?* She risked getting closer. Flashes of tentacles moved around the smaller person inside the guard, like a shield. *Is that the Mother Abbess?*

"Please," Miranda begged. She lifted her left arm like a sacrificial offering. "I've lost so much. I keep losing so much. Won't god make me whole?"

"Move aside," a boy, the Holy Child, said from within the statues.

"Your Holiness, you must not," a woman said inside the guard.

"I must. Let me do this one kind thing here."

The statues began to move away from another; inch by inch, they gave R'lyeh a precious glimpse into the heart of the guard. Through a sliver, she saw the Holy Child standing there, in dirty robes, his right arm, Corrupted like everyone else's, on full display.

"Oh, thank you, thank you," Miranda said. She started to come to her feet.

And then the statues stepped even farther apart and R'lyeh began to see a portion of the woman standing beside the Holy Child. First her foot, then her leg, and then a maelstrom of tentacles, like a ball of snakes, and—

A carrion bird screeched through the air, sank its enormous talons into Miranda's shoulders, and tore her off the ground.

R'lyeh shoved her forearm into her mouth, to stop her from screaming and giving herself away.

Elizabeth didn't care, however. She vaulted over R'lyeh. The statues surrounding the Holy Child and the Mother Abbess closed their ranks and quickly shuffled them away, deeper into the encampment.

"No, no!" Elizabeth swung her sword at the carrion bird, but it was too high to reach. "R'lyeh," she cried. "Please, oh god, please help me!"

R'lyeh jumped to her feet. Daggers out, she quickly scanned the area for something to stand on, or something to fucking throw. Anything to—

The carrion bird lifted Miranda higher. Screaming out buckets of blood, she bucked in the beast's grasp, but it would not break. Intestinal appendages began to uncurl out of the bird's torso. At the end of the appendage, a tooth-lined mouth opened, yawned, and—

"Miranda!" Elizabeth shouted.

—it bore down on Miranda's head, covering it completely. The torso mouth forced itself down to her throat, and started chewing and sucking on her flesh and bones. While it did this, the carrion bird ripped its talons out of her shoulders. It clamped one claw into her breast and another into her thigh.

"Stop!" R'lyeh could hardly make out what was going on, she was crying so hard. "Stop!" She took both the Cruel Mother's talons and hurled them at the carrion bird. It was one of the last things she had of Vrana's, but if it helped… if it helped…

It didn't. The Cruel Mother's talons sailed right past the carrion bird and disappeared somewhere among the tents beyond. The giant bird cackled, as if amused, and tore Miranda apart, ripping her sloppily from her hip to her armpit. A hot, steaming deluge of blood and organs slipped out of Miranda's two halves and splatted against the ground. The carrion bird twisted off her head, sucked it down with the torso mouth, and dropped the rest of Miranda in front of Elizabeth and R'lyeh.

The carrion bird, fat on the flesh and blood of their friend, stretched its wings and took off toward the battlefield.

"Elizabeth," R'lyeh said, completely numb inside. "Elizabeth." She started towards the last, true Deadly Beauty. "Eliza—"

"Get the horses." Elizabeth shoved R'lyeh away and pointed to the stables and horses sixty feet away.

"Eliza—"

Elizabeth dropped her sword as more carrion birds passed by over-head. She found Miranda's still-sputtering bottom half and grabbed it by the ankles. "Get the horses," she said, rolling up Miranda's pant legs. "Get them."

R'lyeh nodded and took off towards the stables. There were three horses left there, and she took all three of them with her, just so one wouldn't have to be alone. It was easier to do than to think, so she led the three back to Elizabeth and thought nothing of how much of a target she must look to the carrion birds above. Maybe it was the numbness talking, but at this moment, with Miranda's blood in her hair, she didn't really care what happened next.

"Elizabeth," she said again, the spooked horses trailing behind her. Any other horse, any other time, would've run. But they wanted to be out of here just as badly as they did. "Elizabeth, I got them."

Elizabeth nodded. She was kneeling down beside Miranda's bottom half, her hand around the ankle. In her other hand, Elizabeth was holding an ankle bracelet made out of seashells. She closed her eyes, whispered something under her breath, and stood.

"Three horses," R'lyeh said. "Miranda can ride back with us."

Eyes still shut, tears seeping out from underneath them, Elizabeth smiled and said, "She can't."

"She will, I'm sure." R'lyeh bit her lip. "Was that bracelet hers?"

"We all had one." Elizabeth opened her eyes, sniffled her nose. "Now, I have them all."

R'lyeh and Elizabeth mounted the horses and kicked them until the beasts wouldn't go any faster. They tore through the encampment. In the sky, more carrion birds had arrived to assault Penance's army. As they reached the southern end of the encampment, the small bands of Arachne clambered in through the northern side.

R'lyeh didn't bother looking back by the time they hit the woods outside the Divide. The only way this could end well for everyone was if both sides died. And if she looked back, she knew she would be disappointed in what she saw. Total annihilation was the only remedy for her sickened soul.

They rode for days back to Gallows. During that time, neither R'lyeh, nor Elizabeth said a word to one another. There was nothing that needed to be said. They had ridden to Rime, failed their mission, and lost a friend on the way back. What had they learned that a few scouts and messenger birds couldn't have? How cruel the world was? How badly their hearts could ache? In all this time, they had done nothing but bear witness to atrocities. Maybe for a man who was only bones there was something to learn from all that suffering, but not for R'lyeh, and certainly not for Elizabeth.

I can't do this, R'lyeh decided at the end of the week, at the end of the day. Gallows wasn't far now, just over the hill ahead. She had found some poisonbite berries along the way, and now slipped them into her mouth. Elizabeth saw her, but didn't say anything. Elizabeth didn't do much of anything. Sometimes, R'lyeh had to remind her to breathe.

I have to fight, she thought, her, Elizabeth, and the third horse, starting up the hill. *If it's a threat, it has to die. I could have saved her, but I didn't. I was closer than Elizabeth.* She scratched her horse behind its twitching ear. *Everyone around me dies. I can't be around anything alive.*

R'lyeh wiped her eyes, turned to Elizabeth, and meekly said, "We're here."

Elizabeth's dull eyes shifted. Her mouth, white with dried drool, cracked the smallest of smiles.

R'lyeh nodded and rode the horse over the crest of the hill. She squeezed her legs against the beast, grabbed its mane, and said, "Shit, shit. Stop."

At the center of Gallows, in the lake of blood, a giant bat floated on its back. On the mangy beast's belly, tens of pale children moved back and forth between the lake and the bat; some rubbed the blood into its fur, while others nursed it into the creature's panting mouth.

R'lyeh threw out her arm, to block Elizabeth, but Elizabeth rode at full-speed past her.

"Great," Elizabeth kept saying, over and over. "Great!"

R'lyeh untethered the third horse. It smartly took off for the country-side. *Don't stop, don't stare.* R'lyeh swallowed her hesitation and rode down the hill towards Gallows.

They didn't know the passphrase for entry, but the cabalists in the sentry towers let them through, regardless. Elizabeth was the first to make it to the dock. When she did, she dismounted from her horse and booked it toward Operations.

R'lyeh, ten seconds behind, hit the docks, and did the same. She kept the giant bat and the pale children in her periphery, but only in her periphery. If she stopped, if she stared, something could happen to Elizabeth. She couldn't lose another one. Not now. Not ever. Not again. Not if she could—

Halfway up the ramp to the second level, Elizabeth braced herself and shouted, "You mother fucker!"

Cabalists across Gallows stopped what they were doing. The pale children in the lake of blood levitated above their bat god and exchanged dark whispers with one another.

R'lyeh, with a stitch in her side, hoofed it towards and up the ramp to the second level. At the top of it, the Skeleton stood, his arms folded across his ribcage.

"What are they doing here?" Elizabeth ran at the Skeleton. She threw her arms at him. He caught them and held her there, a prisoner to her own grief and rage. "What are they... what are they?"

Behind the Skeleton, Warren emerged from Operations and asked Elizabeth, "Where's Miranda?"

Elizabeth went limp in the Skeleton's hands and collapsed onto the ramp, a sobbing mess.

R'lyeh ran up the ramp, dropped down, and pulled Elizabeth against her. Peeling her hair off her hot face, R'lyeh said to the Skeleton, "What the fuck is going on?"

"Allies." The Skeleton looked past R'lyeh and then asked, "Where's Audra?"

R'lyeh shook her head. She held Elizabeth tighter as she tried to pull away.

The Skeleton nodded. He went sideways just as Hex emerged from Operations, too.

"What happened?" she asked, hand covering her mouth. "Audra?"

"No," the Skeleton said.

Hex's face went tight. Her neck tented; she grabbed onto Warren.

"We tried it your way," the Skeleton said. He then turned back to R'lyeh and stepped towards her and Elizabeth. "I'm sorry, Elizabeth."

Face buried in R'lyeh's chest, Elizabeth said, muffled, "You knew, and you called them here, anyways." She spit at the Skeleton. "You're a fucking monster. Get away from us!"

The Skeleton's veiny, glassy eyes focused on R'lyeh. Fat, black, salamander-like tongue flopping around inside his jaw, the Skeleton said, "When the battle is over, whoever wins will come here next. You will be leaving."

R'lyeh shook her head. "No. No! I'm not going anywhere. I'm not running anymore."

"Everyone is running." The Skeleton touched the Black Hour's heart beneath his robe. "Hex's plan failed. Mine will not."

"You're not coming with us?" R'lyeh let go of Elizabeth and stood up, face to face, with the Skeleton. "You're abandoning us?" She pushed him; when she touched him, an orgy of blood and steel stabbed through her skull.

"Hex is going to lead the Marrow Cabal to our new base of operations—" the Skeleton sighed, "—and I'm going to the Dead City to put an end to all of this, once and for all. Now, get Elizabeth out of here, before Gemma sees her."

CHAPTER XVII

Technically speaking, there were two Nameless Forests on the continent, or so Aeson liked to think. The first was the most famous, and the only one anyone cared about—that wooded nightmare to the east that was quickly becoming the Disciples of the Deep's new Mecca. The second Nameless Forest, while at this point nearly forgotten by all, was much older than its spotlight-hungry sibling and, in some ways, or, again, so Aeson liked to think, the more interesting of the two.

But to call it the Nameless Forest would be disingenuous, because unlike the home of the Dread Clock, this second forest was truly nameless. In the countless stories Aeson had read about the place, it was obvious people had tried to give it a name; however, one would never stick for long. Purgatory Pointe, the Dark Woods, the Winding Haunt, Bleak's Holdout—these names, while all similar in tone, were just a few of hundreds attributed to the forest over the remaining recorded years.

Before the Trauma, the humans were calling it the Garden of Sleep. The forest had been annexed by a local state park. Deemed too unstable for general use, it quickly became a Mecca of its own for the many youths who willingly trespassed into the area.

Suicide forests had been in style at the time; when dead teenagers started washing up in the creeks, rivers, and lakes of the state park, the locals panicked. They figured their sons and daughters were going into the Garden of Sleep to kill themselves, but each body that was recovered suggested otherwise. Of the sixty who died in the Garden of Sleep, not one of them was determined to have died by suicide.

The next logical conclusion was that the sixty had been murdered, either by their peers, or by a person or persons residing in the forest. But the medical reports and newspaper clippings Aeson had read were quick to dismiss this suggestion, as well. The teenagers hadn't killed themselves, nor had they been killed by anyone else. They had simply stopped living.

The Trauma happened shortly thereafter, and the humans never got the answers they wanted. But because Aeson was an Archivist (eight years ago he had more time on his hands than did most clocks), he realized in his haphazard researching a precedence in that place for similar mysterious deaths. Back when it had been known as Purgatory Pointe in the 1800s, the Dark Woods in 1910, the Winding Haunt in 1975, and Bleak's Holdout in 2012, there were cases of corpses with unexplainable causes of death. Children or adults, it didn't matter; every year, bodies would be found that appeared to have given up on living altogether, as if the thread of life itself had been snipped from their souls. Myths were made, and creatures were created, and the wrong people were blamed for these eerie wrongdoings. But like the forest itself, the deaths were quickly forgotten, with each subsequent case just as shocking to the public as the first. Not only was the Garden of Sleep—the best name given to the forest, or so Aeson claimed—capable of killing undetected, but it had hanging about it a fog of unfailing amnesia.

Eight years ago, at age eleven, Aeson began making connections in the case about the same time he started hearing stories about the forest from those in Caldera. He had developed an obsession with the Garden of Sleep, not only because of its history, but because the forest was only a half a day's journey to the west from the village. It was an obsession his eight-year-old self at the time couldn't believe no one else had. And yet, it was an obsession only his eight-year-old self and those unfortunately similar to him could have. For what child, orphaned by their parents' suicides, wouldn't take interest in the home of Death?

Ghost stories were for the gullible, and Aeson, with the Old World at his fingertips, was beyond gullible. Hearing that Death dwelled in the Garden of Sleep, he began to see Death in all its corners and corridors. And more specifically, he began to see the rare flower, Death's Dilemma, in all the cases and corpses. Whether it was in the 1800s or on the eve of the Trauma, the flower, or something similar to it, was present in every story from back then, as well as all the ghost stories he kept hearing as a child.

To him, the eight-year-old who thought himself three times his age, the solution was simple: People had gone to Death over the years, and death was what they had gotten. The Garden of Sleep was a gateway to the Abyss—to the great cemetery in which all souls slept. There were reports of a Ferry Woman to take people to Death, but that just seemed like nothing more than pure ceremony. For months, Aeson had wanted to take the trip, to the forest and Death's seamless domain. But as with others, the passage of time had taken his will, his motivation, and eventually, his memory. He never forgot the forest or what it was capable of, and yet, at the same time, he did.

Many people often described Death as a disease, but now, standing here in the outskirts of the Garden of Sleep with Bjørn at his side, Aeson realized the living were the disease. Death had rejected his advances before. But now they were weak and desperate, and clinging to a poisoned hope—they had to have worn Death down. It would have no choice but to accept them.

"The Ferry Woman shouldn't be far," Bjørn said, begrudgingly.

Aeson checked his bag for *The Blood of Before*. "How do you know?"

"Everyone who comes through here has seen her. She's always in the same place."

"When Vrana got back from Geharra, she told me she saw her." Aeson sighed. "Said the Ferry Woman was holding a dead bird."

Bjørn shook his head. Pointing forward, he said, "Home isn't far."

It wasn't. From where they stood, they could see the peaks of Kistvaen through the forest's dying canopy. Caldera wasn't a stone's throw away, but it was close enough to make them second guess themselves every second their journey put them closer to the village. If they returned to Caldera, then they could ask the elders for help. Instead of seeking out Death and some mythical weapon, they could try to throw together a group of Caldera's best and go to Angheuawl to put an end to the witches and their Choir of flesh fiends. And yet to Aeson and Bjørn, both these options somehow sounded unreasonable. Any delay would be a death sentence for Vrana. Any attack that didn't assure the complete eradication of Joy and Pain couldn't be trusted.

But, deep down, Aeson knew the real reason why they felt so confident in courting Death. Bjørn didn't say it, of course, but he didn't need to. Both men had known Death all their lives, and more than once, It had taken someone they loved away from them. Aeson knew Death through books, and Bjørn through deeds; however, with Ichor's dinner party, there was no doubt in either's mind that they were equals in their experiences. The living might have been the disease, but a disease had to keep on living. If they were meant to die, they should've already. Like a carless debtor, Death had taken too much; now it was time to take some of it back.

"You alright?" Bjørn asked.

The swamp in front of them gave an unenthusiastic belch. Aeson couldn't have given a better response. He appreciated the Bear's concern, but for now and years to come, concern was something that cut rather than healed. So he lied and said, "Yeah," and got moving.

This nameless forest west of Caldera was mostly swamp; and those places that weren't appeared to be there just for show. For all the chaos in the landscape—the steep hills and even steeper valleys; the impenetrable black ashes and almost-illusory bald cypresses—there appeared to be a kind of primal order to it. Maybe it was something left over from its days as a state park, or maybe Death had done some redecorating of Its own, but the forest seemed to funnel them through it down a definite path. Those who entered clearly weren't meant to linger long, which made Aeson wonder: *Is the Garden of Sleep really supposed to be here?*

Grunting and groaning, they made their way to the edge of the swamp. The water looked more like an oil spill than anything else. Choked with debris and dead animals, and probably a hell of a lot deeper than it looked, it was obvious they would be skirting around the swamp, not swimming straight through it.

Bjørn took out his giant sword and gave it the once-over. "A few things we have to worry about in here," he said. Then, sheathing the sword: "Came here a few years back for the nethers oil I used on Vrana's daggers. Things should still be the same."

"Wisps," Aeson said.

"Yeah."

"And whatever lives at the bottom of the swamp."

"You don't know, either?"

"No one does.

"Don't think its Death?"

Aeson shook his head. "Not the kind we're going to see."

"Nethers shouldn't be out at this time, but we do have to watch for the lamias. Colder it gets, the more active they get." Bjørn scanned the swamp for the best place to cross. "They hollow-out trees and live inside them. There's some local people that live in this forest—"

"They feed their third-born child to them. The lamias are always female; top half looks human, bottom half, like a snake. Legend says they were too evil for even the Nameless Forest to take them in. It's October, though. We won't see them until mid-November." Aeson smiled a shitty smile and then, feeling guilty, said, "Sorry."

"We don't have to do this." Bjørn wrung the sweat out of his mullet. "You haven't slept since the Sticks."

Vrana had nightmares about the Witch before she took her, Aeson thought. *How long until the flesh fiend comes for me?* He pulled a cloak out of his bag, threw it over his shoulders, and plodded forward. Winter would be here by the time this was all over. If it froze the land, could it freeze him, too? Could winter lay its hands upon him and encase in ice all those terrible feelings wreaking havoc inside him? Holy Child, he couldn't go an hour without feeling as if his heart were going to beat out of his chest. But worse were the noises, the smells. Was it his memory or misinterpretations of his environment? A rattle here, the breaking of branches there. He often smelled the fecal stench of bad breath, and the cloying, eye-watering odor of unwashed flesh. He always jumped; cold sweats were now the norm, and it didn't take much to take him back there, the front lawn of House Gloom, where the flesh fiend had mounted him and fucked its way into his head.

In the Old World, they called his condition Post-Traumatic Stress Disorder. He had learned a lot of their mental diagnoses about six years ago, thinking that mental health might make a resurgence. But it was more than that. At night, when it was darkest, and Bjørn wasn't more than a snoring pile of dirt-covered muscles, the flashbacks (fleshbacks, he once called them, pathetically) were so overwhelming that they stopped afflicting him, and started becoming him. Or he started becoming them. A mental illness could do that to a person, couldn't it? Change them? He heard and smelled the foul breaths, and sometimes, they seemed to be coming from him. The rattling, too, and the breaking of branches, which seemed to be his own bones cracking. And what of the flesh? The unwashed flesh, stinking like mildewed clothes, soiled and soaked through? Sometimes, his flesh felt wrong, like it didn't belong, like it was something he had borrowed and forgotten wasn't really his.

Aeson knew he wasn't turning into a flesh fiend, nor had he been born one. But something was happening to him. Just like something had happened to Vrana. Adelyn had asked him to love her, no matter what. Who would ask her to do the same for him?

It was slow going through the swamp. What little they had of a trail to work with alternated between fat roots and pitfalls. Even though they were on the edge of the swamp, it didn't seem as if it grew shallower the more it tapered towards the shore. One wrong step and they would be up to their necks or worse in the oily water.

And whatever was beneath those black waters definitely knew they were there. There were too many ripples and teasing emergences. Clambering over a fallen tree, Aeson had seen, for a split second, what appeared to be a mushroom-shaped trunk and a single arm covered in serrated rings, like suckers.

"Are there swamp squids?" Aeson asked, the creature submerging before Bjørn could think him anything but crazy.

"You're the Archivist." Bjørn broke right through the tree, his thighs like battering rams. "I wouldn't doubt it, though."

The swamp's end wasn't far off now. It was midday, and they had plenty of light left to get to the dark place they were going. The Ferry Woman was said to be near an inlet shrouded in weeping willows, not far from where the forest let out. She had a boat, and it was by this boat a person could reach the Garden of Sleep. If there was a procedure to this insane plan of his, he didn't know it; those from Caldera who had been seen taking a ride with the Ferry Woman were never seen again. It was a one-way trip. How he planned to get back, he couldn't say. It was best he didn't.

Leaves fell around Aeson and Bjørn as they cleared the last of the swamp. In the canopy, a small lamia slithered down into a tree and hid there—its eyes two yellow diamonds fixed and hungry. Hand on his sword, Aeson watched the tree and those unblinking eyes. In his mind, the afterimage of the creature had stuck but now started to fade. The top half was the nude torso of what could've passed for a fifteen-year-old, slightly stunted, girl. The bottom half, beginning at a false navel, had fused together and scaled over into a long tail checkered with yellow diamonds. The color of the patterns on a lamia's tail were said to match their eyes, as well as temperament and toxicity. If given the chance to do terrible things to him and Bjørn, the lamia would. He could respect that, though. There was a beauty to its construction, a personality to the way it was put together; that is, some semblance that said the thing was meant to be.

Flesh fiends, however, received no such appreciation from Aeson. Not for what they had done to him, or anyone else, but because they weren't meant to be. There was nothing about them that suggested they should've been here, on this earth, doing what they did best. Only Corrupted could create such a cruel beast and somehow pass it off as purposeful. And they did, didn't they? It was from their wombs, and the wombs of the Night Terrors they impregnated, that those devils sometimes emerged. Even after the Trauma, the humans were still leaving little traumas where they could. Where was the balance in that?

Bjørn pointed to his eyes and then pointed at the lamia to let it know he knew it was there. Bear mask sliding down his face, he fixed it and then passed Aeson, taking the lead. Not once but twice, he walked straight into the swamp, going chest deep into the black waters. He quickly recovered, and after a third almost-misstep, he brought them out of the swamp and back into the forest.

"Could have been worse," he said, soaking wet.

Aeson kicked the mud off his shoes. A blue and gold wisp shot past his head. A few more, white, and looking like fractals, rose out of the ground, buzzed around his ear.

"Fuck off," he said, swatting them away.

The wisps bit at his hand with what felt like an electric discharge and spiraled back into the ground.

Bjørn rolled an uprooted tree trunk out of the underbrush and took a seat on it. "Don't tempt them. Everything answers to something. I heard the wisps are the spirits of the dead children the lamias ate."

Aeson shook his head. "What are you doing?"

"Sitting." Bjørn crossed his arms and leaned back as far as he could. "We're almost there. I'm scared shitless, man."

"Yeah." Aeson looked for something to sit on and settled on the ground instead. Without thinking, he dug into his bag and took out *The Blood of Before*. "Me too."

"Can't breathe right." Bjørn leaned forward, elbows to his knees, and held his chin and his mask's chin like a child. "Doesn't feel right."

Can't think about it. Don't want to think about anything. Aeson opened *The Blood of Before* to where he left off and started working on deciphering that passage again.

Skivv ovh veqvin kbcv gvvo lktnvo. Bofxpn, Oxlsvb, boq Abtebo hpee ivyeblv Fpnvenb, Cvibs, boq Jvnkxff. Fpnveb'n ltoqpspto kbn htinvovq, boq vcpqvolv nxffvnsn nkv jbr gv ivnytonpgev ati skv jxiqvi ta Jvnkxff.

Skviv kbcv gvvo jxiqvin po Sibvnz epozvq st skv teqvns

jvjgvin ta skv cpeebfv. Opfks Sviitin biv ots zotho st epcv etof epcvn, boq sktnv skbs qt kbcv qvjtonsibsvq b lbyblpsr ati cptevolv gvrtoq hkbs pn ivdxpivq st nvv skv gbebolv jbposbpovq. Qvnypsv skpn boq skv hbiopof aitj Ipjv'n veqvin, Bofxpn, Oxlsvb, boq Abtebo kbcv ivdxvnsvq bqqpsptobe ivntx-ilvn gv fpcvo st skv avispepsr yituvlsn po gtsk Veq boq Eblxob. Vmyvqpspto svbjn kbcv ivsxiovq aitj skv Qvbq Lpsr. Ta skv shvosr nvos st pocvnspfbsv skv bivb, apcv ivjbpo; skv tskvi shvosr yvipnkvq st skv letxq ta qpnvbnvn skbs vocvetyv skv lpsr. Skv nxicpctin biv ots vmyvlsvq st jbzv ps skitxfk skv hvvz. Skvpi ivytisn, hkpev qpaaplxes st ateeth, biv ltonpnsvos: Skviv pn epav po skv Qvbq Lpsr, boq bgtcv ps, nsbin biv abeepof aitj skv nzr.

Skpn hpee gv jr apobe vosir. Bofxpn kbn tiqvivq skbs ovh bilkpcpnsn ivyeblv jv.

Ati bee txi vaatisn st hbnk ps bhbr, nspee hv biv ltcvivq po skv gettq ta gvativ.

Aeson didn't have to decipher this entry to know that there was something wrong about it. The previous entry, which marked the first actual entry by his parents, was simple and to the point.

Anguis has elected myself (Quinn) and my expecting wife (Mika) to the position of Archivist, which we will share with **equal** responsibility.

A famine (possibly related to the returning expeditionary force) has struck the village.

Gisela has been exonerated, and she will be removed from the village (whereabouts unknown).

The previous Archivist, Emmanuel, is nowhere to be found anymore.

"Aeson," Bjørn said.

But Aeson pretended not to hear him. *Not now,* he thought, flipping back and forth between the pages. Doing this, he noticed a small splotch of blood near the spine. Had it been his parents'? Or the previous Archivist's?

"Now's not the time."

Yes, it is. He took out his own journal. There had been a hint in his parents' first entry—a partial equation. Either they hadn't finished writing it into their own entry, or the previous Archivist hadn't told them the method by which they could decipher his text.

Thoughts of Vrana crept across his mind, like the shadows of doctors gathering over the anesthetized. He could feel her talons tugging from deep within. Wings battered his ears like a fighter's fists. She wasn't here, he told himself, even though she had always been, ever since they first met, when they were young and stupid and dared each other to eat every bug they found.

The equation. The equation. He shook his head and consulted the equation in his journal, which was this: $d(x) = a(x - b) \bmod m$. It was almost complete, but what was missing?

An exponent. The equation had been written through his parents' entry, with each part of it being unsubtly bolded to make it stand out. But this was an Affine cipher, he was sure of it, which meant he needed the co-prime exponent to see how far the Archivist had shifted the letters in the alphabet to—

Bjørn cleared his throat with about as much passive aggression as an old lady at PTA meeting.

One, three, five, seven—the possibilities for the exponent could go even higher than that. But he had to have been missing something. The equation was obvious; therefore, the missing exponent had to be, too. One seemed too easy and… and if he could count anything in the entry, it was names. Anguis, Quinn, Mika, Gisela, and Emmanuel. Five. It wasn't a bad place to start.

"What's it say?" Bjørn asked, finally relenting.

Aeson held up one finger, and with the other hand, started deciphering. It took several blissful minutes of complete focus and total ignorance to get there, but he got there. If he was glad for anything the elders had made him learn, code breaking was certainly it.

When he finished, Aeson read what he had decrypted aloud. It was this:

Three new elders have been chosen. Anguis, Nuctea, and Faolan will replace Giselsa, Verat, and Meshugg. Gisela's condition has worsened, and evidence suggests she may be responsible for the murder of Meshugg.
There have been murders in Traesk linked to the oldest members of the village. Night Terrors are not known to live

long lives, and those that do have demonstrated a capacity for violence beyond what is required to see the balance maintained. Despite this, and the warning from Rime's elders, Anguis, Nuctea, and Faolan have requested additional resources be given to the fertility projects in both Eld and Lacuna.

Expedition teams have returned from the Dead City. Of the twenty sent to investigate the area, five remain; the other twenty perished to the cloud of diseases that envelope the city. The survivors are not expected to make it through the week. Their reports, while difficult to follow, are consistent: There is life in the Dead City, and above it, stars are falling from the sky.

This will be my final entry. Anguis has ordered that new archivists replace me.

For all our efforts to wash it away, still we are covered in the blood of before.

Bjørn made a humming sound and dug his heel into the dirt. "That takes me back."

Still we are covered in the blood of before. Aeson snapped out of it and asked, "How old are you?"

"Forty-nine."

"Do you remember the old elders and Archivist?"

Another lamia slithered through the branches overhead. It gave out a hiss, and then it was gone.

"Goddamn things. I, uh—" Bjørn shrugged, "—yeah, a little. When I was fifteen, they sent me up to Traesk and the Divide. My childhood... I don't remember much. Don't really want to." He started to stand; poised to strike, he mumbled, "Goddamn things."

Childhood. The word sent him reeling ten years into the past, when Vrana was just Vrana, and Aeson was Aeson, and they didn't need masks to be sure of that. He remembered she had been the first to approach him—her knees skinned and scabby, her face grubby, and her nails dark. He remembered she smelled differently (figured it was a girl thing), but now, thinking back, thinking darkly, she smelled just like the flesh fiend.

"This book," Aeson said, forcing out the words and the recollection, "isn't a history. It keeps harping on the same thing. It keeps coming back to our people trying to populate. If this really is our history, then... I mean... is that all that matters?"

"Doesn't matter what you do, as long as you're here," Bjørn said.

And here we are, not far from Death's doorstep.

Bjørn took off his mask and laid it on his lap. "What're you thinking?"

I'm stalling, Aeson thought. Bjørn knew it, too. But the Bear's feigned interest wasn't bait he was about take. He pressed on.

"Every entry so far has been about Lacuna, or the Children of Lacuna, or the Night Terrors' infertility. I never realized how obsessed our people, or, at least, Anguis, Nuctea, and Faolan, are with figuring out how to reproduce. It keeps coming back to that. But it's not just the infertility issue. How many elderly Night Terrors do you know?"

Bjørn shrugged.

"I can't think of anyone over sixty in our village."

"There've been a few, but I can't say what happened to them."

"Did you know Gisela and Verat are spellweavers now? They're still alive."

Bjørn's mouth dropped open. "I figured they went somewhere. Verat was a young elder. Younger than you. They're the ones under Kistvaen making it disappear?" He laughed. "That fucking Snake. He put them there. Gisela must be... what? Eighty?"

"Eight-four. And she's insane. Lucid, but a complete cannibal. The book says she murdered Meshugg, and she would have been about sixty-four at the time.

"We can't reproduce like we ought to, and it seems like we're not supposed to live past a certain age."

"Yeah, but how long has this been going on? That Archivist, Emmanuel, mentioned expedition teams that came back from the Dead City, diseased. And then after that? Your parents wrote about famine in Caldera."

Aeson nodded, said, "Yeah. I think he worded it badly. It made it sound like only one team was sent out, but what if all of the villages, or even just a few, sent teams to the Dead City? What if they all brought something back that made some of our people infertile? It's not completely widespread—"

"—Gisela was insane before the teams returned," Bjørn added.

"Could be separate." Aeson bit his lip and re-read the entry. "Could be that hadn't been the first time they tried to go into the City. They haven't been back since. What if we were meant to die with the Trauma? Like most of the Corrupted? Anguis and the others... all they've been doing, it seems, is trying to keep the tribe alive."

Bjørn laughed and put his mask back on. "And yet here we are, the last place where anything living should want to be."

"What's the blood of before, though?" Aeson asked, sensing his diversion coming to an end. "They went to the homunculi for help, and they said they were disappointed in what we had become. 'We' as in the homunculi? Or us?"

Bjørn's shoulders went tense. He laid his sword across his lap and started rubbing his hands together. The diversion was over; the delay had ended. Aeson closed *The Blood of Before* and his notebook, because what good was history to those who might not be alive much longer to use it?

Above them, shafts of sunlight cut through the canopy, but even still, they were no match for the darkness here. Where the light touched, the darkness deepened, as if it fed off the very thing that was supposed to kill it.

Behind them, the not-too-distant swamp beckoned them back to its black waters. Loud crashes of water careened through the forest wildly, the sound waves, like the waves that had spawned them, chaotic and desperate. Aeson could hear something beating the surface of the lake, drumming out sharp, crackling notes, as if to say: "Here I am. Come and see what you missed."

And before them... before them lay the greatest temptation of all: Kistvaen, and the sight, a sliver though it may be, of the fields outside the forest, between here and home. Autumn hadn't left much in the fields, but what was there was enough. Tall grass, brittle and wind-bent, glowing a cool yellow beneath the retreating sun.

Bjørn must've seen what he had seen, too, because he cleared his throat and said, "Death's coming for us at some point. Maybe it is best we meet It halfway."

"I'm not changing my mind," Aeson said. "This was my idea."

"I know that, but Death's in the business of death. It's going to try to sell you Itself, and with the way you've been acting, I don't know if you're going to be able to tell It no."

Aeson's face started to burn. A muscle spasm wriggled like snakes in his neck. He closed his eyes, gritted his teeth, and thought of Vrana, not as she had been before, but as she was now.

"What did you lose?" he asked Bjørn.

"Huh?"

"When the Witch took her. What did you lose?"

"You being sincere? Or are you trying to fight me again?"

"You see a pattern? You get lost in that book, then you break down, and right before you get anywhere, you clam back up." Bjørn gathered his breath and exhaled slowly. "What did you lose, Aeson? That's what you're really getting at, anyways. I lost a friend. I lost a daughter, even if she wasn't mine. I failed her. She came back to Caldera after Geharra, and she told me about the elders sending her to Lacuna, and I let her go there, anyways. That's me. That's what I lost. My good sense, and the only good goddamn thing in my life besides her mother that I care about. What'd you lose? You and I both know we aren't talking about the person, but ourselves. Maybe I don't talk a lot, but I know things. What's gone from you, Skull Boy? What's there now?"

Bjørn stopped himself. He reached for his mask at his feet, as if to shield his grief-stricken face, but then sat back up. "Please. You got to let it out. I know what it can do to a person if you don't. You got time to heal later."

Aeson pushed himself off the ground and walked over to Bjørn. For the first time in his life, and probably the last, he stood over the Bear. *Was Death watching them?* he wondered. When they were finished baring their souls to one another, would Death come to snatch their souls from them? He stared at Bjørn, but saw something impossible instead: Bjørn rushing to a tree, cutting Aeson down from the rope around his neck, while his mother and father swung overhead, the tips of their toes brushing against his scalp.

"I lost a part of me," Aeson said. "Vrana has been in my life for so long that it's like she was... is a part of me. I mean—" He growled and considered giving up. "—I'm not trying to say she isn't..." His cheek twitched. "I am not me without her. She was with me, even when she wasn't. I love her for her, for who she made me." A weight began to lift off his chest. He sighed and closed his eyes. "It's not because she was my girlfriend. Hell, we were only dating for like five minutes before she left for Geharra."

Bjørn laughed, and when he stopped, there was still a small smile on his face. "You two were dating since they day you met. Just didn't know it."

"I just... I just wanted—" The smell of rotting flesh; the click of talons; the flesh fiend filling herself with him. "I just... want... wanted... want her back. I knew she would be different. I think... I'm okay with that. I have to be. I want to be. But I need to be better. I've always relied on her and... she saw it."

"The flesh fiend."

Aeson nodded, said, "Yeah," and started tugging on his earlobe—something which he hadn't done in years. "Maybe it would've been easier if she hadn't seen it happen—"

"It wouldn't have," Bjørn said.

"—but she did. I couldn't do anything. I let it happen."

"Aeson, no, you didn't."

"She saw it. She had to save me. I'm... we... we're supposed to save her."

"She needs help, not saving." Bjørn furrowed his brow. "You know that. She will know how far you went and what you went through to bring her home."

"That's the thing." Aeson backed away, until he backed into a tree. "I don't want her to."

Shaking his head, Bjørn said, "That's not how it works. You're not any less of a man because of what happened."

Yes, I am, Aeson thought.

"She doesn't care who you are, as long as you are you." Bjørn shook his head. "You're sitting here convincing yourself you have to be something else."

"You told me to be," Aeson said, spitting. "You dragged me out here. You armed me, told me to kill."

"I'm sorry," Bjørn said. Finally, he came to his feet. "I'm a blacksmith. I beat things into the only shape I know. Vrana took to it, but not you. We wouldn't be here if it weren't for you."

"Yeah, but look where we are." Aeson threw up his arms. "This shouldn't even be an option."

"You should have died. Vrana should have died. I've lost count of how many times I've dodged death in battles and brawls. I'm not sure if there is a better option for people like us. But you have to promise me we are going to Death to get the weapons."

Aeson cocked his head. "Why else would we be here?"

"You know why."

"I'm not my parents. I'm not that weak." He went to his skull mask and put it on. "I don't want to die."

Bjørn cleared his throat. "I did, for a long time. Like I said, I chased Death when I could."

"Do you still want to? Die, I mean?"

"No," Bjørn said, grabbing his mask off the ground. "I've never wanted to live more than I do today. Told myself all my life I was one thing. Starting to see I might be something else, too." He smiled and slicked back his hair. "I'm sorry I let these things happen to you. It's going to get worse."

I know, Aeson thought.

"But when it does, you'll have Vrana. It's easier to heal when you're whole, right?"

"I don't know," Aeson said, memory after memory molesting every inch of his body. "Is it?"

Bjørn shrugged. "That's what they say."

Aeson and Bjørn didn't move for the next few minutes. They stared at one another in silence. For Aeson, it felt as if he had stepped outside himself, like he'd had enough of his body and needed a break from all the bullshit inside it. When he finally came to, Bjørn came to, too. Neither man spoke to the other after that.

The Ferry Woman had been waiting for them this whole time, Aeson was sure of it. Fifteen minutes deeper into the forest and they found several tall, clinically depressed weeping willows standing defeatedly beside an inlet. Beyond them, beside a small boat, the Ferry Woman stood, tracking their every movement. Like the Witch's sister, Joy, the Ferry Woman wore a white dress; but unlike Joy, the Ferry Woman's body was only visible where the fabric rested against it. She wore a veil over her face, which kept her head, neck, and shoulders perceptible, but where the dress was open or loose, such as her wrists and hands, ankles and feet, and her legs where the split in the dress didn't touch, there was nothing.

Bjørn, wading through the willows' limp branches, went to the Ferry Woman first. He kept his distance, and his sword in its sheathe. From the forest to the boat, the Ferry Woman watched him every step of the way. When he reached the waters, inches away from the apparition, she outstretched her arm, as if she were offering him something from her invisible hand.

Bjørn looked back at Aeson; and that made Aeson feel better than it should have.

The Ferry Woman nodded. Carefully, Bjørn reached for her hand. As it closed around the place it would be, a piece of crystalline rope wavered into existence. Bjørn took it, and the mirage-like fabric went taught, from his palm to the edge of the boat, where it was connected. Again, the Ferry

Woman nodded. At the speed of a guilty child, Bjørn shuffled to the boat and, with the tether still in his hand, took a seat inside it, his back to Aeson.

Aeson took a deep breath and did his best to follow Bjørn's lead. The weeping willows washed over him, baptizing him with the drowsy softness of their touch. The trees smelled like his bed smelled—cool and clean, with an undertone of earth. Stepping up to the inlet, he found himself suddenly drawn to the boat, as if it had its own center of gravity. It didn't pull him forward, necessarily, but down; the same way sleep would pull his head to a pillow. He found it hard to keep his eyes open, even with the Ferry Woman standing so close at his side.

And now that he was near enough to touch her, if she could be touched, he noticed that the white satin dress she wore was torn in places, and shredded in others. The neckline had been ravaged. The dress' skirt had been split up the middle, not by fashion, but ferocity. This close to Ferry Woman, he could see that the dress was something that might be better suited for a corpse in a casket.

Aeson glanced at Bjørn in the boat, who was sitting in it so complacently. Was he breathing? His skin did look paler. *Turn around. Make some stupid macho comment.*

The Ferry Woman outstretched her arm in front of Aeson. The white satin fabric that ended at her wrist slid back loosely. With it went the shape of her forearm, all the way up to her elbow. He couldn't see what she held, and yet his hand found hers, anyway. Carefully, one eye open and cringing, Aeson clutched the space where the Ferry Woman's hand should have been. As had happened with Bjørn, a crystalline rope materialized from an unseen dimension and coiled itself inside his palm. He clutched it tightly and that, too, ran from him to the front of the boat.

Tugging on the rope, Aeson felt a tugging inside him. It was a dense force that gripped his bones like the hand of Death Itself. He pulled the tether again, and he could've sworn if he had pulled any harder, his ribcage would've been ripped from his chest. A terrible thought was then born into his mind: did he literally hold his life in his hands? And what would happen if he were to let go?

The crystalline rope tightened on its own. The hand that held it shot out. He stumbled towards the boat. Nineteen years he'd managed, and now it was time to set sail. He let the tether take him where it willed, because the pain of resistance was too great to endure. Inside his head, however, he couldn't be farther from this place. Great walls inscribed with passages from *The Blood of Before* encircled his mind, sealing it off from the very real possibility that he'd made a mistake, that he was going to die.

Night Terrors become more violent the longer they live.

The tether tugged again, and Aeson stepped up to the back of the boat.

Scouts from the Dead City brought a disease back to the villages. The Night Terrors started to become infertile.

Aeson's hand burned as the rope brought him around the side of the boat, past Bjørn.

The elders tried to use the homunculi to learn how to repopulate the tribe. Then they used the Blue Worm on Lacuna.

The stream the boat sat in glittered with an otherworldly light; it was dusk at the place it reflected, and soon the yellow and orange waters would turn dark.

The Blue Worm taught them how to calm Kistvaen from erupting and to make it disappear; and it gave the ability to reproduce again.

Aeson stepped into the boat. Bjørn, now before him, didn't so much as budge. He was as stone; a witness paralyzed by his own personal cataclysm.

The Night Terrors should've died in the Trauma. They should've died with Kistvaen going off. We weren't supposed to breed. We weren't supposed to grow old. We aren't supposed to be here.

The crystalline rope jerked downwards. Aeson's heart stopped, and then restarted again. Cold and clammy, and certain he had just died, he sat opposite Bjørn.

Mom and Dad knew it. And they knew what waited in the Ossuary. Were they saving me from It? Or from us? From what we would do? From what we could become to survive again? What the hell are—

The walls came down, and Aeson looked up. The Ferry Woman waited at the edge of the inlet, her arms out and held high, like a priest giving thanks for a holy sacrament. There was no point in hiding; they had come this far, and now they had no choice but to go farther.

As the boat began to move on its own down the stream, Aeson closed his eyes and thought terrible thoughts, for what better place for nightmares than the Garden of Sleep? He woke the memory of the flesh fiend who had raped him and let it rape him again and again until the sick subsided from his throat. He wrestled Vrana's true image from the memory she could no longer be, and gave witness, over and over again, to the terrifying and grotesque thing she had become; until his repulsion retreated like waves upon a shore, and the love he thought he had lost for her lay bare, like unearthed treasures washed up upon the sands.

Then he thought of the witches—Pain and Joy—and all the hate and horror and endless despair they had let loose upon the world, unchecked and unchallenged, over the countless years. He thought of the Children of Lacuna on their pilgrimage, a forced death march; and of the flesh fiends, and their Choir of depravity spreading its righteous, wretched song across the continent.

And then, with his eyes still closed, and sleep seconds away, Aeson thought of Death and Its weapons, and the sweet satisfaction of plunging them into the witches' hearts, and knowing that finally, after so much bloodshed, after so much loss, the weight of his deeds to be done had always been too great a weight for the tree that his parents had hung him from to hold.

The boat came to a sudden stop. As if awoken from the lightest of sleeps, Aeson's eyes snapped open. Bjørn was sprawled out in front of him, his arms and legs every-which-way, grasping at the edge of the boat. They were surrounded by an immutable blackness that stretched forever in front and above them; it was the ground and the sky, and everything else their minds couldn't possibly comprehend. The only source of light was below them, eons beyond their reach—billions of blinking stars as far as their limited vision could see.

Bjørn lifted his head. Drowsily, he said, "Turn around, Aeson."

Behind Aeson, beginning where the boat had stopped, was a small landmass completely covered in thousands of different types of flowers. In this Abyss, the floating Garden was an island comprised not of soil or rock, but merely the flowers and their roots. Kneeling down, Aeson could see underneath the Garden, and through it, too. Like the Ferry Woman, it was solid, but only where the flowers could give credence to its solidity.

Death must've had a sense of humor, Aeson thought, coming to his feet, because Its Garden was filled to the brim with flowers that could cause it. He couldn't name all of them, but because of his time with Adelyn, he could identify a few: water hemlock, Black Chrism, Grave Soil, deadly nightshade, white snakeroot, Purgatory, rosary pea, oleander, Fey Blood, monkshood, and Decay. There were even small clumps of vermillion veins, but they appeared to be quarantined off from the rest of the garden, as if Death had no intention of letting the roots spread here.

And while there were many more that Aeson couldn't name, in colors he could hardly register, he still found himself drawn to the flowers that ran up and down the Garden by the hundreds, before meeting in a dense circle at its center. Death's Dilemma. Bone-white petals tucked beneath an icy blue stalk—the image was always the same, regardless of the story being told, and the consequence for trampling them just as permanent. To crush a Death's Dilemma would result in that person's immediate death. And if Aeson and Bjørn were going to step into the Garden, they would have to crush hundreds of them to reach its center.

"What do we do?" Bjørn asked, coming up to Aeson from behind.

"I… I don't know." He started to put one foot forward, and then quickly withdrew it. "I don't know."

Bjørn grabbed Aeson's shoulder—his hands were wet and trembling badly—and whispered, "What's that?"

At the back of the Garden, where the infinite blackness began, figures emerged from that space and stepped onto the island. They were women, all of them, with long, blonde hair that poured out from underneath their large, tattered hats. They wore long leather jackets and boots that were more buckles than boot. In each of their hands, they held wicked looking crooks that were wrapped in what appeared to be bandages or gauze. To Aeson, the women looked like shepherds.

"Are you okay?" Aeson whispered, not looking back.

"I don't know. I'm not anything." Bjørn finally let go of him. "Are we dead?"

And then from above, behind the sounds of beating wings, a woman whispered softly, "Not yet."

Aeson and Bjørn both looked up. In the blackness above, a massive red ring had formed. Inside it, in the shifting darkness of that great space, there appeared to be a portal to another place; a kind of tunnel, with ribbed, flesh-like walls, that was filled with sinewy strands of light moving aimlessly through it.

"I don't see anything," Bjørn said, his teeth chattering. "Do you see anything?"

Aeson shook his head, and then, pointing, said, "Wait. What is that?"

Across the ring's fiery rim, a shape darted into the blackness.

"I think that's It," Aeson started. "I think that's—"

And then from right beside them, the same woman spoke again. "Over here," she said slowly.

Aeson's body went completely numb. He reached for his earlobe and pulled on it. Swallowing hard, and about to pass out, he lowered his head and chanced a glance at what might be his certain demise.

At the edge of the Garden of Sleep, a moth-like creature waited. Its body and wings were mottled brown, like the bark of a molded tree. Deeper within the creature's fur were striking iridescent stretches of purple and pink. Lining the outside of the moth's wings, from their apex to the outer margin, were pale, white, satin-like markings in the shape of skulls and eyes.

The moth arched its back, as if a spine ran throughout its thorax and abdomen, and stood on its four thin, jointed legs. Out of the moth's chest, just below its head, a set of arms lowered; the four fingers on each hand, fused in pairs to give the appearance of scissors, glinted with their sharpness.

Then the creature's antennae began to move about its head, as if to get a measure of the intruders that stood before it. The moth's eyes, those large, black bulbs attached to both sides of its head, twitched, and when they twitched, specks of light glowed, like the stars below, across the creature's compound eyes.

Aeson opened his mouth to speak, but he was too transfixed to manage anything but a whimper.

The moth reared farther back, revealing the underside of its abdomen. Covered in the same fur as its wings, here the color wasn't mottled brown, but bone-white and icy blue; just like the plants that grew out of the space where the creature now stood.

A jaw lowered from the moth's bulbous head. With a distinctively human shape, the jaw separated into a thin, somewhat feminine and furless mouth. The lips, which were not truly lips, but two hard pieces of iridescent cartilage, split and revealed a hollow mouth lined in silk.

"I am Death," the moth said, offering one hand to Aeson, the other to Bjørn. "I am Death, and as I understand it, you've come here to ask me to help you kill my daughters."

CHAPTER XVIII

R'lyeh ripped off her octopus mask and hurled it across the barracks. Fists balled and teeth clenched, she paced back and forth between the rows of beds, getting angrier and angrier at every sound she heard coming from outside. Senses sharpened by sheer hate, she couldn't stand the smells of the barracks any longer. The warm musk of feet, the cloying vapors of sweat; she could smell the oil stains on the pillows, the drunken desperation on the sheets and dried puddles on the floorboards. But outside was worse. Outside, there were those goddamn stupid sounds in place of what should've been mutinous silence. It was the sounds of raised voices and excited whispers, and rapid footsteps of those running rabidly to load their belongings, already ready to be on their way. The Skeleton had given his orders to the cabalists of Gallows, and the fucking idiots took them to heart as if Bone Daddy were the Undead Lord and Savior. And sure, yeah, sure, R'lyeh really couldn't blame them. When it came to hells on earth, Gallows, at least in appearance, didn't have much competition. Who wanted to live on a lake of blood? Not R'lyeh, and certainly not these cabalists. But the Boney Bastard was sending them away, into the mountains, to some village whose name was harder to pronounce than R'lyeh's own. And he was sending them with the very same company of vampyres who had brought Elizabeth to her knees and tears at the sight of them? And have Hex leading the way? No, no, this wasn't going to work. Maybe it would for the cabalists. Maybe it would for Hex and Warren, and James and Herbert North, too. Hell, maybe even Clementine and Will wouldn't pitch a fit. But this wasn't going to work, not for R'lyeh. She wasn't Corrupted. She was a Night Terror. She was above this. She was better than this. She had given up Vrana; there was no fucking way she was going to give up the Skeleton. He was going to the Dead City? Fine, then she was, too. Neither of them seemed able to die, anyways. All things considered, wasn't that the perfect place for them to go? Besides, it was far away. It would take months to get there. She wouldn't have to stop, or look back, to see the corpses that trailed behind her, trying to show her the greatness of the grave. She was ready for a lot of things, but she wasn't ready to die. She liked the look of death, and the way it made her feel, but she wasn't ready to commit to it just yet. She had so much more to do, though what that was, she couldn't really say. After all, she was only thirteen.

R'lyeh stopped pacing. Her head was swimming. She reached inside herself and found the seeds of a plan in the darkness there—which one had given rise to the other, she didn't know. But it was the only plan she had, so holding it tightly with every part of her being, she took it and stormed out of the barracks, leaving her octopus mask behind.

The giant bat's name was Camazotz. Like a baby in a bathtub, it was lying contentedly in the blood lake, its ten-foot-long wings flapping slowly, forcefully, creating red waterfalls with every beat. Going to the edge of the dock, R'lyeh saw that the beast's pale minions were still at it, still rubbing and spitting gore into Camazotz's black, matted fur.

The vampyres were children, like Elizabeth and Miranda had said. It was hard to tell how many there were, but most of them, aside from the odd seven- or eight-year-old, looked to be about R'lyeh's age, or a few years older. Gemma, the skinny thirteen-year-old with the dark hair and permanent smirk, was the leader of this hand-fanged gang. R'lyeh knew the girl was older than she looked, probably by about a thousand years or so, but that didn't change the fact Gemma was her age, and in charge. And she liked that.

For the longest time, R'lyeh had only wanted to fit in, to find a place to be comfortable and forgotten. But that left too much to chance and the whims of those more powerful than herself. She didn't want a blood lake or a Marrow Cabal, or even a tribe. She just wanted to have a say when someone else was saying she had to go.

R'lyeh pulled away from the sight of the lake and turned towards Operations. A gasp caught in her throat as she found Gemma beside her, her dirty bare feet floating every-so-slightly above the boards.

"You're the one with the mask?" Gemma asked.

R'lyeh wrinkled her forehead and looked around. They weren't alone—cabalists were moving back and forth in a steady stream from one level to the next—but there was no one nearby, either. They had never been kind to the Night Terror, and now that she was consorting with a vampyre, they gave her the kind of wide berth that made her feel like she was already diseased.

Gemma fussed with the bloodstained linen wrapped around each of her palms. "I like your mask." She tilted her head towards R'lyeh, sniffed, and said, "We never met many Night Terrors, but your kind don't really have your own scent, you know?"

R'lyeh didn't know what to say.

"Bunch of copycats, you Night Terrors." Gemma laughed, made a cocking sound with her mouth, pointed her fingers at R'lyeh, and pretended to shoot her. "What's up?"

R'lyeh still didn't know what to say.

Gemma rubbed her ankles together, but still she stayed suspended. "Any other kids around here?"

Kids? R'lyeh often though about her age, but not the fact she wasn't far out from having once been a kid herself. *Kids?* She scoffed.

Gemma didn't notice, or didn't care, and kept on with: "The Skeleton said you're the only Night Terror here, too. You must be some kind of celebrity. I wouldn't be too bummed about not bringing Audra back. Pretty sure the Skeleton was banking on that."

R'lyeh peered across Gallows, to Mr. Haemo's haunt. The mosquito's home at the center of the lake was still shrouded in pink fog, but it was thinner than before; and if she wasn't going crazy, and there was no guarantee on that, there appeared to be several shapes inside the fog, talking. The Skeleton was the only one who ever made the harrowing jaunt into the bug's den. Who the hell else was in there?

"Earth to R'lyeh."

"Why's t-that?" she stammered.

"Why didn't he want you guys to bring back Audra?" Gemma rolled her eyes and then finally brought her feet to the ground. "I mean, he's got plans, hasn't he? Obviously. Plus, dude's got the Black Hour's heart in his chest. Got to cut him some slack for not thinking too clearly."

"How do you know that? The Black Hour heart thing, I mean."

"I was there when he got it. Well, I showed him where the Dread Clock was. The Dread Clock and I go way back."

Sensing bullshit, R'lyeh said, "Oh, really?"

"Yeah, the Dread Clock completely ruined my life. Mom brought it home once, and it made my parents do awful things, and then it made them get rid of me. Dumped me at the Orphanage, and I never left.

"During the Trauma, I hunted that fucker down and dragged it into the Nameless Forest with us. I mean, it helped it was right outside, but still… I think that worked out better than I thought it would…" She laughed. "You don't believe me, do you?"

R'lyeh laughed and looked away from the vampyre girl. Should she believe her? Did it really even matter? They weren't friends, and they weren't about to be, either.

Camazotz let out a high-pitched squeak that bore through R'lyeh's brain. Vision trembling, she stumbled backwards, only to have Gemma reach out and catch her by the wrist. The girl's hand was clammy to the touch, and it pricked her skin, as if it were covered in thorns.

Realizing what was going on, R'lyeh ripped her wrist away from Gemma and shouted, "Stop!"

Amused, Gemma turned her hand over, the linen that once wrapped it hanging loosely around it. Her palm was slit open, from her middle finger to the heel. The womb-like wound quivered; inside it, glistening muscles throbbed out cloudy secretions. There were teeth, too, like the thorns R'lyeh had thought she felt. They were farther back—a hungry wreath of curved fangs—slowly making their way to the front of the slit, to feast.

R'lyeh went for her daggers, but they weren't there. They were on the Divide, in the mud, somewhere near Miranda's mutilated corpse. "What the fuck did you just do?"

"Nothing. You're fine." Gemma wrapped her hand back up. "The offer is there, just so you know."

Had the bitch bit her? Or were these the phantom pangs of paranoia she felt on her wrist? She rubbed her skin and searched for marks, but there was nothing there—only drool.

"Elizabeth told me about you and your Orphanage."

Gemma straightened out the red collar of her green dress. A few fat spiders scurried out of the gaping seams and ran back inside. "I'm sure she did. I'd really like to like you, R'lyeh. You seem cool."

What the hell is she doing?

The October wind buffeted Gallows from the North. The ramshackle town of reclaimed wood and ruins rattled and wavered, as if it didn't have much time left until it gave up for good. The Skeleton and his crew had made of it what they could, but even R'lyeh knew its time was up. She went for her faerie silk cloak, realized it wasn't on her, and hugged some warmth into herself, instead. Geharra was gone. Alluvia was gone. And by winter, Gallows would be gone, too. And she didn't have shit to show for anything, except for the shit she had inside her head, and no one was going to see that unless—

"What're you thinking about, R'lyeh?" Gemma asked coyly.

Need to keep moving, she thought, and started past Gemma.

"I'm sorry about Miranda."

R'lyeh stopped in her tracks, giving a start to the cabalists behind her. They went around her, grumbling.

"I'm sorry about all of them—Elizabeth, Jessie, and Miranda—but they should've never grown up. I warned them about adults and becoming one." Gemma started unraveling the linen on her hand again. "It's not worth it, R'lyeh. Seems like it is, but it isn't. I've tasted a lot of them. They all taste the same."

"What... do you want Gemma?"

"A... friend, I think." The vampyre gave a half-hearted shrug. "I heard you're ferocious, and you're a monster like me. But it's fine. Whatever." Gemma closed her eyes, looked away at Camazotz.

A friend? R'lyeh couldn't be anyone's friend. Miranda had been ripped apart, and Vrana wasn't much more than a name that haunted her like a curse.

"You can ride with us tomorrow morning, when we leave," Gemma offered. Then, disinterestedly: "You know, if you want."

"Didn't you know any Night Terrors back during the Trauma?" R'lyeh asked, completely changing the subject.

Hurt like lightning flashed across Gemma's face. It was there for a moment, and then it was gone. "No," she said, resolutely. "There were no Night Terrors back then."

"Yes, there were."

"I don't mean to be a bitch, but were you alive back then?"

Bitch, R'lyeh thought.

Gemma smiled; she sniffed R'lyeh once more. "Ride with us tomorrow morning. If these humans really appreciated you, you'd still have your mask on."

"And you're saying you appreciate me?"

Gemma smiled smugly. "Just saying I'll actually make the effort."

What the hell was going on? R'lyeh stormed her way up to the second level of the platform and zeroed in on Operations. Had she been talking aloud? Was Hex reading her mind? Or had Gemma? She hugged herself harder and remembered Rime and its Rot that had tried so hard to wrack her body. She was a good friend to have—she could take a beating and her heart would keep on beating—but she didn't need to have any friends of her own. Only poisons, and poisonous distractions.

R'lyeh threw the doors to Operations open and gasped. Where was everything? The tables were empty, the walls stripped bare. Gone were the maps, documents, field reports, and artifacts. Gone were the sections of the room dedicated to the progress of the Disciples of the Deep and the Holy Order of Penance. Every piece of evidence and data that had been collected was gone, vanished, either into a box or into shreds. R'lyeh started down the center, crouching and standing as she went, searching for the stacks of mandatory readings of *The Disciples of the Deep, Helminth's Way,* and *The Sinner and the Shadows,* but they were gone, too. All that was left was the Skeleton's desk, and even that looked ransacked.

There was moving, and then there was moving on. Gemma had said the Skeleton wanted R'lyeh and the Beauties to come back empty-handed, and that made sense to her now. But if he had done all of this for his family, then why the hell wasn't he taking his family with him?

R'lyeh ran to the Skeleton's desk and started ripping out the drawers. Empty, empty, empty—not a speck of dust, not that that was all too great a feat for a man with no skin. Where were the maps? Where were the drawings with the buildings and the word "bomb" written all over them? She dropped to her knees and worked free the last drawer. Before she could get it out, she could hear something rattling inside.

"What did you forget?"

She tugged, and the drawer gave. Falling back on her ass, the drawer going all the way to her crotch, she caught her breath, and caught a glimpse of what was inside.

At the bottom of the drawer, atop of a bedding of cloth, sat a vial of thick, gritty liquid. It was the vial of Thanatos she had stolen from him and then returned before leaving for Rime. A little bit of it was missing, but that was okay. It was just what she needed.

With death in her pocket, R'lyeh hurried out of Operations and headed to the bottom level of Gallows. Because of Camazotz's thrashing in the blood lake, most of the docks on the lower level were so slick with blood it was like trying to walk across ice. The mosquitoes were worse there, too; as the cabalists were trying their hardest to shift supplies from the town to the caravan, the insects moved in thick, ballooning clouds, sucking up the excess blood the fat bat had spilled. If anyone was glad to have the Marrow Cabal leaving this place, clearly it was Mr. Haemo. And that's exactly who she needed to see.

Another burst of wind rocked Gallows. R'lyeh reeled and slipped on the slippery docks. She crashed into the blood-soaked boards and cracked her funny bone. A stomach-churning sensation flared throughout her arm, up to her neck.

"Goddamn it!" she belted, her hands skating across the docks as she pushed off them and onto her feet. Swift as a knife, the mosquitoes slashed across her body, and when they were gone, it was clean—not a speck or spot of blood left on her.

Mr. Haemo could kill of us anytime he wants, R'lyeh thought, rubbing her elbow. *He won't because of the Skeleton. But if the Skeleton leaves…*

In a matter of seconds, all oddities became ill omens no longer possible to ignore.

The cold wind, ripe with decay, crept like a killer across the town, working its destructive charms on the unguarded and weak. Standing there, bearing the violent blasts, R'lyeh could almost feel the static of intent, as if the air were a discharge from some yet unseen plot.

Gallows was alive, but only because of the living desperate to be gone from it. At first, R'lyeh had mistaken the Marrow Cabal's response to the Skeleton as loyalty to the cause. Now, she realized that wasn't the case at all. Cabalists came and went, but their expressions remained the same: horror chancing relief. Watching them now was like watching prisoners who had woken to find their cells unlocked. How many cabalists were there, exactly? The number seemed to dwindle every time R'lyeh bothered to notice. And what exactly did the Skeleton have them doing? He had far more bodies to command than commands to give out. Like the Deadly Beauties' mission to retrieve Audra, it seemed the Marrow Cabal had been mostly for show.

Then there was the lake of blood and the beasts that worshiped it. Camazotz had been having a field day with the red stuff ever since she arrived, but it wasn't just her flailing that was making the blood churn. At the edge of the dock, the lake lapping like a dog at the supports below her, R'lyeh found something in the waves. Every time the blood moved, small spirals formed, in the same way water would ripple when rain would hit it. And it wasn't only that they were the shapes of spirals, but they were spirals turning inwards, like whirlpools, as if every inch of the lake was its own part, and every part was being drained.

R'lyeh went to one knee and pressed her ear as close as she dared to the lake. Gallows was loud today, but the blood was louder. There was something inside the spirals, speaking. Words inside the whirlpools. A seething rhythm; puerile poetry. Trying to make sense of what she was hearing made her brain burn and eardrums swell.

As if the speaker knew she was listening, the words suddenly stopped. R'lyeh's heart sank. Feeling caught, she looked up from the blood. Camazotz wasn't moving, and the vampyre children servicing the bat were staring directly at R'lyeh, letting the blood in their mouths run down their chins.

She had seen something wasn't supposed to have seen; heard something she wasn't supposed to have heard. Something was going on here.

"Are you ready to go?"

R'lyeh let out a shout. She looked back. Will was behind her, a bag slung over his shoulder. His face was covered in patches of stubble that he kept touching, proud to have finally grown them. She had felt that way once with her breasts, before Penance's soldiers got ahold of them. It didn't seem fair. As soon as you grew up, something always came along and made you wish you hadn't.

Will smiled at her like she was nuts. "You look like you're about to jump in."

"Heh." R'lyeh came to her feet, shaking her head. "Not a very good swimmer."

"I didn't know you were back. Sorry I didn't—" He twisted his mouth. "I'm glad you're back."

"Me, too."

"I know you told my dad about the shepherd in Bedlam. I'm not mad."

That was like two months ago; I completely forgot.

"Where's your mask?"

R'lyeh blushed. "Oh, I—"

Camzotz and the vampyres went back to making a loud mess in the lake.

"—I, uh, it's back in the Barracks."

"Weird seeing you without it." Then, quickly, he added, "I didn't mean it like that."

"You think I'm hideous?" R'lyeh made a fist, and then she remembered her plan. With that, she no longer felt like playing. "It's alright. How's your mom?"

"Same old same old," Will said. "She's happy to leave. Me, too. Hey, R'lyeh?"

Looking at the center of the lake, R'lyeh said, "Yeah?"

"Did my dad talk to you yet?"

"No, I don't know where he is," she said, but that was a lie. She knew exactly where he was. She could almost see his boney silhouette beyond the fog surrounding Mr. Haemo's Haunt. He was there with the bug and who knows what else, putting some terrible thing into motion.

"Oh. Oh, well, Elizabeth is gone."

Something snapped in R'lyeh's chest. "What?" Instinctively, she searched Gallows for the Deadly Beauty. "What? What do you mean?"

"She disappeared. I heard about Miranda…" Will's eyes went watery. Miranda had been his and his mom's guardian; by R'lyeh's guess, she'd probably spent more time with them than the Skeleton had lately. "Dad was going to ask her to watch over us, but she left."

She's gone? R'lyeh's eyes went watery, too. Her jaw locked; she tasted snot at the back of her throat—that universal flavor of sadness. *She left me.*

"Dad's going to ask you to help watch over us. Probably with Warren, too, but… yeah. Will you? My dad's crazy. It's good to take a break from him."

"I'm as old as you. I… what can I do?" R'lyeh remembered the Divide, and when she, Elizabeth, and Miranda had breakfast on it. "You have shepherds following you."

Will shook his head. "No, we don't."

"Come on, dude." There she was, using Gemma's word. "I saw it."

"I know, but I don't think it was a shepherd. A real one." He readjusted the strap of the bag over his shoulder. "Mom and I've been lying to him. Telling him we've been seeing shepherds. I freaked out on you on purpose. I'm sorry."

Stunned, R'lyeh asked, "The hell? Why?"

"Mom said he needed reminders. Something to keep him focused on us. He has the heart. He can make things… happen. I think when shepherds show up, it's because he's making it happen and doesn't even realize it. They should've taken us by now. I think Dad was so scared a shepherd was going to show up while we were in Bedlam, he made one appear—probably while he was sleeping. Or pretending to."

R'lyeh stepped away from Will. She had a plan. She had a plan. What the hell was going on? What the hell were these distractions? Did everyone know? Or was it just the blood? Her blood was in there, wasn't it? A bit from Geharra carried here to Gallows. It wasn't paranoid to think that it would be enough to form a connection between her and the lake and the forces that controlled it. She had a plan, and something didn't want her to see it through.

"What's wrong?" Will had noticed her uncertainty. "I swear, it's true."

R'lyeh backpedaled, going farther and farther down the dock, towards the untended walkway that would lead to the center.

"Don't go in there. R'lyeh, stop." Will reached for her, but he didn't follow. "Did he tell you something else? Did he change his mind?" His voice shook as he said, "Please, stay with us."

"He didn't tell me anything," R'lyeh said, slipping her hand into her pocket and gripping the vial of Thanatos. "I'm doing this myself."

"Doing what?" he shouted after her.

She didn't answer.

R'lyeh ran down the lone path that led to the center of the lake. She passed the point where she had spoken to the Skeleton earlier before leaving to rescue Audra, and kept going. If she slowed down, she'd stop, and if she stopped, she'd be back with Will, or even Gemma, doing something someone else wanted her to do. That wasn't going to happen. It couldn't happen. That was the life of a girl who might've been, if Miranda hadn't died, and Elizabeth might've stayed, and the Skeleton hadn't dumped her like a bad date five minutes into dinner.

Elizabeth and Miranda told her she didn't want to hurt herself or others so much, that there were other ways. But those ways were shut to her now. There was blood in her past and present. Who was she to expect anything different from the future?

Reaching the place where the pink fog covered the path, R'lyeh took a deep breath and pushed through it. Like a barrier, it bucked, but her will was stronger than its rule to keep her out. She closed her eyes and pressed her body into the fog. With every inch gained, another was lost. She screamed and threw fists, beating at the air like the mire it mimicked.

A foot in, and she could feel the fog breaking apart, giving itself to her. It enveloped her, filling in the hole she had made with her pigheaded desperation. Not wanting to do it, but doing it anyway, R'lyeh opened her eyes slightly to make sure she hadn't steered off course.

The dock still lay before her, but there wasn't much left of it. A few feet farther and she would've plunged straight into the bloody waters. But that wasn't the worst of it. This was Mr. Haemo, and when it came to Mr. Haemo, he could always be counted on to deliver disgust.

Out of the water, and seemingly reality itself, giant, shit-colored rafts of mosquito eggs had grown. It wasn't a matter of deciding if there were hundreds or thousands, but millions or billions. Fixed to the air, to the fabric of space, they curved over the dock like tooth-lined jaws—the spit they dripped the fluid from the wriggling larvae contained inside. Looking into the rafts, especially those on the surface of the lake, was like looking down on a city from the sky; the rafts were impossibly deep—deeper, maybe, than even the lake itself. Millions of eggs? Billions of eggs? No, much more than that. The rafts weren't parts of a nest, but countries of a continent—small, surface-level glimpses of the great, unimaginable horrors beyond the Membrane of this world.

Others would've stopped, but R'lyeh kept going. She took out the vial of Thanatos and, with both hands, pressed it to her heart.

"Where are you?" she called out, going to the end of the dock. "I know you're here."

A buzzing broke from the shit-colored heavens above. R'lyeh tipped her head back, but there was nothing there. Again, a buzzing; this time, to her right. In her mind, she drew Vrana's ax and faced that direction. And again, there was nothing there.

"Stop!"

Like vibrations across a wire, one after the other, the rafts of eggs shivered out wet, slopping sounds. A whole nation of larvae was watching her, waiting to get at her; to be her first, and her last.

The pink fog hadn't forgotten her. It rose up from in between the gaps in the dock and immediately overtook her. R'lyeh closed her eyes and her mouth, but it didn't matter. The fog was blood, sentient blood, and her pores were like doors to it. It seeped inside her, filled her lungs to capacity. Choking, vision dimming, she remembered the Ashen Man and how he had filled her lungs with flies. She had dodged Death once. That was more than most could hope for.

"Let her go," she heard the Skeleton say.

The fog rushed out of her lungs, up her throat, and exploded from her mouth. R'lyeh reared back, doubled-over. Shaking, she took big, greedy gulps of air while the fog dissipated around her.

"I'm g-going with y-you," R'lyeh stammered.

She swallowed hard and stood upright. The scene was the same, and different. Instead of the dock dead-ending at the borders of uncharted hell, it was checked by a single tree that twisted out of the lake. Its branches were bare, and its midsection massively engorged, so that it gave the appearance of being pregnant. Sitting atop the bulge was Mr. Haemo, and at the foot of the tree, on the edge of the dock, stood Herbert North and the Skeleton.

"Iä! Iä! R'lyeh fhtagn!" Herbert North cried, wringing his hands. He smiled a guilty smile and tried to block R'lyeh's view of the lake beyond.

There was smoke coming off the lake, behind the tree. R'lyeh hurried forward. Herbert North stepped aside, but the Skeleton stepped in front of her.

"You can't come," he said.

R'lyeh shoved him—

Celibate circuitry singing psalms to the achromatic tower. Sickness in the stars.

—shook off his Black Hour touch, and went to the edge of the dock.

"Shouldn't be here," Mr. Haemo buzzed, legs spread over the tree's bulge. "What'd you see?" He leaned forward, claws deep in bark, his huge proboscis inches from her head. "It's our secret."

R'lyeh ignored him and, pointing at the lake, said, "What the hell is this?"

Between the end of the dock and the base of the tree, a man-sized whirlpool churned. It was from here that the black smoke poured, but it wasn't because of the whirlpool itself, or the spells that had woven it. The smoke was coming out of the images inside the whirlpool, the scenes that played out shakily on every constricting layer. Earth and stone; cave and causeway; prison bars and ruddy opulence. Like the Skeleton's caress, the whirlpool was a mere fraction of a maelstrom of experiences. And the images? They weren't reflections, but etchings; Mr. Haemo and the Skeleton were burning their way through reality, the same way the mosquito had hitched his brood into the invisible grooves of time and space.

R'lyeh had seen this before. Months ago, when the Skeleton had destroyed the Red Worm and saved his family. Everyone knew Mr. Haemo was using Gallows as a blood well. But the smoke? The images? The sons of bitches had opened another portal.

"You can't come." The Skeleton put himself in front of R'lyeh, and then stepped forward, pushing her back. "The Dead City isn't a place for you. I want you with my family. I'm not going to be moved on this."

"I thought… you were… going to—"

"Walk?" Mr. Haemo clicked out laughter. "Our Fearless Leader is above such mortal things."

Herbert North's eyes pleaded with R'lyeh. He reached out as if to touch her, but stopped himself. "I knew a girl who went through hell, and when the time came, she thought hell was all she deserved." He nodded back towards Gallows.

Gemma? "How do you—"

"I saved her from the Dread Clock once. But I underestimated its effect on her family. This is Atticus' curse. It doesn't have to be yours." He smiled. "I'm going to Angheuawl, too, with Hex and the others. I know you want to know all about the Old World. I'll tell you everything. But this isn't—"

The Skeleton pulled his ratty cloak closed. "There's nothing to discuss. The Dead City is covered in sickness and disease. You'll die. I won't. That's all there is to it."

"No, that's the thing. I won't." R'lyeh finally took her hand away from her breast and revealed the vial of Thanatos inside it. "I'd say ask Elizabeth or Miranda…" A tear snuck out, and she quickly wiped it away. "That stuff doesn't hurt me. I'm immune."

"What is this? I'm intrigued," Mr. Haemo said, flashing his wings. "You been holding out on us, girl?"

The Skeleton cocked his skull. "What's that in your hand?"

The pink fog pressed in on them from every direction. From the whirlpool, the sounds of a cavern emerged, amplified.

"Deathshade, malingas, poisonbite berries," R'lyeh started. "Darkslick frogs, gloom caps. I've eaten or been bit, or both, by all of them and more.

"When I went to Rime? I was immune to the Rot in less than thirty minutes. And you know the Crossbreed couldn't have affected me. I wouldn't be here if it had. I want to go with you. I can help you."

"Is that the Thanatos?" The Skeleton chattered his jaw. "Give it here. Killed me once. It'll kill you."

Herbert North shouted, "No, don't."

And Mr. Haemo leaned farther in, his bulbous red eyes glinting with sadistic curiosity.

R'lyeh took the stopper out of the vial. The Thanatos' odor found her nostrils immediately and coated it with that sweet, intestinal smell. She pressed the vial to her lips; the poison clung like barnacles to the vial, so she had to shake it loose. One drop was enough to kill a man. But she wasn't a man, nor was she a human. So maybe, just maybe, this could work.

"What're you trying to prove?" the Skeleton said, inching closer to her.

"Never you mind," R'lyeh said, mocking his accent.

She opened her mouth and flicked the vial. The Thanatos dribbled onto her lips, sealing their cracks with the stuff of Death. By the time the poison had reached her tongue, she was blind. And by the time the thick, black spread had coated the back of her throat, she was dead.

And then she wasn't.

R'lyeh shot up from off the ground, her nose bleeding, her eyes watering; the tips of her fingers and toes feeling as if they were on fire. Her chest hurt so bad she had to check it to make sure it hadn't caved in completely. Mouth and throat still filled with the Thanatos, R'lyeh clawed over to the edge of the dock and splashed the blood into her mouth; guzzling it, gargling it, she spat and swallowed and made herself vomit, over and over again, until the taste of blood was stronger than that of Death.

"Goddamn," she heard Mr. Haemo say. "Atticus, you got some competition."

R'lyeh didn't respond. She couldn't. Every inch of her, inside and out, felt as if hooks had dug into her, like she had been reeled out of the underworld.

"What did you see?" The Skeleton stepped up next to her. "R'lyeh, what did you see?"

"Nothing."

That was a lie, of course. She had seen something. She could still see it even now, the residual image like needlepoint upon her eyelids. There had been mostly darkness; bridges of light. And a moth and two skulls, and red words amongst the stars. But the Skeleton didn't need to know that. The jackass had tried to call her bluff, and failed. Now, she was calling the shots.

"Are you okay?" Herbert North's voice shook as he spoke. "Oh god, are you okay? Big Bug, do something!"

R'lyeh batted at the air, just in case someone actually tried to help her. Carefully, smiling with her bloodstained teeth, she rose to her feet. "I told you," she belted to the lot of them. "I fucking told you."

Mr. Haemo rubbed his claws together and hopped down from the tree's swollen trunk. The dock gave a little as the seven-foot mosquito's weight crashed into it. He pulled the hood of the skin cloak he wore over his head and giggled like a child.

Herbert touched the wound on his neck. "Atticus, she's been through enough."

"He doesn't have a choice," Mr. Haemo said, starting to pace back and forth in front of the whirlpool. "Take the girl, Gravedigger, or I close the portal. Don't trust you do this on your own. Not with that shit in your chest."

The Skeleton ran his fat, black tongue over the top of his jaw. His bloodshot eyes darted back and forth, between Mr. Haemo and Herbert North. "We're leaving now."

R'lyeh nodded. But she couldn't help herself: "What about the others?"

"Got to go now," the Skeleton said. "Won't if we don't. Blood will take us to the Dead City, and that's how we'll get back. There's weapons in the City; guns, explosives. The Vermillion God is coming. The humans killed It before with those things. We can do it again. The Marrow Cabal will wait in Angheuawl until we get back."

"How do you know all that?"

Herbert North looked away, ashamed.

"But... you have the Black Hour's heart." R'lyeh wiped her mouth. "You can do anything. You don't need to go to the Dead City."

The Skeleton shook his head. "Penance is going to be here soon. Eldrus, too, probably."

"Do the others know that's why they have to leave?" R'lyeh curled her lip. "Is that what you told your wife and son?"

The Skeleton looked over his shoulder. "Never you mind that. Are you coming?"

"N-now?" R'lyeh looked around the dock. "We don't have any supplies."

"I don't eat or drink. And I don't need no weapons when I have these—" The Skeleton held up his boney hands.

Hebert North cleared his throat. "Stay, R'lyeh. Being immune to one thing doesn't mean you're immune to everything. You don't want to go in there."

R'lyeh raised an eyebrow and looked into the whirlpool. The images in the blood were growing more intense. Earth and stone, and towers covered in gold and rust.

"Is that the Dead City?"

Mr. Haemo finally stopped pacing and launched off the dock into the air. "It's one of them."

The Skeleton grumbled, took off down the dock, and dropped into the whirlpool. A downdraft formed at the center of the lake, transforming the whirlpool into a smoking vortex.

The white hairs on Herbert North's head whipped back and forth. "Don't," he said. "He did everything for Clementine and Will to get them back, and now he can't bear to be around them. He's not the man he used to—"

R'lyeh waved off the old man and staggered to the end of the dock. The Thanatos was still in her system, but she didn't have time to wait it out.

"You have to admit," she said, staring into the swirling vortex, "this makes sense."

"No, it doesn't," Herbert said. "This isn't fate."

R'lyeh put one leg over the edge of the dock. "Then what is it?"

"A little girl who went through hell, and who now thinks hell is all she deserves."

She shook her head and tongued the last of the fresh Thanatos hidden behind her teeth. One drop was enough to kill her, and this time, she didn't even feel a thing.

R'lyeh closed her eyes, told the old man and giant bug she'd see them again soon, and fell forward into the vortex.

The blood swallowed her whole; seconds later, it spat her back out. She fell from one body of gore to another, before washing up on a dim, stony shore. Disorientated, she clawed her way across the rocks, out of the pool of blood. She could hear the Skeleton nearby, doing the same, but her eyes hadn't adjusted to the light.

"R'lyeh?" she heard the Skeleton call out.

R'lyeh blinked and blinked until her pupils were large enough to work with. This was a cave, she surmised; some sort of underground place. Body sticking to the stones, she flipped over from her belly to her back and stared up at the ceiling of the place.

But there was no ceiling, no true ceiling; only a gigantic hole at the top of the cave through which the evening sun poured. The rocks around the fissure were stained with blood, as if some massive torrent had blown through the cave.

R'lyeh's heart sank. Her eyes became jittery as they danced around the hollow. Fixed to the walls were pieces of what appeared to be a spiraling platform; they ran from the top of the hollow, all the way to the blood from which she and the Skeleton had emerged.

She could see the Skeleton in her periphery, watching her as she put the pieces together. He was holding a red stone in his hand that had strange markings across it.

R'lyeh scurried backwards and looked over her shoulder, where she found another piece of a ramp, and a hole in the wall where a few prison cells had been built. Then she was on her feet, staring at the closing portal, noticing how the lake of blood seemed to go deeper still.

R'lyeh glanced back up at the fissure. She could see the sun and the clouds, but there was more than that, too. There were buildings. Large, towering buildings, gilded and glowing, that were so rich just looking at them made her teeth hurt.

She looked back down, at the blood, and at the sheer walls that fed into the lake, forming a funnel. She noticed doorways on one of the overlooks, and what appeared to be skinny corpses piled there.

The Skeleton told her not to worry, that she was safe.

But how could she be safe when she was back where this started? Where she had been beaten and abused, and forced into a cell for days on end. Where she had watched children being raped, and made to rape one another. Where she had seen her mom and dad murdered during the day that'd happened, and all the nights that'd followed. Where ten thousand Corrupted and hundreds of Night Terrors had been brutalized and degraded, so that the holy could keep their hold on heaven. Where flesh fiends had risen out of the waters she now stared at, to feed on fresh flesh, rather than the rotted muck they then wore.

Where a woman named Vrana had saved her, who she couldn't even save in return.

She was safe? R'lyeh started to laugh and cry at the same time. She was safe? How could she be safe when she was back again at the Pit of Geharra?

CHAPTER XIX

Other than the Garden of Sleep and the stars that shone below it, there wasn't much color when it came to the Abyss. At least, that's what Aeson thought, until Death pointed to a place in the dark, distant and gray. It was hard to see, but once he had, it was impossible to see anything else. Shapeless and senseless, the gray cloud sprawled out across the blackness like a nebula. Little light emerged from the astral splatter, but it was enough to let everyone who saw it know that, though it may have been forgotten, it was not unoccupied.

Staring at the gray nebula filled Aeson with such an intense sadness that he almost started crying. It was radiating emotions, the same way the Dead City was said to give off sickness and disease. But the Dead City, however unearthly, was a physical place. Aeson couldn't explain it, but the distant nebula made him feel as if he were peering into a mind, rather than a universe; into a place that had never been, or could ever be, ever again.

"Pain and Joy are my daughters," Death said, "and that gray place is the Void in which they reside. They are never far from me."

Death crossed her arms, closing her wings around her body. The antennae twitched on her head, the same way someone's lip might if they were starting to tear up. Using her scissor-like fingers, she made shapes in the air—sign language, perhaps, for the forever sleeping—and then turned her back to Aeson and Bjørn.

"Come with me," she said, leaving the helm of their boat, going deeper into the Garden.

Aeson and Bjørn both looked down. No matter where they planted their feet, the life-stealing plant that was Death's Dilemma would be crushed. Their attentions focused on them, the flowers ducked their heads even farther beneath their stalks, as if embarrassed.

Death went sideways. Her mouth opened, but didn't move, as she said, "You're as far away from living as possible. Those flowers won't hurt you." She paused, added, "They're not for you. They never were for anyone," and kept walking towards the center of the Garden.

Aeson looked at Bjørn, and Bjørn looked at Aeson. They didn't need to take off their masks to know the expression on each other's faces.

"She's right," Bjørn said. "There's nothing to lose."

"Right now, she has everything," Aeson said.

"Death always did."

Bjørn took a deep breath, even though there was no air to breathe here, and stepped out of the boat. Carefully at first, and then brutishly, he crushed a patch of Death's Dilemma with both his feet. The flowers melted like ice underneath Bjørn, but he did not die.

Okay, Aeson told himself. *You can do this.* And so he stepped out of the boat, into the Garden, and onto a patch of Death's Dilemma so thick he should've died ten times over.

Bjørn laughed.

Aeson couldn't help but do the same.

"They were the first," Death said. "I wouldn't call them daughters, but they are mine."

She was referring to the shepherds that kept appearing and disappearing at random intervals around the Garden of Sleep. They didn't seem to be alive or dead; rather, merely being; creatures of focus and a singular purpose. The shepherds were nearly identical to one another; the only discrepancy was the color of their nail polish. It was as if Death had decided they had to be human, and female, and because Death was neither, superficiality was the only tool at her disposal she was competent enough with to use.

"The entropy of existence can be difficult to manage. Things, on occasion, do slip through my fingers."

Death flexed her hands; Aeson could hear the sharpness of her claws. They looked like scissors, but were far more delicate in shape and curve. Scalpels, maybe, meant to cut out the dead tissue of the World.

Death continued through the Garden, her footsteps leaving no impression, no destruction. She was there, and yet, she wasn't.

"My shepherds maintain those who resist the Abyss, and those who have been called from it." Death stopped at the center, where her name-sake flowers were at their thickest, looked at Aeson and Bjørn, and said, "You have already taken the first step. A few more will not kill you."

At the same time, Aeson and Bjørn moved forward, side-by-side, like two friends approaching oblivion. The Garden of Sleep withered and died in every place that their feet touched it. If they had some life in them, then this was no place for it.

"Are… are Pain and Joy shepherds?" Aeson asked.

"I cannot give life," Death said. "I can only give a part of myself. The shepherds are simply extensions of my purpose. But Pain and Joy were pieces I tore from myself and molded into something new. They began as me, and then, over time, became something else.

"After watching the living for so long, I realized how lonely I was in the Abyss. The lights below us—"

Aeson looked down, through the groundless Garden, at the countless stars that filled the fathomless dimensions of the Abyss.

"—are those that have died. I used to snuff souls out of existence, but over time, I started to collect them. Once I did this, things began to weave spells to steal from my collection. I did not mind this. I liked the challenge, and the idea of a second chance. I did not know such things.

"So, I collected souls to keep me company, but the dead are poor companions. They do not speak, and they are far from me. Those who were resurrected were eager to go, so I formed my shepherds to return them to the flock. But the shepherds are mirrors, and already myself was not enough. For all that I created and coveted, I was still alone.

"I reached inside myself and tore out of a piece of my heart. I gave it my blood and breath, and because my loneliness had grown so painful, Pain is what I grew."

Aeson and Bjørn had reached the center of the Garden. Behind them, their treacherous trek had left a path of ruin. He didn't know if the plants would grow again, and because they appeared to be all Death had, he felt guilty; more so than for courting a mother to help kill her daughters.

The skulls and eyes on Death's wings rotated and blinked. Her stomach, colored in accordance to her Dilemmas, shimmered. She continued: "Humans interest me. There are better, more evolved creatures, but I am fascinated by their flaws. I modeled the shepherds after them, and in time, Pain began to take on their appearance, too. Even when she was nothing more than tissue and fluids, she was beautiful. I had one daughter. I needed another.

"I reached into my heart and tore another piece from it. I gave it my blood and breath, and because I was overjoyed with what I had done, Joy is what I grew."

Watching Death retell her tale, Aeson began to worry. He noticed the way her antennae moved, and the way parts of her bulbous eyes swelled. She stiffened, too, as if on the defense. And she kept twitching her fingers, striking blade against blade. If she managed to finish her story without finishing them first, would she still help them? Was it making it better? Or making it worse?

Aeson took off his mask and held it at his side. "What happened next?" he asked Death, all his flaws on display.

"Children are observers," Death said, cocking her head, fascinated by his appearance. She looked at Bjørn.

And Bjørn quickly took off his mask and held it at his side. His face was flushed, and sagging; he looked two times older than what he claimed. All the years he had dodged Death were finally caching up with him.

"I wanted them to observe something other than the Abyss." Death sounded pleased; her iridescent jaw quivered. "They were not much then, so I carried them like dust upon my wings. We flew the Membrane, even the worlds no one will ever know, but because a child is, in part, their parent, it was humans and the places they had colonized to which my daughters were drawn."

Bjørn cleared his throat. "Were they… always… always the way they are now?"

"No," Death said, turning to the gray Void clinging like mold to the rim of the Abyss. "I made them much, much worse.

"They grew up too quickly. Pain and Joy had bodies of their own before I knew it. Thoughts, too, and beliefs that I had not put there. They were me, this is true, but I had left most of them empty, so that they could be filled and made something else. Different kinds of Death, if you will; two that had taken different paths from their mother, and yet would still arrive at the same place. That is, here, in the Abyss, with me.

"I was never a child. I was never anything but what I am now. I did not know childhood. Pain and Joy were difficult children. They were cruel, and covetous. They teased and tortured my shepherds—"

Aeson glanced over at the creatures. Though they had been arriving and leaving the Garden of Sleep in silence, each with bandages in their hands, their gaze was always fixed on Death. It wasn't that they didn't know the story she was telling. It was almost as if, and this was a guess, because their long, blonde hair blocked their faces, they wanted to hear how she was telling it. If it would reach the end they all clearly wanted.

"—and when I left them with the humans, mostly on Earth, they would sow mischief and misery. Parents lie to themselves about the quality of their children. I did not."

Aeson's throat tightened. Because of Death's words, he remembered something Adelyn had said: To love Vrana, no matter what she had become.

"For a long time, I did lie to myself about Pain and Joy. They were cruel and mischievous, and mean-spirited, but darkness breeds darkness, and darkness is what we had here at the edge of everything. Difficult as it may be to imagine now, Pain and Joy did develop kindness and consideration. They showed affection in kisses, and even played with the shepherds. Joy grew the Garden, to make me happy and to gather friends, while Pain tended to the souls below, to study them and quantify the deeds that led to their deaths.

"No, it was not their quality about which I lied to myself, but their necessity.

"In my daughters, I saw my own doubt, and perhaps, my own downfall. Death does not have a lineage, and yet I formed successors. Pain and Joy were killers, while I merely collected those that needed to be killed. In my daughters, I saw competition, and perhaps, my own obsolescence."

The shepherds stopped coming to the Garden. Above, the red ring that let out to the fleshy tunnel beyond seared itself shut. Below, the stars of souls grew smaller and smaller, while the gray Void appeared to be expanding. Death was steering them closer to her daughters' domain.

"I know the end of all things. Not how it will happen, or when, but only that it will. I know when you will die Aeson—"

Aeson swallowed hard and stared at Death's wings.

"—and when you will die, Bjørn."

Bjørn nodded, whispered, "Is it soon?"

Death ignored him. "I knew that my daughters would die, too. But death does not know Her own death, and never had I worried about my place until those two girls were standing in my shadow. By creating Pain and Joy, I had violated something sacred and profound. I loved them. I love them dearly. But in the end, as it had always been, I loved myself more."

Again, Death's torso shimmered blue and white. She bent down and plucked a Death's Dilemma from the ground and held it outwards. The melancholic petals caught the gray Void's light and glowed like a grave at dusk.

"Pain and Joy had lived for a very long time, but if you had seen them at the moment I decided to kill them, you would have thought they were five years old."

Death dropped the flower, and her Dilemma was dust before it could hit the ground.

"I brought them to Earth with a lie. I told them we were going to live amongst the humans for a while—something which they had greatly enjoyed in the past. We settled on a small town in the mountains that has since been renamed Angheuawl."

That's where the Cult of the Worm is gathering, Aeson realized, heart thudding in his chest.

"There are many beautiful lakes in the area. Hot springs, too, from the volcanic activity of Kistvaen. Pain and Joy played with the children during the day, and their parents at night, while I debated and debased myself away from a decision. I think my daughters knew something was wrong, but among the living, they were, in their own way, gods. The Abyss never had satisfied their cravings. How could it? They were creatures born of my curiosity in humanity. They wanted power, and companionship.

"I knew they could no longer be, so I woke them early one morning, packed food for a picnic, and took them to Angheuawl's most secluded lake. While they were laying out the blanket and setting out the food, I took a rock and bashed their heads in. They did not die. I knew that it would not be that easy, but I could not bring myself to destroy them so brutally. While they were unconscious, I dragged them to the lake. I held them under the water for hours, until the sun had risen and fallen and risen once more. They were full of water, and they were no longer moving. When I looked upon their bloated corpses, I, for the first time in my existence, wept.

"And then I left them there, because despite all my strength, I was not and could never be strong enough to carry what I had done back to the Abyss with me."

Death sighed, clicked her claws against one another. The Garden of Sleep slowed to a halt. The gray Void wasn't close enough to touch, but it was near enough that Aeson could see shapes inside it. Pillars, and walls, and landscapes of its own pock-marked by black, roaming clouds.

She's in there, Aeson thought. *Vrana's in there. She's right there. If only I could just...*

"Why didn't they die?" Bjørn asked.

"I do not know," Death said. "They had a part of me, and so perhaps that gave them an immunity to me. They were curious creatures, like myself, and I know they had spent much time in the Membrane, exploring the worlds it ran between.

"Some time passed before I realized Pain and Joy had not perished. Souls began to join the Abyss that had died by their hands. My daughters were alive, and they were an unstoppable force, moving through the world, building their own myth, constructing their own lore. They gave themselves strengths and limitations, and simple goals to achieve. The humans they terrorized and tortured were instrumental in providing my daughters a purpose. Pain and Joy could have murdered the world in those days, but they preferred to make it suffer, instead.

"I could not kill them again. I could have, but I had failed once, and I knew, in part, their slaughtering was an attempt to spite me. I could not face them; that is the truth of it."

"The Void," Aeson said, nodding towards it. "What is it?"

"I gave half my heart to have my daughters, and half my heart to kill them. The void that was left behind is my weakness, and the Void made of it is their power.

"I do not know if it was I who made it, or them, but when I realized they had not died, I then realized the Void was there. It is where they live; they cannot be harmed there. In the shadow of Death, one is immortal."

Death bent over once more and plucked another Dilemma. In a whisper, she said, "Humans are terrible storytellers. In a matter of seconds, a tale can change. Tell me, Bear, what is this flower's story?"

"It's, uh, meant to represent... represent someone you loved," Bjørn said, sweating. "And someone who loved you. An... impossible union."

"No," Death said, shaking her head. "I formed these flowers after I learned my daughters were still alive. Death's Dilemma is not a weapon, but an invitation. I could not kill them by my own hand, but if they would take one of these flowers, they would be accepting death on their own terms.

"I planted Death's Dilemma across the Earth, and every place my daughters were known to go. Everything they do is to hurt me; I wanted them to know that I was watching, listening, and that the Abyss would have them, if they would have it."

"The flowers are said to snip your soul if you pick it," Aeson whispered.

Death flicked her fingers, like scissor blades.

"Even if it's not your daughters picking them, you kill the person?"

"The flowers, like the shepherds, are extensions of myself. They do, and if they do not, they are nothing."

Death crumbled the flower. "It interests me that a few years ago, Joy was having a similar conversation to ours now with King Edgar in the Nameless Forest."

Aeson and Bjørn exchanged glances.

"Pain and Joy have been together as much as they have been apart. They loathe each other's company as much as they love it. After the Trauma, they went their separate ways. Pain retreated to the Void, while Joy settled in the Nameless Forest.

"She had a family. Joy had always wanted a family, or at least, playthings. Throughout history, she has formed families, only to destroy them or cause them to destroy themselves. But for the first time, in the Nameless Forest, she had a family of four boys that just so happened to be descendants of King Edgar. So many had tried to kill them in the past, to claim the Forest, and every time, Joy stopped them, even though she had wanted to do the same herself. But when King Edgar arrived, she finally lost all interest in her sons, and she promised him the Forest and its secrets if he did. And he did.

"And so here we are now, you beseeching me to destroy my daughters—my daughters, who I cannot kill, and yet think of killing every day. At any other moment in time, I would have collected you for the dark, but in this moment, I will help you.

"Because, you see, children truly are their parents. I tortured and mutilated myself to create tortured and mutilated companions—my shepherds, my Pain and Joy. What does Pain do if not torture and mutilate in the pursuit of companionship and power? I leave Death's Dilemma, and my daughter leaves traps. She is me, and I am her.

"I formed beings because I was lonely. Despite the terrible existences they have lived, I formed them, regardless. I have done it before, and I will do it again, and again. I collect. I am covetous. I need nothing, and yet I want. What does Joy do if not collect and covet in the pursuit of happiness and higher purpose? I form extensions of myself, and my daughter does the same. She is me, and I am her.

"Today, I want them dead. Tomorrow, I may not. I do not see the future. I do not know if this was meant to be. You seek a Red Death weapon? I would have to forge one anew."

"Will it take long?" Aeson asked.

And Bjørn followed with: "How does it work?"

Death lightly flapped her wings and lifted slightly off the ground. "I created the Red Death weapons for creatures to combat threats beyond their capabilities. Humans have created replicas through the use of spell-weaving, but a true Red Death weapon holds the power of myself and the Abyss."

"It can kill anything?" Aeson asked.

Death nodded.

"Even a Worm?"

"Worms do not answer to this Death," she said.

"But it will kill the Witches?" Bjørn asked.

"No," Death said, "but it will be strong enough to sever their connection to this place, to me. It will close them off from the Void, and they will be as human and weak as they've told themselves they would be without it."

Aeson said, "But they have to be out of the Void."

"They will be," Death said. "Abandoned children crave attention. The Cult of the Worm will reach the end of its pilgrimage soon. You can be sure they will be there, in attendance."

Aeson didn't want to ask it. He didn't want to ask anything, anymore. He wanted to be on his way, out of here, with what they had, and nothing else. But he had to ask it, and so he did. "Will it take long to make a new weapon?"

"It is already ready," Death said. She lowered herself back onto the Garden. "If things were different, I may have given the weapon to you two freely."

Aeson's heart sank.

Bjørn literally sank beside him.

"But between you, Aeson, and you, Bjørn, and Vrana, the woman you mean to save, I have been cheated. Each of you were meant to die. You did not die."

Bjørn started whispering underneath his breath.

"One soul for one weapon. I do not care whose soul it is. I could take you both, and one day, I will have you both, but for now, one will do."

Aeson quivered. "Bjørn," he said. "I… we… you're strong… you're stronger…" He wanted to say that he should die in the Bear's place, but the words weren't coming to him. He didn't want to die. He had suffered and suffered, but he didn't want to die. "You have a better…"

Bjørn stepped up to Death. He dropped his mask into the flowers. "Take me," he said.

"What?" Aeson shouted. He reached for Bjørn—

But before he could touch him, and tell him no, this wasn't right, that he shouldn't be the one to die; that he was the one who should save Vrana, just like he had saved Vrana before; that Aeson should have died on the tree with his parents—

Death swept forward and closed her wings around Bjørn. Her form overtook him, and he disappeared completely in her embrace. There was something like a sigh, and then Death pulled back, away.

Bjørn's pale, lifeless body fell down on its knees. It lingered there a moment, his eyes dim, his mouth slack. And then he fell on his haunches and onto his back, crushing all the beautiful, killing flowers under his dead weight.

"Bjørn," Aeson whispered, eyes bulging from their sockets, drool dripping from his jaws.

Death hummed and leaned over Bjørn's body. With one blade-like finger, she sliced through the Bear's breastplate, shirt, and chest. His body split open like a clam, revealing his glistening, useless innards.

"Don't," Aeson said, barely able to speak.

But Death continued, anyway. She reached into Bjørn's chest, grabbed one of his ribs, and broke it off. Then the moth stood up, twisted off her own finger, and jammed it through the rib, so that it protruded from it like a blade. She held the weapon up to her iridescent mouth, and the words she spoke materialized as runes upon the air. They slithered onto the rib and burned into the bone as vibrant, red shapes.

"Here," Death said, offering the Red Death weapon to Aeson. "Now, if you give up, you will not only betray your love, but your friend as well."

Aeson closed his eyes, and then closed his grip around the rib. He was crying so hard, he almost nicked his finger on Death's finger blade.

"You can go now," Death said. "When you open your eyes, you will be back where you started, in the swamp, outside your home of Caldera. If you are surprised that I do not offer any more assistance, you should not be. You are going to kill my daughters.

"As for your friend, weep not. His suffering is over. He will no longer know pain, nor joy. Only the finality of the Abyss. In this existence, for a man like Bjørn, there is no greater kindness."

"Why didn't you kill him before?" Aeson said, eyes squeezed shut. "Why did you let him go? With me? With Vrana?"

"Why does the Skeleton live when he's died more than the whole of the world combined?" He heard Death laugh. "If I knew everything, there would be nothing. Nothing is best... for everything."

"You must be strong now, Aeson," Death said. "Is a human skull truly the right mask for you?"

Aeson felt his mask leave his hand, and another one, a larger one, go in its place.

"Remember me as I am today. So that when we meet again, we meet as friends."

Aeson slowly opened his eyes. Death was gone, and so were the Abyss and the Garden of Sleep. He was back in the swamp, amongst the Weeping Willows, with Ferry Woman a few feet away, standing diligently by her boat.

Aeson looked down. In one hand, he held the Red Death weapon, and in the other, Bjørn's mask. He fixed the rib to his belt, and slowly, more carefully than he had been with the Red Death weapon, he lowered the bear skull over his head.

It was too large. It didn't fit right. But it would, in time. It had to.

CHAPTER XX

The Ossuary hadn't stopped stirring ever since King Edgar and his guard had arrived. He had heard stories that the desert was actually comprised of bone, not sand, but even he, the man who had taken the Nameless Forest and witnessed the Vermillion God, struggled to believe them. According to maps, the Ossuary was just as large, if not larger, than the rest of the continent. The number of bones needed to be crushed and spread over that vast distance was made all the more gut-wrenching by imagining how many bodies had to be pulverized to achieve such a goal. But whereas before he might've been put off by the notion, today, Edgar was not. For with his knees on the ground, the bones of the earth running between his fingers, he knew he knelt not before the graveyard of graveyards, but the gates and wastes of his God's great and inevitable heaven.

Edgar made a fist, some sand still inside it, and pressed it to his parched lips. He breathed in the dead, until he coughed them right back out. Heaven was a heavy weight to carry. He had been bearing it for years now; at first, reluctantly, but now he carried it because he hadn't the help to set it down. It drove him. It kept the ghost away.

The desert was a furnace, and Edgar and his companions seemed to be the coals off which it fed. They had been in the Ossuary for two days and two nights. Whether it was morning or evening, the heat was constant, and consistently unbearable. It was a searing omen of death to come—like the hot breath trapped against one's mouth and the pillow meant to smother. Even with Archivist Amon's collection at his disposal, Edgar hadn't been able to find much in the way of research on the desert. Most expeditions failed due to dehydration or death, or the futility of

271

trying to understand such a hostile frontier. But where previous explorers were wrong was in their assumption that such a place was meant to be discovered. It was never meant to be charted. Like a shipwreck upon a shore, it was never meant to be here at all.

Edgar wiped the bone off his brow and rose to his feet. It was hard to look at the sun, not only because of how bright it was, but because he was fairly certain it wasn't their sun. The blazing, seemingly melting orb hung in the sky like a meteor in low orbit—an apocalypse in stasis.

There were footsteps behind him, but he didn't want to acknowledge them. For the first time since Edgar could remember, he had found some semblance of peace. Between murdering his family, overtaking the Nameless Forest, and unleashing the Disciples of the Deep upon the mainland, he'd had no reprieve. It had been years since this task was forced upon him, and yet when he looked back, the years seemed to be nothing more than a single day he'd stretched beyond what should've been its limits. Archivist Amon, Alexander Blodworth, Crestfallen, the Anointed One, Lotus—they each had coaxed and coerced him into doing awful, terrible, unforgettable things. But he had been complacent, too, in the planting of the Crossbreed in Geharra, the spreading of the vermillion veins, and the torturing of the Marrow Cabal and their leader, the Gravedigger. To call an end to the years-long day would require some acceptance of the events. And accept them Edgar could not, not until this was over. It all had to have been for something, and that something had to be good.

Edgar took a few steps forward, until the plateau they'd made camp on fell away to a fifteen-foot drop. They were deep enough in the Ossuary to be able to look back and not see the world from which they'd come. Standing there, surveying the seamless sand and endless sky, he could fully feel and appreciate the allure of heaven. After so much wrongdoing, he felt right inside. This was the gift he wanted to share with the world; not only with the Disciples of the Deep, but everyone, even the non-believers. It was a shame he had to denounce the Holy Order of Penance, but he needed as little division as possible. The Trauma wasn't a scar, but a wound still sore to the touch. When the Vermillion God woke, he had to be sure that wound wasn't going to open again. Otherwise, this time, there would be no saving the world from drowning in its own ignorant blood.

At the bottom of the plateau, dried-out vermillion veins rose and fell out of the sands, like coils of razor nettle. God's fluids still pumped through the growths, but in a thick, inconsumable broth of blood and bone. Addiction made Edgar salivate at the sight, so he reached into his pocket, pulled out a fresher vein, put it in his mouth, and sucked his Lord out of it.

The footsteps stopped. The shadow of the person behind him joined his own.

"We need to go farther."

Edgar turned to face the Anointed One. The boy he'd brought out of the Nameless Forest looked twelve years old now—the same age as the Holy Child. In fact, the Anointed One appeared to imitate the Holy Child every chance he could get, be it in mannerism, speech, and appearance. He had even given himself a secret, common name—Valac—which only Edgar was to call him by.

Edgar had only known Amon in his twilight years; he had never realized how much these pieces of the Vermillion God were truly creatures of mimicry. The Anointed One was the harbinger of their Lord, and yet he looked to false prophets for inspiration. Sometimes, it made Edgar worry; other times, he laughed, instead.

Valac's entire mouth and throat were stained with the Vermillion God's blood. His teeth were red, and so were his fingertips. The boy was twelve years old, but of late, he looked closer to his actual age, which had to be in the hundreds of thousands to millions. It was the gut that gave him away. Before they had left Eldrus for the Ossuary, Valac had finished assimilating Amon into his body, gaining all his knowledge and experience in the process. The drawback was that now the boy's stomach was completely swollen with the corpse of the old man he had consumed. If the reminders of cooking weren't enough, to Edgar, Valac looked like a potbelly stove.

"We have to find the communing place," Valac said. And then, gravely, he added, "Before nightfall."

The temperature in the Ossuary spiked another two or three degrees, as if to add a fiery underscore to Valac's warning. Edgar wasn't wearing armor, but mumiya wraps, which were thin strips of skin that, when wrapped around a body, kept it fairly resistant to the elements, especially sunlight. The mumiya were extinct, mummy-like creatures that were said to have migrated from the other side of the world. Most of their remains were kept in Eldrus, with Archivist Amon's collection; however, there were reports of women in possession of the wraps, too. Blonde women, with large, battered hats and thick, brutal crooks. Like shepherds that had taken a sinister turn.

Picking at the wraps to air out his flesh some, Edgar said, "I understand making the pilgrimage out of tradition. But look at what we've accomplished. I have to be the Speaker."

"I have collated with the Blood in Us All," Valac said, changing the topic. "I have updates to share."

The Blood in Us All. He'd heard that phrase before, from Crestfallen, when she spoke on her connection to his lineage. But Valac wasn't talking about that. The Blood in Us All was the God's blood that flowed through the vermillion veins and, possibly, all Corrupted. Because it was too difficult to keep up on the current events of the continent, Valac used the blood as a means by which he and Edgar could remain informed. It took a long time, and it took a toll. Valac looked sicker and sicker after every collation.

Edgar turned to face the endless Ossuary and asked, "Did they find Audra?"

"Yes."

Somehow, he shivered. "Is she alive?"

"Yes, but Isla Taggart was not able to secure her." Valac's face flashed fear for a moment. "The Winnowers' Chapter took Rime, but your sister escaped with the help of a Night Terror."

"Do you think she knows we sent Isla in after her?"

Valac shook his head, said, "I don't know." The boy wrung his hands and then, with a fake smile: "But there is good news—"

As long as Audra was alive and anywhere but at his side, how could there truly be good news? She was the last of him. If he lost her to hate or death—

"—concerning the continent."

Like an Old World switchboard, something changed over in Edgar's mind. A new channel of thoughts and concerns overwhelmed him. Audra became background noise to his ego and pride.

"Did Lotus and the Arachne overtake Penance on the Divide?" he asked, excitedly.

"Many veins were damaged or destroyed in the attack. The reports are inconsistent. Lotus lives, but hundreds of Arachne were killed."

Edgar shrugged.

"Penance is still there, but only by a thread. A second attack would surely crush the survivors. The Arachne are refusing to fight, however."

Edgar scoffed. "They must have a different definition of 'good news' in the Deep."

Valac's flesh-fattened face grinned. He bared his small, vermillion-colored teeth. At the back of his throat, veins swirled.

"What?"

"The Mother Abbess Justine has revealed herself for what she truly is," Valac said. "A Worm of the Earth."

Edgar couldn't help but laugh as he said, "A Worm of the Earth? You're sure?"

Valac nodded.

"You didn't know? Again, good news?"

"Only God can track the Worms; Its pieces cannot, nor can the Worms. She has revealed herself, I expect, to draw faith and devotion. But in truth, she has placed a target on her head. The Worms, if nothing else, are a unifying enemy. Most of our flock are sheep that have strayed from hers. They still possess sympathy or allegiance to the Holy Order."

"We've been telling the Disciples that their old religion was a false religion," Edgar said. "Now that they can see there's been a demon the whole time at the head of their church…" Edgar covered his mouth; he could almost cry he was so happy. "Our people will tear Penance apart. They were lied to, made fools of. They'll have to kill the religion, as if to prove they were never truly a part of it."

Valac rubbed his distended belly; it made a sloshing sound of satisfaction. "Good news, then?"

"Take us farther," Edgar said, turning his attention towards their camp. "Bring us to the Deep."

To avoid attention, they hadn't brought many soldiers for the journey, so there wasn't much to the camp other than three tents, ten horses, and bags and boxes of supplies from Kres—the last Corrupted settlement before entering the Ossuary. Adding to the subterfuge, Edgar had abandoned all of his kingly attire, while his guard dressed themselves in the rattiest garbs not even rats would wear. The goal was to look like traders, or traitors, and so far, unmolested and unnoticed by all, they were succeeding.

Captain Yelena muscled her way out of her tent. A few feet of sand caught her foot and nearly sent her face-first into the ground.

"This is Hell," Yelena said, trying to catch her balance. "I hate this place."

"That borders on blasphemy," Edgar said.

Yelena straightened up and got it together. With her black skin and the ocean of sweat running down it, she looked as close as one could get to a living piece of obsidian. And like obsidian, she was rigid, and sharp. Bringing the Skeleton to Ghostgrave had won her respect with Edgar; everything afterward had won her assignment here. She was obsidian, but only because of the fire inside her, that volcanic violence that put even Kistvaen to shame.

Valac waddled up beside Edgar and told Yelena, "Pray for forgiveness."

"And while you're doing that," Edgar said, "ready the rest. We're moving out."

Yelena mopped her brow with her sleeve. Her lips looked like two pieces of burnt bacon, she was so dehydrated. If Edgar gave her the order to die, she probably would, and gratefully. Most of his soldiers wouldn't make it home. In fact, he didn't expect any of them to, except Valac and himself. Any other day, he might've minded this, but he had chosen these hateful ass-kissers for a reason. No one would mourn them, not even him.

"Pack it up!" Captain Yelena screamed. With her order, seven additional soldiers emerged from the tents. They stretched their arms and legs, cracked their necks and backs; the cramped confines had done them no favors. Edgar let them sleep most of the time, especially here in the Ossuary. If he was under any threat, it was from God, and nothing here, in the desert, on this planet, or from this universe, was going to stop God.

They broke apart camp in ten minutes. Seconds later, they were well on their way, down the plateau, and towards the bone-dusted horizon. Their horses were born and bred to withstand the intense climate, but the farther they went into the desert, the clearer it became the beasts weren't going to make it.

The terrain became more and more alien; the dunes and flat stretches took on subtle, eldritch shapes that called to mind great, faded tattoos. When the horses' hooves touched these designs, the horses shook and stumbled, and belted out short, sharp screams. The horses stayed their course, if only to reach Death and her final release.

The atmosphere took a hit, too. While the heat was relentless, even more so on the desert floor, the air and the gravity were undergoing changes with every step they took. Oxygen became sparse, thin as paper and just as filling; and, in places, there were pockets of sand rising off the ground, as if something were breathing the Ossuary in from the depths of space. Again, the horses struggled; but it was the royals and those loyal to them that struggled the most. Edgar and Valac were practically lying down in their saddles, while most of the soldiers had to ride close enough to one another to stop each other from falling off the horses.

"We… are… close," Valac said, each word a struggle. "Do you see it?"

Lost in a reverie, Edgar wasn't seeing anything that wasn't already in his mind. He felt the pained movements of his horse, that brutal Braille all living things can read, but in a way, it was a language he was more fluent in than anything else.

Thoughts gathered on the surface of his mind. Vaporous and bubbling, they came as quickly as they went, but the film of their filth stayed. Thoughts of the continent, and thoughts of the country it could be.

It had been three years since the Nameless Forest. Despite doubt and rebellion, the vermillion veins and the Disciples of the Deep were everywhere. People were no longer believing passively, but emphatically. With every follower gained, the specter of Penance was further exorcised from the Heartland, and the cracks the Trauma had created in the collective unconscious could begin to heal.

The Night Terrors sought balance through division bordering on segregation. But humans were social creatures by nature. Their balance wasn't external, but internal. Equilibrium was impossible, but so were advancements without some sort of togetherness. From Eldrus' suffer centers to today's religious organizations, Edgar had found a way to finally help others in a way that actually mattered.

Soon, God would be here. The oldest question would be answered. Edgar would give to the human race the kindest closure. People would hate him, and they would try to hurt him, but for the first time, they would know. In the Old World, the humans were too blind to see the truth that towered over them. They killed God because they did not recognize It. That wasn't going to happen again.

"My lord?" Valac tried again.

But once more, Edgar was gone. He could taste bone in his mouth. It was packing up his ears. He had the sense gravity was trying to lift him from the saddle. Was this what it felt like to die? Was he dead? He remembered Lotus. His heart started beating again.

And then he thought of Audra, and it stopped once more.

"Captain Yelena, would you check our King?"

If you see what I've done, you'll understand. He blinked some bugs out of his eyes. *You created the Crossbreed. You can't judge me.* He ran his tongue over his teeth, the inside of his cheeks, in search of some sort of sustenance. *I killed them. I killed them, but they were all doomed to die. If I hadn't, you would've. They would've made you. Made you like they made me. Made you like they made—*

"My lord?" Captain Yelena grabbed Edgar by the back of his wraps.

Edgar's thoughts dispersed. He shot up on his own, slinging a wave of sweat across Yelena's face. For a moment, he was cold—the ghost tended to do that to him—but when it passed, so did the chill. He looked at the other soldiers—Paxton, Lawrence, Marc, Katherine, Colleen, and Amir—and did his best to be the king everyone had told themselves he was supposed to be.

"I'm fine. I had a vision." That was a lie. He had never heard from God before in his life, but that was about to change. "Where is it, Valac?"

Valac wheeled his horse around Edgar, stopped, and pointed to where the dunes met in a cross-shaped ridge.

Night was near. The sun wasn't falling past the skyline, but retreating into the distance, retiring from its assault for the day. Other than Edgar and the others, there wasn't much to cast shadows in the area. Yet, in the place to which Valac pointed, there were thousands of shadows, growing and shrinking and slinking across the sands.

"Stop, and make camp," Valac said.

The soldiers looked to Edgar for confirmation.

"Go ahead," he said, "and kill the horses, before they spoil."

"My lord," Amir said, dismounting in unison with the other soldiers, "how will we get home?"

"Have faith," Edgar said. "God will guide us from our desert."

With the help of Yelena, Edgar dropped from his horse. He caught himself against her, and then caught his breath. The air was thin, but now it was filled with sand. A storm was mounting.

"There is an altar inside the shadows," Valac said.

Edgar let Yelena feed him a mash of poultry and produce. It was the same thing they fed to the poor and starving at the suffer centers. Paxton flanked him with a flagon of water, and he downed, that, too. For as little concern as he paid to their wellbeing, they gave great care to his. He knew it wasn't genuine, even now on the precipice of delirium, but it was nice all the same.

"I'll take it from here," Edgar said, reaching for the food and water.

But Valac intervened and stayed Edgar's hand. "Bring as little reminders of living that you can. Your flesh will be enough to set the shadows on edge."

Edgar nodded, jammed some more mash into his mouth, and washed it down with a thirty-second chug of one-hundred-degree water. The sun was farther back, and there were more shadows huddled around the still unseen altar. They hated the living, Valac had told him once, these shadows. They were the dead who had denied God and were now condemned to an eternity of pain and regret. For the Vermillion God, Heaven and Hell were one and the same. The exulted existed alongside the ex-communicated. The sinners supped with the saints.

And yet, where were the exulted? Where were the saints? Audra spoke and wove with the shadows, but never their betters. Probably in the Deep, he told himself. They were probably in the Deep.

"Go to the altar, and listen!" Valac shouted over the worsening sandstorm. "You will know It when you hear It!"

Edgar nodded. Pulling his wraps tighter across his face, so that his eyes were almost completely covered, he said, "What if I can't?"

Valac's face darkened. He mouthed a word—was that 'Audra' he had whispered?—and turned and headed towards the makings of their camp. The soldiers were moving as fast possible, which, given the cutting circumstances, wasn't all that fast at all.

Edgar wrapped his arms around himself and pushed through the storm. Most of the light had left the desert, but even now, he could see the wind tearing the Ossuary apart, unmaking it, so that by the next day, everything here would look completely different.

And he would be no different. The mumiya wraps weren't strong enough to resist the sand. With every choking blast, the storm ripped through the wraps. It did it in pieces, a kind of methodical disrobing. First his arms, then his legs; then his chest, and finally, his face. If he were to go to God, he had to go to God bloody and raw—the same way he came into this world, and the same way he expected to leave it.

Not far from the shadows and the altar, Edgar had to stop. He put a piece of vermillion vein from his pocket into his mouth and chewed on it like a pacifier. The air was so filled with bone that, even if he wanted to breathe, he almost couldn't. Like a fish out of water, he gulped pathetically for something that wasn't there. The desert was up to his knees; he fell over, planted his hands in the sand. Looking forward, he saw the shadows were watching him, their silver fangs bared, their red eyes glowing like embers.

He had to die to meet God, and so dead-like he had to be. He waited for the sandstorm to flay him some, until he was bloody and raw, and then let the ghost in.

The ghost wanted to stand, and so Edgar stood. The sandstorm kicked up a few miles faster. He couldn't see past his feet, but that didn't matter. The ghost was nothing if not determined. He was impervious to pain, to doubt, and the sticky mire of morality. In the desert of bones, the boneless was king.

How did the ghost always end up covered in blood? He laughed, pushed deeper into the storm. Black shapes darted in and out of his view. The ghost stopped. The shadows surged forward. Hundreds of them, thousands; free-standing, three-dimensional. Drool poured down their ephemeral lips as they salivated at the sight of the ghost and his host.

The ghost remembered a little boy telling him about the shadows once, and how their forms were cast from nothing more than the memories they held of themselves. According to the little boy, their punishment was that, although they could remember who they had been, they could not recognize or be recognized by the shadows around them. They reached out to the living mostly to hurt them, but some, like those who had been in communication with Audra, did it to show that they could. To be something more than what their God had told them they could be.

With a wave of his hands, the shadows broke apart. The amorphous mass split and left a path between him and the altar they'd been guarding.

The altar was a slab of stone, four-feet high, from which vermillion veins jutted outwards, like horns. Moving closer, the ghost noticed intricate etchings running across the surface of the slab, covering it completely. Here, the sand couldn't gather; when it fell across the altar, the reduced gravity carried it away.

The ghost went to his knees and put his palms on top of the altar. One by one, the etchings began to glow. Red, white, and blue; yellow, silver, green and purple—the colors emerged from the etching as light, and then evolved, one by one, into flaming helixes.

A shifting shape caught Edgar's eye from a distant dune. The dying light touched it—it looked like a huge maggot—and then the shape was gone.

"My ears are yours, Lord," the ghost said, ignoring the image, closing his eyes, and pressing his head to the altar. "I am listening."

Edgar came out of the desert and the storm, naked but for the blood that covered him. The mumiya warps that hadn't been torn from him were now a part of him, adhered to his skin by the Ossuary's brutality. The ghost had gotten him this far; he had to get himself the rest of the way. Even dead inside and offering dominion, Edgar hadn't been good enough for God.

Valac came running out of the camp. Yelena and Amir followed closely behind, torches in each of their hands. There was no moon in the sky, and yet the Anointed One had sensed him all the same.

Edgar collapsed. The bones beneath his feet caught him in their pale embrace. He had given his ears to God, and now all he heard was the Deep; its fathomless depths, its impenetrable dark. He could hear the ruin of worlds, and all those tainted treasures being stirred and shifted and transmuted. He could hear massive limbs lumbering, rending the space through which they passed. He could hear the halo of smoke, and the dying breaths it was actually comprised of. He could hear God's words, each one an orb of uncountable languages, and when they met his mind, they shattered into incomprehensible shards.

"What did It say?" Valac clamored.

Amir threw a blanket over Edgar. Almost immediately, his blood soaked it through.

Yelena helped Edgar to his feet, and then Amir rushed in and steadied him on his shoulder.

"Go back," Valac said, pushing Yelena and Amir away. "Leave us!"

Edgar fell forward, but Valac grabbed him by the chest and held him there. The boy's arms rippled as the vermillion veins inside him leant him their strength.

"I'm not... I'm not... the Speaker," Edgar said. "I'm not."

Valac closed his eyes and sighed.

"You knew that." Edgar planted one bloody paw on the back of Valac's neck and started to crush it. "You knew!" He shook his head, played with the blood in his mouth. "Her—" He spit on the boy's feet. "Audra. You were so goddamn eager to get her back."

"She is the Speaker," Valac said. "A Speaker first speaks to heaven and hell—the shadows—and then to God Itself. Alexander Blodworth must have known. That is why he hid her in Penance, to use her against us. Not for the murders, but because without her, we are deaf to God's will."

"We're doing just fine… just fine without her," Edgar said.

Valac shoved Edgar backwards, sending him into the sand. "We need a Speaker when God wakes. Amon assured me it was you, but he lied. He led me on. Once God wakes, we will need to hear Its word."

"Then I'll find her," Edgar said, sitting up. "I have to find her, anyways. I'll find her. I'll explain everything. She'll understand."

Valac shook his head. "She doesn't have to understand. She just has to die."

"What?" Edgar kicked at Valac's ankle. "What the fuck did you say?"

"Kill her, and her blessing as Speaker will be gifted to you."

"No." Edgar tried to get to his feet, but he was too weak.

"It does not have to be you," Valac said, his belly rumbling, "but it should be. You killed the rest of your family. You might as well finish the job."

"Fuck you."

"We are one catastrophe away from God's awakening. The world is ready. It just needs a reason, a surge of belief. Did you know that you are not the only one to make a pilgrimage this year? People from Penance are going to Cathedra, to try and make it the new seat of the Holy Order. The Disciples of the Deep are going to Penance, to bring the Word to the heretics.

"And have you heard of the Cult of the Worm? They are new to me, too, but the Blood in Us All does not lie. They are led by two powerful witches under the Disciples' banner. Their ranks are flesh fiends and Night Terrors and Corrupted from all across the continent. They are gathering in Angheuawl soon. I do not know what their intentions are or where their allegiances truly lie, but with this many people on the move, causing so much unrest, all the while war is raging all around them, can you not agree God is needed now more than ever?"

Edgar nodded, reluctantly.

"Can you not agree your work has been good and just?"

Again, Edgar nodded. He was bleeding out of every pore and orifice.

"You do not invite a guest to dinner, only to ignore them for the whole evening. God is coming. You have made sure of that. A God without a tongue speaks only in the syllables of slaughter. What matters more? One life, or many?"

He hated to say, but he said it: "Many."

"Find her, kill her, it does not matter. We must collect your sister."

"If I don't find her... if she doesn't... die." Edgar breathed in the Ossuary. "Can she use the shadows against us?"

"Yes," Valac said.

"Can they stop us?"

Valac narrowed his eyes. His silence said it all.

CHAPTER XXI

R'lyeh must've passed out, because when she opened her eyes, she was in the Skeleton's arms. He was carrying her through the streets of Geharra. She started to say something, but her mouth wouldn't work. She tried to shift her weight, to signal she was awake, but her limbs wouldn't listen. All that she had was all that she could see, inside and out, and most of it made for the poorest company.

She blinked and blinked, but the blurriness in her vision would not break. She sniffed and sniffed, but the stench of the pit would not lift. Her ears were clogged; she moved her jaws to pop them, and instead, she tasted blood and poison and the hot, lingering residue of stomach acids. R'lyeh's body was a prison, kind of like the cells beneath the city. Abandoned and ignored; dilapidated and desecrated; good for one thing, and not much else. If she had only looked back, she might've seen this coming.

Like a ghost, Geharra crept towards her. Second by second, stone by stone, the city-state closed in on her—its advance unavoidable, her anxiety undeniable. With its towering buildings, it reached out to her. With its upturned streets, it dared to touch her. Its breath was a cold cocktail she couldn't place; a drowsy mixture of things not human. It smelled like earth and milk, and something else she knew but had forgotten.

R'lyeh could see better now, and now she saw that Geharra was wild. The Red Worm's awakening had ruptured the Northern District through which they passed. With no humans to heal the wound, Mother Nature had made the effort instead. Trees and plants had overrun the city-state. Where there had once been the main thoroughfare, there were only weeds. She saw cats and dogs, too, and hundreds of birds in the high towers and low wreckages. For a place that had once been covered in the Red Worm's bloody afterbirth, it was far greener here than she would've ever thought possible.

The Skeleton glanced down. R'lyeh closed her eyes, but she was pretty sure he'd seen her, anyway. He didn't say anything, and neither did she. When a couple seconds passed, she opened her eyes again, only to find them moving through the Northern District's gate.

The heart of Geharra stood before them. R'lyeh could still remember the layout fairly well. To the south, the Southern District, and beyond, the fields of Elys; to the east, the main gate and the market; to the west, the Western District, and all its fisheries and abattoirs.

When Penance had drugged Alluvia, they marched R'lyeh and her people through the main gate. From there to here and the pit beneath them, she knew every twist and turn, and street name, real or imagined. She could recall all the buildings they passed. She could see all the faces that should've helped, but couldn't have, because of the Crossbreed inside them. R'lyeh was an expert on poisons. What was Geharra if not another poison? This was her second dose of the place. She was scared, but she was also content. Could she become immune to memories, too?

The Skeleton shifted R'lyeh in his arms. He held her like a dead body, but with a layer of leather and fabric between them. The leather came from the glove he always wore, and the fabric from the cloak that never left his gangly frame. If not for the forethought, his touch would've been transferring images from the Black Hour's heart to her every second. It made R'lyeh's own heart flutter to know he'd made the effort. And, blushing, she hoped he couldn't tell.

R'lyeh rolled her eyes and settled on a distant sight. It was the entrance to the Marketplace. There were still stalls there, but the goods were gone; taken by thieves, or animals with a penchant for sparkling things. Seeing the market, she then saw echoes; not real Echoes—not the Earth's Echoes—but her own echoes—hallucinations, if she were being honest, of Deimos, Lucan, Serra, and Vrana. They were beat up, short of breath; they kept looking over their shoulders, for the flesh fiends that had attacked them, and the Red Worm that, at that moment, was rampaging outside the city-state's walls. R'lyeh should've seen herself in the memory, right next to Vrana, but she wasn't there, because she was here, right here, being taken care of once again, being led out of hell once more.

A single tear slipped down R'lyeh's cheek. It fell off her face and onto the Skeleton's glove. He twitched, as if the piece of leather were now an extension of himself, with skin and nerve endings. But he didn't look down.

She steadied her breathing as they turned eastward. And then stopped breathing, for what she saw stole the air from her. All across the buildings, alleys, and streets were long, thick, green roots. Large trunks, snake-like, with dark eyelets. The growths had nubs, like nipples, and dribbling out of them was a milky discharge that filled in the gaps of the road.

The Crossbreed, R'lyeh thought, teeth slicing into her tongue. She closed her eyes until her tears got the hint and went away. *Serra.* She opened her eyes, turned her head slightly. *Shit, shit.* Now that she knew they were there, she saw the Crossbreed's roots everywhere; coming out of windows, coming out of wells; parks and churches, and the town hall, too. *Why's it still alive?*

She called out Serra's name in her mind. Maybe because he had been mute, and a spellweaver, she expected him to somehow respond. But if he had responded, he responded silently, and most likely from the grave. Deimos and Lucan had left Geharra to join with Penance. Vrana and R'lyeh had been sent back to Caldera, to inform the elders of what had happened. Serra… She could still see the final image of the Piranha. They had followed him to the waterworks in the Western District. Before they could follow any further, he set the doorway on fire and disappeared behind the smoke. He was supposed to burn the Crossbreed; kill it for good.

Teeth clenched, she strained herself to stop from shaking. R'lyeh hadn't known Serra well, but he had saved her. Deimos was an idiot to send the Piranha in alone, and she and Vrana were dumbasses for letting him do it.

The Crossbreed. Holy Child, it really was everywhere. At this point, she didn't care if the Skeleton knew she was awake. From the smallest stalks to the tree-sized roots, she searched the city for any sign that the plant was nearby. Of course, last time, it had been in the waterworks, but maybe it had moved. It owned Geharra now. And that taste that was in the air? That itching smell that made her eyelids heavy? She knew what it was. It was the Crossbreed dousing the city in its fluids. If she hadn't been immune, and the Skeleton hadn't been immortal, they wouldn't be standing here. They'd be lying in the streets without a will of their own, waiting for someone or something to come along and whisper to them the new meaning of their sad, pathetic lives.

Serra, R'lyeh called out again with her thoughts. There was no response. She wasn't about to fool herself with ideas of saving him. If he was here, he was dead. And if he wasn't dead, then he might as well be. She had failed Vrana. She would fail him. In the history of Night Terrors, she barely registered as a bad dream.

"Back when I was a boy," the Skeleton said, "we called Death's home the Garden of Sleep. All these roots round here got me thinking Death might want a change of residence."

"How long was I out?"

"Long enough to start snoring. About five minutes, actually." The Skeleton readjusted her weight. "Herbert warned you about following me. Should've listened."

R'lyeh said through her teeth, "Did you see anyone else?"

"Bunch of flesh fiends that were picked clean. Nothing living. Dead City's going to have to work hard to keep its claim to the name with Geharra the way it is." The Skeleton ran his fat, black tongue over his teeth. "You alright?"

"Better than I thought I'd be."

The Skeleton's glassy eyes met hers, and he said, "You're strong, Vale."

"What?"

"How many times you been here?" the Skeleton asked, ignoring her.

"A lot," R'lyeh said, catching his meaning. Not a day went by that she didn't visit this place in her mind.

"I used to see the Membrane a lot. Got old after a while."

"You went so much you got immune to it."

R'lyeh tipped her head back and made the city upside-down. The sky became stained stone and crumbling brickwork. The clouds hardened over into the tops of buildings, pointed and blunted. From out of space, the Crossbreed's roots twisted, puncturing everything they came into contact with, and binding it together. There was blood, too, behind the green. It was dried now, and some of it had faded, but it was there, like stars that had long since died and yet shone all the same. And vermillion veins. Yes, there they were here. Nests of them, in the gutters and sewers of heaven. Parasites preying on a paralyzed sky, waiting for the eternal night.

Upside-down, Geharra made sense. It stopped being a puzzle her mind couldn't solve. It turned into a tapestry weaved by the Crossbreed's needle-like roots. Each thread was a piece of the past forever immortalized in the amber of greed and gore. But the tapestry didn't start here, nor would it stop here. It ran clear across the continent, to Eldrus, to Penance, and to all the places in between, doubling back and forth upon itself, each layer growing tighter and tighter, and harder to break.

There was a place for R'lyeh in the tapestry. Even though she was above ground, she could see it. A tiny black spot in Geharra's depths. A hole she had fallen into, and then torn herself from.

She wasn't meant to die here, because she was meant for something else. There was something waiting for her in the Dead City. She could see that now. She couldn't before, not with Vrana's belongings weighing her down, or the octopus mask blinding her. Elizabeth and Miranda… had done their best to convince her she could be good, but they just wanted her to be what they couldn't have.

R'lyeh lifted her head up and shed one last tear for Serra. She hadn't tried to, but it happened all the same.

The Skeleton grunted. He turned onto a large, windy boardwalk. Geharra's outer walls grew before them. Not far from where they were, but farther away than it looked, was the Eastern Gate—the actual gate completely demolished, reduced to debris.

"You can put me down," R'lyeh said, wiggling her legs.

The Skeleton nodded, said, "I know."

He didn't put her down.

And R'lyeh didn't bring it up again.

Inside, Geharra was dead, but outside the city, there was more life than R'lyeh had seen in a while. The fish-like, humanoid Mer creatures were not only still here, but they had expanded their scaly kingdom across Geharra's two rivers and the marshes in between. Their homes were spheres—large, hollowed-out orbs of mucus that floated upon the bodies of waters weightlessly. There had to have been about sixty or seventy of the orbs, and the way they trailed off into the ocean made R'lyeh think there were even more of them, and the creatures, in the sea.

The Mer, sometimes crawling, sometimes slithering, were in a state of alarm. They moved quickly through the waters and atop the glassy pleating they'd drooled and molded onto it. They spoke, too, in high, reptilian hisses, and low, watery growls. It wasn't R'lyeh and the Skeleton they were concerned about. Not yet, at least. It was something else. Something in the mist that surrounded the outskirts.

R'lyeh knew this, because she'd seen a village under attack. Twice now. In Alluvia, they went willingly, because of the Crossbreed in their bellies. In Rime, the people had been much like the Mer were today: angry, stiff; constantly pacing back and forth, while their attentions were fixed on the unseen threat. Alexander Blodworth's soldiers; vermillion veins; the Winnowers' Chapter; vermillion veins; and that caustic bitch, Isla Taggart—and if she had stayed in Gallows, she might've even met King Edgar and his Arachne, or the Holy Child and his Mother Worm… No, it was all too much to take. Too many violent strangers she couldn't sell violent ends. The Mer had helped them once, by weaving the illusion of Corruption onto Deimos and Lucan, but this time, they were on their own.

R'lyeh dropped out of the Skeleton's arms. Her legs were weak, half-asleep. She steadied herself on the road. The places where his shielded body had touched her were hot, as if the Black Hour had been trying to burn through the leather and cloth to get to her.

She started to say something to the Skeleton, but as he pointed to the mist, the words were lost to her.

Out of the mist, Corrupted came. Dirty and emaciated, and clad in crookedly cut leathers, they shuffled and shambled through the marsh. There were too many of them to count, but every age and sex seemed to be represented, even on that saw-toothed front. Because they looked so pathetic, R'lyeh thought they might have been refugees—escapees, possibly—from Geharra finally returning home. But then she saw the spears and the torches, and heard prayers on the air, and knew better.

"Scavengers," R'lyeh whispered.

Though the great, achromatic tower was days away, she swore she could see it in the mist, looming; a vaporous silhouette, overbearing and enduring, that trailed the Scavengers and their not-so-good name. One didn't seem to exist without the other. If the Scavengers were here at the gates of Geharra, then surely their object of obsession was, too. If Worms could be born, why couldn't towers move? In a world as insane as R'lyeh's, what was impossibility if not a minor challenge on the road to greater, terrible things?

"Don't know much about them," the Skeleton said. "Herbert might've mentioned them before we left. Can't say for sure. Old man talks a lot once you get him going."

R'lyeh pressed herself closer to Bone Daddy, not for his warmth, because he hadn't any to share, but for the warmth of his cloak. "They're from south of here—"

The Scavengers continued to amble through the mist, their broken bodies like breaking waves upon the Mer's newfound shore.

"—and they worship this big metal tower. All they do every day is dig around its base, trying to find a way in."

Groups of Mer, on their hands and stomachs, clawed and slithered to the Scavengers. The creatures cut through the marsh in stiff, hate-driven movements. Scales sparkling, they looked like beautiful shards of glass speeding towards all that flesh. Where they passed through, be it in the grassy shallows or depths of Geharra's outskirts, spikes shot out of the ground. Subtly sentient, they waved like reeds and clicked out insectile chitters.

The Skeleton nudged R'lyeh, signaling her it was time to go on. "What're they worshiping in that tower of theirs?"

"God," she said.

The first of the Scavengers stopped just outside the Mer's village, where the land gave way to the river, and the spherical homes were suspended. The approaching Mer hadn't made it to this point, and yet the spikes shot out of the ground all the same.

"They think god is inside the tower."

The spikes arched backward. Thin, glistening tubes worked their way up each spike and emerged from the tip. They weren't traps, R'lyeh realized, but artillery. And they weren't weapons. The movements... the sounds. These strange growths were alive.

The Skeleton marched onwards, going to where the road from Geharra split and veered north.

"Guess if someone looks hard enough, they can see god in just about anything," he said.

R'lyeh was having a hard time tearing herself away from the sight of the Scavengers and their standstill on the edge of Mer territory. The mist had started to break. More Scavengers waited farther back, not with supplies or the makings of future homes, but killing tools.

How're there so many? To call them walking corpses would be an insult to walking corpses. They were malnourished, malformed; sunburnt, and scarred. Their clothes were sacks, and their hair nests. The Corruption on their arms was such a bright red that it had taken on the color and texture of a seething wound. The closest thing the Scavengers resembled were flesh fiends, and now that R'lyeh had made that connection, flesh fiends were all she saw.

The Mer met the Scavengers outside their village. The humanoids puffed out their chests and started spitting out words that hit R'lyeh's ears like wet punches. The Scavengers stood their ground, all the while shoring up their ranks.

"R'lyeh," the Skeleton said, frustrated.

R'lyeh faced the Skeleton, his impatience having broken the scene's spell over her.

He went for the northern road, and then: "Maybe they're on a pilgrimage. Like everyone else these days."

Pilgrimage. R'lyeh's thoughts lurched as something deep in her subconscious hit the brakes. *Pilgrimage.* A word she had never heard or said before in her life, and yet now couldn't shake. Hex had said it first, when she'd lost her shit and tried to shank R'lyeh. Then Ghelys in Rime had said the Children of Lacuna in his village were on a pilgrimage, and Deimos had told her later they were trying to get Angheuawl... Angheuawl. Hex's hometown. And where the Skeleton had just sent his family and most of the Marrow Cabal. Did he know? He said Hex was better, but he had to have talked to her. Holy Child, did he know and send them there, anyway?

"Might be their god told them to go to Geharra to get something," the Skeleton carried on.

Shit, shit, shit. I have to tell him. Maybe he doesn't know. Fuck. If they get there and the Witch and the Lucanans... Vrana could be... I could still do something to save...

"Don't know what those fish creatures are doing outside the city," the Skeleton said, "but if I had to hazard a guess, I'd say the Scavengers came for this."

The Skeleton's disturbing grin seemed to stretch as he dug into his cloak and, briefly, flashed the object he held in his hand. It was a red stone with jagged marks etched into its surface. R'lyeh had noticed him carrying it when they came out of the pit. But this wasn't the first time she'd seen something like it. Vrana had one, too, except it was blue. She had used it to put to sleep the Blue Worm.

"Summon a Worm, and it leaves a stone behind to seal it away again," the Skeleton said, pocketing the object. "Kill a Worm, and it leaves behind a necklace to summon it again. We got it all now."

"Who... who has the necklace?" R'lyeh asked, suddenly wanting it more than she had ever wanted anything else in her life. "Who has it?"

"Herbert. One of the God's minions buried a similar necklace in his neck once, but he lost it. Guess he's trying to do penance."

"Is that why we're here?"

"We were coming here all the same. Stone was a bonus. Don't worry."

R'lyeh trembled. "You're not going to try to summon it again, are you?"

The Skeleton looked at her like the idiot she felt.

"Were you going to say something?" he asked her.

"What?"

"Just now. Looked like you were thinking about something."

R'lyeh didn't answer him, nor did she look away. Instead, she stared into his crazed eyes and saw the world reflected on their glassy, vein-choked surface. Surrounded by creatures that could kill her, she felt immortal at his side. Angheuawl didn't hold answers, only bitter reminders and battles she couldn't win. She had given up on saving Vrana. Maybe the Skeleton had given up on saving his family.

So when the Skeleton asked her again if she had something to say, R'lyeh didn't say anything at all.

"We have a lot of ground to cover," the Skeleton said. "Let's be on our way before your fish friends stop being so friendly."

Friends. Choking down her secret, she remembered that day she and Vrana had watched Deimos and Lucan from Geharra's walls. They had gone to the Mer, and in exchange for their armor and masks, the creatures wove a spell of Corruption onto each man's arm, so they could infiltrate Penance's approaching convoy.

R'lyeh squeezed the corners of her eyes, to stem the tide of tears. Deimos' and Lucan's masks were probably still in the marshes, in one of the Mer's caches for safekeeping. They were never going to get them back, she thought, just like she wasn't ever going to get her octopus mask back. Without Deimos or Lucan, or herself, the masks were nothing more than pieces of dead animals. Someone would find them one day, and they would think nothing of them. It hurt R'lyeh to think something so meaningful could be, at the same time, so meaningless.

R'lyeh and the Skeleton walked for hours without stopping, talking, eating, or drinking. By the time they had reached the highlands northwest of Geharra, the moon had usurped the sun from the sky, and there was blood in R'lyeh's boots. Her feet were sore and calloused, and her ankles had been rubbed raw. Her stomach sounded like a symphony of dying frogs, and her shoulders hurt so badly, it felt as if they were tightening inward, as if to pop her head off her body, like a cork from a bottle. She wasn't carrying anything, and yet her muscles burned as if they had reached their limit. And maybe they hadn't, but she had. She kept this to herself, though. Any sign of weakness, or mortality, and the Skeleton just might shake her.

It was midnight when the Skeleton put a stop to R'lyeh's stubbornness. She knew it was midnight, because the Skeleton's chest started to glow. Even without a clock, the Black Hour's heart had a job to do. The Skeleton parked them on top of a hill surrounded by mountains. He didn't prepare camp, because like the Scavengers, he hadn't brought supplies to do so. By foot or horse, the Skeleton had intended to make this journey alone, and without stopping. He didn't need to eat or drink or sleep, or simply take in his surroundings. Without flesh, he was beyond all earthly distractions.

R'lyeh lay on the ground, the grass her blanket and roots her pillow. Exhaustion was a poison for which she had no natural immunity. She could feel her body filling up with something that felt like water. Second after second, she was sinking into herself, succumbing to weakness.

"I can... keep... watch," R'lyeh mumbled, looking past her toes at the Skeleton.

"Shut your mouth and sleep," he said.

"I'm sorry."

"It's better this way. More time to think."

"About... what?"

"What needs to be done."

R'lyeh went to respond, but when she finally did, a few hours had already passed. She jerked out of her uninvited sleep. A blanket, a real blanket, slid down her body, while her grasping hands closed around the pillow, a real pillow, her head had been on.

The Skeleton was where she had left him: on the side of the hill, staring off into the mountains that circled them. The moon was higher now. From their lonely rest, R'lyeh noticed where the mountain chain had been cleaved in two; there was a pass there, and beyond that, the lowlands that twisted towards the Dead City's diseased peninsula.

R'lyeh, sitting up, blanket and pillow in hand: "Where'd you get these?"

"From 2017." The Skeleton looked over his shoulder and touched his chest. "Go back to bed."

The Black Hour. Lying back down, she asked, "They're not tainted, are they?"

"Not any more than anything else you or I touch."

Fatigue forced another question from her lips: "Do you really want to stop the Vermillion God?"

"Eh?" The Skeleton knitted his boney fingers over his boney knee. "What do you mean?"

"You have the heart of the Black Hour." R'lyeh bit her lip and pinched her skin to stay awake. "You... traveled to Lacuna with it. Killed the Red Worm. And these—" She pulled up a part of the blanket and pillow, and laughed. "We don't have to go to the City to kill God."

"Isn't that why you're here?"

"To kill God?"

"To go to the Dead City."

"No, I'm—"

"You sure? Figured you followed because you had something to prove."

R'lyeh stopped pinching her skin. The Skeleton was getting her good and pissed. She didn't need pain to stay awake. "What?" She shot up. "What about you? You could end this now."

"Doesn't mean I should. You talked to Clementine plenty. Don't you know I like to make things complicated?" The Skeleton sighed and shook his head. "Can't use the heart, not for something like this. Heart's never been in something living before. It's shown me things. Spoken to me. The more I use it, the more it'll use me. Understand? It wants something, and I don't know what. If I reach into the past for something strong enough to stop God, I think something else might just come through with whatever I bring back.

"Humans stopped the Vermillion God before. What was good enough then should be good enough now. I'll carry the heart as long as I can, because I can. Besides, it's freezing—"

It was freezing. R'lyeh could already tell she would be sick in the morning. If her body had stopped hurting, it was only because she was too numb to feel much else.

"—and I figured it wouldn't hurt to use it to give you something to warm you up. Something small."

"Thank you," she said, holding the blanking tightly.

"Yeah." He grumbled. "Guess I could've conjured up a roaring fire, but in the heart, seconds can turn into hours. It was the best I could do."

"I appreciate it."

The Skeleton threw his hood over his skull. "I forget what it's like sometimes, to have skin."

"Do you miss it?"

"The skin?"

"Yourself."

"Oh." He tongued his teeth and gawked at the moon. "I'm the same."

"Then... why aren't you with your family?"

"Nothing's changed. I don't expect you to know that, not knowing me as long as the others."

R'lyeh passed out for another half an hour. Then, waking up, as if it were seconds later, she pressed him with: "But you fought so hard—"

The Skeleton stood up. He had a sword now, somehow. His cloak fell from his body and, for the first time in a long time, she saw him unraveled. He was all bones, that part of him hadn't changed. But now the dark growths spreading from the Black Hour's heart had covered his entire ribcage, and a portion of his pelvis. At this rate, if he waited long enough, there wouldn't be anything left of the Skeleton, or the remnants of the man once called Atticus.

"I'm s-sorry," R'lyeh stuttered. "I... I—"

His hands became claws. Against the white moon, the blackening Skeleton was demonic. "Why aren't you with your friend Vrana? What happened to saving her? You aren't going to find her here."

"Fuck you," R'lyeh said through her teeth. "I know that. I just—"

"Needed to get away?"

"Yeah."

The Skeleton picked up his cloak and put it back on. "Going to the Dead City isn't for anyone but myself."

R'lyeh sniffled her nose, said, "Me, too."

"I gave everything to get my family back." The Skeleton's voice quivered. "And now I come up with every excuse I can to get away from them."

"Yeah." R'lyeh wiped her eyes. "I don't think Vrana would like who I am."

"Clementine and Will like me plenty the way I am," the Skeleton said. "That's the problem."

"I don't know who I am," R'lyeh said, lying down.

"You're young. You're not supposed to." The Skeleton wandered

SCOTT HALE

over and looked down on her. "What's my excuse?"

R'lyeh woke at dawn to a small fire and two skinned rabbits that had been roasted over it. Starving, she didn't ask where the Skeleton had gotten them from. The gesture was enough.

It would take most of the day to reach the mountain pass. The highlands were comprised of sheer cliffs and heart-stopping plummets. Paths were luxuries this part of the world couldn't afford. R'lyeh did the best she could, where she could, but often times, it wasn't enough. She found herself sliding down slopes, knees first, and paralyzed with fear in higher places—that damn phobia she often forgot about finally getting the better of her.

"My best friend's name was Gary," the Skeleton said, urging her along the last of the many narrow, open-faced trails they'd traversed.

R'lyeh nodded, hearing, but not really hearing what the Skeleton was saying. If she stepped forward, she'd fall for a good ten seconds before splatting on the forest floor below.

"He was a ghoul. You would've liked him."

R'lyeh shimmied sideways, gripping the cliff behind her for dear life. "Was he a-afraid of heights, too?"

"No." The Skeleton prodded her side, making her pick up the pace. "Just wanted to tell you that."

By nightfall, they made it to the pass. At that point, R'lyeh's knees were covered in blood, bruises, and scrapes; and her hands had been rubbed so raw, they put most scullers' mitts to shame. All things considered, she had made it out fairly well. The Skeleton had died twice on their journey from the lonely hill to the desolate cleave. Once from bad footing that sent him skull first into a boulder, and secondly, randomly. He called these random deaths 'hiccups.' Said they happened out of nowhere, and didn't stop until they felt like it.

R'lyeh's battle scars had cost them a couple of hours. The Skeleton's death… about twenty seconds. When it came to who was burdening who, the choice was clear, and yet Bone Daddy didn't bring that kind of talking up anymore.

Coming out of the mountain pass, R'lyeh fell against the rocks there and caught her breath. Besides all the bones the Skeleton had broken on the way here, it was the first actual break she'd had herself.

The Skeleton, ahead of her, stopped and turned to face her. "It's not far."

R'lyeh licked her lips and lifted herself off the rocks. He was right. The Dead City wasn't far at all. If she stretched out her hands, she could almost grasp it.

At the farthest end of the lowlands, the Dead City looked to be about twelve hours away. In the dark, it wasn't much. Just skyscraper after sky-scraper at what most maps seemed to suggest was the end of the world. In the light, like most things, the city would be different. She would see it for what it really was, and at that point, she would have to decide if she really wanted to go through with what she had come here to do.

"Even from here, I can taste it," the Skeleton said, doubling-back to her.

She could, too. The disease, the sickness. It was faint, but it was there, in the air—tiny morsels of temptation from Death's unending banquet. Defiant as ever, R'lyeh breathed in deeply, filling her lungs with that in-fected oxygen, beginning the inoculation process.

"You alright?" he asked.

R'lyeh didn't know if she was or wasn't, so she played it safe, said she was, and took the lead. The Dead City was twelve hours away. She'd get them there in ten.

Fifteen hours later, and on her last legs, R'lyeh stood trembling before the beginning of the peninsula that led out to the Dead City. The crooked piece of land wound across the ocean under a thick, green cloud of countless contagions. Whether or not it was actually land that connected the continent with the City, R'lyeh couldn't really say. The peninsula wasn't soil, but a thick, black, tar-like substance that shone like plastic garbage bags. It was as if something else had been built here at some point, but an intense heat had melted it down, beyond recognition.

Then there was the Dead City itself. She had spent the majority of the journey from the mountain pass to here staring at it, but it was so much easier to appreciate up close, in its diseased presence. In fact, it wasn't until she was here that she could even make sense of it. The Dead City was unlike anything she had ever seen before. The height of the build-ings, the intricacy of the architecture. The City was almost too dense for R'lyeh to fully realize. The streets, signs, and storefronts; the highways, advertisements, and neighborhoods; the cars, trucks, and toppled trams—all of it was there, on display, scattered or piled high. It looked as if a hurricane had hit the City hard and tried to drown it in its own excess.

There was no doubt in R'lyeh's mind that whatever modern weaponry the Skeleton was looking for was probably inside the Dead City. But how he was going to find it—

R'lyeh stumbled backward, having blacked out for a moment. She gripped her head, where it throbbed with a sudden, monstrous migraine.

"R'lyeh," the Skeleton said, touching her arm with his gloved hand.

She shook him off. Opening her stinging eyes, she saw the green cloud that blanketed the peninsula and City taunting her, testing her. Her lungs started to burn. Breaths became shallow. That was how it killed you, she'd heard before. The cloud attacked your lungs, and then you suffocated on your own blood.

"I'm fine," she said, feeling anything but. "I'm ready."

The Skeleton didn't stop her as she took the lead. Walking alone into the haze of disease, R'lyeh wished he had. The green cloud swelled around her as she pressed into its sickly embrace. Carefully, so as to not ingest too much of whatever foulness was floating around her, she took small, measured breaths. If she gave her body enough time to process the cloud, then maybe it wouldn't kill her. The Skeleton had said he had died so much he didn't even really notice when it happened anymore. Like blinking, it became an invisible eventuality. If it worked for him, then maybe—

R'lyeh's legs went out from under her and she hit the black ground hard. The tar-like surface rippled from the impact, like the water over which it spanned would. Sticky, she peeled herself from it and managed to get to her hands and knees. Her body was fire. Her lungs felt like two twisted rags hung out to dry in the heat. She was bleeding, too. Somewhere. She couldn't be sure where.

No, no. Her heart was beating so fast she could hear it in her ears. A pillar of nausea exploded out of her stomach and rammed itself up her neck. *Goddamn it, no.* She covered her mouth, bit into her fingers to stop the pathetic sounds coming out of her mouth. She tried to take another breath, but the air caught in her chest and sat there, and she choked on the very thing she needed more than anything else at this point.

"Son of a bitch," the Skeleton said, hurrying towards her from behind. "I told you!"

R'lyeh collapsed onto the ground. Her body twisted to the rhythm of its convulsions. Heaving hoarsely, she balled her fists and buried them in her stomach, because she was pretty sure if she didn't, she just might cough it up.

I'm not dying, she told herself, and yet she could hardly believe it, with green death pressing in all around her. She tried to breathe again, and puked up blood instead. *No, no, no.* She buried her face in the trash bag-colored soil and huffed its virus-laced fragments. She ground her body into the ground; kicking and clawing, an indentation formed beneath her of her body—the only grave, perhaps, she could've hoped for.

"Get!"

The Skeleton yanked R'lyeh off the ground and into his arms. She writhed in his grip, kicking and screaming and spitting out chunks of stinking blood into his face.

"I don't know why I let you do this."

The Skeleton strengthened his hold on her and turned them back towards the mainland. But R'lyeh took him by the front of his cloak and shouted, "Don't!"

She jerked out of his arms and, spinning, slammed back into the ground. The impact busted her chin, but somehow, had opened up her lungs. She gasped wretchedly. Digging her knuckles and toes into the black dirt, she went rigid and forced herself to breathe. Every breath was like surgery. Each one she took, she could feel her lungs tearing open, separating, as if the cloud and its diseases had fused them together.

"I'm…"

The spasms stopped in her arms and legs.

"I'm…"

She pressed her forehead into the ground and forced herself to vomit out the white foam that had been clogging up her throat.

"I'm…"

The migraine dispersed along her scalp, retreated behind her ears.

"I'm okay." She stayed prostrated on the ground, because every muscle in her body was one movement away from cramping. "I'm okay," she said, looking back, between her legs, at the Skeleton. "I told you… I'd be—"

"Get, goddamn it," the Skeleton said. "We have company."

R'lyeh, not moving, looked up. There were two… things standing ten feet away. They wore heavy, bulky, dirty white polyester suits that made them move as if they were underwater. Yellow tubes wrapped around the suits, from their backpacks and into their helmets, which were in the shapes of diamonds. The faceplates of the helmets, although transparent, were too filthy and scuffed to see into. The things looked like humans, but there was something wrong with their right arms. Those parts of the suits were engorged, as if something had been stuffed alongside their limbs. Lights, too; there were lights, blinking behind the fabric. Red lights, the color of Corruption.

"You are… alive," one of the suits said. It was a woman's voice. Her words were garbled, drenched in noise from the broken communicator she spoke through on the side of her mask.

The second suit: "Have you come to witness it?" This one was male, and his voice was even harder to understand. Not because of the communicator, but because it didn't seem as if he had spoken to anyone in a long time.

R'lyeh swallowed hard, dipped her head forward. She sipped on the green death like a strong drink. Slowly, sweating, and cramping like she thought she would, with the Skeleton's help, she rose back to her feet.

"Witness what?" the Skeleton asked gruffly, holding R'lyeh in place.

"The Putrid Prince," the woman said, the tubing in her back vibrating as she spoke.

"As it rises to claim its kingdom in the stars," the man added.

"No, we'll pass," the Skeleton said. "We're just here to rob the place."

The man in the suit shook his head. "Anything you take, you take a part of it with you. The Prince has filled your lungs, little girl, and yet you live."

"Barely," R'lyeh rumbled.

"And I don't know what you are, skeleton—"

"Skeleton will do, actually."

"—but if you're here, then…"

The woman in the suit started to shake excitedly.

"…then maybe the world is finally ready."

The Skeleton tugged R'lyeh backwards, closer towards him and the sword at his side. Carefully, she reached back and grabbed its hilt.

"Ready for what?" the Skeleton asked.

"I'm confused," the woman in the suit said. "Aren't you here to see it? Aren't you here to bask in the glory of the great, Green Worm?"

R'lyeh eyes widened. "Green Worm?" She ripped the sword from the Skeleton and pointed it at the man and woman. "Another Worm? Are you fucking kidding me?"

CHAPTER XXII

The mining town of Angheuawl was part of a trade route that ran through the backwoods of Cathedra and the foothills of Kistvaen. The route was meant to meet up with the trail, Adelaide's Hollow, which connected Cathedra with the eastern chamber of the Heartland, but thieves and carnivorous trees saw that the expansion never came to be. If the two had been connected, Aeson had once read, then it would've brought enough prosperity to the Heartland to sever their ties to their benefactors in Eldrus. Several towns, along with Angheuawl, had been erected along the route, in preparation for the Heartland's new age of independence.

Caldera's Night Terrors let the Corrupted settlements build up in Kistvaen's range, and then they sabotaged the route and planted the carnivorous trees to ensure no one would ever use it. The thieves that appeared later were just icing on the cake. Most of the Corrupted fled from these company towns, while those who stayed did so only because they had the Dismal Sticks' special brand of stupidity weighing them down.

Forty miles from Caldera, in a basin, the first of the five settlements had been established. Older maps called the town Llyn, but newer ones didn't even bother listing it at all. Because of its close proximity to Caldera, the Night Terrors took it upon themselves to slaughter every man, woman, and child in the town, several times over, until the Corrupted got the hint to stop populating it.

So when Aeson arrived at Llyn a few days later from the Garden of Sleep, he wasn't surprised to find the town abandoned. What surprised him were all the freshly flayed and fucked corpses that littered it. Corrupted, Night Terrors, flesh fiends; all ages and sex; color and creed; and every beautiful trait and wretched imperfection—they were all accounted for, in every home and alley, on every street and dock. The Choir had already been here, and in the dead, they left their heavenly psalms.

He had to go around Llyn, rather than through it. Because of the area, it cost him some time, but saved him some sanity. The sight of the ravaged reminded him of his rapist; even then, convinced he had moved on, he swore he could still feel her following him and reveling in his taste.

Eighty miles out of Caldera, thirty from Llyn, Aeson snuck into the meadows of Trist, the second town on the route. It wasn't a hard place to find, but because, again, the Night Terrors had murdered everyone that once lived there, the place had been forgotten. There were no proper buildings to speak of. Nature had swallowed them up. The overgrown regurgitation—a large, hairball-looking hill impaled by wood beams and stone chips—was all that remained.

Death wasn't here. After meeting Death face-to-face, that statement meant more for Aeson than most. Instead of slaughter, he found a sacristy. There was flesh and blood, of course, but not the defiled variety. The flaps of skin, sewn-together muscles, and organ ornaments stashed inside the hill weren't trophies, but uniforms. Like someone's Sunday best, they were laid out with great care, wrinkle-free, except for those hides that came from the elderly. There weren't enough uniforms to dress the whole of the Cult of the Worm, which Aeson reasoned must be in the hundreds, but the sight was, despite obvious reasons, disturbing all the same. Not for what it was, which was revolting, but for what it represented, which was ritual, intent—something more than senseless debauchery. Above all else, there was meaning.

There was that, and then there was the Cult of the Worm's symbol. One gigantic, double-headed stick figure icon that appeared to have been painted onto the hill with the celestial colors of the Abyss. Unlike the symbols of the Cult Aeson had seen previously, this one was different. The body of the stick figure was thicker; it had depth. It wasn't because of the hill, or some trick of the light. The line was a gouge.

Pushing aside Bjørn's bear mask, Aeson put his eye to the line, and recoiled. There were sights inside the symbol. Grayness, and a solitary retreat suspended in darkness. The Void. It was here, just out of reach, waiting to be called forth. What was holding it back? Why here, rather than Angheuawl?

The road to Marwaidd was paved with bad intentions. The third town on the route straddled an impassable swamp and an impossibly thick wood in the deepest part of Kistvaen's range. Following the route through each of the settlements was the only reliable way to reach Angheuawl, but by the time Aeson hit Marwaidd, he started to consider other options.

Half of his hesitation came from the vermillion veins that had sprung up like weeds in the area—six-foot, pitcher plant-like weeds that followed him as he passed. The other half came from the songs rolling out of Marwaidd, and the fact that he couldn't find anyone singing them.

He was getting used to Bjørn's bear mask, but when panic set in, it was the first thing he took off. The Night Terrors wore the dead on a daily basis. But wearing the skull of his dead friend, even if it wasn't really his skull, made Aeson feel like a flesh fiend. And he couldn't deal with that shit right now.

"Okay, okay," Aeson said, slipping off Marwaidd's road, towards the swamp side of the area. There weren't any vermillion veins there. Not yet, at least.

He stopped beside the water's edge. Catching his reflection, the air caught in his throat. Mask or no mask, he looked like a flesh fiend. His hair was greasy and hung unevenly above his shoulders. His eyes and his cheeks were sunken; pallid, he wasn't palatable to even vultures. He didn't know what he'd weighed before leaving home, but he had to have been twenty or more pounds lighter now. He had muscles, sure, like Bjørn would've wanted, but they were the cheated kind. The kind that showed when there was barely an ounce of fat on someone's body. The kind that was soaked in adrenaline, and would be useless to him as soon as they did what they had to do.

Death had spared him, but for how long? If he killed the Witches, would the moth cart him off before Vrana made it to his arms? Better yet, would she even recognize him? He laughed, thinking that Vrana could hardly be picky about his appearance given her own, but she could, couldn't she? He wore his hurt inside and out, now. He was supposed to be her reflection. An image of strength, like she had always been for him.

Aeson found a tree and leaned against it. If he sat, he was liable to not get up again. Digging into his bag, he pulled out a squirrel he'd cooked and finished it off. It tasted awful; he'd probably pay the consequences for his poor cooking skills later in the day. He knew how to survive in the wild, the same way a rat knew how to survive in the wild. He had all the knowledge, and yet all he did was scavenge. He was doing the best he could, but if Bjørn were here… if Bjørn were here he would be doing so much better.

The Blood of Before brushed against Aeson's fingers. He took it out and opened to the last page he'd been trying to decipher. The eerie songs from Marwaidd swelled into a teeth-aching howl, but he ignored them. He had to ignore them; otherwise, every note would take him back to that night in the Dismal Sticks, and Ichor's dinner party at House Gloom.

Tssnrt sa nrie su osri k.caiesheZ

Aeson was a little less than three-fourths of the way through *The Blood of Before*. After the entry about the Dead City and the disease the Night Terrors brought back from the place, there had been several more of little significance. He was getting closer to the portion of the book where the words were written in blood. The only thing stopping him? This entry here. One sentence. Either it was the strain of the journey, or his mind had finally snapped, but either way, he could not figure out how to decipher it. He had stared at it for so long, he didn't even read it anymore. But until he understood its meaning, he couldn't go forward (or rather, backward in time, since the book was in reverse chronology).

He put *The Blood of Before* away and closed his eyes. He thought about Bjørn, how little he had truly known him, and how much he missed him. Aeson reached behind his breastplate, where he carefully hid the Red Death weapon. Keeping the Bear's rib close was what kept him going. He would've liked to have said it was Vrana, but this weapon and Bjørn's sacrifice was the only thing that gave him enough hope to finish the mission.

A piece of parchment fell out of his bag and landed over his feet. He snatched it up before the wind could. It was the small list of names of the Children of Lacuna Anguis had given him to investigate. How many "Children" were there these days, he wondered. Children of Lacuna: they were either Night Terrors or Corrupted, or some indiscernible combination of the two. Children of the Witches made more sense, though. Thinking this, he thought back to House Gloom and how he'd seen Joy carrying babies back into the Void. There were more children coming, he knew. Not flesh fiends, Corrupted, or Night Terrors. Abominations. Grotesque playthings of the two daughters spurned for eternity by their heartless mother.

Fuck, he should've asked for more Red Death weapons. Bjørn would've been pissed knowing the rest of his ribs went to waste.

The songs of Marwaidd stuck with Aeson as he made his way to the next town. The verses and chorus swirled inside his head—a ravenous repetition that feasted on his senses, leaving him deaf to his environment, and nearly blind to himself. As if such a thing were possible, the song gave him a mild case of synesthesia; except the only color he saw in the songs was blue. Blue, like the Worm the Witches were using Vrana to somehow draw from. If Pain and Joy had managed a way to harness a fraction of the Worm's power without actually having to summon one...

The fourth town, Rhyfel, found him before he found it. Lost in the greasy lines of the Cult and Choir's horrendous art, he walked into the town without even realizing it. He couldn't remember what Rhyfel had been before the Cult took it over, but they had turned the town into a factory. The wide, open spaces between buildings and the poor creatures shuffling from them gave Rhyfel the appearance of an internment camp.

Aeson ducked behind one of the buildings. Damn near sweating through his armor, he inched along the stone, three-story building, carefully minding the scrap that had built up behind it. Voices and footsteps rose and fell around him, in a language that wasn't a language, much like the song reverberating through his head. But he could recognize orders when they were being given. And progress, too; the sound of creation; intense metalwork, furious crafting. Hammers and anvils, knives and leather; the jangle of chains; the hiss of steam. Progress, of a nefarious purpose.

Already he could feel his body breaking down, giving itself over to his own personal Trauma. Like the continent he called home, his insides shifted and memories twisted, and suddenly even the most recognizable things became foreign to him. From the piles of scrap, fingers, like worms, wriggled through the gaps and beckoned him to them.

"Stop it," he said to the visions, just as angry as he was afraid. "Stop!"

Aeson slid alongside the building to where it stopped. He was tired of this shit. Not a day or night went by that he didn't find himself reminded of House Gloom and... her... it. He knew his mind was trying to make it easy on him, because the memory of what'd happened to him was getting hazier and hazier. The narrative was always the same, but the details that made it kept going missing. Like the disease that afflicted his people from the Dead City, or the Corruption that tainted the Corrupted's arms, his rape was a sickness his body was trying to push out.

But his body didn't forget the sounds, the sensations. The wound would heal, but the phantom pains would haunt him until he was a haunt himself.

Through his teeth, he said, "Fucking stop," and leaned out from behind the building.

Night Terrors and Corrupted—members of the Cult of the Worm—were working too hard to notice him. Their eyes were a dazzling blue that was far prettier than they deserved to be. He couldn't get a good fix on how many people were here, but after a few minutes of observing, he knew what they were doing.

They were forging weapons and armor, and what the hell was that? Aeson rubbed the gunk—weeks'-worth of travel—out of his eyes to clear his vision. From one of the farther buildings, a crumpled silo, several Cult members carried out three large, very heavy-looking wreaths. But the rings of the wreaths weren't comprised of flowers, leaves, and twigs, but skin and bone tied together with tendons and stretched intestines. Blood and a dark putty—undoubtedly some torturous extract—acted as the glue that kept the structure together. Attached to the sides of the wreath and running down its center was, for Aeson, a familiar sight: the two-headed stick figure symbol.

Whatever the wreath was, it was, if nothing else, a testament to the Witches' lack of creativity.

There were no flesh fiends here, except for those that roamed the corridors of Aeson's brain, and that, although relieving, confused him.

Llyn was a slaughtering ground, Aeson thought, slipping back behind the building. *In Trist, there were the uniforms and that big ass symbol... and in Marwaidd the Choir was somewhere. Underground, I guess.*

Footsteps. Aeson straightened up and drew his sword. He had the Red Death weapon, but who knows how many deaths it had in it before the thing would break.

Heavy breathing, a cough: a shadow stretched past the edge of the building. Then the footsteps stopped.

A wicked smile stretched across Aeson's face. He hadn't killed anything but animals since the Dismal Sticks.

Still out of sight, Aeson watched the person's shadow for movement. The shadow sighed; it raised its arms. Fluttering wings, and then a snap: the person threw a dead raven into the grass and then, laughing, walked away.

Rhyfel... He shook his head, crept along the building, to the edge, again. *It's an armory.*

He heard shouting, and more wings flapping. He leaned out once more. From the wreaths, a handful of ravens had emerged. The cultists were scrambling after them.

Was Llyn a slaughter ground? Or a training yard?

He steadied his breathing. Watching the cultists rip the ravens out of the air and break them. It made his heart hurt.

Llyn… a training ground. Trist… a place to be fitted, or initiated. Marwaidd… a chapel. And here, Rhyfel… an armory. The towns aren't that far off from each other. And they're right in the middle of the continent. Easy access to the North and South, but especially the Heartland.

Aeson started away from the town, and as he did so, thought: *If all the towns have a purpose… then the Witches have everything covered. What the hell are they doing in Angheuawl?*

When he finally reached Angheuawl, it was the first afternoon of November, and it was snowing. There was about an inch of snow on the ground, but most of it had been reduced to a red slush. Because even as Aeson crept towards the town from the distance, there were still flesh fiends and cultists pouring into the town from every direction, and wherever they went, blood flowed; be it from their own wounds, or the wounds they made in passing on their brothers and sisters. It seemed as if the Witches' congregations couldn't go a second without tearing a piece out of one another. Even as they finally finished the climb to the hill upon which Angheuawl sat, the flesh fiends were fondling with and chewing on everything they could get their claws on. And the strange thing was that the cultists, whether they were Children of Lacuna or new initiates who had bought into the sisters' bullshit, didn't seem to mind. They welcomed the mutilation. Disappearing into the town, Aeson could still hear them clamoring for "communion."

Aeson dropped down into the bushes. There was no wind, and yet the raucous cries of the Choir deep inside Angheuawl seemed to move through the area the way wind would—the sound waves flattening the foliage, bending trees. He checked the Red Death weapon, even though he knew it was there, in his armor, and again, stowed it away.

I'm here, I did it. He glanced up at Angheuawl. There was blue smoke in the air, rising from the center of the village. *Vrana's here. I can do this.*

He started for his feet, and then stopped. What was that? He had heard—

A curse wolf padded through the undergrowth, its stark-white face sizing him up, and headed towards the hill to Angheuawl. The wolves were said to be portents of Death, but Aeson knew what was going on. She was watching him, waiting to see how dirty he was willing to get to do her dirty work.

How the hell am I going to get up there? he thought. *Will they even notice if I'm not one of them?* The Cult of the Worm didn't seem to be part of some hive-mind. *If I'm with people that look like me...* He shivered. *I could ignore them. I could ignore the flesh fiends. I could walk right past them. Hell, they might even think I'm a flesh fiend given—*

The curse wolf stopped halfway up the hill and stared into the woods, directly at Aeson. A pack of Night Terrors in heavy furs—Rimeans— lumbered past the curse wolf, as if it wasn't there.

Despite his pep talk, Aeson immediately caved. "I can't," he said under his breath. "I can't do it."

A sharp pain pricked his chest. A tunnel of pressure slammed into his forehead; his eyes filled with black light. Something scratched his skin again from behind his breastplate. Mindful of the Red Death weapon, but frantic, he reached into his armor and took it out.

Death's finger, which she had fixed to Bjørn's rib, was moving slowly, beckoning him forward. Lip quivering, the effects of the weapon's pricks waning, he looked at the curse wolf. The beast gave him a nod and went to the edge of the hill, where the woods were thin and crosshatched with sun shafts.

"Follow," Death seemed to say. And why not? He had been chasing Death his entire life, in one form or another.

Sword in one hand, Red Death weapon in the other, he swallowed the sick in his throat and, skirting the hill, headed towards the wolf. He kept to the trees, bushes, boulders, and anything else he could cower behind. Every time the snow crunched underneath his feet, he swore the cultists climbing the hill could hear him. But no one had, or if they had, they didn't seem to care.

Carefully, Aeson rounded the bottom of the hill. He came up the side of it where the curse wolf waited. Death's familiar shook its head and padded off, away from Angheuawl, into the trees.

This is stupid, Aeson thought. The woods that scaled the hill's slope were not only sparse and sun-soaked, but flooded, too. It wasn't that snow was melting, though it flowed past his feet all the same; it was the lakes in the area. Farther on, where the land flattened at higher elevations, two lakes had flooded.

"Pain and Joy use water to enter our world," Aeson said, crouched, the rushing water up to his shins. "What're they doing here?"

The curse wolf glanced back, as if to say, "You'll see."

Aeson heard splashing not far from where he stood. With the wolf, he hurried towards the thickest grouping of trees he could find and wedged himself there. Sitting on the ground, lower-half soaked, hard-hitting shivers rocked his body. He made himself as small as possible, without relinquishing the weapons, and waited for whatever was up ahead to leave.

Don't see me, don't see me, don't see me.

The splashing grew louder. He could make out limbs wading through the water, as if those who were approaching were down on all-fours. He heard teeth chattering, too, and wheezing.

Aeson cringed as each sound grew louder and louder. They were close enough that he could hear the cracking of their bones; he could feel how uneven their teeth must be, by the way they clicked together. He gripped his sword, started to lean out from the trees, and then quickly retreated.

They were passing right by him.

And there was his reflection in the water, scared shitless and plain as day.

Looking at the wolf, he begged it silently for a plan. But Death's dog had no answers for him. It was as scared as he was.

Ripples from those approaching broke against Aeson's side. A voice, loud enough that it felt as if the speaker were shouting in his ear: "She's h-h-here... I c-c-can smell t-the way s-she tastes."

That voice, Aeson thought. *I know I know that voice.* It was garbled, though, like the speaker's mouth was filled with spit and glass. He couldn't place it, but he knew he knew—

A fat flesh fiend crawled into view, inches away from where he sat. Like a startled animal, Aeson went stiff. He stopped breathing, stopped blinking. He retreated inside himself, to that dark and dead place where not even the most severe suffering could reach him.

The flesh fiend's sagging gut bludgeoned the water with every step it took. It didn't crawl on two hands, but one; and the same was true of the three flesh fiends that traveled with it. Each of them had one of their twisted, mutilated, white-crusted arms extended above and away from them. They were carrying something, sharing together the heavy weight of the unholy load stretched over them.

Above the flesh fiends, held up in their grips, a sedan of charred vermillion veins was suspended. The warped, blackened chunk looked like a comet disgorged from some chaotic plane. The flesh fiends struggled to hold it, but they held it all the same; as if the speaker buried within the mass' center was royalty.

"Take m-me t-to… her," the voice spoke again.

The end of the procession passed Aeson. The four flesh fiends' eyes never left Angheuawl. They had a job to do. Everything else was invisible to them.

"She n-needs… my hurt."

The four flesh fiends and their vermillion cargo reached the hill and headed for town.

The curse wolf nudged Aeson to move, but his body wouldn't budge. He felt Death's finger scratching at his chest again, but the threads of his mortality wouldn't yield.

Get up, he said, coming out of that dark and dead place. *You have to get up.*

And that was true. It was now or never. And never really wasn't an option, because it was the only one that anyone with any sense would choose. The long line of cultists coming into town was thinning. There were only stragglers now, from the north and south; Corrupted and Night Terrors, mostly—some wearing the white garments of Cathedra, others, the mossy armor of Traesk.

Again, the curse wolf nudged him. He stared into the beast's jet-black eyes and saw the luminescent sheen of Death's wings in its pupils.

I have to do it now.

Three dead ravens floated past him.

I have to do this now.

The curse wolf took off through the woods, darting between the trees. Aeson followed as fast as he could, his legs numb from sitting in the icy water for so long. The closer they came to Angheuawl, the less cover they had with which to hide themselves.

Aeson and the curse wolf reached the hill's summit and quickly slid behind a work shed that stood in shambles on the outskirts. They waited until the very last of the cultists passed, and moved deeper into Angheuawl, one wrecked wall and bombed-out building at a time.

So close to the center, to the end of this horrid quest, and yet Aeson couldn't steal but a glimpse into the heart of the Witches' operation. Angheuawl was a mining town, built by miners, on the edges of Southern

Cradle, in a volcanic range. Not much thought went into its construction or aesthetic. It was an uneven, unpainted mess of homes and stores intersecting at odd angles; a plot of garish geometry, streamlined for work, and reluctant to allow for anything else. Squat homes, narrow roofs; woods worth of wood on every corner, along every street—splintered, buckled, and covered in the Cult's graffiti.

But like cattle answering the call, there was an order, despite the meandering. For at the farthest end of Angheuawl, there was the mine. Aeson couldn't see it from where he was, but he saw the top portion of façade that had been built over it; a wooden steeple jutting high into the sky, and a name—Nicholas Harrington—painted boldly in black on a horizontal beam between the supports. That was where the blue smoke was coming from, and the singing, and the—

Aeson dropped the sword and held the Red Death weapon against his chest. He couldn't do it. He couldn't pretend to ignore it anymore. The Cult of the Worm was everywhere.

Holy Child in hell there were hundreds of them. Clogging the streets, moving in and out of the business and homes. Adults, mostly, except for the childish flesh fiends that slinked along the rooftops, biting the heads off the ravens in their hands. Night Terror, Corrupted, Child of Lacuna, or Cultist—it didn't matter. Other than the presence of Corruption, who these people were or what they believed was impossible to determine. The distinction between species and sub-species was so blurred it made Aeson cross-eyed trying to figure it out. The only way he could identify them was by the culture they clothed themselves in.

There, Night Terrors from Rime and Traesk, and a few elderlies from Eld. Shit, was that the Wasp and Boar from Caldera?

There, Corrupted from Nora, Nyxis, and, yes, hunters of the Blasted Woodland. And goddamn, soldiers from Eldrus and Penance, too?

But that wasn't all. There were more, many more, up ahead, shuffling towards the mine, damn near walking hand-in-hand with the flesh fiends at their sides. Flesh fiends. Subterranean sadists, subdued, almost docile. He'd hoped the creatures at the Dismal Sticks had been a fluke, but, no, it was true: The Witches had discovered a way to control them. And there were so many of them. More than the humans and humanoids with blue light dripping from their eyes. For every piece of flesh, there were five fiends. Like roaches on their best behavior, they seemed to be playing a part, biding their time, for the great feast to come.

Shrill laughter swept through the town, from the mine upon which the Cult was converging. It was Pain's voice he heard, and behind it, pathetically, there was a croaking. And beating wings. And scrabbling claws. And another woman, Joy, screaming at the yet unseen, still love of his life—the Winged Horror.

The curse wolf started for the next building, an infirmary. Aeson cleared his thoughts and thought of nothing else but Vrana. She was his blessing, his boon; the backbone he'd been born without. He never would've come this far for anyone else. No one else could've brought him this far.

They slipped into the infirmary through a backdoor. It smelled sour inside. Most of the beds were nothing more than frames. The supply cabinets had already been emptied and filled again; this time with cobwebs. Unless someone was seeking a radical cure for arachnophobia, no healing was going to happen here anytime soon.

The curse wolf kept going. Aeson did, too. They hurried into an administrative office and back into the streets. The wolf stopped, barred his path. The tail end of the four flesh fiends and the vermillion sedan passed by. And then the coast was clear; they were off again.

They snaked through the edge of Angheuawl, never daring the main road. From the infirmary, they went into a chapel and out its window and into a string of residences. They were getting closer to the meeting point—the Choir's throaty hymns were absolutely deafening—but the dread inside Aeson told him they were never going to get close enough. The lack of guards was surprising, but when he thought about it, it really wasn't. No one except for himself was going to be stupid enough to come into a town crawling with flesh fiends. And Pain and Joy had nothing to fear. So long as they had the Void, they had everything.

The curse wolf crept out of the last house, paused, and huffed at Aeson to give chase. He hurried down the porch. Just then, a Night Terror and Corrupted, both women, naked and still covered in the sweat of their sex, came trudging down the street. They locked eyes with him, and he with them.

"Have you come to open yourself?" the Corrupted asked.

Aeson nodded.

The Night Terror was holding her mask. It was a monkey. "There's a void in us all. One to fill the other." She smiled, slipped on her skull, and walked on with her lover.

About to shit his pants, Aeson ran after the curse wolf into the saloon. The place was covered in the Cult's two-headed stick figure symbols, as if a child had gone to work on the walls.

"Fuck." Aeson gasped and propped himself up against the bar. "Fuck, that was close."

"Goddamn it," a woman rumbled behind him.

Aeson's stomach sank.

The curse wolf's lips peeled back into a terrifying snarl. Its teeth were Death's nails.

Aeson spun around. Behind the bar, there was Belia, the one-armed servant flesh fiend from House Gloom. She was still wearing the dress Ichor had given her, except she wasn't really wearing it; rather, it was now a part of her. When the house had burned down, the heat must've fused the corset and cage crinoline to her body. There was pus oozing down her chest; and her breasts looked like two deflated balloons covered in hair. When she caught Aeson gazing at her, she covered herself up, as if embarrassed.

"Goddamn it!" she screamed, hurling herself at him.

Aeson stumbled backwards. He dropped the Red Death weapon beside the curse wolf, not wanting to waste it.

Belia hobbled across the saloon, spitting and swinging her claws. Her left leg, shorter than the right, slowed her down badly.

"Goddamn it, goddamn it!" she said, over and over, the only phrase she was capable of. "Goddamn it!" Her voice was an alarm he couldn't afford to have going off any longer.

Belia sped up and flung herself at him. Aeson went sideways. Her grasping claws hooked onto his breastplate and yanked him onto the ground with her. Aeson broke his fall on her hip. She took the blow like a champ, oriented herself, and came after him, on her hands and feet.

Aeson scooted backwards, the nails in the wooden floor catching on his ass. Feeling bad for Belia, he pulled the sword back, ready to bust her with the pommel. But as she vaulted towards him, she stopped being Belia, and started being her, it, the fiend that had fucked him.

He felt an invisible weight on his groin. And heat from the fire that burned Gloom down. And the wet grass, soaking his back.

"Goddamn it!" Belia lunged.

Aeson's sympathy was the finality of steel. At the last second, he twisted his hand and drove the sword through Belia's mouth. It scraped against her teeth, made a mush of her gums. The flesh fiend's momentum drove her down on the sword. The tip blew out the back of her skull. It wasn't until her bleeding face hit the hilt that she stopped.

"Goddamn it," Aeson said, standing up. Belia slid off his sword like meat from a skewer. "Thanks for the help," he said to the curse wolf, stepping over Belia and retrieving the Red Death weapon.

Vrana. Vrana. Vrana. Aeson repeated the name over and over as he and the curse wolf ran out of the saloon before anyone might come investigate the noise. *I'm coming. It's almost over.*

Angheuawl's streets had all but cleared. Aeson and the curse wolf skirted along the sides of a general store, waiting for two flesh fiend children to catch up with their brethren at the town's center.

The falling snow started to thicken. The flurries fattened and came in sideways. As if his eyes were failing him, the town was suddenly rendered in a gray tone, and visibility fell off after fifteen feet. Convenient. Maybe it was the work of whatever spells the Witches were weaving ahead, or maybe, just maybe, Mother Nature wanted these bitches dead as much as he did.

Vrana, I'm so sorry I took so long.

Aeson went low when the wolf seemed to tell him to get low. Like the beast he followed, he crawled along the ground, to the last turn in this maze of a mining town. After that, he'd be close enough to the center to see everything.

I don't care what you are now.

The curse wolf glanced back, to make sure Aeson was still there.

I know you won't care what I've become.

"Get up," the curse wolf said with a yelp.

We've both gone to pieces.

Aeson got up and slinked over to the alley that let out from Angheuawl's center.

I'd rather be broken than broken-hearted.

He moved down the alley, the snowflakes that pelted him melting around him, as if he gave off an aura of intense heat. He set his sword against the wall, within reach, and holding the Red Death weapon with both hands, peered out at the center of town.

The Cult of the Worm was everywhere. On every roof, in every doorway. There was no ground to walk on, because the cultists blanketed it with their bodies. The Night Terrors, Corrupted, and flesh fiends were here by the hundreds, and all of them, every single one of them, were on their backs, their arms interlocked with their neighbors', singing a single eldritch note no creature of this planet should've been able to create. There was no blood or gore; no senseless slaughter, no mass rape; just body after body, bound by their limbs, looking up into the sky, weeping diamonds of light, as blue smoke swept across the congregation and poured into their quivering mouths.

Wicked laughter lifted Aeson's attention from the demonstration. At the back of Angheuawl, where he had expected to find them, Pain and Joy stood. They were in front of the entrance to the drift mine, except the mine wasn't a mine anymore; its doorway was now a gray, swirling portal that let out into the Void itself.

And there was Vrana. There she was. It hurt to look at her, the same way it hurt to look at the sun, but despite the pain, he needed them all the same. Vrana was between Pain and Joy, her arms and wings crucified to the support beams that formed the opening of the mine. Her head was tipped back; the blue smoke that roamed Angheuawl was pouring out of her beak. Around Vrana's neck, the Blue Worm's silver necklace shone with an intense, throbbing light.

Between here and the witches were hundreds of their minions, all willing at any moment to tear Aeson to pieces. He gripped the Red Death weapon until it felt as if his knuckles were going to tear, and retreated into the alley. The curse wolf was gone. He had to do this alone.

"Bring out the babies," Pain cried. "Let them see the world they're going to inherit."

Joy stepped in front of Vrana. Her white satin dress swished around her legs. Black bloodstains ran up and down the front and the back of the fabric from all her miscarriages. She held up her arms and said, "Are you sure?"

Pain grinned, spit on her sister, and laughed. Her wild eyes, black orbs pricked with red, rolled in their sockets. "Better late than never!"

"We should finish what we're doing first—"

Pain walked over to Joy and slit her throat with her fingernail. Joy dropped to her knees, blood sputtering out of the wound in thick, almost comical geysers. It doused Vrana, but Vrana didn't stir. At this point, Aeson couldn't tell if she was alive or dead.

Pain held out her pale, slimy hand, and Joy took it. By the time she was back on her feet, the wound had healed.

"They're coming!" Pain screamed giddily into Joy's ear. "Give them a good show!"

Joy nodded and held up her arms again. The Void portal contracted, and a tendril of it reached out and touched her between the legs. The black bloodstains dripped off the dress and slithered into the Void.

"Not all of them," Pain conceded, sounding annoyed.

Joy's body jerked. The black bloodstains whipped out of the Void, like chains, and hooked upon their ends were the most terrifying abominations Aeson had ever seen.

From the Void, the bloodstains brought out huge cancerous masses that had been formed from the bodies of children. They were sick amalgamations of body parts, fitted together in such a way to allow for movement. Its lower half was a hard crust, like a massive callous, comprised of legs and arms, and some combination of the two that had been melted together into what amounted to tails and tentacles. The upper half was like a piece of severed fruit; a glistening bi-section of tiny bodies and heads constantly crying out in garbled, childish pleas. Like rotted seeds, babies and infants were lodged into the top of the Horror of the Womb. From their split bellies, ropes of intestines flailed in the air, flinging blood and shit across the nearby cultists.

One after the other, Joy conjured these creatures from the Void, until there were four of them. Then, the last of black bloodstains wrenched a fifth Horror from the Void—their mother.

The Mother Horror wasn't Death, but a mockery of Her. The Horror came tumbling out of the Void, end over end, until it was checked by Joy's trembling legs. Slowly, it rose off the ground—gallons of clear, steaming fluids pouring off it. The Mother Horror grew exponentially in size as it gathered itself. Beginning as a dripping grub, it soon sprouted sets of arms and legs, and then two moth-eaten, moth-like wings. It wasn't beautiful in the way Death was beautiful; it was horrible to behold. Its body was oily; the furs that covered it matted and knotted. A head burst from the top of the grub, and it was a single black bulb, with no eyes or antennae; simply a sneering grin painted on with what appeared to be nail polish.

Joy dropped her arms. Pain, rubbing her hands together like the villainess she was, shouldered past her sister and, flailing her arms, screamed at the Horrors, "Go! Go!"

The white satin dress practically swallowed Joy as she dropped to her knees, spent. The black bloodstains returned to their place on the fabric. "They can't fend for themselves."

"Neither could we," Pain said, taking Joy by the chin. "Look at us now."

The Mother Horror, now a good twenty feet long, lifted off the ground. Gracelessly, it drifted like a kite over the Horrors of the Womb.

One by one, with its arms and legs, it picked up the oversized ovaries and hauled them off, over Angheuawl and into the snowy distance.

With the Horrors gone, Aeson let himself breathe again. *I can't do this,* he said to himself. Crying, and shaking, he fell like Joy, crumpling on the floor of the alleyway. Out the corner of his eyes, he stared at Vrana, crucified; her feathered body struggling in a kind of epileptic shock. She was covered in every kind of fluid imaginable. There were fresh scars all over her body, and her legs looked gnarled. *I shouldn't do this. I can't save you to kill you. Killing you is the only way to save you. I can't—*

"What's that?" Pain hollered.

Her voice found him like an arrow and pierced him through. He looked back at the Witches.

The Witches were looking back at him.

"Is that…" Pain tilted her head; her ashen hair fell across her face. "It is! Joy, fetch him!"

No, no, no. Aeson hurried to his feet.

But Joy was faster. She rose out of her dress and glided over the still lying, still singing Cult of the Worm. She cleared the distance in a blur. One second, and she was there, in the alley with him.

"Do I know you?" Joy asked, slowing her words to sound sultry. She was flirting with him.

Aeson slipped the Red Death weapon behind his back.

But it was too late. She had already seen it.

"What do you have there?" she whispered. Her eyes narrowed. She bared her teeth and winked. "I can keep a secret."

Aeson shook his head.

"Bring him here!" Pain yelled.

Joy rolled her eyes, turned her head: "Have some fucking patience for—"

Aeson swung the Red Death weapon at Joy's side.

But before it touched her, she caught his arm by the wrist and stopped him.

"What is it?" Pain asked.

Joy's face turned paler than it already was. Death's nail was an inch away from her side, and already it was going to work on her, burning through her dress, eating through her skin.

"Do… do you…" Joy stared at Aeson; her lip quivered. "Do you know who… this is?" she asked Pain.

"Yes, yes! Bring him here. I have someone special to show him!"

Aeson could feel Joy's grip loosening on his wrist. She was breathing heavily now. There was a pop; boils and blisters spread across her skin.

"You're going to miss your babies! They're almost there," Pain said.

Joy's eyes began to water. A smile flashed across her face. Knitting her brow, she let go of Aeson's wrist. They stood there a moment in silence, staring one another down, as the snow built up around their feet, and the ice melted from their hearts.

"We're coming," Joy said, with a nod.

Aeson took the Red Death weapon and stowed it behind his breast-plate. Hesitant at first, Joy finally took him by both hands. She was careful with him; gentle, even. She whispered a word. His feet left the ground. And then they were off, floating over the Cult of the Worm.

The Maiden of Pain could hardly control herself. "Come here, come here," she said.

Joy landed the both of them beside Vrana. Aeson tried to look away from her, but Pain quickly came up beside him, took him by the head, and forced him to stare at her.

"Like what you see?" Pain whispered into his ear; her breath smelled of mildew. Her touch was like touching a cold, moss-covered stone. "She did everything for me. I'm sure she would do anything for you.

"You came a long way, didn't you? That night I burned your shitty little village… I couldn't even bring myself to kill you—"

He remembered. She had just laughed at him, instead.

"—and here you are. They say you shouldn't judge a book by its cover and, what do you know—" Joy slapped the bear mask off his head, "—this book has a new cover. Look, Vrana, at who's come to see you!"

For the first time since he'd seen her, Vrana moved on her own. She was alive. Yes, somehow, she was alive. The smoke stopped spewing from her beak. She twisted her neck and, with one pained eye, looked at him.

"It's Aeson, isn't it?" Pain scoffed at Joy, who was pacing nervously. "Oh, just go! Go!"

Joy lifted into the air and left Angheuawl in the same direction her Horrors had.

Pain nudged Aeson and spun him around to face the Cult of the Worm. "What do you think?"

Bide your time, he told himself. *Bide your time.* Every centimeter of his body tensed. He could feel it breaking down on the inside, the acid of anxiety eating away at his core. *Bide your time.*

"I wish I had someone love me as much as you do her," Pain said, smirking. She picked a raven feather out of her ratty dress. "Soon, though, soon."

"Please…" Aeson closed his eyes, pretended he was somewhere else, so he could get this out. "I don't believe…"

"Believe this is happening?" Pain laughed. "Do you even know what is happening?"

Aeson shook his head.

Pain pointed to one of the double-headed stick figure icons on the wall. Her eyes rolled back into her skull and she screamed, "Kvuxl Vkxul!

The Cult of the Worm's symbol crumpled, sucked inside itself, and a vortex opened behind it. A gray portal that, like the one behind them, led into the Void.

"Kvuxl Vkxul!"

Another symbol was torn apart by the spell; where it had once been, a swirling gate now stood, as if it had been there the whole time, simply waiting to be called forth.

"Kvuxl Vkxul! Kvuxl Vkxul!"

Two more portals opened at the center of Angheuawl. And every time one did, the Choir sang louder from the ground.

"This isn't the first time you've seen our symbol, is it, Skull Boy?"

It wasn't. They were everywhere in Angheuawl, and in most, if not all, the towns he had passed through getting here. He had seen the symbol in the Dismal Sticks and… Caldera.

Aeson covered his mouth. When Pain had attacked Caldera, she had burnt an image into the ground. No matter what they did, they could never get the image to go away. Like a brand, it was there forever.

"Alone no more," Pain said. "We will be everywhere soon, in every village, town, and city. King Edgar had the right idea with the vermillion veins. But our idea was better."

"H-how?"

Pain grabbed Aeson by the shoulders and bit off a piece of his cheek. She spat the bloody hunk his face, and then kissed him, forcing her bristled tongue deep inside his mouth.

Aeson broke free of her grasp. He pressed one hand to his cheek, and crossed his arm over his chest. The Red Death weapon had almost fallen out.

"Belief. We have so many believers now, and we're about to have more. Come here." Pain snapped her fingers. Aeson was levitating again.

"Come and see."

Pain pushed Aeson into the sky and urged him forward; far enough away that he could see what was going on outside the town. There was Joy and her Horrors... and what appeared to be a small army of Corrupted battling in the snow. Below him, the vermillion sedan burst out of Angheuawl and headed for the fight. For a moment, it looked up at him, and he saw buried inside the writhing mass the burnt face of Ichor.

"Ever heard of the Marrow Cabal?" Pain asked, lowering him back into the town beside her.

Aeson stumbled and landed near Vrana's feet. She was panting. She had been watching him the whole time.

Almost, he wanted to tell her. *Almost.*

"They'll be ours by the end of the day," Pain said.

Aeson crawled forward. He took Vrana's feathered ankle in his hand and kissed it. She had to know. If he didn't save her, she had to at least know he still loved her.

With a spell, Pain yanked him to his feet and put him in front of her. "Joy's stupid children can't fight for shit. They're just there—"

"For fear," Aeson said, shivering, on the brink of collapsing.

"For fear. I like that. When I drink your blood tonight, it will be to fear that I toast."

"What's the point?" Aeson asked, crossing his arms over his breastplate.

"It brings me joy," Pain said, "to bring them pain."

Joy returned to Angheuawl and floated down beside her sister. "They will be here soon," she said, smoothing out her white satin dress.

"Good. Is that Skeleton with them?"

Joy shook her head.

"Next time. Prepare the Cult, we're opening all the—"

Joy reached out and touched Pain's face.

"What?" Pain asked, confused.

One look. Joy gave Aeson one look.

He pulled the Red Death weapon out of his breastplate and, with every ounce of hate and sadness, malice and madness; with every ounce self-doubt, self-loathing, and self-harm; with every burning piece of filth inside him, filling him, polluting him, ruining him, he drove Death's touch into Her daughter's heart.

Pain screamed louder than the Choir that praised her. She touched the Red Death weapon still protruding from her chest. It crumbled into nothingness, but the damage was already done. Behind her, and all around her, the portals to the Void began to react violently.

Joy looked at Aeson as if she hated him more than anything else in the world and ran into the Void, the gateway closing behind her.

Pain, gasping for air, dropped to her knees and dug at the wound in her chest. Her mother's touch was poison. She cupped her breast and drank the wound, trying to suck out the force that had severed her tie to the Void.

"No," Pain said, and Aeson heard her clear as day, for the Cult of the Worm had stopped singing. The light had left their eyes. There was a moment of silence, mutual confusion, and then the flesh fiends turned on those they had once held hands with.

There was another sound. A tearing of skin, and a loud thump.

Aeson turned around to find Vrana standing behind him. She tore off the Blue Worm's silver necklace, threw it at him, and ran at Pain.

Vrana's wings closed around the Witch. She picked her off the ground as if she weighed nothing at all, then threw her down, breaking her face on the hard soil. Vrana straddled Pain, pinned her limbs back. And then she started eating her.

Vrana raked Pain's flesh, splitting it into strands. She made six strands at a time, and then shoved them down her beak. Pain screamed out in agony.

Vrana ripped her jaw off, tore her tongue out of her mouth, and gobbled down both of them. Warm, hot blood poured out of the Witch. Vrana cupped her claws together and drank it like soup.

The Witch, somehow still alive, beat Vrana's side. Vrana bore her beak down on each of Pain's arm sockets, until they were easy enough to rip away from her body. And once they were, Vrana did just that. And then she ate them, too.

Blood and muscle and tendons spilled out of Pain's shaking torso. Vrana gathered them with her twitching talons and sucked them off each of her fingers.

Pain was laughing now, so Vrana tore open her gut and buried her face inside it, and one by one, ate every organ inside. They popped and hissed and squirted inside Vrana's beak.

Then, leaving the rib cage and head, Vrana mutilated Pain's pelvis, until it was so mashed and beaten, she had to lick it off the ground.

She worked her way down to Pain's disembodied legs and choked them down her throat whole. It took her a moment to swallow them, but she did.

Vrana reared back, completely covered in blood and gore. She glanced at Aeson, and Aeson made no attempt to stop her.

Vrana grabbed Pain's torso and ripped the ribs out of it. She ate them, one by one, leaving no scrap of flesh or cartilage unconsumed. And then, slowly, considerately, she closed her claws around Pain's severed head, bashed it open until it split in two like a rock, and gulped down everything inside it, bones, too.

And then, when there was nothing left of the Witch but the few pints of blood that had escaped Vrana's lips, Vrana stood up and wiped her mouth.

"Twenty pieces a person, for every person the Witch killed in Caldera that night. I promised Caldera that's what I'd take from Pain when I found her," Vrana said, blood and chewed-up body parts pouring out of her mouth. "There are two-hundred-and-six bones in the body, and seventy-eight organs. Between those, and everything else, I think everyone's covered."

Aeson nodded, and he was lucky he could do that. Blood splashed across his shoes. A few feet away, the Cult of the Worm were slaughtering one another, raping one another; completely annihilating one another. There were no words to describe the carnage. It was carnage beyond comprehension. Something only the blind could comprehend, for the eyes couldn't behold what the other senses could sample. The overwhelming stench of violence and lust, the discharge of seminal and vaginal fluids, and balled fists holding clumps of shit like trophies. Too many bodies. Too much blood. Holes where there shouldn't have been holes. It was, for the Cult of the Worm and the God they claimed to worship, their greatest masterpiece.

Vrana took Aeson into her wings and lifted them into the sky, where he morbidly thought to himself how fortunate he must be to be one of the few to see the eradication of an entire species.

His species.

There was no coming back from this.

CHAPTER XXIII

R'lyeh covered her mouth and coughed as quietly as she could into her hand, so as to not alarm the Skeleton. She closed her palm, sealing the blood she'd spat up into her lifeline. It wasn't much, and it was watery, like it'd been diluted. It smelled sweet, too, like fruit. She went to wipe it on her pant leg, but there was already so much hacked-up gunk there it was starting to get obvious; so, she smeared it on the park bench, instead.

When it came to its name and lore, the Dead City didn't disappoint. Caving inwards upon itself, like the slowest closing pop-up book, the place had all the charms and amenities of a sepulcher. Gray stone, old dirt; filthy glass, rusted metalwork—the true source of color in the city came from the green clouds of sickness and disease that roamed through it. Because the clouds were constantly moving, the Dead City appeared to be constantly breathing. The skyscrapers and subway stations, and businesses and apartments were transformed from decayed corpses to rotting corpses, and then back again, depending upon the time of day, and how much infection was spewing from their splintered, shattered, broken-down, busted-through lips.

The Dead City was dead, but the Green Worm had taken its husk and, with it, had given itself a form. The Green Worm was the city. Every street and highway, road and lane; every business district and residential span; every park and playground and putrid pothole that plummeted into the sewers below. Like a ghost beneath a sheet, or a spirit inside a doll, the Green Worm was what it possessed. That's what the weird people in the suits had told R'lyeh and the Skeleton, and that's what R'lyeh was thinking about now, as she filled her lungs with the same kind of creature that had taken everything from her.

R'lyeh coughed again, but no blood came out. A good sign. As with every other infection or poison, her body was rejecting the Worm. Hell, how could it not? This was the third time she'd crossed paths with their kind. Fourth, maybe, if the Mother Hydra was one. Is that what she was meant to be? A hunter of Worms? She liked the idea as much as she hated it. But wasn't that why most people did the things they loved? To stop the things they hated?

The Skeleton paced back and forth near the small merry-go-round, giving it a good spin here and there. Ever since they had been escorted into the City, he had been acting strange. Aloof, that was how her mom would describe it. He'd come so far, and yet it seemed like this was the last place he wanted to be.

It's the Worm, R'lyeh thought. *He thinks he has to kill another one.*

The Skeleton stopped near a demolished drinking fountain and adjusted his cloak. The Black Hour's heart's growth appeared as if it had stopped for the time being. The black moss hadn't spread any further. Maybe he didn't want to be here, because this was exactly where it wanted to be.

I want to kill it. R'lyeh tapped her fingers on the blade of the sword across her lap. *I want to kill something.*

R'lyeh rose to her feet. Unsteady, she took a deep breath and waited for the nausea to pass. Another cough; no blood. Swinging the sword at her side, she made her way towards the Skeleton. With him, the past couldn't touch her; he was the boney barrier that kept the bad memories back. He couldn't die, so neither could she. That's how these things worked. The Green Worm was this city, and she was the company she kept. No different than anybody else.

"I used to be obsessed with the Old World," R'lyeh said, going to the merry-go-ground.

The Skeleton stopped at a toilet, the last standing part of a bathroom that used to be here. "That so? Don't look like you're having a field day."

R'lyeh stifled a cough. "I wanted to be a librarian." She grinned. "A badass librarian."

"Hate to be a bearer of bad news, but I can't say I've ever met something of the sort. I think being a librarian and kicking ass are two mutually exclusive things."

"I got the ass kicking part down."

The Skeleton laughed. "Hope so. Expect we'll be fighting our way out of here soon."

"Okay," R'lyeh said, swinging the sword a little faster. "That's fine."

The Skeleton threw on his hood, and then took it back off. He strolled over to the edge of the park, where the sidewalk was split and a telephone pole had fallen through. Across the street, a storefront had been spray painted over with a mess of graffiti. It was hard to make out most of it, but there was a phrase separate from the rest. It read: Don't Assume My God.

"I take it Elizabeth and Miranda's teachings of non-violence didn't take?" the Skeleton asked.

"No—" R'lyeh's eyes wandered over the city, noticing that same phrase was repeated again and again across walls and billboards, "—not really." And then, forcing the image of Miranda's mutilated body out of her mind: "Wait, were they supposed to work?"

"They wanted them to."

"Why?"

"Because they thought you could be more than a killer."

R'lyeh twisted her mouth. "I am more."

"Never said you weren't."

"I've been through hell."

"Me and you both."

R'lyeh stormed over to the Skeleton. "You see that there?" She pointed to a cell phone store. "That's where people would go and buy phones, things that let them talk to each other, no matter where they were in the world."

"Fascinating," the Skeleton said, unimpressed.

"And that—" R'lyeh drew his attention to what appeared to be a courthouse, "—was where people were judged, to decide if they were innocent or guilty of crimes."

"Yeah, alright."

"That's a gym, where people worked out to get stronger. And that's a—" she coughed, "—place where people who didn't have a lot of money got help from the government." She smacked the Skeleton's arm—

Black winter; red summer.

—and shook off the Black Hour's image. "That's... that's a library. There're probably computers in there. For a lot of people, that and the Internet was everything—"

"R'lyeh."

"—because it had everything. You didn't have to wait for someone to tell you something, or spend your whole life looking for something. If something bad was coming, you'd know about it. You'd have time to get—"

"R'lyeh."

"What?!" she shouted, a knot in her forehead. "Sorry, what?"

"You're here," the Skeleton said, "isn't that enough? That's better than most, if not all—me withstanding, of course."

R'lyeh covered her mouth, fought back the urge to wheeze.

"The only past that should concern you is yours. What's all this—" he held out his skeletal arms, "—going to do for you? Fill the shelves in your head with all this knowledge, and for what?"

"Seriously?" She shook her head. "Isn't that why we're here? To use whatever weapons they made in the past to fight?"

The Skeleton stared at her, his crazed eyes glistening in their sockets. "I don't want to be another Poe."

"I don't know what that is."

The Skeleton sighed. "Doesn't matter."

"Then why'd you say it?"

"Can you say no to me?" The Skeleton stepped up to her; his crooked, bare smile sending a chill down her spine. "Can you say no to anyone you trust?"

"Yes, yes, I fucking can," R'lyeh said. "I'm not a child. I'm a Night Terror. I'm not like you."

"Without your mask, you are." The Skeleton touched his chest. "I'm not always me, not with this inside me. Neither are you, what with all you've got locked away. I am getting worse. I don't know you well enough to say if you're getting better."

"I'm fine," R'lyeh said, resolutely. "I'm fine... Atticus."

The Skeleton grunted. "People used to call me the Gravedigger. Wish I could get back to that. People ever call you something different?"

"No, just R'lyeh."

"You still R'lyeh? Or do we need something fancier, on account of you being a badass librarian now?"

"R'lyeh works," she said, trying not to smile. "I guess."

"Get your Vrana back after this," the Skeleton said.

R'lyeh pretended not to hear him. She coughed blood up and quickly wiped it off her lips.

The Skeleton pretended not to see her. He touched the heart again and quickly pulled away.

They waited another good twenty minutes in the park before the man, Arbo, and woman, Merna, who had met them outside the City, returned. This time, it was more than the two of them. They were flanked by six suits which were somehow bulkier and cruder than their own. Large, flimsy white tubes twisted out of each of the individual's backpacks, into their suits and masks. Like Arbo and Merna, it was impossible to see their masks. Unlike Arbo and Merna, these six were armed. With guns.

The Skeleton stepped in front of R'lyeh and said to those approaching, "What's this all about?"

Rifles? Automatic rifles? R'lyeh hadn't really learned much about guns in school; most of her knowledge came from the books she devoured. She peeked around the Skeleton. They were definitely rifles. Looking down at her sword, she didn't feel so immortal anymore. And with the Skeleton having no flesh of his own, he didn't even make a very good human shield. She coughed again, and bad thoughts starting brewing at the back of her skull.

This is just like Rime, just like Geharra. Bad choices always bring you back to where you belong. Her mom used to say that, but R'lyeh never knew what it meant, and she still didn't.

"It's okay," Merna said, approaching slowly, signaling for the others, including Arbo, to stay behind. "Trust me. We do not want to hurt you."

A thick, green cloud rolled across the playground, and then took a sharp turn down a street.

"The last time anyone made it this far into the city was decades ago," Arbo said, going to Merna. "People with animal skulls on their heads. There was a large party of them."

The Night Terrors were here? R'lyeh wondered.

Arbo went on: "They lasted about an hour. Most of them died before reaching the outskirts. It has been a long, long time of watching, and waiting. This—" he gestured to the six behind him, "—is just necessity. There aren't a lot of us left."

Not wanting to look weak, R'lyeh stepped out from behind the Skeleton and stood at his side.

"Not a lot of anything left nowadays," the Skeleton said. "You said waiting. What've you been waiting for?"

Merna spoke up. "A sign, and a chance to leave."

"Leave the Dead City?" R'lyeh asked, her eyes never lifting from the rifles.

"Walk with us, to where we live. If the Putrid Prince hasn't rotted you already, then we must assume you are honored guests."

"Answer the girl," the Skeleton said.

Merna adjusted the voice modulator on her suit and said, "Yes, we want to leave the city. We want to leave this whole planet behind."

They called themselves Virion, and their home was at the center of the Dead City, where the buildings leaned into one another at impossible angles, creating the image of an enormous triangle looming over the city. With the overwhelming amount of green clouds roiling there, it appeared this was the Green Worm's epicenter. That was where R'lyeh and the Skeleton were now headed. And if it had been any other Worm, R'lyeh wouldn't have been able to make the walk. But it was a Worm without form, and apparently, without an effect on her. No, this was easy; what was going to be hard was what the Virions seemed so excited to show them—that large shape, blinking and screaming, they kept getting glimpses of the closer they drew to the pyramid.

"As far as we know, the Green Worm has been awake the longest out of all the other Worms," Merna said, directing them down the narrow streets. "Humanity did not summon it. God did."

"The Vermillion God?" R'lyeh whispered.

"Yes. When the Vermillion God brought about the Trauma, It gave Its most loyal followers Its crimson blessing." Merna stopped and stared at R'lyeh's right arm. "You do not have the 'Corruption,' child."

R'lyeh kept her mouth shut.

Merna tapped her faceplate, the same way she might've her chin in contemplation. "And yet you are still… here."

Arbo piped up: "Skeleton, were you human?"

"Still am," the Skeleton said, looking not at him, but the six armed guards surrounding them. "What about it?"

"Those that did not receive the crimson blessing were ostracized, but still they thrived. God did not like this," Merna said, "nor did It have any interest in this world any longer. As It fell into Its long slumber, It woke the Green Worm and let it loose upon the Earth, to infect and kill anything that did not bear the mark."

"I should be—" R'lyeh coughed, and then tasted blood, "—dead, then."

"Dead? No. Changed," Arbo said, voice wreathed in static through the modulator. "The Green Worm used to kill the unbelievers, but now it changes them. It makes believers out of everyone, eventually."

"You see a lot of walking, talking skeletons around these parts?" the Skeleton asked. "Don't see much moved by my being here."

"We don't," Merna said, sounding elated inside her suit. "I see two people unchanged in the presence of the Putrid Prince, who both came here of their own accord. I see hope."

R'lyeh's attention bounced back and forth between the Virions and the cityscape that surrounded them. It was the middle of the afternoon, but the sky wasn't so much a sky, but an infected slab of marbled meat that rendered the sun in a drunken blur. Light should've been faint, and yet it wasn't. R'lyeh hadn't realized it before, because it wasn't something she was accustomed to seeing, but yes, holy shit, the Virions were supplying electricity to this stretch of the Dead City.

She started: "You're just another—"

Street lights flickering; lone bulbs in coffee shops, computer stores; Christmas strings in a tax refund business; an art gallery on full-blast; an adult entertainment store drenched in seedy red.

"You're just another—"

More coffee shops; a college university smashed between leaning apartment buildings, light bleeding from its abstract cracks. From a scalped police station, an alarm strobed out a thousand years of late warning.

The Skeleton leaned in, asked her if she was okay.

She nodded and finished: "You're just another Cult of the Worm. Eldrus, Penance... the Witches—"

The Skeleton cocked his head, started to say something.

"—and here. All worshiping Worms. It's always the same. Everywhere." R'lyeh said to the Skeleton, "They're not going to help us."

"Witches..." the Skeleton mumbled.

"We do not worship the Green Worm," Arbo said.

"Not at all," Merna agreed.

"Besides, for all these Cults you say are out there, there is only one true Worm. The others are merely segments of It. Heralds."

That's not what Deimos said, R'lyeh thought, remembering the Bat's words back at Geharra. "An apocalypse, that's all they can bring.

"Yes," Merna said, "an apocalypse. A shattering revelation."

The Skeleton was glaring at R'lyeh as he said, "Don't know about any revelations. Only thing the Worms seem good for is turning the rest of us into fertilizer."

"Exactly," Arbo buzzed. He fiddled with some dials on his suit. "They break humanity down to their rawest forms. And with that naked, desperate fear, the Worms reveal to us the most obvious, odious mystery."

"That we need God. That without God, we are all nothing but worms ourselves, stuck in the soil of our miseries. The Worms are what they represent, are they not?" Merna stopped. "Violence, hidden knowledge. Religion, disease. Greed, lust. They are what they are, and they come from sacrifices done in the name of what each Worm represents. Worms are just as human as we are, if not more so, because what do humans sacrifice if not themselves?"

"But we don't worship the Green Worm, nor does it expect us to," Arbo interjected. "We appreciate what it is has done for us, for all the life it has given us. You're here to find a way to stop the Vermillion God? Understandable. But you say there are more Worms summoned? Wouldn't you think our need for God is greater than ever?"

The armed guards raised their rifles and pressed in towards R'lyeh and the Skeleton.

Arbo raised up his large, gloved hand. "We will help you find what you want. You will not succeed, but we will help all the same. The Green Worm is more than disease and sickness; it is a parasite, and we've grown used to a parasitic style of living. Hurt us and what we believe in, but that is fine so long as the host is whole."

The Skeleton spun around and batted away the guns. The armed suits hesitated, but they didn't open fire.

"I'm not as smart as you city folk seem to be," he said, his hands clawed, his voice dripping with vitriol, "but if you love your Putrid Prince so much, then why the hell you dressed like that? Why're you hiding from it?"

Merna's voice came out garbled from her modulator. Arbo responded in the same unintelligible speech.

She pressed her hands to the sides of her helmet.

Belting out a distorted dialect that sounded like English crossed with a drainpipe, his arm shot out, and he grabbed at her.

"Stop, Arbo," Merna said.

Click, hiss—she flipped two switches and broke a seal on the left side of her helmet.

"There's not enough," Arbo said, his voice nearly normal again.

"They have to know," she said, her voice sounded scared.

Click, hiss—she flipped two switches and broke a seal on the right side of the helmet. Hesitation; her fingers fiddled with the switches, as if to lock them back into place. Green sludge dripped out from underneath the helmet, where the connectors that lined it had separated from the neck of the suit. As she slowly lifted her helmet off, a gelatinous hunk of mucus fell with a splat onto the toe of her boot.

Liquid syllables, laced with agony—Merna said, "They have to see," and removed the helmet completely.

After everything she'd been through, R'lyeh wasn't one to startle easily, and yet the image of Merna sent her reeling. Only a place without humanity could convince someone else that she was human. Merna's neck and head had the shape and color of entwined kelp; a single appendage that flared outwards in random directions, and moved freely to an invisible current. She had a nose and a mouth, ears and eyes, but they were sunken into the swaying kelp, and held in place by the gaseous swells and seething pustules. Beyond the soft, almost tranquil exterior of Merna's face were hard, translucent tubes; ribbed, and quivering, they mimicked the tubes that ran out of her backpack; and actually—R'lyeh circled Merna—they were one and the same.

"We do not wear these suits to keep the Green Worm out," Merna said, each word a struggle without the modulator. She put her helmet back on and locked it into place. "We wear these suits to keep the Green Worm in."

R'lyeh drifted closer to the Skeleton. When the Green Worm had been threats as empty as the clouds it traveled in, she could deal with it. But now she felt the dark stirrings inside her; the murderous tendons tugging out murderous tendencies. Six guns at her back, and two freaks in front of her. In a city as large as this, it couldn't have felt any smaller. She knew a corner when she saw one, because everywhere she turned, there seemed to be one.

The Skeleton must've smelled the Trauma on her. As she raised the sword to strike, he touched her—

Sprawling fields of flowers, and a cool, babbling spring.

—and stayed her hand.

"You all look like that?" he asked.

Arbo said, "Yes, and there are not many of us left."

"Why's that?"

"The Putrid Prince did kill," Merna said. "God wanted the bloodlines that swore allegiance to It to prosper, while It wanted those bloodlines that rejected God to die. But disease and sickness cannot survive with hosts—"

"Sacrifices," R'lyeh spat.

"The Vermillion God and Its pieces are bound by rigid rules. Our Prince knew it would be needed again, so rather than fall into slumber after wiping out most of the unbelievers, it stayed awake, here, in the Dead City, and sustained itself on those that were able to resist its power."

"First came the change," Arbo said, flexing his gloved hands, "and then the realization the Putrid Prince's presence had left its hosts infertile. All of us carry the Green Worm with us. We need it as much as it needs us. But the Vermillion God is coming, and soon the world will be Its. Eventually, It will grow tired of this world and seek out others. We want to be on each of them when this happens, to see our Prince restored to its former glory."

Merna added, "We believe in the Vermillion God, but we owe our lives to the Prince. It has been good to us. We were once heretics, but now we are more."

"We're here to kill God," R'lyeh said.

"You're here to try," Merna corrected. "We are all Worms in our own ways. You are the Red," she said to R'lyeh. "You are the Black," she said to the Skeleton.

He cocked his skull, looked at his arms, and laughed. "Is it still so obvious?"

"And we are the Green," Merna said. "Through and through, forever, until we are never again."

Shaking her head, R'lyeh said, "They want something."

"We do," Merna said, "but before we ask, here is what we offer."

R'lyeh scanned the street, searching for weapons, bombs—any kind of anything that might deliver a good dose of deicide. In her searching, she noticed things she hadn't before: massive tubes, running in and out of the buildings, down the street towards the leaning buildings—tubes not unlike those in the Virions' suits and bodies. They reminded her of the Crossbreed's roots, the way they had overtaken Geharra, went where they willed. Great appendages of a greater being, searching for fuel amongst the dead.

"I don't see anything…" R'lyeh furrowed her brow. "Bag of Bones, I don't think this is a good—"

"The Dead City," the Skeleton said. "That's your offer?"

"Yes," Arbo said, modulator on the fritz. "Once we leave, the Green

Worm will be gone from it. You will have all the destruction you could ever want at your fingertips. You could even bring your followers here. You have followers, don't you?"

"Yeah," the Skeleton said, reluctantly.

"If you don't take this place, others will," Merna said. "If you do not succeed, the Vermillion God will wake again, and It will claim this city."

"And It'll get rid of you," R'lyeh said. "It'll seal the Green Worm away. You'll die."

"Replication is the key to a pathogen's survival," Arbo said. "We cannot replicate, so we must be selfish, instead."

"Assuming you got what I want..." the Skeleton chewed on his words, "... what do you want?"

Merna and Arbor told them to follow, and so with six guns at their backs, R'lyeh and the Skeleton followed.

The Dead City became less of a city and more of a machine the deeper they plunged into its narrowing streets. The tubes R'lyeh had spotted were everywhere, connected to everything. Like umbilical cords, they had been attached, or had attached themselves to everything capable of giving them electrifying life. The buildings, which were leaning so badly against one another R'lyeh was now certain they would topple, stopped being buildings and transitioned into moldy obelisks decorated with dials and jittery screens, and rows of lights, large and small, behind and between the miles of wiring that webbed the buildings. R'lyeh had seen a computer once, inside and out, and it didn't look much different to the Dead City; the only difference was the scale... and the intent.

When they reached the center point, where the leaning skyscrapers formed that menacing pyramid in the sky, they were greeted by more Virions. More cumbersome suits with impenetrable visors, all in various shades of white, as if those that wore the dirtier suits had been around longer than the rest. Some were armed with rifles, others had handguns; but mostly, they held their arms outwards, to welcome R'lyeh and the Skeleton into their own makeshift Inner Sanctum.

Merna, Arbo, and the six silent soldiers they'd brought with them left R'lyeh and the Skeleton and went to the greeting party. They seemed eager enough to meet their guests, but nevertheless, they were blocking the way.

"What do they want?" R'lyeh said, leaning into the Skeleton. "Obviously, they think you can get it for them."

The Skeleton ran his fat, black tongue over his teeth. "Something out of reach, I expect. Something guarded. They're terrified of dying. I'm bored of it."

Screaming from the center, below the pyramid. Not a human screaming, but a machine. Lights flickered around the Dead City. The massive tubes hummed out numbing vibrations. Whirring, clicks… the sharp discharge of energy. A pungent smell drifted from the center; something she'd never smelled before; it made her eyes water. And then finally, thankfully, silence.

On edge, R'lyeh said, "What the hell is that?"

"Don't know."

"Are you going to give them what they want?"

Merna and Arbo turned around and headed back their way.

"Depends on what they want."

"They worship God, though," R'lyeh said.

"Been friends with a lot of people who worship God," the Skeleton said, his hands becoming claws again. "Killed a lot of them, too. Makes no difference to me."

"Cool," R'lyeh said, and coughed. "You're going to get me killed."

"Most likely be the other way around."

R'lyeh coughed again, and wanting to test the Skeleton, said, "Sorry I keep coughing."

Before the Skeleton could say anything, if he was going to say anything, Merna and Arbo rejoined them. A trail of green clouds followed them everywhere they went. The tubes running out of their backpacks and into their helmets trembled. As the seconds passed, the two seemed to move more quickly, more fluidly. They were feeding off the Green Worm, but it was more than that. It was like… it was like they were filtering out the rest of the stuff around them. As if, to them, this world was the contaminant. It was probably the thirteen-year-old inside her talking, but R'lyeh could get behind them on that. She'd slit their neck afterwards, but until then…

"I am sorry for keeping you in the dark," Merna said, her speech clearer than it had ever been. "Our secret is all that we have. The others needed to be convinced it was worth sharing with you."

"Let's see it, then," the Skeleton said. "My partner here—"

Partner?

"—is of the fleshy variety. It's cold, and we had a long trip. She's not… neither of us are feeling too good. You want to be gone? Me too, so let's get."

Arbo and Merna led them to and through the entrance, the gap, rather, between the buildings held up by one another. Passing through the skyscraper passage was like moving through a cave system on some distant, alien planet. The facades weren't natural, and neither were the growths and wiring that covered them, and yet it all came together in such a way that, to R'lyeh, it made sense. A new kind of force. A happy marriage—her father's favorite phrase—of man and earth. Mother Nature's bio-mechanical sister.

Scaffolding began to take form in the green dark of the entryway. Virions roamed the upper levels, buzzing back and forth to one another. She didn't know if they were civilians or soldiers, but that didn't seem to matter. They were observing them, sizing them up, breaking them down. No different than the citizens of Geharra, or the soldiers of Penance, R'lyeh found herself fighting back image after image of that day she'd been paraded through the city-state's streets.

Go away, she screamed at the memories. *I don't need you anymore.* She gulped down the Green Worm's vapors, to spite the flashbacks, to show herself she was stronger than her mind gave her credit for. She coughed, of course, and there was blood, of course, but that was like someone mentioning the sky was blue. For her, these things went without saying. And it was working—her immunity. She was here, with the Skeleton, about to finally, hopefully, do something that mattered. No more fuck-ups like in Bedlam or Rime. She'd had more failures than successes; if she kept it up, she'd be no better than those teenagers whose diaries she'd read back in Gallows. Thirteen, sure, in human years.

"You would've liked my wife and son," the Skeleton said to her, out of the blue.

R'lyeh looked at him like he was insane. "Would've?"

He ground his teeth, stared at her as if she wasn't there, and then kept going.

"Before the Vermillion God woke in the Old World," Merna said, "the humans had finished construction on a space vessel called the *Vigilant.*"

"Turn here," Arbo said, leading them through the busted wall of one of the skyscrapers. They passed through a stock trading exchange, and came out the other side. Once they broke through the green clouds ahead, they'd be at the center, directly underneath the pyramid.

"When the Vermillion God took Its place upon the Earth, the humans scrambled to be rid of It. While they assaulted It endlessly, the rich and the affluent scrambled to have the *Vigilant* launched into space."

The Skeleton, with his gloved hand, took R'lyeh's.

The hell is wrong with you? she wondered.

And then, with his other hand, he touched his chest, where the Black Hour's heart was lodged.

Together, Arbo and Merna behind them, they stepped into the green cloud. Visibility dropped to zero. R'lyeh felt him squeezing her fingers, as if he, the Skeleton, Bone Daddy, Bag of Bones, their Undead Lord and Savior, were scared.

Merna's voice, taking on once more its watery tone, closed in around them. "The *Vigilant* left the Earth's atmosphere successfully, unfinished and unfurnished, and without proper stock. They did not make it far before malfunctions grounded the *Vigilant* at the rim of the system. The Trauma made communications impossible with Earth, so they resorted to stasis to maintain their lifespans."

What is she getting at? R'lyeh squinted. The green clouds, the Green Worm's true body, were beginning to disperse. Again, she heard that metallic screaming, that wretched whirring. It pierced her ears deeper than any blade ever could. *They're nuts. He can't send them into fucking space.*

Arbo passed in front of them, and disappeared into the field of color. "About thirty years ago, we began receiving transmissions from the *Vigilant*. The Dead City had been the launch site, and amidst the wreckage, we found portions of the facility. Communications devices."

"Atticus," R'lyeh said. She coughed, and tried to wriggle her hand free of his grasp. "You're hurting me."

She was able to see the Skeleton at her side; despite her pleas, he didn't seem to give a damn.

"There are people who are still alive aboard the *Vigilant*," Merna said. R'lyeh could see her, too. "They are the ones who told us where we could find it."

It? It? R'lyeh opened her mouth to ask just what it was, but then the green fog lifted from the center, and she saw her answer, instead.

Surrounded by skyscrapers and the machines and labs that had been built around, the 'it' was a spacecraft. A vessel. A fucking technological marvel. More advanced than anything R'lyeh had seen before, she couldn't even begin to fathom the components that it was comprised of. It looked like a ship, except it was supported by four pillars, and it was from these pillars the sounds and the harsh light, like bursts of fire, were merging. The body of the craft was sleek, but panel after panel had been torn away or replaced entirely, giving it a checkerboard-like appearance. The nose was covered in concave glass; inside, she spotted more Virions, working at terminals. The massive tubes R'lyeh had seen earlier in the city were here, too, connected to the back of the spacecraft, feeding it energy.

Arbo said, "When the crew of the *Vigilant* realized they would not be able to make it back to Earth, they sent an emergency vessel to return to the point of origin, this Dead City, for help. The vessel crashed, and those piloting it died. After we made contact with the *Vigilant*, they gave us the coordinates of the crash, and we unburied it."

"Restoring the vessel has been a long-term project," Merna said. "The materials we have to work with are limited, and not what was intended. But we are close, so close, to finishing what we and our predecessors set out to accomplish years ago."

Above, the nebulous body of the Green Worm billowed and churned; growing impatient and restless, it kept reaching through the cracks in the buildings, already eager to begin its conquest for the stars.

"What do you need?" the Skeleton asked, coyly. "Where is it?"

"Not on Earth," Arbo said.

"Sorry about your luck, then," the Skeleton said.

"Not on this Earth," Merna corrected, "but the one we knew from before."

Oh, shit. No. Shit, shit, shit. R'lyeh drew her sword and stepped in front of the Skeleton; this time, she would be his shield, to stop him from doing something mighty stupid.

"You have the heart of the Black Hour," Merna said.

And once she said that, every Virion, in their bulky suits, behind their blank helmets, turned their heads towards R'lyeh and the Skeleton.

"We know this, because the Putrid Prince knows this," Arbo said.

"The Prince said you can use it for anything. We do not want anything. We want only what we need."

Merna moved towards the Skeleton, but R'lyeh stabbed her sword outward, placing the tip centimeters away from Merna's chest.

Undeterred, Merna continued. "We only need a few components. We can show you what they look like, what they are called. We have records of the day and time of when they were here, in the City. We do not want the heart... we... it—"

The Green Worm's clouds formed violent, emerald nimbuses.

"—cannot have it. If you do this, then the Dead City is yours."

"Haven't seen the weapons. Haven't seen why I'd want this place in the first place," the Skeleton said.

"No, you can't," R'lyeh said, looking over her shoulder. "What the hell did we come here for if you're going to use the heart, anyways?"

The Skeleton's crazed eyes told her to be quiet.

And so she was.

"We want to rejoin the *Vigilant*," Merna said. "We want to go into the infinite dark, and bring those lost there into the light."

"You all aren't going to fit," the Skeleton said.

"We will become as one," Arbo said. "It has happened before."

The Skeleton clicked his teeth together. He flexed his hand, the leather glove that covered it stretching, almost ripping. What the hell was this? He was actually considering what they had to say?

R'lyeh lowered her sword, turned around, and pushed the Skeleton back. "What the fuck is wrong with you? You can't do this."

"R'lyeh, stop," the Skeleton said.

"You know what'll happen if you use that thing for even a minute!"

"I haven't even made up my mind."

"Yes, you have." R'lyeh rolled her eyes. "I can tell. Don't. You can't."

"It's that, or kill all of them."

"Fine, let's kill all of them," R'lyeh pleaded.

Arbo held up his hands. "Now, wait, just wait. We do have guns—"

"Shut the fuck up." R'lyeh grabbed the Skeleton's cloak. "Don't. Don't leave me… with them."

The Skeleton, looking down upon her, like a pale demon not even hell had room for, whispered, "I'm not leaving with you any—"

R'lyeh forced herself to cough. The Skeleton straightened up. Again, she made herself cough, but louder this time. She dug deep inside herself; she constricted her throat. Each cough exploded out of her mouth. She doubled-over. The Skeleton reached for her, and she batted his hand away. She had his attention. She had their attention. She coughed and coughed and spit up a little blood. As long as all eyes were on her, they weren't on the Black Hour's heart.

When she couldn't keep coughing, because it hurt too much, R'lyeh gathered herself, closed her mouth, and locked her watering eyes with the Skeleton's.

"My partner and I need to discuss your offer," he said. "If anything happens to her—"

And then R'lyeh was coughing again. Deep, burning coughs that bar-reled up her throat like fists. Blood exploded from her mouth. She dropped to her knees and tried to hold her breath, but it was impossible. She couldn't breathe. She wasn't faking it, not anymore. She couldn't stop it. She wanted to ask for help, but now she was vomiting all over her hands.

And then there was the Skeleton, picking her up like she weighed nothing at all.

And then there were the Virions swarming him, tearing into his cloak, reaching over her, clawing at his ribcage, tearing at the Black Hour's heart.

And then nothing.

CHAPTER XXIV

Vrana's appearance was a puzzle Aeson's mind couldn't wrap itself around. Every time he began to recognize something, it immediately became unrecognizable. He was so desperate to find something to cling onto that he found himself scrambling between her features, like a panicked climber scrabbling carelessly between holds, searching for anything that might give him the slightest reprieve. He was making it about him, he knew, as his eyes darted from her eyes to her beak, from her talons to her wings, but he didn't mean to. He'd told himself he wouldn't do this. Pain and Joy had treated her like their own personal pet. The last thing she needed was another person gawking at her as if she were still stuck in the Witches' grotesque zoo.

Kneading her forearms, Vrana caught Aeson's gaze. "It's not glamour," she said. "It's not going away."

Her hands and feet were still bloody, open wounds from where the witches had crucified her. She didn't seem to mind, though. They had scavenged the area for what curatives they could find, but Vrana wasn't worried one way or another. She had told him she'd been through a lot these last few months; that if she made a list of all the terrible things Pain and Joy had done to her, a few holes in her body would be sitting near the bottom, right under pissing on her.

"I'll be able to fly again soon," Vrana said. She smiled, or at least it seemed as if she were smiling. With the raven mask now fused to her face and threaded into her muscles and bones, it was hard to tell. If she was putting on a show, Aeson couldn't say. But he knew how quickly agony could bring out the actor in everyone.

"Take your time," he said, touching his seething cheek, where Pain had taken a chunk out of it. "We're in no rush." He stared at her some more. "This is all I wanted. To be here with you. If you need forever—" Had every feather been jammed into her skin? "—then forever is fine with me."

Here. Where was here, exactly? Vrana had flown them east of Angheuawl for about twenty minutes before her strength gave out. She landed them high in Kistvaen's range, where the peaks were white from the constant snowfall. Aeson was freezing; sitting there, he was so tightly balled up that he looked like an egg. And with the giant raven across from him, that kind of imagery hit a little closer to home than he would've liked.

There was so much blood in Vrana's feathers the snow under her had turned red. It spread across the ground in veiny patterns, and like fingers, they reached out to touch him. Violence wasn't something they'd had in common before, but not anymore. It was the bond between them that kept them from snapping. They were two gore-encrusted mirrors reflecting one another, simultaneously embodying every atrocity, as well as every strength. Her calmness became his calmness. His humanity became her humanity. For in all the ways they had changed, for all the pieces into which they had shattered, even sitting here, in the bloodied snow, raw and violated, trading exchanges like rare currencies, it seemed that, somehow, in some way, they could come together again, and fit where they hadn't fitted before.

Aeson felt closer to Vrana than he ever had before. And yet, why the distance? Just because she looked like a wounded animal didn't mean he had to treat her like one. he scooted forward, the cold snow stinging his nerves, until his feet touched the talons where her toes should've been.

"I missed you," Aeson said.

Vrana wiped her eyes. "I missed you, too."

He reached backwards for Bjørn's bear mask and set it on his lap. He hadn't worn it since he'd saved Vrana.

"He still didn't let it go to bone?" she asked, her beak barely moving.

Aeson ran his hand through the fur. Patches were missing, but not much. For everything the man had done, he still wore a mask whose "rank," so to speak, was no better than an initiate's. But that was how he'd liked things. Understated, without pretention. Being a hard-ass for the sake of being a hard-ass.

"He must've been a treat to travel with," Vrana said, staring at the mask.

He hadn't told her Bjørn had died. Apparently, he didn't need to.

Vrana leaned forward, outstretching her wings. Aeson got the hint and moved closer, until his body was against hers, and her wings were wrapped around him. She wasn't warm, but she wasn't cold, either. She was somewhere in between; a tepid state. Having stayed inside the Void for so long, Vrana's body was probably still working out the concept of temperature and what it meant to it.

Closer to Vrana, Aeson could see the human features that had otherwise been obscured by her feathers. Tenderly, he traced the outline of her face and the remainder of her jaw. He touched her neck, pressed carefully down on her clavicle. There were holes in her beak; through them, he could see her lips, sensual and inviting, and then… and then, when she breathed, her stretched-out tongue and toothless mouth.

Vrana's wings slid over him as she moved to touch him, too. Her hand was tough and taut, and the skin that covered it the color of ash. It was all bones and tendons; he could tell by her touch her hands had taken many lives. Whereas he had been tender, she was anxious, unsure. The talons were a part of it—one extra ounce of strength, and his flesh would be flayed from his face, but it was something else, too. She was touching him—his face, his ears, his lips, his chin and chest—as if she hadn't done this before, or in a very long time. Like she'd forgotten she could do this, without resorting to mutilation.

"You saved me," she said. She went in, as if to kiss him, but with her break, it was never going to happen. She pressed her forehead to his, instead, and whispered, "Not going to lie. Figured it'd always be me saving you."

Aeson snorted, sucked up some saliva. "You did. You are. Right now."

"Tell me what happened," Vrana said. "How the hell you and Bjørn… did this."

Aeson tried to wrangle his memories together into something more manageable. This journey had a definite beginning, and so far, a definite end. She knew about the Dismal Sticks. She'd been the one to… save him from the flesh fiend. But did she know what she was? That she was born on Lacuna? Did she know about her father? Or that Bjørn had saved her from Death Herself? If he hit her with too many revelations, would she be ripped apart? And if she was, did he even have the right vocabulary to comfort her? Did anyone?

"You first," he said, instead. "I always go first."

Vrana's hands made the shape of scissors, to beat the paper he always picked. "Play you for it."

Aeson laughed; he noticed he'd stopped shivering. "You know I'll lose."

"Maybe not." Vrana's breath smelled of blood and gore, and every fluid and substance with which the Witch had been made. "I spent every day preparing myself for this."

"Rock-paper-scissors?"

Was that a smirk? He couldn't tell. "No. Seeing you… I mean, you seeing me. I know I'm… fucked up-looking."

He wanted to compare himself to her, to show her she wasn't as bad as she thought, but whereas he had scars and cuts and fresh wounds, she had transformed entirely. Sure, maybe he had undergone a transformation himself, on the inside, but how could he articulate that? Besides, he didn't even know what it was.

"You're still Vrana," Aeson said. "That's all that matters."

"It's not," she said, running her talons down where her breasts used to be, to her feathered stomach and emaciated hips, "but thank you."

"I don't care about that," he said.

Vrana's eyes moistened. "I do. I care about everything those fucking bitches took from me."

Aeson pressed himself closer to Vrana; the cold had found him again. "Did you think it would be me who came for you?" He shook his head. "The scared Archivist who never left home?"

Vrana cleared her throat, let her eyes wander over the mountain range.

"Wow," Aeson said. "Thanks a lot."

"At first, I thought maybe it would be R'lyeh… but when I saw you at the Dismal Sticks… god, I wanted so badly to go with you. To even talk to you." Vrana held his hand as carefully as she could. "I knew you wouldn't stop."

Changing the subject from the Dismal Sticks, he asked, "R'lyeh sent Caldera a letter saying the Witches took you."

"That was Pain and Joy, not R'lyeh."

Aeson thought back to the day the letter arrived; he remembered how strange it felt to hold, and a purplish hue to it, as if it had been written in the colors of the cosmos. It seemed so obvious now, but then, it had just been a piece of hope in an otherwise hopeless situation.

"Pain wanted Caldera to send more people looking for me, to keep

spreading word of the Witches, because it's belief that powers them."
Vrana snorted. "Look how well that worked out for Pain."

"Probably didn't expect to see me," Aeson said.

"I think I'm good to fly again," Vrana said.

"No, I can walk—"

"Come on, it's freezing. After everything, you want frostbite to be the
thing that takes you out?" Vrana rose to her feet and stretched out her
wings. "We can find a cave, at least; build a fire."

Aeson, brushing the snow off his soaked backside, stood and dropped
his arms to his sides. "How do you do it?"

"Be so positive?"

"Yeah, actually. Yeah."

Vrana stepped up to him and wrapped her arms around him. She held
him so tightly that it hurt, but he wasn't about to complain. Her talons
hooked his armor, and some of his skin, to keep a better hold on him. If
she dropped him, he wasn't sure if she could recover him mid-air. But
he'd accomplished what he'd set out to do. That was enough.

"It's not that I'm being positive."

Her body tightened; holding him, she crouched down, to push herself
off the mountain.

"A lot of things happened to me I couldn't stop. And if I'd stopped
to beat myself up about it, I would've been a bloody pulp my first week
into the Void."

She began beating her wings.

"I've numbed myself to everything; everything except you and the few
people I actually care about. The Witches knew that, and tried to use it
against me, but it was worth it."

She flapped her wings forward; her feet left the ground. "They
couldn't kill me, so instead, they just tried to kill every part of me. I gave
them almost everything."

Higher and higher, she flew into the whitened sky.

"But I wouldn't give them my love. They wanted, and hated, that the
most."

Vrana flew them through Kistvaen's range for another thirty minutes
before winding down into the naked, pale woods somewhere outside of
Rhyfel. As promised, she found them a cave. They'd seen what appeared
to be flesh fiends in the area in their fly-by, so they scouted the cave
before building a fire. They heard the creatures killing animals, or one
another, but by the time the sun began to set, the sounds of slaughter

had died away. It turned Aeson's stomach to think of where the flesh fiends were headed next, but he didn't care. At last, he could say he was done with them.

Aeson sat as close as he could to the fire without sustaining first-degree burns. Down to his plainclothes, and glistening with sweat, he felt purified by the flames. But it wasn't just the heat that was healing him; it was Vrana beside him, not above him or below him, or reaching out to him from the darkest recesses of his most terrible nightmares. She still had the Blue Worm's necklace—she kept in a fleshy pouch in her side—but not once had she made any attempt to use it. She was a child of Lacuna, with the possibility of some flesh fiend cross-contamination playing havoc with her genetics, and yet she had been nothing but gentle, as she had always been. Yes, she had literally eaten Pain whole, but he was pretty sure she would've done something similar whether she was half-raven or not.

"Alright," Aeson said, clearing his throat and nose, "I'll do it."

"Hmm?"

"I'll tell you everything. From the beginning."

Vrana nodded, and held his hand. "I know where I was born, how I was born. I know about my dad." She paused. "You don't have to hold anything back."

And Aeson didn't. He told her everything. From the day he left Caldera, with the list of Lacunans, to the Dismal Sticks and Ichor's deranged dinner party.

"Do you want to… talk about it?" Vrana asked, regarding the flesh fiend who'd raped him.

Aeson shook his head. "I've been over it enough," he said, as he smelled the female flesh fiend and her rank lust. He heard nails scratching on the cave of the floor, and claws, clicking, carrying out the Choir's piercing tune; the deep dins of desire. They were calling to him, even now, when he was at his strongest, safest.

He took a moment for himself, and then told Vrana about Death, Her daughters, and the dagger She'd made to kill one of them.

"That makes… so much fucking sense," Vrana said. "They never mentioned Death, but that makes… I can't believe you and Bjørn did that."

Aeson placed the bear skull on his lap. "He loved you. More than anything else, I think."

"Yeah," she said, wiping her eyes. "I've killed so many people. So many people have died because of me."

"It's not your fault—"

"I know," she said, cutting him off. "I know."

While Vrana sat in contemplation, Aeson removed *The Blood of Before* from his bag and handed it to her.

"What's this?" she asked, taking it.

"Anguis gave it to me. It's supposed to be our history."

She opened the book, screwed up her face as she tried to read it.

"It's encrypted. I'm almost finished. My parents wrote in it."

"Shit." Vrana handed it back to him. "They did?"

"When my parents killed themselves, they tried to kill me, too. They tried to hang me with them, but Bjørn cut me down. They thought something was coming; they wanted to spare me—"

"The Vermillion God," Vrana whispered, still stuck on his previous statement. "Aeson, I'm so—"

"There's something wrong with the Night Terrors. Something very wrong." He chewed on his lip. "Everything we do seems to just lead to our extinction. If we get too old, we lose our minds. And I think we brought something back from the Dead City—"

"The Dead City?"

"Yeah. The elders sent Night Terrors to search for something. And then they came back diseased, and birth rates plummeted. And then there's this shit with Lacuna and Corrupted and flesh fiends? And you know… you know Caldera was built under Kistvaen for the sole purpose of eventually being wiped out? It's like… it's like our ancestors knew we were fuck-ups, knew this shit had to end, but someone kept it going all these years. And we haven't done anything worthwhile since."

Breathlessly, Vrana said, "I didn't know that. But, hey, Aeson, are you talking about our people, or us?"

"I just… I look at you and I… every second I'm convincing myself things are better. And then I remember. And I don't even know what you had to go through. I… I just—" he swallowed hard and started to laugh pathetically, "—you know, we judge the Corrupted because of their Corruption and what they've done."

"You want to be judged?"

"No. I just… don't want to hurt anymore."

Vrana scooted closer to him, wrapped her arm and wing around him. "Neither do I, but that's not always up to us. Best we can do is hurt the ones who'll try to hurt us."

"Then it's just that same circular shit again."

"Pain and Joy are always going to be with me," Vrana said.

Aeson cleared his throat. "Well, you did eat Pain."

"Would it have helped if the flesh fiend had a name?"

A choking ball of anger rose through Aeson's chest and throat. *What the hell?* he shouted inside his skull. *What the hell does that mean?* But he knew what she was getting at. Her tormentors were two of a kind; with names and faces and well-defined legacies. The ghost that owned his body was none of those things. She was one of many, and identical to the many she was one of. He would never see her coming, and in each flesh fiend, she'd be coming.

"Bjørn saved you, too," Aeson said. "He said he ran into Death once, while he was carrying you home from Lacuna."

"And Death stepped aside," Vrana said, finishing his sentence. Her eyes were brighter now, with or without the flames in front of them. "I don't even know…" She laid her head on Aeson's shoulder. "I don't think my story is going to make you feel any better, but can I tell you it?"

Her head was heavy, and her bones cut into his skin. Afraid to move or complain, he said, "Of course," and tried his best to stop thinking of his goddamn self.

"I killed fifty-three men, forty-one women, and ninety-nine children for Pain and Joy," Vrana started. "They were saving the hundredth child for something special. Pain thought it would be funny. Joy couldn't wait.

"I think I've been to every town, village, and city at this point. I helped them track down Lacunans, and I convinced most of them to leave their homes and families to join the Cult. Pain and Joy used fear and manipulation to convince regular Corrupted to follow them; some people were part of the Holy Order of Penance, others were from The Disciples of the Deep. I lost track of how many we'd converted, but not everyone came to Angheuawl. There are still supporters out there.

"The Choir was Joy's idea. Pain called the flesh fiends angels, and I think because Pain approved of them, Joy wanted to make them part of the family. Pain twisted things, but Joy wanted to make things, form her own bloodline. The flesh fiends are perfect. Night Terror and Corrupted fuck? One month, and there's a kid. Flesh fiend and flesh fiend together? A few weeks, sometimes less. They just had… pits… everywhere. They'd throw people in. Cultists, or people they made me capture. Flesh fiends would fuck them, or eat them, or both. Some of those pits are still out there, still going. Flesh fiends develop quickly. Their children can give birth shortly after they're born."

Aeson remembered the Horrors of the Womb, how Pain had sent all four of them not to attack the Marrow Cabal, but to terrify them. A sacrificial offering in honor of the god of fear.

"Those were the offspring of the Cult, from Lacunans, Night Terrors, Corrupted, or flesh fiends. Joy collected them, like dolls. She was going to build her family with them, and then, like we did on Lacuna, when they were ready, she was going to release them from the Void into the world.

"Pain thought it would be better if the children were turned into the Horrors and used as instruments of fear. Joy... I'd never seen Joy so mad before."

"She let me kill Pain," Aeson whispered.

"She saved herself. Pain was always obsessed with being with her sister. But Joy always did better on her own. She ran the Nameless Forest for hundreds of years, Aeson. She's... she has connections with Eldrus. And all these other families from the Old World." Vrana squeezed the sides of her head. "You—"

"I killed the wrong Witch," Aeson said, realizing what Vrana was getting at.

"You got me away from them." She made a sniffing sound. Did she still have a nose? "But this isn't over."

What did they do to you, Vrana? Aeson held her hand tighter. *You can't even say it.*

"Joy is going to come for you, Aeson," Vrana said. "Even though she let it happen, you still killed Pain. All they had was each other. It doesn't make sense, I know, but she's going to want revenge. I know she will."

He could hear them again—the flesh fiends—calling for his skin. "Does she... still have enough power to?"

Vrana's voice was barely above a whisper. "She can't control the Lacunans anymore without me or the necklace. But she still has her followers, maybe the Choir; and... the portals."

"But everyone who came to Angheuawl has to be dead by now," Aeson said.

"That was for show," Vrana said. "They didn't need to do that. But I guarantee you Joy will start spreading stories about what happened there, and her power will... skyrocket once people see the proof. I think she can still manage to open another portal."

"Caldera." Aeson tipped his head back; tears ran down the side of his face. "The mark in Caldera."

"They set up outposts in these mountains."

Llyn, Trist, Marwaidd, Rhyfel… Angheuawl. I knew it.

"Whether she can control them or not, this place is going to be swarming with flesh fiends soon."

"I don't think Death is going to give me another weapon to defend myself," Aeson said, the statement making him laugh. "I don't think I want to ask again, either."

"We'll figure out something," Vrana said. "We're together. That's all that matters."

Aeson nodded and cast his eyes into the heart of the fire, where he should have cast any notions of hope as well. How the hell was he thinking that this was over? His days might've begun and ended with thoughts of Vrana, and that was okay for him, but the rest of the world? It wasn't going to stop, and nothing was going to be the same. He remembered the day he had given her the third trial, and wondered, if he hadn't, would they be here, in this cave, contemplating ways to kill the inevitable? His parents had wanted him to die with them, to spare him from the wretched world to come. They weren't wrong.

Stop it, he said to himself. *Get it together.* "Should we go after R'lyeh?"

"No, I think she's found her people. She'll be okay. The woman I saw her through, Hex, had a lot of love for her. Listen, I don't know if you noticed—"

"Maybe we could spellweave some of the feathers off you. Shorten the beak."

"Aeson—" Vrana touched his neck, "—we have to leave."

"Right now?" He turned away from the fire, faced her. "Why? What's wrong?"

Aeson's ears pricked; he picked up sounds outside the cave—rustling in the overgrowth; something crunching through the accumulating snow. He smelled shit and blood and the stomach-churning musk of damp, matted hair. Movement stirred on his lap; shocked, as if he had been bitten, he screamed and jumped to his feet, as he grasped for the sword that was nowhere nearby.

"Hey…"

With a mouthful of spit and a fistful of sweat, he checked the cave entrance and found it empty. Vrana was staring at him. Her eyes, dark like a bird's, considered every inch of him. Slowly, she rose, shedding feathers from her body, which the wintry wind fed to the fire. She was taller now, lankier; stretched out; her form inhuman enough to be unsettling. The closer she came to him, the closer her beak came to piercing him like a bladder, so that she could guzzle out the gore, the same way she had with Pain. The farther she moved away from the light, the deeper the darkness around her became. It wasn't new. It was as if it had always been there. A piece of the Void she had brought with her, visible only when he was at his weakest, his most embarrassed. She would comfort him, until she would consume him.

"Aeson."

Clenching his eyes shut, he shook his head and blubbered, "I'm sorry. I lost everything, too. I'm not as strong as you."

"Don't start that." Vrana took a deep breath; he could tell she was losing her patience with him. "Look outside, to the west."

He gulped like a child.

"Go," she said. "We're safe, but look to the west, man."

Don't take your shit out on her, Aeson told himself, nodding at Vrana. *You're an Archivist. You're an Archivist.* Having started to become something else, he had forgotten what he was before, so it bore repeating. *You're an Archivist. Stop this. Stop acting like everyone else. You're not. You're better.*

Outside the cave, night had fallen to the Earth with violent reluctance. Aeson couldn't remember what things had looked like before, even though it hadn't been that long ago since they'd arrived, but he was certain that, somehow, something was different. December was still a few days away, and yet it was everywhere he looked: in the bright sheets of snow reflecting the moon's mourning light; in the slinking shadows leaving darkness like gifts for those shunned by the sun; in the way land was jagged silhouettes, as if the cave were a throat, and everything else was simply teeth and bone and tongue of the invisible, inevitable evil that had swallowed this orb eons ago. And just like his parents had tried to warn everyone, this beast, be it from the Deep, the Nameless Forest, or the Ossuary—whether it was the Vermillion God or something worse—was waking, and it was hungry. The world was different. This was the first time he'd ever seen it outside of paper, ink, and binding, and even he knew that.

Vrana came up behind him and pointed over his shoulder to the massive mountain in the distance. "It's Kistvaen. The last time I was able to see it outside Caldera, it was when Pain attacked the village—"

"And killed the spellweavers," Aeson whispered. "How? How is she there?"

Vrana ignored him, started batting her wings.

Aeson ran back into the cave, grabbed his bag with *The Blood of Before,* and his sword. "How is Joy already there?" he screamed at Vrana. "Why won't this end?"

Caldera wasn't close. At first, they went by wing, and then by foot, and then, by a stroke of luck, they stumbled upon a wild horse and Vrana scared it into servitude. They flew, walked, and rode straight through Kistvaen's range, never stopping to eat, drink, or relieve themselves. They slept in shifts, and never for long. With Kistvaen looming over them, rest wasn't something that came easily. Anything could be happening in Caldera right now; and if it could've been avoided if he hadn't saved Vrana at all...

They ditched the horse the first of December; Vrana, fighting against obvious exhaustion, carried Aeson through Caldera's outskirts, before dropping him in the harvested fields.

They had everyone's attention the moment their feet hit the ground. An Archivist and a giant half-human raven would do that to a village. It was day again, and there were Night Terrors everywhere. They should've been at home, with their families, but they were outside, in the streets, and they kept looking at Kistvaen. The mountain's illusion had been dispelled days ago, and yet the Calderans still seemed surprised.

Aeson searched everyone's faces and masks for signs of distress. He looked past them as they gathered on the edge of the fields, to where the first symbol of the Cult of the Worm had been burned into the ground. It was still there, but it hadn't been activated.

"Your mom has to be around here," Aeson said to Vrana. "She'll want to see you. Anguis, Faolan, and Nuctea... they have to be inside the mountain."

Vrana told him, "No," and with his hand in hers, they took off through the silent crowd, to the house of the elders.

The house was dark and empty, no different than it had ever been. Though it felt as if it had been ages since he'd been here, Aeson knew the ritual for accessing Kistvaen by heart.

"I don't know if it'll let you in," he told Vrana, taking her to the room of perpetual, seamless darkness, where the obsidian boulder—the gateway to Kistvaen—was supposed to be. "I know how to do it right, though."

"I know," she said, following him into the room. "I trust you."

Aeson went to the boulder and went through the motions as quickly as he could. He splayed his fingers and placed them into the five grooves alongside the boulder; waiting five seconds, he then pulled away, his fingertips covered in black, and plunged them into the pond beside the boulder.

"Used to be so scared of messing this up," Aeson told Vrana. "After hanging out with Death, though, I guess it's not so bad."

Vrana, standing over him, squeezed his shoulder. "After you witness your Void, not much is."

The black stains ran off Aeson's fingers and colored the pond black.

"Eil'en'kul," he said, the pond scabbing over with a volcanic crust.

"You're amazing," Vrana said. "This is amazing."

"But if there's any killing to be done—" Aeson pressed both hands against the boulder, and slotted each of his fingers into the ten hidden grooves, "—I'll leave it to you."

Vrana nodded, said, "You killed Pain. You're the only person who ever did. Not a bad thing to retire on."

"Yeah," he said, his smile quickly falling into a frown.

"What?" Vrana asked.

The boulder… Aeson pressed his body against the obsidian boulder. "It's hot, like it's on fire on the inside."

"Is that bad?"

"It's never happened… Nyxannul." He spit on the pond and made sure Vrana was standing on it with him. "Nyxannul."

The surface shattered, and Aeson and Vrana fell through, straight down, until in minutes—not seconds, like it should've been—they were standing upright, upon the top of the same pond; except the transparent grass was gone and so, too, were the mushrooms, sprites, and the ceiling of sky. Now, they were no longer in the house of the elders, but a mile outside the village, deep inside the mountain, Kistvaen.

And there, in front of them, framed by the jagged walls and prismatic pillars, stood Anguis, Faolan, and Nuctea. They weren't moving, nor were they speaking; they were simply standing in silent awe as Gisela the spellweaver paraded around the inside of the volcano, with spellweavers Enaar's and Verat's innards streaming off her body, like the red robes of royalty.

Aeson didn't know why he thought it, but the line from *The Blood of Before* he couldn't decipher came into his mind, and seeing Gisela doused in the blood of her brethren, he knew what it meant.

Tssnrt sa nrie su osri k.caiesheZ.

Disease. It always came back to disease. A fundamental flaw in the Night Terrors that the tribe was always trying to correct. Disease was the key to understanding the phrase, and with it, he unlocked its meaning.

"There is a sickness in our stars," Aeson said aloud. He took out *The Blood of Before* and held it before him, its ancient knowledge now his only shield. "There is a sickness in our stars," he repeated.

Anguis was the first to turn around from the sickening spectacle. "Yes, there is," he hissed behind his snake skull. "Flesh, as you can see—" he glanced at Vrana, and then returned to Gisela, "—makes fiends of us all."

CHAPTER XXV

Hebert North wasn't a fan of this planet; never had been, and at this rate, the way things were going, never was going to be. From the day of his birth in 1870, to the day of his death in 2026, the bones of the Earth had, in most cases, never changed. A crack here, a fracture there; at times they broke, but at the same time, they were quick to mend. The framework was always the same; once you figured it out, even the unexpected became trivial.

As Gemma so often put it in her own snide, hundreds of years old adolescent way, "We all have the same Skeleton in our futures."

He'd spent most of his living life hunting supernatural creatures, to prevent them from overtaking the world. Apparently, he hadn't hunted them hard enough, because they ended up calling the shots, anyway. Perhaps it had been foolish to expect that his work who-the-hell-knows long ago would've meant something, but when Ruth Ashcroft finally found him and put him down for good in 2026, he had hoped, as his eyes dimmed and his unnaturally long life came to an end, that he'd made a difference.

Because he'd known monsters better than he did Man. He'd even been one himself once (monster, not man; well, both, actually; whatever). The sum total of his friendships could be counted on one hand, whereas his knowledge of the occult, beasts, and the Membrane would take a couple of hours of hair metal and whiskey to get through (so it goes without saying, he'd never really bared his soul; the hair metal was generally a deal-breaker, and now, much to his dismay, extinct).

Ghouls, ghosts, and nethers; zombies, vampyres, and werewolves;

mumiya, haunted dolls, and goredrinkers; marionettes, corpse collectors, and soul consumers; he knew witches like the back of his hand, and on the back of his hand, bore their scars, too; Argentos, they were a treat, and the Keeper of the Dread Clock? he was glad to be rid of it, even if another one seemed to have taken its place. He used to have books filled to the brim with entries and illustrations about these creatures and the hundreds, if not thousands, of others he'd come into contact with, or had heard about in passing.

The vermillion veins hadn't been absent from his work, either; but like the man desperate to discover a cure, he mistook them, perhaps the most important species of all his encounters, as being inconsequential. He'd even had run-ins with their gardener, Amon Ashcroft, back in the day. They'd scuffled here and there, but not much came of it. If Seth had been with him, maybe he would have taken Amon a little more seriously; he might've followed the vermillion veins to their unearthly source and scorched them from the back of that Winged Heaven. But he hadn't. He didn't take anything seriously, ever.

It was a bunch of bullshit, if you asked him, which no one did, and probably because that was the answer they were expecting to get. He had devoted over one hundred years of his life to a world that went and fucked itself over, anyway. Was it too much to ask? It wasn't like he had been a police officer, and that he had expected to rise from the grave to find the world rid of crime. No, he had been a supernatural investigator, spiriting around the world, closing doorways and chasing out the things that had slipped through them. It was hard work, but like philosophy professors, the demand wasn't exactly through the roof. But... apparently, it was. So, again, bullshit.

Because here he was, in the thick of it again, everything exactly the way he'd left it. The skin was different, and the muscles were different, but the bones were the same. The old man in him (what was he? One-hundred-and-fifty-five going on oblivion?) wanted to break out that creaky phrase that everything had been better back in his day; that, goddamn it, monsters had class back then, and they weren't running around with skin hanging down their asses; but he knew better. It was bullshit, all of it. The same bullshit, every day of the month, every month of every year, from here until the hereafter.

This fact hadn't really hit him when the Skeleton pulled his kin and him out of the Membrane. Nor had it in the months that followed, when he was hanging out with the Marrow Cabal on a lake of blood governed by a giant mosquito he swore to splat back in 2020. Gemma was the first sign that something was fucky; but no, it wasn't until today that he realized just how truly powerless he and those around him were to the forces that had ensnared this, quite literally, god-forsaken planet.

Today. Eight hours ago, to be exact. That's when the shit hit the fan and he got his wake-up call. He and the Marrow Cabal had marched into Angheuawl on the Skeleton's orders in search of a safe haven. What was the opposite of a safe haven? Connor had always been the writer. If he were still here, he'd know.

Hell. At first, Herbert had thought the Membrane was hell, but after a few stretches of seeming timelessness, he got used to it. At least, when he was there, he had a goal in mind. But no, the Membrane was hell as much as he was a heterosexual. He could look the part, but when it got down to the nitty gritty, most parties either ended up disappointed, or far more pleased than they would've expected. Needless to say (the epitaph of Herbert's life), in a world so gray, Herbert still kept vigil for those fantastical, never-having-existed days of black and white.

"I'm older than you," Gemma said, floating across the battlefield outside Angheuawl, "so how am I doing more than you?"

Hebert ignored the girl and kept his ass firmly planted within the confines of the Marrow Cabal's guard. Because outside it, between here and Angheuawl, was a quarter-mile catastrophe. Eight hours ago, a foul abomination—some terrible combination of moth, bird, and grub—lifted out of the village and dropped four, ovary-shaped Horrors on top of the Marrow Cabal. The massive balls were like the aborted leftovers of some cruelly fertile womb. Comprised solely of children and their tiny parts, the Horrors were defenseless amalgamations. Two of them cracked open upon being dropped, dousing the Marrow Cabal in gallons of blood and amniotic fluid, while the other two Horrors sat, crying and shrieking, as the Cabal cut them to pieces. Because of their size and density, each Horror of the Womb took fifteen minutes each to kill. As for the Mother Horror, it died on its own. After dropping the ovaries, it ran itself into the ground, breaking its neck in a suicidal dive.

Herbert shook his head and waved off Gemma, as the vampyre was drawing closer, despite his insistence that she go away. Behind where he sat were the tents of Clementine, Will, and James. After the real attack, they had refused to come outside. And how could he blame them? Their husband, father, and best friend had sent them here. Nothing supposedly got past the Bone Man, except, apparently, the things that mattered.

"What's wrong?" Gemma chided. "Bunions got you down? Hemorrhoids acting up?" She glided right up to and landed in front of him. Her green dress from the Orphanage was covered in blood. "You're a lover, not a fighter, huh? Explains a lot."

The Mother Horror and her despicable cargo didn't count when it came to the attack. They were the shock before the awe. The attack started seven and a half hours ago; in small pockets of this cold mountainside, it was still happening.

It started shortly after the Witch, Joy, left the sky. That was a face he wasn't expecting to see again. When she returned to Angheuawl, something happened. He could feel the change in the atmosphere, as if a great force had been released. Then, another shape took to the sky. Herbert had thought it was Seth, but then saw it was a raven, not a man covered in flies, and it was the greatest sight he had ever seen. He didn't know when Pain had rid herself or had been rid of Seth, and no, he hadn't been in the Membrane to find his friend during his descent, like he'd intended, like he'd meant to when he fought to stay in that place to begin with, but needless to say, he was moved to tears knowing that his love, his best friend, was no longer the bitch's pet.

Whatever the Raven had done, she had tampered with the forces of hell in the process. Because out of Angheuawl, hell came; in a wave of flesh and blood, like one wet sheet of canvas torn from humanity's depraved portrait, hell came. The cabalists called them flesh fiends, and the name made sense. But watching the monstrosities pour of Angheuawl in every direction, attacking one another and the poor cabalists and vampyres on the front lines, Herbert got to thinking about another kind of creature he'd encountered in the so-called Old World. What they used to call them, though, he couldn't remember. But the resemblance, aesthetically and behaviorally, was damn near identical. God, what did they call them?

Gemma stopped beside Herbert. Slowly, she lowered herself to the ground, until her bare feet were touching it. The girl's hands were stained; and the mouths in her palms were so swollen with blood, she looked as if she were developing an allergic reaction to the drink. The vampyrism had changed her in some ways, but not as much as one might've expected. The first and last time he had met her face-to-face, he had pulled her out of the Dread Clock, after she had gone inside it to save her mother and father. Even then, she'd been a rough child; no smooth edges—all cuts and bruises in a stew of simmering deviance. She was a girl who could handle herself, true, but his mistake was thinking that she could handle herself after the Dread Clock had its way with her and her family. It manipulated them to disown her, so she found a new family at the Orphanage, instead. Herbert should've seen it coming. In his later years, he learned that was where all the children who'd survived encounters with the Dread Clock ended up, as if it were collecting them, saving them. And then, as irony would have it, it was they, the Orphans, who ended up collecting the Clock in the Nameless Forest.

"What're you thinking about?" Gemma asked, childishly, as the stink of death rolled off her in a choking fog. She turned towards the tents. "James in there?"

"Leave him alone," Herbert said, his breath fog upon the cold air.

Gemma huffed. "So, for real, what're you thinking about?"

"Just—" he gestured the battlefield before them, "—all of this."

"Yeah, I don't think Atta-boy would've sent us here if he knew." She flexed her hands, so that more blood would run into the mouths on her palms. "See any shepherds?"

"Not one since we left the Membrane."

"That's good."

"I don't know." Herbert crossed his arms and pulled on their flab. "Don't think I'd be too bent out of shape if one came for me."

Gemma laughed; her eyes were back on the tent again, probing it for shapes of James. "What? You don't like all this?"

He didn't have any whiskey or hair metal, and as all the good cops in bad cop movies used to say, he was getting too old for this shit, so he wasn't about to give her his spiel. But no, Herbert North didn't like all this.

He didn't like he'd left the comfy confines of the Membrane thinking he'd come topside and be the lovable curmudgeon some strange farming family had taken in because he'd done them a solid once.

He didn't like he'd become part of some pathetic resistance group hell-bent on stopping the hell that was already here—a resistance group that was fronted by an immortal who couldn't give two shits about it, but was, in fact, actually led by a batshit crazy, blue-haired woman who only wanted the best, and yet went about achieving it in the worst ways possible.

He didn't like that he was sitting here, alone (aside from the blood-sucking nuisance beside him), watching as gullible cabalists and relentless cultists crashed into one another, trading blows and bodily fluids—fucking one another into the dirt, or decimating one another into an early grave; each group giving everything they had for nothing in return; trampling the dead and the dying in their desperate dance to win the praise and attention of overlords that weren't even watching; leaving corpses, like brambles, to twist out of the earth, to be stepped on and reduced to dust, and forgotten, until that day some sad piece of shit like Herbert North, but not Herbert North, is called to the site, to put down some unholy uprising, some spiritual succession; until that day some poor bastard has to go in and play doctor with a wound that has been festering for years; a wound like all wounds everyone everywhere carries; the same old wounds—different sizes and shapes, but from all the same sources all the same: politics, power, and the pursuit of grace; he'd been here before, a thousand times before; new flesh, old bones.

But most of all, he didn't like that, when he was at his most needed, and so far into his element they'd have to make a spot for him on the periodic table, he was completely, one hundred percent useless. He was an old man who couldn't fight worth a damn. He used to have all kinds of potions and powders and a few Red Death weapons at his disposal; he used to have eyes and ears in the community, keeping tabs on targets and carrying out jobs when he couldn't make it. He'd taken out a good chunk of the Ashcroft line, and had even harbored the Dread Clock for a time. He'd gone toe-to-toe with Gemma's master, Camazotz, and a whole clutch of succubae and their queen, Agrat. And then there was that time with Scarlet…

Herbert sighed and shook his head at himself. That's what it came to. All tell and no show. The most he could lay claim to these days were the mind-numbing farts he let loose amongst the ranks. Crop-dusting, that's what they used to call it. Sure, he had knowledge of the Old World, but look where it got them. It got them here, in Angheuawl, their numbers thinned and morale mere motes on the wind. And it was his fault they were here. And it would be his fault if the Skeleton did or didn't come back with all the guns, all the bombs—all the terrible things humanity had covered with their ashes.

Gemma made a shocking sound and pinched Herbert's side. "Buzz, buzz. What's the matter, Grandpa?"

Herbert started to stand, but then most of his bones cracked, and he sat back down, annoyed. "What's Hex's next play?"

Gemma shrugged. "I don't know. She's still… indisposed. Most of the cultists inside the village killed each other. Some ran away. Can't really stay in the village with it looking the way it does, but… the cultists that ran may come back. So I don't know what to do."

Herbert squinted as he watched a cabalist bi-sect a flesh fiend. "Just keeping killing."

"You're welcome, by the way, for saving all of you." Gemma stuck her tongue out.

"I'm the one who saved you. If I hadn't been stupid and left you with your parents, you might not be here right now, saving everyone else."

"I guess every turd has a silver lining," Gemma said. "Well, I better get back to making you look bad."

"Gemma—" Herbert grabbed her collar and yanked until she crouched down, closer to his face. "How did you get ahold of the Dread Clock again? Connor and I sealed the hell out of that thing."

"Well, I wanted it to get some sweet revenge on," Gemma said, "but then the Trauma happened… and the Orphanage got stuck in the Nameless Forest." She laughed and shook her head. "Only in a world as crazy as this can I say what I'm about to say and not look insane."

Herbert looked at Gemma, the mouths in her palm, and said, "Words are the least of your worries, you little creep."

"You smell like prune juice," Gemma said, wrinkling her nose.

"Not sure prune juice exists anymore. You're going to need better insults if you're going to keep pretending you're a kid."

Gemma jerked out of Herbert's grasp. Her blood-speckled face tightened into a grimace. And then, when it seemed she was done talking to him, she said, "A big ass maggot dropped the Dread Clock off at our doorstep."

Screams, from Angheuawl; feet pattering across the empty spaces; the thud of a body going down to a chorus of clanging swords.

"A maggot?" Herbert asked.

"Yeah, a real big sucker. I'd say it was… I don't know. Seven hundred pounds? Color of pus. It had the Dread Clock on its back."

"And… it just left it there?"

Gemma nodded, stood. "Uh, huh, yeah."

"Why?"

"It said not to move it, no matter what. And I wasn't planning on moving it. But we were in the Nameless Forest a really long time, and then Edgar started sending soldiers in trying to take it out, and then the Gravedigger popped up and he actually seemed like he could take it out, and… I just wanted to leave. Seemed like my only chance to get my family away from the Forest."

"Do you think it was hiding it from something?"

"No," Gemma said, "I think it was trying to stop something from getting back in."

"What… God?"

"Probably. I mean, once Bone Man took the Dread Clock out, the vermillion veins were everywhere. And the Disciples of the Deep, too. There's a gateway to God deep in the Forest. Makes sense that somehow the Dread Clock was holding it back. It was holding everything back."

"And… you don't care you might be responsible for… everything?"

"We all have the same Skeleton in our futures," Gemma said, coy as she could be.

Hebert waved her off, and then: "The hell does that even mean?"

"The Black Hour's Keeper told me that once. I just think it sounds gangster."

Hebert sank down in his seat and pinched the bridge of his nose. As Gemma levitated herself off the ground and headed for the field again, he called after her. "What happened to that maggot?"

She shrugged, shouted, "Don't know. Went South. Said it had more work to do."

Herbert sat there awhile longer, not thinking about much of anything. Instead, his eyes simply wandered over the scene, capturing each grotesquerie like a photograph for the vaults of his dusty mind. He wanted to remember the naked cultists face-down in the mud, the flesh fiends entwined in their balls of death, having died together like breeding cockroaches. He wanted to cherish the sight of the cabalists and vampyres marauding in and out of the village; every time they came back, a little more missing from them. He wanted to capture, in the amber of his memory, all those who had died here, all the life that could've been better spent somewhere else, rather than in the form of blood and semen and sweat. He wanted to immortalize the Horrors of the Womb and the Mother Horror, still dead upon the field and now host to a horde of skittering, slithering, snacking smaller horrors filling their bodies and eating their innards. He wanted it all, in crystal clear clarity, so that the next time anyone offered him any proposition other than to have a cheap beer, he'd say, "No thank you, buddy," and be on his way.

When the blood from the field began to stream underneath his toes,

Herbert got up, went past the cabalists guarding the tent, and visited Clementine and Will.

The first thing Clementine said to him as he drew back the flap was, "Please, not right now, Herbert."

"You got rid of my dad," Will said, his eyes following Herbert like a predator's, "and you promised you wouldn't."

Herbert shook off the snow that had gathered on his shoulders. He didn't pay them any attention. Invitations weren't something he was accustomed to receiving, anyway. Clementine and Will's tent was spacious but sparse; having spent so long outside of the earth, they had, apparently, given up all need for earthly belongings. To the Skeleton, this had been a warning sign that something wasn't quite right with his wife and son. To Herbert, it just made good sense. Because what the hell was the point of building a life back up if a shepherd was just going to come along to knock it back down? It wasn't just Death that had changed them, but also a distaste for bitter disappointment. All they had wanted was the husband and father who had wanted them most of all. He tried to explain this to the Skeleton on numerous occasions, but the stubborn bastard hadn't wanted to hear it. To be fair, though, Herbert was surprised the Skeleton could hear anything these days, what with the Black Hour constantly whispering into his non-existent ears.

Clementine combed her fingers through her hair. For a moment, she looked like a spellweaver conjuring a crown of silken fire atop her head. Herbert could see why the Skeleton had sacrificed life and limb for her. She was beautiful, and she was sharp; a rare gem, not to be collected, but to be cherished. She had an effect on everything she came into contact with. And Herbert was fairly certain that, if she told the Marrow Cabal to pack it up and turn this ship around, back to Gallows, they'd do just that. It wasn't infatuation or fear she was working with, but a genuine personality. The Skeleton had said everyone was obsessed with him and her and their relationship back in the day—small town sweethearts, if you will. Herbert could tell that, when the Skeleton told him this, he missed those days, the same way the starving may fantasize about food. It was a fleeting sustenance currently unsustainable in this vermillion hell. And that's why, if anyone asked Herbert, he thought the Skeleton had caught himself a ride to the Dead City. To find a way to wipe the slate clean, before it was dirtied for good.

"How is it out there?" Clementine finally spoke up. "How much more killing needs to be done?"

"A bit," Herbert said. And then, to Will: "I didn't get rid of your dad. You know I wouldn't do that. Your dad isn't someone you can say no to."

Will crossed his arms and looked cross. The Skeleton and Clementine had led storied lives, even before he lost his flesh and she, possibly, her mind. But Will wasn't either of them in any respect. He wasn't going to become the criminals they'd once been, or the pillars of this hodgepodge community they'd become. He was young—fourteen—but he had his future written across his face, and etched into every action he made. He was good. He was kind. And despite being gored by one of Eldrus' soldiers, dying, and then coming back to life again, he was still those things. The Marrow Cabal was no place for him. Neither was Angheuawl. He reminded Herbert of Connor: gullible, hyperbolic; more capable than he gave himself credit for. In a different place, in a different time, Herbert might've tried to make something of Will. A partner in investigations, maybe, or the son he'd never have.

"I thought Mr. Haemo was coming with us, to bring him back," Will said. "There's enough blood here to do it, right?"

"I don't know," Herbert said, shrugging. "I don't think the mosquito is giving up Gallows without a fight."

"How's Dad going to get back?"

"He said he had something in mind. Your dad is going to be fine, I swear." Herbert smiled as he nodded and said, "He really will be. Nothing can stand up to him."

"Except the heart he's carrying around." Will dug his heel into the dirt. "It's making him crazy."

"Your father just doesn't do anything simple," Clementine said, "but he always comes through."

Will agreed, begrudgingly.

"He's going to arm the Marrow Cabal with whatever's in the Dead City, right?" Clementine asked.

"Right," Herbert said. "If he can do that, he can stop Eldrus before they wake up the Vermillion God. This... world is so regressed. It might be good to give it some new technology. Move things forward."

"Then it's not going to stop," Will said. "Dad, I mean, isn't going to stop. He doesn't care about any of this."

Dull screams passed through the tent like the phantoms of the dead who'd let them out.

"He doesn't have to listen to anybody, but he lets Hex boss him around."

"We owe a lot to Hex," Clementine said. "Herbert?"

"Yeah?"

"We're here. What's next?"

"We're to wait." Herbert strained his ears; someone was approaching the guard. "He should be back in the next day or two."

Will's face tightened. He ground his teeth together in deliberation.

"What's wrong?" Herbert asked.

"Did he know it'd be like this here?"

"No way, no. I don't think so. He wouldn't send you guys into danger." Herbert laughed uncomfortably. "What makes you say that?"

Clementine touched Will's arm, but he shook her off and said, "The heart might be making him try to get rid of us."

Clementine was silent. She'd been with the Skeleton at the most intimate of moments. Her silence was her unspoken agreement with her son.

"I mean, Hex tried to kill R'lyeh. She was nuts. And Dad put her back in charge, anyway. He could've sent us anywhere away from Eldrus or Penance." Will closed his eyes and balled his fists. "You think R'lyeh is okay?"

Herbert didn't need a teenager of his own to know a crush when he saw one. "Yeah, she's a tough kid. I'm sure she's the one keeping him out of trouble. She's going to be fine."

Will nodded. Was that what he was actually worried about? With his dad, he always seemed distant. And according to the Skeleton, his son was always distant. They were two planets drifting out of one another's orbits—the need for the other no longer necessary.

"Clementine," Hebert said, "I'm sorry if I made this worse. He pulled me from the Membrane. He didn't want to use the Black Hour's heart. I didn't know he'd haul ass—"

Voices, from outside the tent.

Clementine smiled the saddest smile Herbert had ever seen. "We've been through worse, he and I. Have you seen any shepherds lately, Herbert?"

Shepherds? No one had, not as far as he could tell. She knew that. The only time anyone saw shepherds was when Clementine and Will claimed to have seen some themselves, to keep the Skeleton at their side.

"No, I haven't," he said.

"Let me know if you do," she said, the sad smile never falling from her face. "Let us both know."

Cocking his head, Herbert said, "Clem, I don't..." *I'm not getting into this, not in front of Will,* he thought. He changed the subject. "Where the hell's James?"

Will pointed his finger, a tear in his eye, and said, "Behind you."

Herbert turned—"Holy shit!"—and jumped sideways as he caught James standing behind him, his body half inside the tent.

"Jesus Christ," Herbert said, grabbing his chest. "You about broke my ticker."

James drove his stump of a hand into Herbert's side and said, "Hex wants to see you."

Warren had been waiting for Herbert and James outside the tent. Like Gemma, but somehow worse, the mountainous man was covered in blood. He didn't have a sword at the moment, just his hands, which had been fists for so long, he was having a hard time making them anything else. Of all those that held the important positions in the Marrow Cabal, Herbert knew very little about Warren. He hadn't been around much, on account of Hex always sending him into the field. And now that he was here, had been here during the move from Gallows, the man said next to nothing. When Elizabeth came back with R'lyeh and he found out Miranda had been killed, Warren's vocabulary had been reduced to cuss words and growls. But ever since Elizabeth ran out on the Marrow Cabal the night before they left, Warren had stopped speaking altogether.

James did most of the talking nowadays, for most everyone. A self-proclaimed gimp, he enjoyed his new job of diplomacy, and as an ex-prostitute, it seemed he couldn't have been a more perfect fit.

Hebert, standing with James and Warren outside the tent, gave the corpse-clogged horizon a once-over and said, "Tell Hex I'm busy."

"It's safe," James said.

Warren squeezed his fists until blood shot out of them.

"What does she want? She pissed at me, too, for sending Bone Daddy away?"

James puffed out his cheeks and blew. "She wants you to look at her brother."

"That thing was her—"

"She wants to see if you know any way to help him."

"It's still alive? How the fuck is it still alive?"

Warren, apparently having tired of the conversation, started forward, each stomp of his feet leaving holes in the snow.

There had been another Horror of Angheuawl, but unlike those of the Womb and the Mother Horror, this one'd had only one target in mind: Hex. It had come screaming out of the village on the backs of flesh fiends. A giant seed pod, completely covered in hundreds, if not thousands of vermillion veins. When the Marrow Cabal cut down the flesh fiends that'd been carrying it, the flailing tumor tightened the veins into limbs to support itself. At that point, Hex had seen it, and it had seen Hex. They took off together, towards the hills and the sun, with tens of scrambling Marrow Cabal in tow.

"Brother?" Herbert repeated, minding the dead strewn across the outskirts. "Isn't Ichor supposed to be… missing?"

James threw up his hand and nub in confusion. "He's not anymore, apparently."

"I don't think I can… bring him back to what he used to be. I'm not a miracle worker."

"She doesn't want you to…" James rolled his eyes. "She just wants to help him."

"What… does that mean?"

Warren cleared his throat and said, "Help him, so she can keep hurting him," and then went silent again.

They all did.

Herbert and the others hurried through the thickening snow to the woods that ran wide around Angheuawl. When they'd first arrived, the area had been reduced to a shallow marsh due to the nearby lakes that had flooded. Over the course of battle, the streams slowed and the waters thinned, as the dead had drifted into one another and built dams with their bodies. Now the corpses had begun to freeze; snow-covered and sparkling, it was about the only time in their lives these mercenaries and murderers could be called beautiful.

Hex was waiting for them at the wood's edge, guarding the mass, her so-called brother, behind her like a mother would her brood. Her blue hair was greasy, knotted; filled with twigs and stones like the bird's nest it resembled. As with almost everyone else here, she was covered in blood, except Herbert could see where she was wounded. A long gash across her face, from her ear to chin, and then down her neck, vertically. Her breastplate had been broken in; the plainclothes behind it shredded, as if something had meant to get at her breasts. Her hands looked as if she had armed herself with thorn bushes as weapons, and her left leg kept giving out. She used her sword like a cane; seeing that, Herbert didn't feel so old anymore.

Ichor, partially obscured by Hex, the trees, and the snowfall, whined. Thick vermillion veins rose and fell from his bulbous husk. Periodically, they would snap off, hit the ground with a loud crunch and thump. One by one, they did this, like ropes being cut from a completed monument. Herbert didn't know anything about Ichor, but he didn't have to know there wasn't anything beyond what he'd become.

He moved to move closer, but Hex intervened. "Don't lay a hand on him."

Herbert held up both his hands. "Trust me, I'd rather not. This is... this is Ichor?"

Two eyes blinked. A mouth opened wide and a tongue of vermillion veins poured out. Ichor trembled as he brought what must've been his hands (they looked like tumorous trunks) to what must've been his face and cleared the snow off it.

Herbert cringed and looked back and forth between James and Warren, to make sure they were doing the same (James was; Warren's eyes weren't even open). Ichor's face was like a piece of paper that had been punctured through and held in place by the hard, vermillion rods jutting from his elephantine head. His neck wasn't a neck, and his body wasn't a body; both were one continuous trunk, tightly wound and teeming with growths. To Herbert, Ichor was God's bezoar: a solid mass of human and the divine; sanctified shit that any priest worth his spit would prop up and proselytize as the ultimate in earthly ascendance. In his own way, Ichor was a monument; he was a representation of what was possible if one were to follow the teachings of the Disciples of the Deep. He was pathetic and disgusting, but in Herbert's experiences, that had never stopped the devout before. Such qualities only made it more attractive. The worse the suffering, the sweeter the reward.

"You can't keep him alive..." Herbert said.

Hex's face hardened.

"I mean... at least... you can't let anyone see him."

"There's r-reports—" James paused as Ichor's mass unraveled and a flesh fiend in a butler's suit fell out. "—reports of others changing across the Heartland once they ingest the seed of heaven. More and more are—"

Infused with the steaming heat of Ichor's digestion, the butler flesh fiend sank into the snow.

"—surviving the change. They're passing seeds out like candy." James covered his mouth with his nub. "I heard the Holy Order's put a bounty on the mutants. They've been calling them Lilin. Killing one is an automatic entry into heaven."

"Hydra's a Worm last I heard. Pot calling the kettle black," Hex said, sounding offended. "Ichor's coming with us."

This grabbed Warren's attention. He struggled with the question, perhaps he was afraid of the answer he'd get, but it came out all the same. "What are you going to... use him for?"

"Intel. Find out what he knows about the Cult. Find out what he knows about the Disciples." Hex knelt down beside her brother and touched his repulsive face. "Study him. Might find a way to use the seeds to our advantage. Take out the Disciples and the Holy Order at the same time, before they go and fuck the Heartland over. This is the Marrow Cabal, isn't it?" She shushed Ichor as he started to whine. "It's what we're meant to do."

"Hex," Herbert started.

Hex pulled her hand away from Ichor's face; a slick webbing clung to her fingers and his torn forehead. "What?"

Don't say it, Herbert told himself. *Let it go. Shoulder your blame. It's not worth...* And then he came out with it, anyway: "Hex, one of those Witches got in your head. You kept going on and on about a pilgrimage. You're from Lacuna. Did you know... what we were walking into?"

Scoffing, Hex stood and started working her blue hair into its trademark braids. "Did the Skeleton?"

James drifted closer to Warren, farther away from both Herbert and Hex.

Hex's grip tightened on her sword. She had Corruption on both of her arms, and they were so red, it was as if they were on fire. "Did you know?"

"Jesus Christ," Herbert said.

"Who's that?" Hex asked.

"No one, no. Listen... I didn't. I thought it was strange he was willing to trust—"

Inches from Herbert, Hex stopped. Despite her buckling leg, she pulled her sword, that makeshift cane of hers, out of the ground and took it in both hands.

"Did you know your brother would be here, too?" Herbert didn't care anymore; bring on the wrath, woman. "You're as crazy as the Bone Man."

Hex smiled. "We hurt the ones we love."

"Alright, Hex." Herbert put out his hand, to drive her sword away. "Come on. What're you doing?"

"I know everyone's been busting your balls about the Skeleton leaving. I'm not all that upset. Problem is he's going to come back, and he's going to come back with more problems for us to deal with."

Hex nodded at James and Warren.

Warren got the hint and headed back towards the Marrow Cabal.

James, on the other hand (his good one, if you will), didn't. "Let's wait it out," he said, as Warren returned to him and ushered him away. "Hex, don't."

Herbert's heart kicked up a notch into something short of full-blown cardiac arrest. "Hey, wait. Don't fucking kill me."

"I'm not going to kill you." Hex stabbed the sword into the ground and leaned onto it. "Eldrus, Penance, or both were going to be on our doorstep eventually, anyways. We had to move."

"Thanks f-f-for c-coming... Sis," Ichor sputtered, his veins writhing in excitement.

Hex kicked him in the face, and he stopped moving.

"But if the Skeleton had been here, you wouldn't have lost so many cabalists," Herbert said, catching her drift. "Vampyres, too."

"Don't give two shits about Atticus' friends," Hex said. "But we had to sacrifice. I have to be better than him now, whether he comes back or not." Her eyes started to glow a vibrant blue color. She closed them, and when the light stopped seeping out from underneath her lids, she opened them again. "Got another sacrifice to make. Look to the woods. Tell me what you see."

Herbert thought about running, but where would he go? Back to camp where no one would defend him? Into the wilds, where a stray flesh fiend could feast on what the cold hadn't taken from him? He was one-hundred-and-fifty-five going on oblivion—the only safe place for him was the comfy confines of a coffin. So he didn't run. He stayed. And looked to the woods.

I'm old, he thought, eyes wandering over the flooded woodland. *But she's wounded.* Trees. Water. The hazy silhouette of mountains, one much larger than the rest—one that he could've sworn hadn't been there before. *I could knock that sword out from under her.* There wasn't anything out here; even if there was, he wouldn't see it, anyway. Not with the snow smearing the scene like television noise. *I'm old, but she's out of her mind.*

Thump, thump, thump.

The sound hit Herbert like a bat to the back of the head. His vision doubled. His stomach lurched. Fight or flight kicked in, but the fear was stronger. Paralysis of the deepest kind. A black hole had opened up inside him, and through it, he'd find the Abyss.

Thump, thump, thump.

Not far from where they stood, the snow had stopped obeying the laws of the universe. Where it should've fallen, it rose, and it swirled, and then it pulsated outward—a bracing nova that left icicles on everything it touched. At the center of the nova, reality had become smudged; he could see what looked like fingerprints in the rawness of space; a kind of genetic code, or molecules, or maybe even the last bit of evidence of a preternatural creator. And then there was a hat, large and battered. And then a face shrouded in blonde hair. And then, a hand, and in it, a crook.

Thump, thump, thump—the rest of the shepherd came through.

"Get it away… g-get it away," Ichor said, flopping around like a seal.

"It's either you, or Clementine and Will. They're a package deal," Hex said. "One's not going without the other. I can't have them gone when Atticus gets back."

The shepherd reached into its cracked leather jacket and took out a roll of pink bandages. This shepherd's nails were gray, like the color of the Void.

"I… I…" For all his bitching, Herbert wasn't exactly ready to die again. "I think Clementine and Will would rather go."

"Not going to work," Hex said. "Skeleton comes back and those two are missing? That's it for everyone. Everything. Won't be no holding the Black Hour's heart back. It's you, Herbert. If Mr. Haemo were here, maybe this could go differently. But he isn't. So be a man and get."

Herbert shook his head. With a scream, he shoved Hex back. Her bad leg gave out and she crumpled upon herself in the snow. Ichor raged and hoisted himself forward, one agonizing centimeter at a time. The shepherd blew its hair out of its face and, holding its hand out to grab him by the neck, hurried forward.

"Get the fuck back!" Herbert grabbed Hex's sword off the ground. "Tell Death if She wants me, She'll have to come and—"

As if some great bond had been broken, an earth-shattering explosion rang out through the woods. A force rushed through the area, knocking Herbert off his feet and the shepherd back into the Membrane. Trees were felled, and the few birds remaining were knocked from the sky.

Herbert, face-down in the snow, exhaled. His body hurt immediately, like it was covered in one large, hideous bruise.

"Fuck," he wheezed, eating the snow while he struggled to breathe. Everything had gone dim. He shook his head, rubbed his eyes. The snow was a different color, a sinister shade of black. He turned over, on his back. The sky. What the hell? He rubbed his eyes harder, but still the image stayed.

The sky had turned red. The color of Corruption. And the clouds were on fire.

CHAPTER XXVI

Green tubing tying off gangrenous arms. Summer heat, knife in meat. Black cloak prowling refuse. Legs spread wide; a whole universe inside. Blood on the banks. Bombs in the blood. Corn fields. Red sky. The Ashen Man strapped to a bed, breeding flies with Pain. A globe in a classroom. Rats running the sewer.

"H-hey... please... stop."

Bodies in the expressway, flashing lights behind their skin. Two lovers in the park. Beds covered in hair. A rope made out of clothes. Lust at a beauty pageant. Chalky arithmetic.

"I can't take..."

The Dread Clock an hourglass. Skull and skin on a scale. Little girls in their fathers' arms. Beaming mothers at a spelling bee. The pull of the Abyss from before even birth. An alligator. A cat. Fast food.

"Just stop. I'm..."

Catheter made of thorns. Green jungle. Red tribesman. Scorpion priest. Bookstore signing. Matted fur. High school stench. Vigilance. Virulence.

R'lyeh forced her eyes open and kicked at the Skeleton's arms until he dropped her.

Shepherds on Sunday. Mourning on Monday. Terror on Tuesday.

The Black Hour images stopped as soon as she was out of his embrace.

R'lyeh flipped over. She did a belly flop on the garbage bag-colored ground. The inorganic material received her with hard indifference. The air blew out of her lungs, and a sickening, empty feeling filled them back up again. She sat up and turned around, and saw that the Dead City was behind them, far behind them. They were back on the peninsula, almost to the mainland, and the Green Worm's fog had all but cleared.

The Skeleton stood over her, his cowl flapping in the quickening wind. For a man who supposedly didn't feel anything anymore, he looked as if he had just had the crap beat out of him. It wasn't that he was wounded. It was the way he held himself. Like the weight of the world was finally getting to him.

R'lyeh was lost in her own twilight. She probably was in pain, too, but her body hadn't realized it, yet. Sweating, not thinking clearly, she stripped off her armor, piece by piece, until she was down to her doused shirt and pants.

She rubbed her eyes, and they felt like stones. She sniffed her nose, and a gallon of snot went down her throat. She farted, and accidentally shat herself. In a place so cold—*Great, here comes the snow,* she thought—she appreciated the warmth, and didn't mind the smell. R'lyeh smacked her lips; it felt as if her gums were flaking.

"What—" her voice sounded as if she she'd been smoking since birth, "—happened back… there?"

The Black Hour's growth had spread farther. It had reached the Skeleton's neck.

"How're you feeling?" he asked.

"If a shit could shit, I'd be that shit," R'lyeh said. She smiled to herself. That wasn't a bad, badass phrase, was it? Oh man, she'd forgotten to work on those. So much to do, she couldn't even remember what it all was. She coughed loudly.

The Skeleton offered his gloved hand and said, "Let's find you somewhere better to rest them bones."

R'lyeh's legs weren't having any of that. Moving sounded like the absolute worst idea in the world, even worse than coming to the Dead City. She shook her head. "I'm good here."

Not far off from where she sat and he stood, on both sides of them, the ocean lapped against the peninsula. There must've been more land here at some point, she considered. If they had just waited for another hundred years or for a terrible hurricane, this bridge between the Old World and New might not have even been here. If only she had gone more slowly, she might still be back in Alluvia, telling Derleth no as he handed her the roots of the Crossbreed and asked her to drop it in the village's well. She coughed again.

Aimlessly, R'lyeh dug out the ground, pulling up piece after piece of the black plastic material that coated it. Occasionally, she'd find a buried trinket, a forgotten memento, or just junk: a locket, a wallet, some laminated business cards; a stuffed animal, with most of the stuffing out of it; coins, and a wedding ring.

"Look at all this stuff."

The Skeleton kept on looking at her, instead.

R'lyeh stopped digging. It was making her tired. "What happened back there?"

Could a place know someone was talking about it? Out of the dreary still life that was the Dead City, the angry sounds of machinery lifted.

"You had a fit. They attacked us." The Skeleton paced, and then he settled on a spot beside her, where he sat. "They were going to kill you. There was nothing I could do to stop them and save you."

"What'd you give them?"

"What they wanted."

R'lyeh covered her mouth, but the force of her cough was strong enough to blow her hand away. She wasn't cold, even though she should've been, but she was shivering, anyway. Her lower back hurt, too. Like she'd been slouching all day. Mom and Dad did warn her about that.

"Wanted parts for their ship," the Skeleton said. "Gave me a time, date, and a place where I could find them."

"You used the heart."

"Yeah. Didn't get everything, but it was enough to get them away, get you out of there. Didn't take long, but I'd say I was in the Black Hour for a good forty-five minutes. Wasn't sure you were going to make it."

Dead-eyed, R'lyeh smiled at the Skeleton, "I'm doing alright. So... we own... the City?"

"Doesn't matter if we do or don't." The Skeleton started digging at the plastic ground, too. "It's going to be ours, regardless. Once I eat them up."

R'lyeh let that last statement slide. It had been a rough day for the both of them. She started coughing again; she put her whole body into it—bones, too. Things were going to start cracking inside her. She had to get this under control.

"Need to get you back to the mainland," the Skeleton said. "I'll carry you."

R'lyeh laughed and rubbed her moist face. Vomit sailed the edge of her esophagus. She pissed on herself, because why not? And then she started coughing again. This time, a sharp bar of pain drove itself through her ribs. She winced, moaned; she smiled at the Skeleton, drool in the corner of her mouth, and pretended she was okay.

"Oh man. Atticus, after everything, I think I'm finally getting sick," she said, wiping her mouth.

The Skeleton didn't say anything. She was hoping he would, but he didn't. Instead, he sat there, cloak flailing around his frame like it meant to get away from him, staring at her. Most of the time, he didn't look any different. How could he? Like a witch's stew, he was eyeballs, tongue, and bone, with that southern broth of sass. But today, right now? He did look different. Maybe it was the shadows in his cheeks, or the glint in his pupils—that little spark of humanity that had somehow escaped the Black Hour's black grip. Or maybe it was the way he carried himself. That kind of sympathetic slouch Dad used to get when R'lyeh would come home with a scrape, or from school after having scrapped in the school yard. Every time she coughed, he'd lean in closer, like a scientist inspecting a specimen. So she coughed a lot, even when she didn't have to, thinking she might get a hug out of this. She didn't need another dad. But she wouldn't mind a good hug.

R'lyeh made herself laugh. "I... I said I think I'm finally getting sick."

The Skeleton's tongue, which at this point had to be infected by the Black Hour, ran over his crooked teeth.

"What?" R'lyeh hacked up a lung, literally; a bloody chunk flew out her mouth, onto the ground. Again, she made herself laugh.

"I think you're getting dying," the Skeleton said.

"Shut up." R'lyeh screwed up her face. "No. The hell? No, I'm not. This—" she gathered her breath, "is just like when we first got here. It's always b-bad, but then it gets better."

"Stand up, then."

R'lyeh fell forward, having almost fallen asleep, but she didn't stand. She couldn't. It took too much effort to even consider standing. Her neck constricted. Her heart began to beat faster. Sweat and snow melted from her scalp, ran down her face. Something was different. Something wasn't right.

"I'm sorry, R'lyeh."

R'lyeh tried to steady her breathing, but it was no use. Every breath she took hurt; every exhale made things move inside her, like the Green

Worm's clouds were growing over her innards, like mold.

"Get me out of here."

The Skeleton didn't stir.

"Get me out of here!" She squeezed her eyes as tears fell from them. "Please."

The Skeleton shook his skull. "Green Worm's in you." He covered his mouth. "Can't get it out."

R'lyeh, shaking her head and coughing, swiped at the Skeleton, but missed. "That's b-bullshit." She tried to push herself off the ground, but her arms gave out. "Help me, Atticus."

As soon as the Skeleton slid an arm under her armpit, an excruciating pain coursed through her body. R'lyeh screamed and jerked away. Her nerve endings were raw, flayed by disease. Like the old woman she sounded like, she wept there in a twisted knot of agony.

"Use it." R'lyeh quivered. "The heart."

"There's no cure for what you got." The Skeleton touched her hand with his gloved one.

Shivering violently, she brought her knees to her chest. "T-then go back in t-time. Don't let me come here."

"No good can come from that." The Skeleton's voice broke.

"Are you kidding me?"

"I didn't even do it for Clementine and Will. There's a lot of things I'd like to change—"

R'lyeh stopped listening to him and started listening to herself. He wasn't going to help her. He had already doomed her to Death. That's what he knew. That's all he knew. She wasn't dying. She wasn't doing good, and this was quickly becoming the worst thing that had ever happened to her, but she wasn't dying. The Worms of the Earth were stronger than anything she had ever dealt with before, but she had dealt with the Red, endured the Blue, and seen through the Green. She was R'lyeh of Alluvia; the Octopus; a member of the Marrow Cabal; sole survivor of Geharra and the only person, besides the Skeleton, to have gone as deep as she had into the Dead City; and a Deadly Beauty. She wasn't dying. She wasn't—

She held her legs tightly. She had so much spit in her mouth, it kept seeping out onto her thighs. The pain from the pressure of sitting and holding herself was getting worse. She tried to move, to find a better position, but everything hurt everywhere. Winter was helping, numbing her where it could. It wasn't enough.

"Please," she said into her knees. "Please."

The Skeleton gently wrapped his arm around her and pressed his bony body against hers. His touch was like rough fingers stirring the pink meat of an open wound. She bared it for him. He bared it for her.

"Cure… Go back in time… I'm…"

He shushed her.

"Are you m-mad at… me?"

"No."

"Why won't you do anything?" R'lyeh tipped her head back, and lost it. Her face was inflamed with agony. Every tear was a knife cutting into her, taking her apart, laying her bare. "The Virions c-changed… I could be changing."

The Skeleton whispered, "You don't want that."

"No," she whimpered. "I don't want to die." Burying her face back into her knees, she wailed, "I don't want to die, Atticus."

"You had a good run."

"Fuck you," she said, her face a smile and a scowl. "Are you kidding me? I'm not just… giving up."

"Not asking you to." The Skeleton's wild eyes met hers and he said, "Just give in."

She tried to shake her head, but her muscles were too taut. "No, no. I'm not done. I haven't done… anything." She coughed and growled out the pain it caused her. "Oh god," she cried, blood dribbling down her chin. "Please. I need—"

"You've done so much," the Skeleton said.

"No, no, stop. Listen to me. I can fight it. I can f-fight. I…" Her airway closed; suffocating, she gripped the fabric of her pants until she could breathe again. "Just… use the heart."

Snow blew across the peninsula in white waves, until the Dead City was gone, and the mainland was gone, and there was nothing else other than him and her and the sounds of the sea.

"I think I can stand."

She couldn't.

R'lyeh was crying again. Muscles she didn't even know she had were wracked with spasms. She had a migraine. There was snow in her eyes— the red kind, the bad kind; the kind that came when your body went. She fell sideways, into the Skeleton's side. The fabric of his cloak blocked her skin from the taint of the Black Hour, but only barely. If he moved, it would consume her.

"I didn't do enough," R'lyeh said. "I didn't do anything."

The Skeleton draped his arm over her.

I didn't do anything, she thought. But she didn't want to be alone right now, in her head. If she wasn't an open book, she'd close for good.

"I fucked up everything," she said. "Every mission you g-gave me. My village. My… parents. Vrana…" Silently, she bawled; those deep, thudding sounds of despair. "Here… You. It's not fair. It's not… fair. I tried so… so hard. Please, you have to… I can't. I can't. I don't want to be… alone again. I'm so—" She coughed and cleared her nose. "I'm afraid. I'm so weak. I'm really scared."

"You did plenty," the Skeleton said, kind as he could probably manage. "You survived Penance attacking your village and Geharra. You went all the way across the continent. You survived Lacuna, too. And Gallows, when the Red Worm came. You scouted for me. You got out of Rime alive. You passed through Penance's army… and Edgar's spider soldiers. You went through a blood portal. You came here. That's not bad. That's not bad at all."

"But it didn't mean… anything."

"It meant everything to me," the Skeleton said. "You saved Audra, I reckon, and Elizabeth, too, in a way. You made my boy happy, even if you didn't much care for him or speak to him."

R'lyeh smiled.

"You didn't have to save the world, but you did save a few souls. Mine's damned for all I've done, but you kept me holding on."

"How?" she whispered.

"Didn't come here for weapons. Came here to get away. Knew no one could follow. But you did."

"But your w-wife… and son."

The Skeleton ground his teeth. "I knew Hex's Cult might be gathering in Angheuawl. I sent them, anyways."

R'lyeh's eyes were as wide as saucers. "Why?"

"Don't know. Don't know why I do the things I do anymore. I think I find ways to keep saving them. If I settle, I'll just be bones.

"Every day my grave gets deeper, and darker. And when the light goes out, all my hours will be black. Dying isn't so bad. It's living you got to watch out for."

"Did I save you?" R'lyeh asked, like the child she was.

The Skeleton shook his head. "Can't save what's lost. But you gave me a little light to see with."

"I didn't know… you were so fucked up." She managed to laugh, and then regretted it.

"I don't expect either of us know each other as well as we should."

"Would you… use the heart… if you did know me?"

"By time I come out of it, you'll be gone. I want to be here, to see you off."

R'lyeh covered her eyes. The tears were finally coming to an end. She didn't have anything left to give, because she had given everything.

"Can I see… it?"

The Skeleton didn't ask her what she meant; death was their bond now; and by its bond, they ran the same wavelength. With his free hand, he reached into his cloak, removed the Red Worm's stone, and laid it on her chest. Then he took out the Red Worm's necklace and gave it to her, too.

"Never again," she said. "It's mine. Thought you said Herbert had it."

"It is yours, and I lied, for some reason."

R'lyeh had another coughing fit; between each violent exhalation, there was blankness—the pages of her so-called open book… there wasn't much written on the ones ahead.

"My name is R'lyeh Akkoro. I'm from Alluvia. My m-mom's name is Anoplo Akkoro and my d-dad's name is Iso Akkoro. I… want to be a badass librarian… and have people think I'm the b-best. I like horses. I like when it… rains." She coughed and fought to stay awake. "I don't like hurting people as much as I thought… I did. I liked… hurting myself… more.

"My best friend was a woman named Vrana, and t-this man named Atticus… or Gravedigger… or Skeleton… or…" She laughed. "He has a lot of names. But he was good to me."

The Skeleton held her closer.

"I'm thirteen years old, but… I think… because I'm so badass… I'll be fourteen now."

"You've earned it," the Skeleton said.

Snow blew into R'lyeh's eyes, and the world was rendered crystalline.

"What… what do I do?" R'lyeh closed her eyes.

"Let go," the Skeleton said.

"Will you come see me in the Membrane?"

"Don't fight and end up there. Go to the Abyss. Everyone's waiting."

"Okay," R'lyeh said.

As she settled into his bones, R'lyeh heard the sound of beating wings.

Thinking it was Vrana, she opened her eyes and saw that there was a giant bat flying above them, weeping its blood everywhere it went into the accumulating snow.

"What's Camazotz… doing here?" she asked.

The Skeleton took out a large fang from his cloak and held it out in front of R'lyeh. "She's our ride. Are you ready to go out in style?"

"Always."

R'lyeh closed her eyes. She could feel the humungous bat drawing closer, the power of its wings parting the wintry air, dusting the snow from the ground. The Skeleton shifted R'lyeh's deadening weight, and she could tell this by the pain he was inflicting on her as he was moving her to his arms.

In her final moments, R'lyeh saw Geharra's pit. It wasn't filled with bodies, but stars. She didn't recognize most of them, but there were a few that shone brighter than the others. Their light was a warm light, distant as it may have been. For the first time in a long time, R'lyeh stopped running. She went to the pit in her mind and met the past it harbored. She peered into its depths and let it have her. It was always hers, and she was always its. Of all the poisons she'd taken, the past was the only one that really mattered.

Something thundered in R'lyeh's ears. It sounded like the world was shattering in two. But she didn't care. She kept focusing on the sound of Camazotz's wings and telling herself they were Vrana's. She couldn't wait to see her again.

CHAPTER XXVII

Gisela had taken it upon herself to redecorate the spellweavers' lair. Their disk-shaped home inside Kistvaen had once been a plate upon which the gaudy niceties of the Old World had been served. It was a place, the things and the people imprisoned within it, that had been entirely fabricated by the elders of Caldera. It must've bothered them to have the spellweavers call their home a lair, because clearly, the elders had meant to make for them a museum, instead. The couches and embroidered chairs; the intricately woven rugs that covered the floor; the curtains that cordoned off sections of the lair with the ancient Roman, Greek, Japanese, and Indian images displayed across them; the desks and the dressers; the grandfather clocks and the newly installed chimes; the grand chandelier, hanging from the high ceiling, weeping candlewax like tears on the shackled below—all of it Aeson had assumed was a desperate attempt by the elders to misdirect themselves, the spellweavers, and others into thinking that what they were doing here was okay, comfortable.

But Gisela had torn everything apart, piece by piece, and covered it in the skin and bone, blood and gore of Verat and Enaar. And in doing so, she had revealed the truth of the elders' efforts: this museum wasn't a museum but a mirage; an image of their empathy warped by the volcanic light. It had to have been hours, if not days, since Gisela had slaughtered the other spellweavers. Not only had Anguis, Faolan, and Nuctea left the remains where they remained, but they had been held up here this entire time, watching Gisela, studying her, giving her a full-run of, arguably, one of the most important and dangerous places on the continent, as if they were curious to see what she might do with it.

Night Terrors weren't human, so they couldn't lay claim to such ideas as humanity, but they did have compassion, and even remorse or regret. Aeson had never known the elders to have any of these things, and watching them as they marched the soiled pentacle carved into the lair's floor, he realized they'd never had them to begin with. They weren't Corrupted, nor were they Night Terrors. They were something else entirely.

Vrana had never been to this place before, but Aeson could tell it somehow must've confirmed her suspicions about the treatment of spellweavers. He should've told her; he should've told her a lot of things.

Straight to the point, Vrana croaked, "What the hell is going on?"

Nuctea hummed behind her owl skull. "Look at you." She adjusted the headdress she wore; the heat inside the volcano was causing it to slip. "You are amazing."

Aeson's eyes roamed the lair. The spherical alcoves in the outskirts had gone dark; the black fires that had once burned there burned no more.

Faolan of the wolf was trotting through the filth that filled the pentacle's ridges. She said, "Aeson is amazing, too. You, both, have gone so far, and have seen so much." She shooed Gisela away as the blind, eighty-four-year-old crone came close to her. "You have what it takes to be elders."

Gisela scoffed and clapped her blood-caked hands together. She stripped off a piece of flesh from her shoulder and wiped her ass with it. Kistvaen rumbled, seemingly pleased with her depravity.

"Answer her," Aeson said, not to Faolan or Nuctea, but to Anguis, who was slithering around the center of the lair, where the spellweavers usually weaved.

Anguis stopped. "That's not your mask."

"It isn't," Aeson said.

Vrana's head tracked Gisela's movements. Hands clawed, she was poised to strike.

"She killed Verat and Enaar," Anguis said.

Gisela laughed and started fondling her breasts.

"How?" Sweat stung Aeson's eyes. "You keep her chained up. Did she break free?"

Gisela shook her head.

"We let her out," Faolan said, shit up to her knees in the trench where the spellweavers relieved themselves.

Vrana outstretched her wings; Pain's encrusted blood flaked off her feathers.

"What?" Aeson shouted. "What the hell? Why?"

"Verat had a stroke," Anguis said. "Without the third, keeping Kistvaen's illusion maintained is too strenuous for the other spellweavers."

"Gisela has always used violence as a way to bolster her abilities," Nuctea said. "We thought she could manage the illusion until replacements arrived if we let her have her way with Verat's body, and Enaar's."

Gisela started licking her fingers with loud, sloppy sounds.

Vrana moved closer to Aeson, her body between his and the cannibalistic spellweaver's.

"It did not work," Anguis said.

"No fucking shit," Vrana barked.

"Wait... wait," Aeson said, "but it's not just the illusion they have to maintain. If you don't get more spellweavers in here, the mountain is going to erupt."

Vrana drew a sharp breath.

"It will," Anguis said.

"It should have a very long time ago," Nuctea added.

Faolan tipped her wolf skull back and whispered, "We were wrong."

"No, wait." Aeson took out *The Blood of Before*. "You can't... What the hell's the point?"

The lair shook. Pieces of stone fell from the ceiling above. The grand chandelier shivered; one if its supports broke free from the stone and it went swinging sideways. It crashed into the rocks, into a million useless, pretty pieces.

"Kistvaen's magma has been building since the Trauma. When we found it, the crust was about to give way," Anguis said. "We did not mean to, but with the Blue Worm's weavings, we were able to contain the eruption. But the magma has continued to build. And now the restraints are free. What is the point, Aeson? To cover the land in lava, to blacken the skies in ash. To kill everyone and everything, and euthanize this existence for good."

Vrana made a clicking sound inside her beak.

Gisela mimicked it, and laughed.

Aeson couldn't tell what was burning hotter, him or the volcano. "Why now?" he said. He imagined beating Anguis' skull with *The Blood of Before*. "There's no reason..."

"There is," Nuctea said.

"There's every reason," Faolan continued. "How far did you get in that book?"

He squeezed it and said, "To where it's written in blood."

"That's where we have all read up to," Faolan said.

"The rest is gibberish. Insane ramblings in a language that existed in a time without time," Nuctea said. "To understand, you would have to go back, and be like Gisela."

Gisela nodded and collapsed. Her slick body made a smacking sound as she hit the stone floor. Eyes closing, she started to snore.

"We have fought for years to maintain the balance between the natural and the supernatural, but it was the internal battle that was the more important of the two," Anguis said. "The scales have shifted."

"Angheuawl..." Aeson caught his balance as the lair rumbled. "It's Angheuawl."

"The Night Terrors were already something of an endangered species," Nuctea said. "We tried with Lacuna, but how many Lacunans died in Angheuawl?"

"Hundreds," Aeson whispered.

"And those that didn't die are lost to us, in the thralls of the Void," Faolan said.

"We are nearing extinction." Anguis stepped up to the center of the lair and cast his beaming gaze upon Gisela. "We cannot reproduce. Those that we did create with the Blue Worm have been killed or made insane. We cannot live a long life. Those that do become as Gisela. Our time has always been limited. And now it has run out."

Vrana clicked her claws on the ground. "You're going to kill everyone because... we're dying out?"

Anguis laughed, said, "We are going to kill everyone because it is the kind thing to do."

Vrana started forward, screaming, "How can you even do something like this?"

Aeson looked at Faolan and Nuctea and nodded. Together, they reached to their stomachs and, with no effort at all, tore away the skin there. Except it wasn't skin. It was a porous material, like a sponge, and behind it, inorganic organs were lodged, pumping clear liquids into the tubing running out of them.

"Without a tongue, one can speak freely, I imagine," Nuctea said.

"Without a mind, one can think freely, I imagine," Faolan said.

"Without a soul, one can be free, I imagine," Anguis said.

"Homunculi." The words were barely words as they escaped Vrana's beak. "You're... you're homunculi."

"Every elder that obeys tradition is," Anguis said. "We can do what you cannot. We are what you and they were supposed to be."

"So close," Nuctea said.

"I could almost touch it," Faolan said.

The lair was beginning to fill with pressure. Behind the stones that surrounded them, they could hear something surging; a great swell in search of release.

"We need to get out of here," Vrana said.

"Not yet." Aeson threw the book at Anguis, but missed. "What the fuck is going on? Why did you give me this? Tell me!"

"The Night Terrors were not meant to survive," Anguis said, placing his fake skin back into his stomach. "They were experiments; man-made creations. They were created by Frederick Ødegaard, his wife, and their team in an attempt to perfect humanity. We were supposed to have all of the humans' best qualities, and none of their weaknesses. We were to be the paragons by which the human race would follow, for it had stagnated in a pool of its own selfishness and greed.

"Then the Vermillion God woke, and the humans rejected It and drove It back into Its slumber. It unleashed Its last teaching, the Trauma, upon the world. In that waking nightmare, the humans were reduced from billions to thousands and made Corrupted. The natural gave way to the supernatural. Though the Night Terrors' numbers were few, we flourished, and picked up the punishment of the Corrupted their God had left for them."

The ceiling split into hundreds of cracks. A large chunk of stone broke free and crashed into the ground, narrowly missing Nuctea. Despite almost dying, she didn't seem to care.

Anguis had to shout, because Kistvaen was tearing itself apart. "We were meant to be better, and so we created a culture around being better. The humans had created the Trauma, the ultimate example of their inferiority and need for guidance. Over time, thinking this, it became easy to convince ourselves we were necessary."

Faolan shouted over the rumbling, "Sounds nice, doesn't it?"

Nuctea joined Anguis. "If you tell yourself something long enough, you begin to believe it. But you cannot wash off the blood of before."

Anguis took off his snake mask and dropped it to the ground. It broke upon impact, and sent shards into the pentacle's trenches.

Vrana took Aeson's hand, gently, not violently, and said, "We need to leave right—"

"What else kills humans? What else wears flesh and bones?" Anguis asked through a toothy grin.

The sounds of Kistvaen's forthcoming eruption died away. Aeson stopped feeling the mountain tearing itself apart. He stopped seeing the lair, and the elders, and Gisela, and Vrana within it. His mind's eye closed, and when it opened again, he saw her, it, clad in flesh, armed with bone, dragging its dripping sex across the folds of his brain.

Vrana answered for him. "Flesh fiends," she said, dropping Aeson's hand. "We're flesh fiends."

"The flesh fiends were not meant to survive," Anguis said, steadying himself. "They were created by Frederick Ødegaard, his wife, and their team in an attempt to perfect humanity. We were supposed to have all of the humans' best qualities, but the experiment was a failure. We acquired only the worst that humanity had to offer. Hunger, lust, greed, selfishness, self-righteousness; unbridled, unrelenting violence. We were deformed, deranged. We bred quickly, and our lifespans were even quicker. Ødegaard tried to teach us, to control us, but we were unreachable. The need to kill and defile was too great.

"Those flesh fiends that had not escaped into the Old World were ordered to be terminated. Then the Vermillion God woke. In the chaos that followed, and the Trauma that twisted this world, the flesh fiends thrived. We murdered and raped our way across the continents, and because we often killed at night, the humans began calling us Night Terrors, instead."

The farthest wall in the lair caved-in. Steam and fire exploded through the fissure.

Aeson couldn't move. And neither would Vrana.

"The Trauma was long, and our evolution faster than most," Anguis said. "During the Trauma, some flesh fiends began to develop small communities. They began to control their urges. Slowly, over time, the need to kill became controlled, and the flaws of the original fiends were bred out. The longer we lived, the more civilized we became."

"When they say… our ancestors used to be much more bloodthirsty…" Aeson mumbled.

"They meant it literally," Nuctea said.

"Even now, we're not all that different," Faolan said. "We've just built a society around it and justified it."

"Flesh makes fiends of us all," Anguis said. "And we are fiends in this flesh. We became civilized, but the more we aged, the greater the likelihood those uncontrollably violent tendencies would emerge."

"Like Gisela," Vrana whispered.

"We had endured the apocalypse and our own biology. We went to the Dead City in search of answers and came back infected, and the plague of infertility spread through the villages. We could not live long, nor could we breed. We tried in Eld and Lacuna to repopulate our ranks, but it was never enough. We were not meant to survive, and it was not until now that we truly realized it.

"Caldera was built under Kistvaen because our predecessors knew that a day would come when we would need to be destroyed. Now, not only do we need to be destroyed, but so, too, does the rest of the world.

"The Vermillion God is waking. The Disciples of the Deep are gaining ground, while the Holy Order of Penance is sacrificing its people by the thousands to regain their monopoly on the religion of the world. The Disciples will win, once the swell of belief is too great for the God to ignore. It will wake and It will ensnare this world in Its vermillion grip. There will not be another Trauma. The Corrupted will yield. And there is nothing we can do about it. More than half of our people died in Angheuawl, or on the roads. Winnowers have taken Rime. Lacuna is gone. We will die out, and so, too, will the world. This world has been dying as long as it has been living. It will be better this way."

Another piece of stone broke free from the walls. Falling, it crushed Nuctea where she stood.

"Goddamn it," Vrana cried. "Aeson, fuck this. Let's go."

"Who are you?!" Aeson yelled.

Faolan went to the center where Gisela lay. The cannibal crone awoke immediately and started tearing her apart.

"How… how can you do this?" Aeson said.

"We are homunculi. We were born and raised in the mokita machines of Ødegaard's hospital. Vrana has seen them. The glass tubes filled with strange liquids in the hidden labs.

"We were the prototypes for the flesh fiends that followed. But we are without flesh. We are the teachers. We are the ones who make the decisions even the cruelest of beasts cannot. When the flesh fiends showed they could be more than instinct, we were the ones to give them purpose. Animal skulls instead of human skulls. Controlled killing rather than senseless killing. The entitlement never went away. We were always better, but it was okay, because no one said it was not.

"The scales are not balanced, you see—"

Gisela let out a gleeful scream as she plunged her hands down Faolan's throat, tearing her mouth agape.

"—but soon they will be."

"Aeson," Vrana growled, "please."

"There's nothing you can do anymore," Anguis said, going to Gisela and kneeling beside her, waiting to be dined upon. "The mass of the eruption will ruin this world. The ash will be enough to choke out all life. God will not claim this planet, and humanity will finally find perfection, in the calmness of the Abyss.

"Go, now, Aeson, with Vrana. Adelyn is looking for her, and I should like the two to be reunited, as we all will be, soon enough, in flames."

CHAPTER XXVIII

The Skeleton lifted R'lyeh's dead body and laid it over Camazotz's back. The bat twisted its head to have a look at its corpse cargo. Its eyes, small in comparison to its bulky head, sized the girl up. The Orphanage had a niche when it came to down-and-out kids who'd been cast aside. Was that sadness in those black orbs, or inky indifference?

Camazotz opened its mouth and bared its nearly toothless mouth. The Skeleton took the fang he'd used to call it here and wedged it back into the bat's mouth. It squeaked, pleased, and in return, left a drop of its blood upon his digits. Its blessing, its boon; a one-way ticket to immortality.

"Appreciate it," the Skeleton said. He wiped the blood on Camazotz's horned nose. "Little one's lived long enough."

The bat stared blankly at the Skeleton, its fetid, blood-fouled breath coloring the snow that fell around it. Camazotz didn't understand why he wouldn't save her. Truth be told, neither did he. He didn't understand much these days. The farther the Black Hour's growth spread across his body, the harder it became to make sense of his thoughts and whether or not they were his, or its. Every suggestion that seeped into his skull could've been of sinister intent. Herbert and Hex had called him paranoid. They weren't wrong about that.

Before mounting Camazotz, the Skeleton brushed R'lyeh's hair aside. Death never made anything pretty. The girl didn't wear It well. She was a slimy thing, with blotched cheeks and torn up lips. Fragile, too, like she might break if he didn't handle her with care. He kept wanting to call her Vale—the baby girl he'd lost—but that wouldn't be fair to her. She

389

wasn't his. They weren't the same.

You let her die, because you wish someone had let you die when you were young.

"That was years ago," the Skeleton said to the heart. "R'lyeh got dealt a raw deal. Worse than my own."

You could not save her. How will you save Clementine and Will again?

"They don't need saving. They just need to be rid of me, 'til I'm right." Camazotz glanced back, confused.

You will never be right. You cannot even remember why you abandoned them to Hex and that Cult.

"To get the weapons…"

That is not what you told R'lyeh.

"The shepherds are tracking me, not them."

You do not believe that.

"I don't trust myself around them, alright?" The Skeleton pulled the cloak closed, as if that would silence chaos. "I get suspicious."

We know.

"Get to thinking I brought them back to a worse kind of hell."

You did.

The Skeleton scoffed and mounted Camazotz's back. He tightened his legs around the bat's body the best that he could, and held onto R'lyeh for dear, albeit fabled, life.

"You know what… Shut up. Heard enough."

You are not sad she is dead.

The Skeleton ignored the Black Hour's attempts to get him good and pissed. He didn't have any skin, so it was easy to get under. With R'lyeh dead, he could offer her the kindness of touch he couldn't before. His hand pressed against her cheek; a firm grip, his bones encaging hers; a hug, which, leaning over, he gave her.

He was sad for the girl, though he couldn't show it as much as he would've liked. That part of him had gotten worse; however, when it came to emotional intelligence, he was, admittedly, dumber than a box of rocks. Might've been the moment when he was R'lyeh's age, and he killed his abusive mother for killing his abusive father. A thing like that would change a person. He went to the local pimp, Poe, for him to make it better, but instead he rubbed that blood in, deep, and blood became the feeling he felt on most occasions, if such a thing were possible.

Yeah, he was sad for R'lyeh, but Death had come many times for the girl before. The Skeleton, of all people, knew that if you refused Death enough, Death may not come back. Things without an end eventually lost their meaning. He'd lost his end; thought it would've been Clementine and Will, but Hex knew the horror he'd become and made no bones about sharing it with them. Maybe he'd made them horrors—Clementine and Will—to make it easier on himself. Or maybe he just wanted to save them again. The dead were known to dance in loops. They laid claim to routine, like Gary had with the graveyard.

The Skeleton was dead, not immortal. There was a difference. If he'd seen it sooner, he wouldn't be here, in the Dead City, with another dead body before him. He'd be amongst the living, learning how to live again.

"Son of a bitch," the Skeleton said. He was a few traumas shy of psychosis, he knew that, but damn, he should've realized this sooner. "I'm a moron."

Camazotz huffed in agreement. It stretched its wings and arched its back and waited for the Skeleton's command.

It is the flesh that fools you.

The purity of bone, the Skeleton thought, touching his chest.

Flesh holds all the secrets. With bone, everything is laid bare. If Clementine and Will did not have their flesh, you would know the truth of their souls.

"I am not going to flay the falsehoods from their bodies."

Fancy talk. You sound like us.

"Always whispering in my ear." The Skeleton corrected his speech. "Can't be helped. Come on, Cammie, let's get."

Camazotz reared back and began beating its mangy wings, creating a blinding wall of snow. Clinging tightly with his legs, the Skeleton leaned forward and pulled R'lyeh's body against his, until her head was lodged underneath his ribcage. He pressed his palm over the Red Worm's stone, making sure that it wouldn't slip off her body. She'd earned it, and he planned on burying it with her in Alluvia. He'd never been to a Night Terror village before. Shame there wouldn't be anyone there to greet him, to give him the chance to talk-up R'lyeh and all she'd done. Dreams of being a librarian never really came to fruition for the Octopus, but being a badass? Never broke a sweat trying. The Skeleton couldn't be sad for her, but he could be her blood and spread it around. It was, after all, the substance of her making; and the sustenance of her undoing.

What about all the weapons? What about all the guns and the vehicles and the fuel depots and that helicopter you saw? The bat

cannot carry all that.

Higher and higher they lifted into the air. The peninsula shrank beneath the Skeleton, from miles in size to meters. Camazotz braced itself against winter's current and rode the frigid tide. The Skeleton held on tightly to R'lyeh, but it wasn't needed; the cold and her skin had begun to form an icicle stitch between her and the bat's fur. Soon, if he wasn't careful, whether he wanted it to happen or not, she'd be a part of Camazotz's Orphans, for the bat had grown fat with the blood of Gallows; in particular, the blood of Penance, and the blood of Alluvia. To think there might be a possibility the girl would be resurrected in a vampyric communion involving the blood of her dead mom and dad didn't sit well with the Skeleton.

"I'll come back," he said, finally acknowledging the heart. "Got to check on Clementine and Will."

You heard what the Virions said. The Green Worm imbues everything that it touches. You will risk exposing the world again.

"Only the unbelievers. Everyone believes in God. It's just no one is going to want It."

She is a liability. Her body is a breeding ground.

"It won't be a problem," the Skeleton said. "If it would be, you wouldn't have said something."

You're getting smarter, country boy.

"I expect that I am."

The Skeleton turned around and gave the Dead City a good gander. Sickly pillars of smoke were pouring out of the Virions' home base beneath the collapsed skyscrapers. He could hear the whirring of their spacecraft, and it didn't sound any better than it had before. He didn't really care if they made their pilgrimage to the stars. In fact, he was kind of hoping they wouldn't. R'lyeh's death, in a way, was on their mutated hands. He wanted some good, old-fashioned revenge before the reckoning.

Clementine and Will would've liked to have seen this place, the Skeleton thought to himself, as Camazotz made of it a miniature with distance. Will always fancied himself something of an archeologist; those holes he'd dig while digging graves years ago led him straight to Ronny's shop and ancient wares. It was there he learned about machinery and inventions; and it was from his son that the Skeleton was educated on such matters. Ships had always been Will's obsession. Vessels to take him places that weren't filled with shit-kickers and dust. He would've liked the spacecraft. A ship for the sea above.

While Clementine's fascination with the Old World came mostly from trying to learn as much as she could about the lives of those who'd lived in it. The Skeleton reckoned she wanted to see if she could find a kindred spirit amongst those millions of spirits; if at some point, someone like her had lived, and if they had, what they'd done with their life until their death. Clementine only managed to connect with those who bore the same scars as her; they were wounds of initiation into the coven of hurt women, of which she was the sole member and leader. He should've brought her something back, a souvenir of some sort. The corpse of R'lyeh was the only thing he had to offer, and while she was a hurt woman through and through, it wasn't the kind of memento those with flesh knew what to do with.

The Skeleton kicked Camazotz's sides. The bat slowed down to spite him. They were crossing the ocean now, and headed southward.

He spied hints of Geharra behind the ragged mountain range, and wondered if the Scavengers and the Mer had stopped beating around the bush and just started the beatings.

Looking to the Frozen North, he saw the endless, glacial fields of Hoarfrost bore the brunt of the snowstorm sweeping across it. Not much could claim dominion in that bitter domain but him and stubborn sons of bitches like him.

Glancing east, he couldn't catch much. The land, in winter, lost much of its detail and most of its color. He could make out the Blasted Wood-land and the mountains near the Southern Cradle, but even then, he wasn't sure. The world was round, but he tended to see things flatly. A series of consequences, or problems followed by solutions. Angheuawl was, at least, hours away, but his pressured mind kept seeing it every-where—on the coast near the Elys, or the hardened crust of the Dires. He'd done the deed of securing armaments; next came rescuing his family from the peril he'd put them in. Salvation had a sweetness that made his black tongue prickle. It would be the last time, he told himself, that he did this to them. But even then, he knew he'd have to leave them again. To go back for the weapons. To go to the Nameless Forest. To go to Eldrus. To go wherever it took to keep the hunger for life at bay.

Would it be easier if you knew they could not die? If you knew they were like you?

"No," the Skeleton said.

There is only one way to find out.

"I do not think I want to know the mystery of what moves my bones."
There you go, talking like us again.
"Oh."
We do not believe you.
"Don't care," he said, correcting his accent again.
Tear us out. Throw us into the sea.
"You'd like that, wouldn't you?"
You wouldn't. That's why you haven't.
Camazotz jerked. She reared up, threw her wings back. They caught the air and she slowed down. The Red Worm's stone slid down R'lyeh's chest, off it, and—
The Skeleton grabbed it before it went singing slaughter to the world below.
"The hell is wrong with you?" He fixed the stone back around R'lyeh's neck and wrapped his arms around her and it. "What's the matter?"
Animals can sense danger.
The Skeleton's eyes rolled around in his skull. He consulted Geharra behind him, the vague, jagged outline of the Heartland before him. Gut sinking, not that he had a gut, he strained his vision, trying, though he knew it was impossible, to see the Nameless Forest from here, thinking that the Vermillion God had begun to stir.
The danger is from within.
"Cammie." The Skeleton grabbed a tuft of fur. "What—"
Camazotz twisted its neck around. The bat's beady eyes were blacker than black; that foul extract of fear itself. Its nose was sniffling, the stench of terror setting on alarm all its senses. She opened her mouth, bloody blessing running over her fractured teeth and scarified gums, and whispered, "Don't."
The Skeleton, taken aback, reached for his chest and gripped the Black Hour's growth.
"What the hell is—"
A flash of light. Shades of red and black. A burning pillar, like one of the supports of hell itself, tearing through the earth.
A boom. An explosion, like a summation of all thunders of all storms. Hell's blaring horns, raging across the continent, beating what it touched into concussions.
A crack. Hundreds of them, like whips; the sounds of demonic taskmasters setting on new, frightened subjects.
The Skeleton's jaw dropped open. In the Southern Cradle, a volcano

had erupted. Magma was spewing out of it in violent, melting arterial patterns. Even from here, hours away, he could see it lobbing massive amounts of lava, dousing and destroying everything they came into contact with.

And then there was the ash. The great, bulbous, boiling pillar of ash, filling the sky, covering the sky, as if the sky had a ceiling and it couldn't escape. The outpour was endless. Winter had been white. Now it was black.

"Angheuawl…" the Skeleton whispered.

The clouds overtook the volcano. The fiery vomit of Kistvaen became glowing shapes behind the choking plume.

"Clem…" The Skeleton gripped the Black Hour's growth on his ribs harder. "Will."

Something snapped inside the Skeleton's skull. The locks he'd had in place inside his mind were undone by the catastrophe, and broken for good by the guilt he'd sown. Angheuawl was under the volcano, not far from its liquefying grip. Clementine and Will. He'd put them there. They were there. He'd put them there. They were there because of him. He would never reach them in time. And if they couldn't die, they'd be just as bone as him, just as blood as him. He had sent them there. They were there—

—because of you.

The Skeleton screamed.

Camazotz bucked to break off his tightened hold, but he wouldn't budge. She started to squeak and cry pathetically.

He tipped his head back and ripped the Black Hour's heart out of his chest. The organ's growths shot up the Skeleton's neck and into his head, and then went downwards, to his feet, until, like Winter's snow, like the land, like the bodies of his loves, his bones were charred black.

"Don't," Camazotz rumbled.

But the Skeleton didn't hear her. He didn't hear anything anymore. With the heart raised high, he dug his fingers into the bat, steered her towards the volcano, and started raining Black Hours down upon the world—laughing and crying, but mostly crying, as he did so.

CHAPTER XXIX

Vrana grabbed Aeson by the hand and tore out of the spellweavers' lair. Behind them, the ceiling opened. A tongue of magma lashed the room, and Anguis and the others were consumed by Kistvaen's unsustainable hunger.

She could tell she was hurting Aeson. Pain had been her mentor. His hand in her claws, arm stretched to the point of dislocation—Vrana ran him through the wispy portal to this place. Coming out on the other side, they hoofed it up the hill of polished stone and prismatic pillars. Fire spewed from widening vents. Lava leapt at them, and it lapped at their feet. Kistvaen wasn't erupting. Kistvaen was dying. From what Aeson and the elders had said, this should've happened long ago. Its life support had been pulled. And so, too, had the Night Terrors'.

They reached the top of the hill. Aeson went down on all fours and frantically worked the puzzle of the obsidian boulders. Vrana stood over him, her wings outstretched, bearing the brunt of the rocks that broke free from above. He was her way out. And she was his. They had to get out together, or they wouldn't at all. In here. In everything.

"Fuck… fuck." Aeson made fists and wiped his eyes. His hands were shaking, and they kept slipping from the boulder. "I can't… I can't."

Vrana didn't want to lie to him and tell him that everything would be okay. Most of what she had known about herself, her birth, her mother and father, and her people had ended up turning into a lie. The same could be said for him and for the struggles he faced, in his mind and memories, where flesh fiends roamed beyond just the helixes of his genes. Lies were like the fingers of Death snipping souls: they could only take so many cuts before the whole of their beings came crashing down.

"There, there. I think…" Aeson took a sharp breath and grabbed onto Vrana's ankle. "Okay, okay!"

Black water formed around their feet. As Kistvaen heaved, launching them off the hill, the black water from the boulder reached out and pulled them into its shallow depths. In one moment, they were in the heart of the growing inferno. The next, they were in the house of the elders, tearing across the seamless room, out into the halls, and towards the doorway rimmed in vermillion light.

Aeson stopped before they reached the front of the house and planted his feet like a pouting child.

Vrana, thinking of her mother, hadn't noticed at first. Reaching the door, almost tearing it open, she spun around and croaked, "What's wrong?"

For the first time since he'd saved her, Aeson looked the way she imagined he would. The way she expected him to look after the all the horrors he'd seen and experienced. Gone was the strength. Gone was the grit. She knew he'd been putting on an act, pretending to be better than he was. But Anguis' news had broken him. He was bent, and panting. Bjørn's bear mask somehow didn't fit him as well as it had before. The firelight from outside filled in the emaciated pockets of his frame. His hands were clawed, too, like hers, and his features were pulled tightly, as if something was beneath his skin—the something beneath all their skin—and it was trying to come through.

"What's the point?" he said with a whimper. "It's just like I said. It's the same bullshit, always!"

Mom, Vrana thought. The house of the elders shook violently. All around them, she could hear things breaking, falling from shelves. Floorboards buckled. A flash of flames exploded out of the seamless room they'd just left; a searing discharge from the portal yet to be closed. *I have to find you, Mom.*

Aeson held his head. "I can't be one of them."

"You're not." Vrana ran for him.

Aeson backpedaled. "We all are!"

I swear to god, Aeson…

"They made me Archivist." He bit on his lip until he drew blood. "Do you… do you think that's why my parents wanted me to die with them?"

The house of the elders sank. A portion of the floor split apart and fell into the pit that had opened up beneath it.

"I don't know!" Vrana screamed at him. "But I don't want to die right here. I have to find my mom. Aeson..." She took both his hands, and then pulled him into her arms. "You're not an Archivist. You're not the elders' lapdog. You're as much a flesh fiend as me or anybody else. You beat Death... twice. What the fuck are you doing going at It for a third time?"

Aeson, shaking, said, "I don't want to become her."

He felt so much smaller in her arm; like the subterranean child he used to be. Alone, under the earth, with only his thoughts and the written word regarding dead worlds. His life support had been pulled, too. And right now, she wasn't enough.

"I don't want to become this," Vrana said, pointing to her feathers and beak. "But I have. And I haven't. We're both fucked up. At least we'll be fucked up together."

Aeson stepped back, nodding. "I don't know how to stop this."

Vrana didn't know if he was talking about Kistvaen's eruption, or his change. And she didn't care. She took off for the front door, and he followed behind.

Outside, there was screaming. And bodies. Not one separate from the other, but melded, entwined; a metamorphosis. The Night Terrors were not only Night Terrors, but a surging stream of unrelenting terror and dread broken down to their baser being. Under the red sky, upon the shaking earth, they crawled and they cried and tore at themselves and one another, as they moved through the streets and through the houses, deciding what to take and if they wanted to stay. They didn't turn on each other, but they seemed to turn on themselves. They became the skulls they wore, and moved like those animals—be it beast, bird, or reptile—through Caldera and its fields.

Vrana saw them as flesh fiends, because she knew they were flesh fiends. Her father had regressed, but that could've been blamed on the Blue Worm and the birthing process. If Kistvaen went off, what would the survivors become? Without the homunculi to shape them, what cruel forms would they take? Aeson was right. She couldn't tell him he was.

"Do you need anything?" Vrana screamed over the cacophony.

Aeson shouted, "No, just you," and took the lead.

Vrana darted through Caldera, somehow never keeping up with Aeson. Her talons clicked against the warming earth, and she caught the gazes of her fellow villagers. Some pointed. Some shouted blame. A few called out her name. But no one stopped.

"Mom!" Vrana cried, her house in sight. "Mom! Mom! Are you—"
A flash of light. Shades of red and black, in a mire of Void and Abyss.
Vrana and Aeson looked to Kistvaen.

A boom. An explosion, like a summation of all thunders of all storms.
And they were flattened to the ground.

A crack. Hundreds of them, like whips scoring the backs of the thousands who'd dared to survive the Trauma.

Vrana pushed herself off the ground and staggered as she took small steps. But the world was quickly darkening. Aeson was disappearing in that darkness. And so was her home.

She made it to Aeson, the air becoming so much hotter and harder to breathe, and together, they cast their eyes to the sky and witnessed the hell coming out of the heavens.

In a roiling cocoon of smoke and ash, great gouts of lava spewed from Kistvaen's peak. The force of the eruption sent the glowing molten cords miles into the air, and in every direction, for as far as Vrana could see. Down the side of the volcano, pyroclastic flows were gaining speed and mass, consuming or obliterating everything the avalanche of ash, lava, and gas came into contact with. A large flow, already the size and span of Caldera, was racing eastward, back the way they'd come, as if Nature meant to wipe from its wilds the Cult of the Worms' outposts, from Llyn to Angheuawl.

Hot chunks of lava rained down upon the village. Vrana came to and hurried for her house. She and Aeson ducked and weaved through the villagers and the pelting rocks ablaze. Some weren't as nimble as them, though. One after the other, Night Terrors crashed into the ground, as the burning hail bore into their bodies and melted them from the inside out.

"Mom!" Vrana yelled, unable to hear her own voice.

Aeson stopped a few feet from her house. He was waving at someone. He'd seen something.

Vrana caught up with him. Hot ash blanketed Caldera. She could barely breathe.

The front door to Vrana's house opened. Adelyn stepped out, a satchel in her hand. She wasn't wearing her raven mask. Her eyes immediately met Vrana's.

Vrana stopped dead in her tracks. Mom. Her mom. She was okay. And shit, she had to see her like this. A big fucking bird. She had to be strong. She couldn't doubt herself, not like Aeson doubted himself. She'd have to fly them both out of here. It was the only way, and if she had to choose…

"Here!" Adelyn threw the satchel at Aeson.

He caught it. "What is this?"

"What we'll need!" Adelyn smiled. She mouthed Vrana's name and ducked back into the house.

As Aeson slung the satchel over his shoulder, Vrana ran to the house, to her mother. "Mom, come on!" she yelled, trying her best to make her voice sound like it used to.

"Hold your horses," Adelyn said, still out of sight.

Vrana, a foot from the doorstep, stopped as Adelyn reappeared, a bag in each hand.

"My girl," Adelyn said, arms going limp.

Ash wept from Vrana's feathers. Tears leapt from Vrana's eyes. She reached for her mother—

—and a massive wave of lava slung across Caldera, slamming into Vrana's home, taking it and her mother with it into a burning pool of fire.

Aeson grabbed Vrana from behind, yanking her away before the magmatic splash hit her.

Mom, Vrana thought, her eyes fixed on the place her home had been, where her mother had been. Now it was nothing more than a black, burning smear; like the trunk of a tree severed by lightning. *Mommy.* Her body shook, and feathers fell from her flesh. She clutched her claws so hard into her palms she bled. *Momma.*

And like that, like Aeson before, she was made a child again.

"No," Aeson said, hyperventilating. "No, no, no."

The fiery expulsions of the initial eruption had gone as high as they could, and now they were falling back to the ground, covering vast areas in lava.

Screams, and the sizzling hiss of souls succumbing to the elders' final solution. Vrana should have felt something—the heat, the hate; the need for flesh and blood in her mouth—but there was nothing. She had saved the love inside her from the torture of Pain and Joy, but now it was gone. R'lyeh had her pit. Aeson had his flesh fiend. And Vrana? Her hell was a smoldering pool of lava and pieces of her mother floating inside it.

The pyroclastic flow had broken apart. The burning mass had scored its way down Kistvaen's south face; it was seconds away from Caldera. If they stayed, it would destroy them. It would destroy all of them. They would be assimilated into it, just as they had assimilated humanity's culture into their own. History would make no note of their accomplishments, for they had accomplished nothing. Their legacy was lunacy.

Vrana grabbed Aeson and pushed off the ground. Her wings, heavy with ash, struggled in the ascent. Carelessly, she dodged the falling lava. She could tell Aeson was beating out fires that had started in her feathers from the debris, but she didn't care. Instead, she kept thinking of Adelyn, and how she had said Vrana's name, and how it was Vrana who had reached out to her, and not the other way around.

Before they were overtaken by the clouded sky, Vrana looked down one last time. An impossible heat washed over her. Black fire poured in melting waves over the mountain range. And where the vermillion veins had grown around the area, the waves were halted, for the growths had become fists, and they held portions of the flows in their grip.

Out of the south came the clapping of hooves.

CHAPTER XXX

The Vermillion God stirred. In Its slumber, It felt want. Long had it been since the Vermillion God felt such a want, such a need. At first, It did not wake, not fully. Instead, It flexed Its veins and was surprised to find how far they'd spread. In Its grasp, there was a world. A world of want, and desperate need.

The blood of before had supped from Its veins. Those It'd chosen and bestowed Its crimson gift upon had drunk in Its communion. The Vermillion God was a God in and of Itself; every mouth and whisper could be accounted for, and every vein counted. A mouth and whisper were gone, sent out into the world, and some of the Worms of Its belly had not yet returned. The Harbinger had heralded Its arrival. The Worms had made right the soil. And the descendants of the Chosen had supped from Its blood.

It was they who spoke to the Vermillion God, the crimson-colored, and they did so with God's blood in their hearts and in their mouths. The request was simple, and it was always the same. "God, help us!" they cried in a unified chorus, their suffering giving to the Vermillion God the greatest of exultations. It searched their beliefs for weakness, but their devotion displayed little desperation. The want was real. The need was palpable. The Vermillion God swirled the faith inside Its maw and found its flavor favorable.

Curious, the Vermillion God emitted a small pulse of Its power. It traveled through the endless expanse of heaven and the ruined worlds collected inside. To the Nameless Forest the signal went. The discharge thereafter was weak, still dampened by the incomprehensible chaos

Time's tapeworm had disgorged upon that gateway. It was open, but the conditions were unclear. Clarity was key. Tradition a necessity.

The Harbinger had been successful, and the belief that this mouth and whisper had propagated was stronger than the Vermillion God had known in eons. It was nearly unanimous. Not even the White Worm's defiance could tarnish the taste of this new congregation.

The Vermillion God, hardly conscious, formed a word and gave it to the shadows to carry. The dead were drawn to the Speaker, for the dead were convinced it would be the Speaker who would save them from their Hell. They were Its subjects. They were bound to Its will. The Vermillion God could tell that the shadows, those heretics of old, had been busy while It slept. Many were missing, and there was much joy amongst their endless ranks. They had found the Speaker, and they delivered Its message to the Speaker, but the Speaker did not respond. Audra, her name was Audra, and when the shadows filled her mind with Its message, she screamed.

The Harbinger had been successful. The want was great. The devotion would be complete. But the Speaker had yet to be brought into the fold. Clarity was key, and it was clear the necessity of tradition had not been followed.

The Vermillion God began to slip into a slumber...

...and then, much to Its own surprise, It opened one of Its many eyes and answered Its Disciples' call.

The Vermillion God awoke. All of Its eyes snapped open. The halo of smoke that crowned Its head began to spin. It stretched Its gargantuan arms and splayed Its fingers—all sixteen of them, fused and unfused. It cleared Its throat of the carnage still lodged within by vomiting half of the Old World onto Its throne of uncountable bones. Then It stretched Its wings—those dusty, reptilian continents of membranous flesh—and spread wide their span.

The Vermillion God placed Its hands upon Its knees and straightened Its back. The thousands of vermillion veins attached went taught, but none broke, for the belief that fueled them had hardened their casings. Satisfied with their strength, It stood tall in the Red Heaven, and the sounds of Its bones cracking and popping shattered the cities It had collected below.

The shadows swarmed the Vermillion God, to give witness to Its waking, to feed Its ego their woe. They formed mountains with their forms, as if they meant to reach out and prevent It from surfacing. But It had made Its decision. To the world It would give one last time their deity.

The Vermillion God flexed Its muscles and fell into the veins that webbed Its back. It searched inside Itself for permission, and Itself, It gave Itself permission.

With belief and purpose, the Vermillion God wrapped all of Its arms around Itself and exerted Its will. Across the continent, the vermillion veins tightened their hold on the land, while others fought to control the catastrophe that threatened to kill it.

The Vermillion God propelled itself backwards, through the Red Heaven. It tore through the ground, millions of miles at a time, through space unfathomable and laws incalculable, until It burst through the sands of the Ossuary and was lifted high into the sunless sky. The frontier had shifted, It saw, for the way to Heaven had not been upon this plane before. The change was unexpected, not in accordance with tradition, but the sands of the Ossuary were inviting—the bones that comprised its sands a testament to its allure—and many more bones would be required if this orb were to hold Its attention.

Reeled backward by the thousands of miles of thick and long vermillion veins, God adjusted Its shape and size to accommodate this laughably small world. With Its spiderous eyes, it spied the object of Its flock's worry and snorted. Fire on the horizon. A volcano smothering the land in ash. These creatures could not be expected to survive alone. They were too weak, and they were too stupid. Their need for God was the same as their need for air.

The vermillion veins pulled God over hundreds of miles, through the southern reaches, towards Kistvaen. Approach slowing, the vermillion veins had shifted and spun themselves around the surrounding area of the volcano, forming a funnel, forming a throne.

It knew It could be seen by Its Disciples below, for belief had bolstered to intoxicating levels. The Vermillion God, ever-proud, unraveled the tentacles from Its body and gave to Its dutiful audience a show of their size and reach. Those before, in the world of Old, had forgotten Its power and challenged God to display It. This world of New would know Its power, and the Trauma It would inflict upon them, should they forget it, would resonate through the stars for eons to come.

The veins tightened to their snapping point. It passed over the lava-covered ruins of Caldera. With Kistvaen completely encased in a throbbing prison of blood, the Vermillion God took Its seat upon Its throne and stifled the flames and ash that would have undoubtedly annihilated this mewling congregation.

The Vermillion God dug Its feet into the cooling lava where Caldera had been and placed Its hands upon Its legs. There It sat—the dead at Its feet, the living on their knees—towering high above the land. God outstretched Its many arms and numerous tentacles, made dark the world with the shadows they cast, and to Itself began to think wickedly.

TO BE CONCLUDED

YOU HAVE BEEN READING

"THE CULTS OF THE WORM."

GLOSSARY

GLOSSARY

The Abyss: Where all who die are said to go.

Amon Ashcroft: The former Archivist of Eldrus.

Arachne: Half-human, half-spider creatures from Atlach.

Alexander Blodworth: Understudy of Samuel Turov, an exemplar of Penance. He was given the task of going to Geharra to create a smokescreen for the disappearance of the Holy Child. Instead, he planted the Crossbreed in the city-state's sewer system and used it to control the entire populace. Along with the people of Alluvia, a neighboring Night Terror village to the city, Geharra's population was sacrificed by Alexander to birth the Red Worm.

Alluvia: The nearest Night Terror village to Geharra. It is the home of R'lyeh.

The Anointed One: Harbinger for the Disciples of the Deep.

Angheuawl: A small mining town in Kistvaen's range. The hometown of Hex and Ichor.

Ashen Man: His real name is Seth Barker. Partner of Herbert North. He was a supernatural investigator from the twentieth century who was investigating deaths and disappearances in the town Nachtla. There, he discovered the Witch, and fell in love with her. She took him into the Void and transformed him into one of her grotesque servants.

Audra: King Edgar's sister. The only other surviving member of the royal family. She is a gifted botanist and has the ability to communicate with and manipulate the shadows of the Deep. She was allowed to escape from her confines in Pyra after being sent there by Alexander Blodworth as a prisoner.

The Binding Road: A road, much like the Spine, that cuts through the Nameless Forest. It is one of the few places untouched by the Forest's chaos.

Black Hour: A temporal aberration that occurs at midnight and lasts for one hour. During this period of time, anything that has happened, will happen, or may never happen is possible.

Bloodless: A mythological plant, like the Crossbreed, that is said to be capable of draining an entire town's worth of blood in one night.

Blue Worm: A Worm of the Earth that was awoken on Lacuna by the Night Terrors to learn ancient knowledge. The Blue Worm taught the Night Terrors about magic, as well as how to procreate more effectively.

Cadence: The small southern village where Vrana leaves the little boy who she later learns was the Holy Child. Upon learning the Holy Child is there, Penance rides into the town, kills everyone, and returns the Holy Child to Penance.

Caldera: Vrana's home, and the southern-most Night Terror village. The village is built at the base of Kistvaen, a massive mountain.

Corrupted: A derogatory term used by the Night Terrors to identify humans. Humans are called this due to the crimson pigmentation in the skin of their right arms. The Night Terrors believe this defect is evidence of humanity's predisposition to violence; they use this as justification to murder the humans.

Corruption: A genetic marker created by the Vermillion God to identify Its followers.

Crossbreed: A massive plant created from ingredients that are not supposed to work together. It secretes fluids that cause those who ingest them to become extremely susceptible to suggestion.

Dead City: An Old World city of skyscrapers and modern technology that is unreachable due to the poisonous fumes that cover the peninsula it sits upon.

Deimos: A Night Terror who wears a bat skull. He was a watcher of Geharra. His husband, Johannes, was killed by Corrupted. He hunted down Johannes' killers, but in doing so neglected his duties of keeping watch over Geharra. This allowed Penance to enter the city and take over its people. He was last seen escaping Pyra with Lucan and Audra.

Derleth: A Night Terror who wears an eel skull. R'lyeh had a crush on him. He is responsible for tricking R'lyeh into planting the Crossbreed's roots in Alluvia's water supply, thus giving Alexander Blodworth the ability to easily take over the village on his way to Penance.

The Disciples of the Deep: Eldrus' new religion.

The Divide: The massive river that cuts through the content, separating the snowy lands of Penance from the Heartland.

The Dread Clock: Rumored to be the origin of the Black Hour; a grandfather clock once located deep in the Nameless Forest. Now, the heart of the Black Hour resides in the Skeleton's chest.

Edgar: The youngest of the royal family of Eldrus. He became King of Eldrus by murdering his family and overtaking the Nameless Forest.

Eldrus: The northern city-state that sits above the Heartland. It is governed by a monarchy that is led by King Edgar.

Exemplars: Six individuals who are meant to be the embodiment of a certain skill or trait. They are meant to be examples for the people of Penance to follow.

Flesh fiends: Subterranean creatures with a conflicted mythology. They wear the flesh and body parts of their victims. When a Corrupted and a Night Terror mate, there is a chance a flesh fiend will be born. They were last spotted in the sacrificial pit of Geharra, as well as near the island of Lacuna.

Geharra: The western-most city-state. The Night Terrors favor this city due to its lack of interest in war and expansion. Now, due to Alexander Blodworth, the entire population is dead; they have become one with the Red Worm.

The Heartland: The lifeblood of Eldrus; many towns and villages exist here, including Gallows, Bedlam, Nyxis, Hrothas, Islaos, and Cathedra.

Herbert North: Seth Barker's (the Ashen Man) partner in supernatural investigations. Freed from the Membrane with the Skeleton and his family and now a part of the Marrow Cabal.

Holy Child: Believed to be the speaker for Penance's god. Only the Mother

413

Abbess is higher than him in importance in the Holy Order of Penance. Samuel Turov stole the Holy Child away into the South for unknown reasons, and kept him there until Vrana killed Samuel. His name is Felix, and his religion is a lie.

Ichor: Hex's brother whose whereabouts are unknown. He and Hex have a troubled relationship where in which they play game to inflict the maximum amount of pain upon one another.

Johannes: A Night Terror who wears a fox skull. He was Deimos' husband.

Kistvaen: The massive mountain that sits behind Caldera. It may be a dormant or extinct volcano.

Lacuna: An island off the eastern coast. It sits within the Widening Gyre, and it is hidden from prying eyes by spellweavers. The Blue Worm was awakened on this island, and used by Mara and other Night Terrors to learn its secrets, as well as to discover a way to repopulate the Night Terror people.

Lucunans: Also know as children of Lacuna, these individuals were born and bred on Lacuna for the purpose of not only repopulating the Night Terrors, but to also act as sleeper agents in Corrupted cities due to their ability to pass for human.

Lotus: The mayor of Threadbare.

Lucan: A Night Terror who wears a beetle skull. He escaped Pyra with Deimos and Audra, albeit badly injured.

The Maiden of Joy: Also known as Crestfallen, Joy, or Adelaide. She is the sister of Pain. She has been reunited with her sister in the Void.

Mara: A Night Terror who wears a mask made out of centipedes. She was in control of Lacuna's fertility project. She has had run-ins with the Witch in the past.

The Marrow Cabal: A resistance group led by the Skeleton and Hex. Notable members include R'lyeh, Elizabeth, Miranda, Warren, James, and Herbert North. And, of course, Mr. Haemo.

The Membrane: A plane that exists between life and death; an area that may connect to additional planes and horrible dwellings. The dead pass through here.

Mother Abbess Justine: The ultimate authority of the Holy Order of Penance. Also known as the Hydra of Penance. She is the White Worm of the Earth.

Nacthla: A small, abandoned town where it is believed a portal may exist into the Witch's Void.

The Nameless Forest: Like the Black Hour, anything is possible here; except the Nameless Forest is not bound by time, so the chaos it contains is constant. It is from here the vermillion veins are said to originate. Now the Dread Clock has been taken out of it, the creatures inside are free to escape.

Night Terror: A race of humanoids whose entire culture and purpose is to understand and murder the Corrupted. They are believed to be supernatural creatures, though their origins are a mystery. The only actual observable difference between Night Terrors and Corrupted is that Night Terrors lack Corruption.

Old World: The world before the Trauma.

Ossuary: A massive desert located at the southern-most point of the continent. No one goes there, and nothing is said to thrive there.

Penance: The eastern-most city-state. It is the home of the Holy Order of Penance.

Pyra: The headquarters for the Holy Order of Penance.

Red Worm: A Worm of the Earth that was summoned from the ten thousand dead that had been raped and murdered in the bowels of Geharra. It was killed by the Skeleton in Gallows.

R'lyeh: A thirteen-year-old Night Terror who wears an octopus as a mask. One of the few survivors from the genocide of Geharra. Her hometown is Alluvia. She was Vrana's companion. She is now a member of the Marrow Cabal.

Samuel Turov: The Exemplar of Restraint. He stole the Holy Child as means by which to stage an attack on Geharra. He was killed by Vrana.

Scavengers: A splinter group of the Lillians (who were an older incarnation of the Holy Order of Penance). They reside outside Geharra, where they worship a large, achromatic tower. They believe god lives inside the tower.

Shadows: Remnants of the unbelievers that were killed and sentenced to eternal damnation by the Vermillion God. They reside in the Membrane, but are able to communicate with Audra.

Silver Necklaces with (colored) gems: Objects which are essential in the rituals used to summon the Worms of the Earth. When a Worm is summoned, it leaves behind a sealing stone, which is used to put the Worm back to sleep. When a Worm is put back to sleep, it leaves behind a silver necklace.

Six Pillars: An older name of Penance.

The Skeleton: A mysterious individual who Vrana sees twice in her journey. She meets him once in the Black Hour, and once again on the island of Lacuna. The Skeleton was instrumental in leading the failed rebellion against King Edgar.

Spellweavers: Individuals who are capable of magic.

The Spine: A massive highway system that once spanned the entire continent but has since fallen into disrepair.

The Trauma: A catastrophic event of unknown origin that has led the world to the state it is in now.

The Void: The home of the Witch.

The Woman in White Satin: Another name for the Maiden of Joy. She is an ancient witch. She ruled over the Nameless Forest for many years. Her sons acted as wardens over the various places in the Nameless Forest.

The Worms of the Earth: Biological weapons of destruction brought about by ritualistic depravity and sacrifice. They are powerful creatures that have to be sustained by death. One Worm generally provokes the birth of another Worm.

Vermillion Veins: Growths thought to only exist in the Nameless Forest. They are the veins of the Vermillion God and a physical representation of Its influence in the world.

Victor Mors: A philosopher who was assassinated for his studies into the Membrane and the Worms of the Earth.

Vrana: A Night Terror who wears the mask of a raven. She was mutated by the Witch into a grotesque raven-like creature, and is now currently imprisoned in the Void.

Winnowers' Chapter: An elitist group of Holy Order members who disagree with the direction the Mother Abbess is taking the religion. They abandoned the Holy Order for the Disciples of the Deep and fled Penance.

The Witch: Also known as the Maiden of Pain, the Witch has been responsible for countless deaths over untold years. She attacked Vrana's village of Caldera, and had been using Vrana as a way by which to spread her influence, so as to increase in power and relevance. The Witch has been influencing individuals in an attempt to build what is referred to as The Cult of the Worm.

ABOUT THE AUTHOR

SCOTT HALE is the author of *The Bones of the Earth* series and screen-writer of *Entropy, Free to a Bad Home, and Effigies.* He is the co-owner of Halehouse Productions. He is a graduate from Northern Kentucky University with a Bachelors in Psychology and Masters in Social Work. He has completed *The Bones of the Earth* series and his standalone horror novel, *In Sheep's Skin.* Scott Hale currently resides in Norwood, Ohio with his wife and frequent collaborator, Hannah Graff, and their three cats, Oona, Bashik, and Bellatrix.

Printed in Great Britain
by Amazon